Stefan Heym

HOSTAGES

A NOVEL

G. P. PUTNAM'S SONS

NEW YORK

BECAUSE MY FATHER WAS A HOSTAGE

ACKNOWLEDGMENT

MY DEEP-FELT THANKS TO GERTRUDE GELBIN
WHOSE HELP IN EDITING AND CORRECTING
THIS BOOK HAS BEEN OF INESTIMABLE VALUE.

S.H.

HOSTAGES

CHAPTER 1

"JANOSHIK! Janoshi-i-i-i-k!"

The shrill voice of the wizened bartender re-echoed through the narrow hallway which led from the grill a dozen steps down to the washroom.

Janoshik slowly opened the door and growled back: "What the hell is the matter?"

The bartender drew in a deep breath. He would give Janoshik a piece of his mind. "Always you hang around up here when I don't need you. But when I need you I've got to holler all over the place. Come on, get moving! And bring along a bucket and the broom."

Janoshik grunted and slammed the door.

He liked the quiet down here. Each time a guest opened the door and walked past him to the toilet, Janoshik resented it, because the guest would bring along a gush of noise from upstairs—voices and erratic bits of melodies from the gramophone.

He liked the quiet. He needed quiet and time to think because he was an orderly and somewhat slow-thinking man who took his or somebody else's impressions and ideas, turned them over and over again before he folded them accurately and stowed them away in specified corners of his brain. Once he had stowed away something, he was able to call on it at will and to use it cleverly and systematically.

Janoshik did not hurry. He never hurried. Of the people who knew him, none ever could recall having seen him in a hurry. Even down in the mine at Kladno, when the shaft caved in and the men, frantically shouting, ran around like trapped mice, he did not hurry. He picked up his tools because he thought he might need them. He carefully adjusted the light in his lamp to conserve the battery. Then he waited till the men, realizing their desperate situation, stopped shouting. And in the terrible silence after the disaster, when the harsh question, "What is to be done?" hit numb minds, he stepped forward as a leader.

Janoshik did not hurry. He heard the bartender call again.

He took broom, bucket and mop out of the closet, then filled the bucket with water from the faucet over the basin, and proceeded upstairs, slowly, with heavy measured steps.

It was good that his feet were accustomed to set themselves solidly on the ground, for down the stairway tumbled a man in a German officer's uniform. The officer, bleary-eyed and sickish white of face, angled for support. He grasped Janoshik's broad shoulder.

"Steady, steady, old man!" Janoshik said. "Just go straight ahead—you'll find it."

But the drunk had other intentions. Using Janoshik's body as a combination support and guide, he slid down to squat on the stairs. He buried his head in his hands and began to sob, a loud, whimpering, ridiculously female sobbing.

It was pitiful, but Janoshik felt no pity. He shrugged his shoulders and walked on.

"I thought you'd never come!" greeted the bartender. "Beg pardon, gentlemen!" and he motioned his hands imploringly.

4

The men standing at the bar made room for Janoshik who was eying the mess. The drunk whom he had encountered on the stairs had vomited on the floor.

Janoshik shook his head, softly and disapprovingly.

"Come on, wipe it up!" a sharp voice spoke in German. Janoshik looked up, looked into the face of a Nazi officer.

"Wipe it up!" the bartender repeated in Czech. And, obviously for the other guests to hear, he continued loudly: "Why did you dawdle? You should ask the pardon of all these gentlemen because they had to wait so long for you to clean up! After all, the grill of the Café Mánes is no pigsty, is it?" He laughed nervously.

Janoshik began to work. The officer turned to a second one and said, "Lazy bunch, those Czechs—slovenly, undisciplined. Just look at that janitor!"

The second officer was not interested in the first one's observations. "We shouldn't have taken along Glasenapp," he muttered. "He's no fun. He can't stand more than a couple of drinks—gets sentimental and pukes all over the place."

The first one insisted on having his way. "Let him puke as much as he wants. I dare those Czechs to throw us out. How respectable and well-behaved they are—don't even say boo, don't even walk out. We've got them nicely trained now, my dear Marschmann. They're afraid, you know, afraid that we'd be offended if they walked out!"

He shouted "Boo!" and began to laugh hysterically, shaking.

The Czech civilians, those sitting at the tables as well as those standing at the bar, had ceased talking. As usual, among better class citizens of Prague—and the Mánes was frequented by this class—almost everybody understood German.

A well-knit young man, who had been sitting at a table in the corner, stood up. "Waiter, my check!" Turning to his companion, he said, "I think we'd better go, Prokosch. The atmosphere is getting a little too sticky."

The officer with political ambitions sidled over to the young man. His steps were not quite steady. When he reached the table he drew himself up to his full height: "I am Captain Patzer, 431st Infantry. And who are you?"

The young man remained silent.

"Who are you?" Patzer repeated, louder.

"My name is Peter Lobkowitz."

"Well, Herr Lobkowitz, you aren't leaving, by any chance, because you dislike me, or Lieutenant Marschmann, or poor Lieutenant Glasenapp who could not stand the rotten schnapps which is served hereabouts, are you?"

Lobkowitz was not sure about the best way to answer the provocative question. This Captain Patzer, obviously, was under the influence of liquor. Anything one said might lead to a fight, and fights of this kind led to speedy intervention on the part of the police—and the police intervened always on the side of the Germans.

But he had to decide quickly.

"I have an appointment," he said.

Patzer grinned. "But you said before that the atmosphere was getting too sticky." He stopped grinning and moved close to Lobkowitz. "If the atmosphere is good enough for me and Lieutenant Marschmann, it certainly is good enough for you Czechs. Is that clear?"

"Quite," said Lobkowitz.

"That's better, much better." Patzer became friendly. "I want you to have a drink with me and Lieutenant Marschmann on that. You see—" and he made a sweeping gesture, addressing everyone—"if you Czechs will only co-operate, we'll get along very well—very well indeed." Grabbing Lobkowitz' arm, the Captain staggered back to the bar.

Janoshik, mopping up the floor, observed the scene with great misgiving. Nobody could foretell what would happen

6

when German officers on the loose took it into their heads to educate the Czech population.

And there, among the guests, was Breda with whom he must speak, and who must get away safely. What if this Captain Patzer were personally offended each time a guest wanted to leave?

Breda was standing at the end of the bar, farthest from the German officers. He was quietly sipping a beer.

Janoshik picked up the bucket. When he righted himself again, his eyes met Breda's. Janoshik motioned his head toward the exit, a signal imperceptible to anyone but Breda.

Going downstairs, Janoshik suddenly remembered that the drunken officer probably was still in the toilet. Janoshik cursed softly. Breda would come down and they would not even be able to talk. Everything went wrong today!

But to his surprise, Janoshik found the coast clear. He checked carefully, but the drunk—what was his name?—ah, yes, Glasenapp—the drunk was definitely not around. Though Janoshik was not much concerned about the drunk's fate, and though uppermost in his mind was the message he was to receive from Breda, he nevertheless could not help thinking of the officer. The man must have gone somewhere!

Perhaps he had stepped through the little side door onto the jetty.

Maybe he should look and make sure? The jetty was not very wide, and there was no railing to keep one from tumbling into the Moldau River.

When Janoshik accepted the job as janitor and handyman of the Café Mánes, one of his inducements had been that little side-door exit to the jetty. A wise man, Janoshik thought, always provides for a retreat.

7

The whole layout of the Café Mánes attracted Janoshik. He had to be at a place where he could be visited and talked to unobtrusively. And how many plans could be discussed and arranged while he was shining his visitor's shoes! Even the mere brushing of a man's collar afforded opportunity to whisper a few words—an address that must be passed on, a warning that must be spread.

Whenever he was off duty, a message could be left in the little medicine chest which contained a few essentials for first aid—a bottle of iodine, gauze, cotton, alcohol. Small packages could be brought in or smuggled out unchecked with the laundry. The laundry boy was safe; in fact it was he who had tipped off Janoshik on the possibilities of the job at the Mánes.

And finally, there was the approach from the water. The Mánes was built on a jetty which reached far out into the Moldau River. Its main floor was occupied by the café; its top floor had been leased for exhibitions before the Nazis marched into Prague. Then the Mánes stopped being a center of budding, modern Czech art.

Through a passage from the café, one reached the bar and grill to the left. To the right was the stairway leading down to the toilet and the storage rooms. At the foot of the stairs was the door to the water.

Janoshik, who could swim like a fish, took the job at very little money. Occasionally he received small tips. Anyway, he was accustomed to living on almost nothing; and had it been necessary, he would have paid to get the job.

He had been at the Mánes for more than four months, and it had been the quietest time of his life. In former years, when he was organizing the miners, or when he lived among the farm workers of Moravia, he had been forced to be on the move all the time—changing his name, changing his room, occasionally staying in jail. But now?—he smiled to himself—he had a warm little hiding place, with a rear

8

exit at that, and it seemed as though the authorities, Czech as well as German, had either forgotten or not yet discovered him.

Oh, Janoshik was no fool. He knew that this could not go on forever. At some time or other he would be arrested, his jig would be up. He had no fear of that. When he had been in the war—and he was in it for four long years—he had known that he might be hit. A soldier had to take such risks. He was a soldier again—this time, however, voluntarily.

The door opened. The man who had been sipping his beer at the bar entered.

"Give me some soap," Breda said.

Janoshik gave him soap and a towel. He observed the man as he was washing his hands—big, well-formed hands, hands which filled one with confidence.

"We can talk," Janoshik began, "but make it short. I want you to get out of here quickly. Those officers up there—"

"They're raising hell," Breda reported, "the loud-mouthed braggarts. They're now picking on somebody you should know—your former boss, I believe."

"My boss?" Janoshik asked.

"Yes—Lev Preissinger, of the Coal Syndicate. He now owns all the mines in Kladno. He's here with some sort of doctor, fellow named Wallerstein. Wallerstein is giving the Nazis a lecture on psychoanalysis; he's talking his head off so as to keep them engaged and quiet. It's really funny."

Breda dried his hands thoroughly and handed the towel back to Janoshik.

"All right," he said, "everything is ready and prepared. Today is Thursday. Next Tuesday, at latest Wednesday, the barges are going to come through. They will be tied up here for a day or so. We do not know exactly at what pier—the longshoremen will have to check on that. As far as my group is concerned, our job is done, the bundles are ready. The longshoremen know that they have to finish their part of the work before the munitions are transferred from the barges to the freight trains. Now get this address: Watzlik, Smíchovská Street 64. Repeat it."

"Watzlik, Smíchovská Street 64," Janoshik said slowly. "I won't forget."

They looked at each other. They felt that perhaps they should say something more, something big and meaningful. But neither carried his feelings on his tongue. They just shook hands.

"If there is anything special, I'll drop around," Breda said.

Janoshik turned to rinse the basin.

Softly, the other closed the door.

So, Janoshik thought, Lev Preissinger is here. And I did not even recognize him. Odd—and I have talked against him so often. How he wouldn't give us new wood to back up the shaft. Wood costs money, lives cost nothing. Those few Kronen—what do they really mean to Lev Preissinger! Well, it's a few Kronen here, a few Kronen there, and it adds up to millions. But Petka's face, when he was crushed under mountains of stone—and Petka was still such a child!

He would go up later and have a good look at Preissinger. Such a good look as he had had at Petka's face. In this life, he thought, one must keep one's records straight.

There were hurried steps on the stairs. The bartender poked his face through the door. "Say—where is that officer? Tell him to hurry up and he shouldn't forget to button his pants."

"I can't tell a German officer to button his pants," Janoshik remarked dryly. "It's against his dignity."

"Tell him Captain Patzer said so," answered the bartender. "He wants to go. Am I glad that they finally got tired of hanging around!" A big sigh followed this statement.

Janoshik wanted time. He wanted time for himself to think, and for Breda to escape.

"Do you know," he asked the bartender, "Otto Krupatschka, who used to own the Golden Angel tavern in Žižkov?"

"I am not concerned about your Otto Krupatschka," answered the bartender. "I've got to hurry back, and will you please give that message to the officer!"

Janoshik stepped to the door and grabbed the bartender's arm. "But if I tell you of Krupatschka, it is important—you understand?"

The bartender winced. "Let me go!"

Janoshik, unruffled, continued: "This Krupatschka had a young wife who was very good at making meatballs, meatballs and a special sauce with lots of pepper in it. There must have been something to that sauce—Krupatschka, in any case, could not quite keep up with her—you understand?"

The bartender was torn between his duty and his desire to hear the end of the story. "I must go," he said, "hurry up, for God's sake!"

"Well," Janoshik developed his tale, "one fine day Krupatschka sends the boy to tell his wife that he would come home early, and that she should have supper ready on time, for he was hungry. And the boy goes, and after a long while he comes back to the Golden Angel—"

"Tell me the rest tomorrow!" the bartender pleaded. "People want drinks. And Captain Patzer is waiting!"

"How can I tell you a story," inquired Janoshik, "if you interrupt me continuously? I would have been through by now if you had listened instead of talked.

"Anyway, as I was saying, the boy comes back to Krupatschka. 'Tell me,' says Krupatschka, 'what did she answer?' So the boy says, 'She did not answer anything. And if I were you, Pane Krupatschka, I would eat out tonight. For your

11

wife, she has run away with a certain Ludwig Polatschek, who is a very nice young man and a medical student...'"

The bartender had succeeded in freeing his arm from Janoshik's grip.

"And why," he asked sternly, "do you keep me from my work by telling me such a story which is stupid and has no point?"

"Because there is a certain parallel, if I may say so," Janoshik explained patiently. "Like poor Otto Krupatschka's wife, who ran away with that fellow Polatschek, your officer must have run away too. He's not here any more. He has disappeared."

"Impossible!" There was fright in the bartender's voice. "Look around yourself!"

The bartender did. He opened the door of each booth; he peered into the dark of the night through the exit to the jetty—there was no trace of Lieutenant Glasenapp.

"Holy Virgin!" he groaned. "This is terrible! This is catastrophical!" And shouting at Janoshik: "Do you know what this means?"

"No," Janoshik answered honestly, "I don't."

The bartender had become utterly pale. He had lost his voice and could only whisper, "You're so dumb I could kill you!"

Janoshik, towering over the shriveled man, asked with an expression of kindly pity, "Why?"

But the bartender did not bother to answer. He was running up the stairs.

The door remained open, and Janoshik could hear the ensuing excitement.

All the while he was making up the Krupatschka story, Janoshik had been thinking hard. He simply could not imagine what might have happened to the officer. However, there was no sense in worrying about it now—he would have to plan his own tactics and behavior. Perhaps it would be

12

best to stick to the truth and tell them he did not know. He last had seen the officer sitting down on the staircase—that was all. He did not know more. He would not tell more. There was not much anybody could do about that, and in all probability the officer was home in his barracks by now.

If only Breda had succeeded in leaving on time!

There was the sound of heavy boots on the stairs. Janoshik saw the Nazi approach—first the boots, then the breeches, finally the whole man. He was no pleasant sight.

Janoshik could read the man's face. Fear was in it, and tyrannical rage. His right hand was brandishing a gun.

"Where is Lieutenant Glasenapp?" Patzer demanded.

"How do I know?" Janoshik asked back. "I'd like to respectfully suggest that I haven't had the honor of ever meeting the Lieutenant."

"Keep your wise remarks to yourself," Patzer replied in an ominous tone. "You know perfectly well that I speak of the officer who came down here to relieve himself. Where is he?"

Janoshik lifted his hands in a helpless gesture. "Honestly, sir, I don't know. I cannot keep check on all the people who come to this room. I am in and out frequently." He turned and began to take out fresh towels from the closet. As far as he, Janoshik, was concerned, the interview was over, and he intended the officer to know it.

But Captain Patzer grew the more enraged, the less headway he made with this stubborn Czech.

"Come along!" he ordered.

"What for? Where to?" asked Janoshik.

Patzer poked his gun between Janoshik's ribs.

"I have a very nervous finger," the Captain growled. "I advise you to obey orders without asking questions—do you get that, blockhead?" And he pushed his gun deeper.

Janoshik smiled the smile of hurt innocence. "Sir—I only inquired because my boss does not like me to loiter away from my job. I appreciate your company. Your invitation honors me. Do you want me to help you look for this—this Lieutenant Glasenapp?"

They were walking upstairs.

Janoshik continued to babble away happily. "People disappear sometimes in the funniest way. I know all about it, sir, because I used to play pinochle with Inspector Jan Poczporek of the twentieth police precinct. He is dead now for over ten years, poor soul, but he was a fine source of information. Not that he played a good game, I couldn't say that for him. . . ."

"Stop talking!" Patzer shouted.

The grill room was buzzing with excitement. Most of the guests were standing at their tables. Some of the more courageous ones tried to ask questions of Lieutenant Marschmann.

"Will we be allowed to go home soon?"

"I must phone my wife—she is waiting for me—may I use the telephone?"

"Why do you hold me? I have nothing to do with this officer. I was sitting here all the time. Why—Dr. Wallerstein —isn't it true?"

To all of which Lieutenant Marschmann did not reply. He displayed his most important face. He could show that he was somebody—like Captain Patzer, he had taken his gun out of its holster. People tried not to look at the vicious black muzzle.

Patzer, returning, took command of the situation. He stepped on a chair, placed his free hand on his hip, and waited. After a little while he found that this action had no visible effect on the attitude of the guests. They were far too upset to stop talking. So he shouted in his most authoritative voice: "Silence!"

Silence was achieved immediately. Captain Patzer looked around. There were faces—many faces; in fact, far too many. Some of the faces he saw double, and in addition, they began to circle around him. Patzer was experienced in such visions. He knew he would get dizzy in a moment.

Therefore, he stepped down from his chair and held on to the back of it.

"Something has occurred," he began slowly in order to control his heavy tongue. "Something has occurred which prompts me to take this drastic action. Lieutenant Glasenapp, the third man in our group, has disappeared. Disappeared mysteriously, without a word, without leaving any trace.

"These are difficult times. We Germans are trying to bring order into this country. Our effort is not always appreciated. Sometimes, some of us are made to disappear.

"Mind you, I am not accusing any of you. Not yet, at least."

"Couldn't it be that he simply went back home to your barracks?" someone interposed.

"Who said that?" Patzer asked sharply.

"I did," Lev Preissinger answered. "I am Lev Preissinger, the Director-General of the Bohemian-Moravian Coal Syndicate."

Janoshik, who had made himself inconspicuous in a corner, turned a quick glance at Preissinger. He saw a thick-set man, a bit stoop-shouldered, with stubby gray hair, small blinking eyes and ruddy complexion.

"Well," Patzer said belligerently, "perhaps you can tell us whether you noticed Lieutenant Glasenapp leave through this door"—he pointed toward the door leading to the street —"and when you noticed him leave?"

"I am sorry," Preissinger replied, "I was busy conversing with my friend, Dr. Wallerstein." And turning to the doctor: "Isn't that so?"

15

"Everybody was busy, apparently," Patzer continued, enjoying the way in which he had disposed of Preissinger. "And we are going to find out what they were busy doing. So—we will have to keep you here till the police arrive. That's official, and our orders will be enforced."

Patzer let the light fall on his gun so that the glint of steel was visible to everybody.

There was an apprehensive silence, interrupted only by the clinking of the glasses which the bartender, unnecessarily and senselessly, was washing and wiping over and over again.

Janoshik leaned his head against the wall and closed his eyes.

He was relaxed and breathed more easily than when Patzer had pushed him upstairs and into the grill room. For Breda was no longer there.

Janoshik's trick had worked. He had kept the bartender downstairs with the help of the unfortunate Otto Krupatschka's marital troubles. These precious minutes had given Breda the chance to escape. And a narrow escape it had been.

As for himself, Janoshik was not much worried. He kept no papers on his person, there was nothing treacherous in the washroom downstairs, and even if they went to the trouble of searching the bare quarters in Královská Street where he slept, they would find nothing.

The whole thing was too ridiculous anyway. Glasenapp might have walked up the jetty and reached the street by crawling over the embankment of the river. He would turn up in his barracks or would be found lying in some gutter.

The police, whom those drunken fools had called, would probably take everybody's address, and that would be that. Certainly they would not bother about Janoshik, a mere keeper of the toilet, who did not look too bright and who

16

had a way of talking which drove every police official to desperation.

Janoshik smiled. He remembered the sergeant in Moravská Ostrava—he had sort of liked the fellow; but when he got through with him, the sergeant collapsed over his desk, crying, "Take him away! Take him away! I don't want to see him any more!"

Those were the good old times.

The Gestapo was different. They were tougher, they had no humor—that, however, might make it all the easier to exasperate them.

Once, Janoshik had read a book about the life of animals. Some there were who had no possible means of self-defense. But they could change color and appear like a dead leaf so that nobody would bother to stoop and pick them up. He was like that, he thought. The only thing that could happen to such an animal was that somebody would step on it accidentally. But this was improbable, one chance in a million.

The big talkers were no good in this fight. Their name, their fame soared like the light of a meteor—only to burst and sink back into darkness. What was glory? In our time it only meant that one exposed oneself to additional dangers. The great art was rather to do one's job and to stay alive in spite of it, for a dead soldier is of no use to anybody.

This had been Janoshik's experience; he had molded his life, his activities, accordingly. Therefore he looked forward confidently to what was to come.

The pause before the arrival of the police lasted unbearably long. The guests became more and more fidgety, and Lieutenant Marschmann and Captain Patzer were beginning to feel silly brandishing their guns.

Marschmann whispered to his superior, "And if Glasenapp

somehow slipped away and is back in the barracks, snoring his head off—what then?"

Patzer did not answer immediately. He was thinking. "In any case," he said finally, "it'll be educational for these people. We're nobody to pull tricks on—they'll learn that. Right?"

Marschmann shook his head sadly. He feared that Patzer's eagerness would bring no end of trouble on their necks, and wished that they had left the drooping Glasenapp at home instead of trying to cheer him up. It was always best, he thought, to leave people to their own damned affairs . . .

His philosophizing was interrupted by the sharp whistle of the approaching police emergency squad.

A sudden hush came over the persons in the room. Captain Patzer pulled down the tunic of his uniform, and lifted his gun higher—to the level of the chests of the guests.

Hobnailed boots clattered on the sidewalk. The door to the bar was torn open noisily.

The patrol of black-coated SS men piled in, led by a rosy-cheeked youngster who looked like an apprentice in a boxing school.

The youngster glanced around quickly and noticed that the two army officers had the situation quite under control. He motioned to one of his men to station himself at the entrance, and then walked up to Captain Patzer.

"My name is Gruber, sir. I am aide-de-camp to Commissioner Reinhardt of the Secret State Police, who, unfortunately, is not at headquarters this evening. I have standing orders to attend to matters during his absence. What seems to be the trouble?"

Patzer felt that he would get all the co-operation in the world from this eager kid. He gave his voice as assured a tone as possible.

"Captain Patzer, 431st Infantry," he replied crisply. "This is a most unfortunate situation, I fear. One of our com-

18

rades, Lieutenant Glasenapp, seems to have been kidnaped —possibly assassinated."

"And these people?" Gruber pointed at the guests who stood around awkwardly.

"Lieutenant Marschmann and I thought it better to keep them here till the police arrived. Any one of them, more likely several, may be involved in the outrage."

Gruber nodded understandingly. "Very good, Captain, very good. I wish we always got such splendid co-operation. And now, can you tell me what actually happened?"

Before Patzer could begin his story, somebody pushed himself through the waiting guests. It was Lev Preissinger.

"You're the commanding police officer?" he demanded of Gruber. "Yes? Why don't you let us go—I mean my friend, Dr. Wallerstein, and myself. I am Lev Preissinger, Director-General of the Bohemian-Moravian Coal Syndicate, and surely—"

Gruber nodded to one of his men. The man stepped forward and pushed Preissinger so hard that he tumbled back and would have fallen if Dr. Wallerstein had not held him up.

Preissinger's face was crimson. He tried to sputter something.

Without turning around to the people he addressed, Gruber remarked, "The next fellow who opens up his big mouth without being asked will be dealt with more appropriately." And to Patzer he said, "Sorry—we were interrupted. How and when did Lieutenant Glasenapp disappear?"

"Around eleven o'clock," Patzer stated. "He took sick and went down to the toilet—and never returned."

"When did you become suspicious?"

"After fifteen, maybe twenty minutes—I sent down this man—"

The bartender grew pale under Gruber's cold stare.

19

Patzer continued: "I sent this man down to fetch Glasenapp. He returned to confess that he could not find the Lieutenant. I myself then went downstairs. I could find no trace of him either. He had mysteriously disappeared."

"I see," Gruber said with as much import as he could manage. "Enzinger! Walters!" he ordered.

"Yes, sir!" The two men stepped forward.

"Go downstairs and check up. See what you can find." Enzinger and Walters trooped off.

"Now let us see—" Gruber asked. "Do you remember, Captain, whether any guests left after Lieutenant Glasenapp had gone to relieve himself?"

Patzer thought for a moment. "To be frank, it is quite possible," he said. "After all, neither Lieutenant Marschmann nor I suspected that such a foul crime was being planned. But I do remember that two of the guests—that young man over there and his companion—were quite obviously set on leaving. However, I kept them here."

"That is very, very interesting!" Gruber exclaimed. "Step forward, you!"

Peter Lobkowitz complied with the order.

"So you wanted to get away?" Gruber demanded sneeringly. "Why?"

"Because I had an appointment," Lobkowitz said quietly.

"With your fellow conspirators, I presume?" Gruber shot back.

"Of course not. I want to state here and now that I am in no way connected with the disappearance of any German officer."

Enzinger and Walters returned from their expedition to the toilet and lined up before Gruber, ready to report.

"We will investigate you later," Gruber said to Lobkowitz, and turned to his men. "Well—what did you find?"

"There's actually no trace of Lieutenant Glasenapp," Enzinger, the older of the two, stated. "But we found some-

20

thing which seems to be important—there is a second exit downstairs which leads onto the jetty—and into the Moldau River."

Gruber grew enthusiastic. This was meat for him. "Ah!" he said. "This is not difficult to reconstruct! Not difficult at all! You see"—he turned to Captain Patzer—"your comrade left you, not in possession of his full powers—some persons either waited for him downstairs, or went after him—cowardly as they are, they overwhelmed him, killed him outright, or merely beat him unconscious, and then disposed of his body in the river."

Patzer shuddered. This fate also could have befallen him.

"A dastardly plot!" Gruber continued. "Devious! Devilish!" And he shouted to the guests: "But we'll uncover the criminals! They'll pay for it!"

A sudden idea struck him. "Was there no attendant to this toilet?" he asked.

Janoshik had been standing in his corner, observing the scene. Ever since the two Gestapo men had gone downstairs, returned and given their report to Gruber, he had expected this cue. Now he stepped forward.

"At your service, sir," he said. "That is my job. I've seen better days, though, I assure you. Why, there were times when I would have looked down on such a man as me. But it's honest work, and, after all, it's hard to make a living these days—"

"Shut up!" Gruber said after he had overcome his first surprise at the cascade of words flowing from Janoshik.

Janoshik complied. But his face expressed clearly that here was a sensitive soul, trying to be helpful, who had been thwarted cruelly.

Gruber looked at him. A little thrill of power ran through the young Gestapo man. The Czech was standing there almost like a dog pleading not to be beaten. We've got them licked, Gruber felt.

21

"You saw Lieutenant Glasenapp go to the toilet. Just answer yes or no!" Gruber added hastily for he had seen Janoshik draw a deep breath.

"That depends," Janoshik said. "I saw him, and again I didn't see him."

"Is that man crazy?" Gruber asked angrily. There was no answer, for obviously this question was not directed to anybody in particular. Finally, the bartender's voice piped up: "He's a bit simple-minded, if you permit, sir."

"What do you mean?" Gruber continued to question Janoshik. "Either you see a man or you don't see him—and you must have seen Glasenapp!"

Janoshik smiled happily. "You said it! Of course! If you put it that way, it's very easy. I saw him—but I didn't see him go to the men's room, sir."

Gruber's eyes narrowed. Deep in the pit of his stomach was an uncertain feeling: was he being fooled? "Where did he go then?"

"To the toilet," Janoshik assured the Gestapo man. "He was very sick. It was a sad sight. I've seen plenty of drunks in my day, but he was one of the worst—if I may say so. He almost fell into my arms, poor chap. He was weeping. Tears were streaming down his face—"

This time Captain Patzer blew up. "Herr Gruber! This lousy Czech is speaking of a German officer! I demand—"

"I don't enjoy this either," Gruber retorted, his voice husky with suppressed anger. "But I must get this story straight. This man said he saw Lieutenant Glasenapp go to the toilet—"

Janoshik shook his head. "No, sir—I did not!"

Gruber shouted, "Goddamn it! You said you did!"

Janoshik raised both his hands in a gesture of desperation. Here and there, some of the guests could not keep their snickering under control.

Gruber's face grew very red. He swallowed hard.

Janoshik knew the youngster's next move. It would be a simple one—Gruber would hit him over the head. But Janoshik did not want to be beaten. He wanted to establish his reputation as a harmless nitwit—he had accomplished that purpose. And he wanted to establish his alibi.

"With your kind permission, sir—I can explain it all. I was making my way upstairs. The barkeeper had called me to wipe the floor. Some mess, I assure you, was left there by the unfortunate Lieutenant, God bless him. This gentleman"—he pointed at Captain Patzer—"he even spoke to me. He told me, most definitely, to clean it up."

Patzer nodded.

"The last I saw of the Lieutenant was when he sat down on the stairs and started to cry his heart out—but whether he ever actually entered the toilet, that I don't know. I was up here for quite a while, because it was such a terrific mess—"

"All right! All right!" Gruber said. "Spare us the details!"

Young Gruber had had very little police training. Right from school he had joined the ranks of the black-uniformed Elite Guard, from which the Gestapo is recruited. One thing, however, had been drilled into his skull—that he and his colleagues lived among enemies, that they were the objects of fierce hatred, and that in any and all cases it was best to use the most ruthless measures.

Justice was something that existed only in a higher sense—as far as it benefited the cause of Germany and of Adolf Hitler. The individual counted only in so far as he furthered that cause. Otherwise he had no rights and was to be dealt with harshly.

Gruber recognized that he could not solve this case here and now. Of course, he could go on quizzing people—but he shied away from the responsibility of keeping some and releasing others. Nazi education, which led to the disregard of the individual, also created fear of individual responsibility in the Nazis themselves.

"Get your things!" he bellowed. "You'll all come along to headquarters."

Pummeled and driven by the Gestapo men, the guests gathered their belongings. They were lined up before the door, and went out in single file. Gruber stood beside the door and counted—there were eighteen in all, eighteen men. Lobkowitz and Prokosch, followed by the bartender and Janoshik, formed the end of the line.

Two, however, remained seated at their table—Lev Preissinger and Dr. Wallerstein.

Preissinger was quietly puffing a cigar, and Wallerstein was studying his companion's stolid features.

Gruber, hands on his hips, strode over to them.

Preissinger kept his cigar between the lips while he said, "I don't presume you want to include me in your little comedy?"

Gruber was sometimes affectionately called "the Kid" by his associates. Now his round face lit up in a smile which was positively childlike. He lifted his right hand and slapped Preissinger's cheek so hard that the cigar sailed into a far corner of the room.

Wallerstein kept his eyes fixed on Preissinger. He was terribly interested in the man's reaction to this attack. The vein on Preissinger's forehead swelled up like a blue rope.

"You'll be damned sorry for that!" he said, and his voice sounded cracked. "It so happens that I'm a friend of Herr Goering. . . ."

"Enzinger!" Gruber called.

Enzinger, who was about to leave the room, returned hurriedly.

Gruber turned to his subordinate and explained: "This gentleman tells us he is a friend of his Excellency, Reich Marshal Goering. I think that he should not be forced to

24

march with the others. Take him, tie him up, and let him ride in the car. If he makes any untoward move, you know what to do!"

Enzinger was an experienced hand at tackling people. Lev Preissinger, Director-General of the Bohemian-Moravian Coal Syndicate, was yanked up from his seat. He felt a sudden stinging pain in the joints of his shoulder—then he passed out.

Dr. Wallerstein saw the limp body being dragged off. He turned to Gruber. "That was a neat job. It might be quite salutary for the old man."

"Who are you?" Gruber asked back. "A wise guy?"

"No. Not exactly," Wallerstein answered in a matter-of-fact way. "I'm a doctor. A psychoanalyst, if you know what that is."

"I don't," Gruber conceded, "and it won't help you any. Come along!"

Wallerstein bowed his great head. He walked awkwardly, with shuffling feet.

"Hey, you!" Gruber said.

Wallerstein stopped.

"Do *you* know what actually happened?" Gruber asked, not very sure of himself.

The doctor looked at the Kid, and his lips stretched in a thin smile. "I don't know," he said. "I will tell you, though, that in an abstract sense the problem begins to interest me very much."

CHAPTER 2

"Is THERE anything else?" the Kid asked.

Reinhardt leafed perfunctorily through the file marked "Erich Glasenapp, First Lieutenant." Then he looked up and saw the Kid staring at him in obvious admiration. Gruber, as always, wore his uniform untidily. The big, fresh, adolescent body seemed to burst out of the tight-fitting clothes. The Kid's pink cheeks were funny in contrast to the silver skull and crossbones on the lapel.

"Something wrong with me?"

"Oh, no, no, sir!" the Kid answered, embarrassed.

"Then stop staring at me. And how often do I have to tell you that your uniform pockets should be buttoned at all times? You do not seem to realize that you represent German authority in these parts."

The Kid blushed, which made his cheeks even pinker and the weak blue of his eyes paler.

"Dismissed! Heil Hitler!" Helmut Reinhardt could crack his words like a whip, especially when he gave orders. He watched their effect on the Kid. The big boy seemed to tighten up, clicked his heels, and tramped off.

Softly, the door closed. Reinhardt was alone, behind his

wide desk which he loved to keep clean of even the slightest speck of dust. This is my battlefield, he was in the habit of saying to himself. *My* part of the front—it must be in exemplary order. Can't work otherwise.

He leaned back in his armchair, stretched himself luxuriously in anticipation of some quiet thinking. Before him was the thin pile of papers marked "Glasenapp." What had the Kid said, in his childish superiority? "A weakling!"

The Kid was beginning to get bothersome with all his hero worship. That he, Reinhardt, should be the hero in the case was all the more awkward, sometimes even disturbing.

Do I look like a hero? Reinhardt asked himself. Oh my God! The receding, weak chin—the dark and piercing eyes, much too narrowly set—the thin nose, quiveringly sensitive —the forehead.... Well, the forehead was fair, it was high enough with a pleasant curve. His was, to say the best, an uneven face.

But perhaps, Reinhardt's mind rambled on, in the Kid's dumb mind his face was impressive. After all, it was the work one did, the authority one exercised, which mattered most. If one looked at Hitler, one would not believe that the man could manage a middle-sized shoe factory, not to mention half of Europe. And yet Hitler did. There were difficulties, of course. But, mused Reinhardt, to eliminate these difficulties, such men as himself were on the job. A tremendous machine, and it worked smoothly. Where on this earth was there anything to compare with it?

So the Kid might be right in his admiration. This is the machine age. Individual bravery is poppycock. The man who makes the machine go—this man is the hero.

At first Reinhardt had cursed old man Gruber who, wanting to save his precious offspring from being smashed by some Soviet tank, had, by devious ways, pushed the boy into the Gestapo service. And now, Gruber, Jr., was entrusted to Reinhardt's competent hands. He had not known what to do with the unnecessary addition to his staff, and had finally made him a more or less glorified office boy. One could never foresee when and where a favor done to old man Gruber would bear interest.

It was not disagreeable to have the Kid around. One needed a lightning rod, sometimes, for one's annoyance. And also—Reinhardt began to see with surprise—one needed a little admiration. It was not enough to know that one did one's duty in the framework of the great national effort. All was impersonal. The men in this delicate machine, the Secret State Police, were not given to words of praise. A job well done—what of it? The Kid provided silent recognition pleasant to receive.

But one must treat him with severity. Otherwise he would permit himself familiarities which could not be tolerated.

Commissioner Reinhardt stopped himself angrily at this point. What business had his thoughts to drift so far?

He rose and stepped to the window of his office.

Downstairs, before the entrance to the building, the steel-helmeted guard walked up and down, up and down. People hurried by, nobody dared stop and idle, look about and talk. With a little thrill of satisfaction Reinhardt's mind registered: We are feared.

He returned to his desk and began to go over the Glasenapp file.

Personal data were scant. Born 1909 in Mainz. Grade school and Gymnasium in Mainz. University in Cologne and Heidelberg—studied Philology. Then teacher at the Girls' Lyceum in Mainz. Member of National Socialist Party since 1934. Reserve Officers' Training School. Commissioned Second Lieutenant in 1938. Mobilized since 1939. Service in Czechoslovakia, Poland, Norway, France. Never in front line —weak eyes, flat feet.

Probably didn't get enough calcium during the first World War, Reinhardt figured.

Was he married?—No. No illegitimate children either. Well, men hardly confess to that, even though we try to make them feel proud of having fathered a future soldier.

Let's see what else there is. Military passbook. Money, two Mark 45 Pfennige, a few Czech Kronen—the thing happened before pay day. A clipping from a newspaper, reporting graduation at the Mainz Girls' Lyceum. How pitiful! How little a man leaves on this earth...

They probably forgot him long ago at the Lyceum.

And here is the letter the Kid mentioned. A letter never finished and never sent—perhaps the only real clue to the case.

Reinhardt read it over slowly.

Dearest Milada—I am pretty desperate as you will see from the fact that I write you at all after what has happened between us. I know how you must feel, and I assure you that I acted with best intentions. What else was there to do? Could I bring him back?

But it made me sad to think of you being without hope. What a fool I was not to realize that some day you were bound to learn the facts. Yes, if you ask me point blank—I concede that I realized it even then.

But sustaining your hope was my only justification for seeing you. And you had grown to be something in my life which is hard to define. My life was not so empty any more—

And now, all this is over. I have no right whatever to ask you—

Reinhardt drummed an impatient march on the desk. He did not like the letter at all. It smacked of suicide. Yet it was too small a segment of the man's life and experience to tell much. Reinhardt felt that, if one only knew to what the dead man referred, one could reconstruct the whole story.

The letter had been in the water with Glasenapp for over

twelve hours. They had done a good job of deciphering and retouching in the laboratory. A soaked piece of paper to go on—an intriguing task, perhaps. Reinhardt's police mind began to operate, he could feel it—it geared itself almost automatically. He just needed to relax and follow the train of his thoughts. Long years of training bore fruit.

He took the photo of Lieutenant Glasenapp which had been sent over by General Headquarters at the Kid's request. He half closed his eyes and took in the dead man's features, slowly penetrating every angle and curve of that face. If one succeeded in letting the man come alive before one's eyes, one would be able to judge how he would act and react, behave and speak. And that would be a tremendous step forward.

But it was a bad picture. The photographer had allowed his flashbulb to reflect on Glasenapp's eyeglasses—there were no eyes in the picture, only two empty, shiny circles. This ironic accident, perhaps, was quite typical. For the entire face was such that one would not have recognized it even if one had passed by the fellow a dozen times. An average face of an average man. The visor of his cap covering the forehead almost in its entirety. The cheeks, it seemed, said most about the man—they were thin and drawn, patterned with shadows of pimples. Bloodless lips of a nondescript character, but a well-formed chin.

What was likely to happen to such a man? Why should anybody be interested in disposing of him? Why?

He decided to telephone General Headquarters. His call to Major Grauthoff was put through, and after the usual palaver about their mutual well-being, he asked:

"Say, Major—this is what I want to know. It's in reference to that stupid Glasenapp case. What did the fellow do? What were his duties? Did he have any occasion to come in conflict with the local populace?"

The voice at the other end, which had been quite cheerful, changed and became bitter.

"Well, Commissioner—you know we all are not exactly loved and esteemed here."

"I know!" Reinhardt grew impatient with the slow army man. "We are not in Prague for purposes of fraternization. But Glasenapp—he was not singled out for any particularly disagreeable job?"

"Not that I know of. The usual rigmarole. Dispersing unruly bread lines, night watches, day watches—boring stuff."

"Was he known as—let's say—strict?"

Major Grauthoff mumbled something. Then his voice became clearer again. "Strict? . . . You mean brutal? No, I wouldn't think so. Rather the contrary. His comrades say he was more on the softish side."

Reinhardt hesitated for a moment. Was there anything else he should ask the officer? No. Over there they knew as little about Glasenapp as he did.

"Well—thanks, Major—any time you want me to do something for you, just call me up. Heil Hitler."

He heard the soft click of the receiver being hung up on the other end. The Major, apparently, did not like to deal with the Gestapo. At General Headquarters they seemed to think that the sooner the whole affair Glasenapp was forgotten, the better. Raking up muck about it might just give a few more of those Czechs unfortunate ideas—how easy it really was to dispose of assorted German officers.

Reinhardt grinned. Nobody likes risking his life on a soft job. Out in the field, they probably would stand up and fight, but here, they all have a hellish fear of the enemy in the dark. You could not see him, you could not grasp him— and yet he was there, you only felt him after he had struck.

Over at General Headquarters they were inclined to placating measures, the damned fools! Didn't they see that

31

any sign of weakness would only increase the stubbornness of the Czechs? Beat them down, beat them down to the ground, don't let them lift their heads even one single solitary inch—this, and this alone was the only workable policy.

Reinhardt crossed his legs. His mind began to retreat from the outside world and concentrate on the elements of the case. Still a few irrelevant factors intruded, but they would disappear soon. There was, for instance, the way in which the black cloth of his breeches firmly closed in on his knee. It made him feel well-dressed, tight and full of disciplined energy. Then everything became more and more blurred, and instead of his office another picture emerged—Glasenapp.

Glasenapp was moving now, with slow steps, hardly lifting his feet from the ground. *"I am pretty desperate . . ."* the man was saying in his soft, ineffectual way. *"It made me sad to think of you as being without hope."*

There was no pity in Reinhardt, he despised him.

"You had grown to be something in my life which is hard to define."

You are sick of mind, Glasenapp, sick of mind and heart and soul, and it is a goddamned shame that I should have to rack my brain over you.

"My life was not so empty any more. And now, all this is over. I have no right whatever to ask you—"

Ask what? And of whom? Come on, you, speak up! I've got to know! We'll unseal your bloodless, grinning lips! You can rely on that!

All right, you don't want to speak. You've shut up forever. It makes no difference. We'll get along without your petty, desperate ideas.

We'll simply take up the threads where you left them. Then we'll arrive at certain concrete questions which can be answered easier than those of your own rhetoric.

32

Reinhardt took a sheet of paper. Absent-mindedly he began to scribble:

1. Who is Milada?—Must make inquiries from officers.
2. What happened between Milada and Glasenapp?—Milada obviously Czech name. Relation, whatever its nature, against army regulations. Threat of blackmail? Improbable, since girl would be implicated herself. Besides, he acted with "best intentions." Doing what?
3. Trying to bring "him" back? Who is this "he"? How did "he" disappear, and where to? Was Glasenapp responsible in some way for "his" disappearance? Glasenapp—or other Germans?
4. Some day she was bound to learn the facts—facts connected with the disappearance of "him"? Probable—but this indication not enough for conclusions.
5. Rest of story pretty clear. G. uses his best intentions as a means to seeing M. New meaning of life....

Reinhardt pushed away the sheet which was now covered from top to bottom with his clear, sharp writing.

This was stupid all around. If Glasenapp had acted like a man and not like a whining pup, one would have no trouble whatever. But was it really so much trouble? All one had to do was to find this Milada woman and grill her, and the matter would be solved.

Solved in so far as Milada was concerned.

He had to decide now whether Glasenapp's death was connected with the Milada affair.

At first sight, he was inclined to think so. There was, of course, always the possibility that outside forces were involved—but General Headquarters had stressed that Glasenapp was in no way outstanding or exposed. This information from Major Grauthoff tallied with the impression

Reinhardt had gained from the Lieutenant's letter and photo.

It was highly improbable that this inconsequential, vapid man would be singled out for a spectacular death by the dark enemy.

Weighing the two sides of the question, pitting the one against the other, Reinhardt had to reach the conclusion that Glasenapp's departure from this world had been by his own wish and action.

He had committed suicide.

Or, perhaps, the man was soused and simply fell into the river, and gave up struggling for his life because he was tired of it, and it had lost its meaning.

Disgusting.

Disgustingly simple.

Reinhardt was disappointed. This was nothing one could get one's teeth into. A file, soon to be forgotten in dusty archives. A few notices in the papers. Less than that, even— a disgrace for Germany. German officers killing themselves! As if there were not enough places where they could be killed to better purpose . . .

One would have to check up on the relatives of the man in Germany. Cases of this kind always raise disagreeable ripples in the country. Things would have to be hushed up.

Why couldn't Glasenapp be a hero? Why couldn't he have died a hero's death against the enemy?

Reinhardt straightened.

Yes—why couldn't he? the Commissioner asked himself slowly.

There was really no reason why he couldn't.

One just had to make him a hero.

The enemy, after all, was real. He was always near, lurking in the dark.

Who was there to know differently? Only the Kid—and that Milada woman. The Kid would not ask questions. And

34

Milada—she probably would be glad if nobody bothered her, and would keep her mouth shut tight, very tight. She had better!

Well, now one had something to work with! He had raised hell with the Kid for indiscriminately hauling in everybody who had been at the Mánes Bar on Thursday night. It was crude, but now it would come in quite handy. Not only were these people suspects—one could use them most advantageously as hostages.

One or several of them could be made to appear in collusion with Glasenapp's murderers.

One of them, maybe, could figure as the assassin!

There would be immense possibilities for publicity. Broadsides on all street corners of the city—30,000 Kronen, nay, 50,000 Kronen reward for whoever would give information leading toward the capture of the infamous murderers of Lieutenant Glasenapp, who was assassinated on the night of Thursday, October 9th, 1941, in or near the bar of the Café Mánes, in Prague.

Twenty hostages will be shot within a week if the murderer or murderers are not delivered to the authorities, or give themselves up.

Reinhardt was a changed man. All signs of inertia vanished. He walked up and down, snapping his fingers, talking to himself, his face flushed with excitement.

Then he snatched another piece of paper and, bending over his desk, wrote down a first draft of the announcement, and rang the bell.

The Kid entered noisily.

"Have this printed immediately, and posted on the walls and billboards," Reinhardt ordered.

The Kid was obviously eager to read the slip.

"Go ahead, read it!" Reinhardt prodded, affably.

35

He watched the Kid, whose eyes moved slowly along the lines.

"You are most clever, Commissioner," the Kid said, his voice reverent. "How did you know he was murdered? After we had deciphered that letter of Glasenapp's, I would have bet my best pair of shoes that he killed himself!"

Reinhardt smiled. When he smiled, his yellow teeth showed.

"You have yet a lot to learn, Gruber. In our work it is the effect that counts. Think that over. And get me the list of the people you rounded in the matter Glasenapp."

"You're going to have them shot?" asked the Kid.

"Not right away. I want to see what develops in this affair. I am quite curious myself. I have a friend who works in the Gestapo office in Paris, Murtenbacher is his name—you may have heard of him."

The Kid nodded.

"Murtenbacher told me that these hostage cases often take the most surprising turns. Murtenbacher said he was fascinated with the widely differing behavior of his hostages. He made quite a study of it. I think he even wrote an article about it in the *Schwarze Korps*. You might look it up if you have the time. And now get me that list, please."

"Yes, sir!" The Kid shot out of the room and was back in so short a time that Reinhardt felt compelled to ask, "You must have kept those papers handy. Did you expect me to request them?"

The Kid did not answer right away. He looked unhappy.

"Well, what's up?"

"I think I'd better tell you," young Gruber said, shuffling his feet. "One of them is, unfortunately, a big man in this country. He's been co-operating with us loyally all along. I only found that out when we took down their personal data at the desk. He received quite a pummelling from our men, because he talked back. But how was I to know?"

Reinhardt took a deep breath. "I wish you would not speak in such a long-winded way. Will you please tell me who the man is?"

Anxiously, the Kid placed the list before Reinhardt and pointed his finger at the name. "I thought of releasing him quietly—but then you took over the case, and I felt that it would be better if you decided . . ."

Reinhardt pushed the Kid's stubby finger away from the paper.

"*Lev Preissinger, Director-General, Bohemian-Moravian Coal Syndicate,*" Reinhardt read.

"By God!" he snapped. "It would be better if you kindly left decisions to me. Didn't I tell you that it is stupid to haul in people indiscriminately? Have you no brains in that thick skull of yours? Everything, but everything is spoiled now!"

Then he caught himself. He saw the big boy trembling, fear in his eyes. He compared his own slight build to the Kid's tremendous muscular body.

"Why are you shaking?" he asked sharply in order to hide his sudden amusement.

"Please, sir," the Kid begged, "don't send me away. I want to stay here. I want to make good. I want to stay here . . ." His voice trailed off.

Reinhardt began to see and to understand. This big, tough-looking boy was afraid of death, terribly afraid. He was afraid that he would be shipped away to the front, that he would have to die as so many others died.

"I will decide later what to do with you," Reinhardt announced casually. "Dismissed!"

Gruber, Jr., shuffled away, broken in spirit.

Let him worry a while, Reinhardt thought, it will be good for him. It will make him nice and pliable. He'll become faithful as a dog as soon as the feeling that his very life depends on me has penetrated the marrow of his bones.

37

He rubbed his hands. Reinhardt enjoyed having power over people.

Then his thoughts returned to the sad fact that among the prisoners of the Glasenapp case was this important Czech industrialist. He did not have much detailed information about the man, but he had heard enough to know that Lev Preissinger made frequent trips to Berlin to hobnob with influential German steel and coal men. He also had read that Preissinger had spoken at a conference on the New Economic Order in Europe, or something of that nature. Reich Minister of Economy Funk had presided at the conference, and Reinhardt knew that what Funk approved, went. Furthermore, the Bohemian-Moravian Coal Syndicate was busy filling German Government orders.

What a mess! At the offices of the Coal Syndicate they probably were moving heaven and earth to find out where their Director-General was. The wires to Berlin must be buzzing. It was lucky that he hadn't given out any report to the press.

Perhaps the Kid was right. If one released Preissinger quietly, with an apology cleverly mixed with hidden threats, the Czech would shut up.

But Reinhardt was not sure.

He probably would have to lay all aspects of the matter before the Protector. Commissioner Reinhardt was not important enough to speak authoritatively to a man of Preissinger's position. However, Heydrich, the Reich Protector in Prague, vested with all the power of the German Government, and himself one of the highest functionaries of the Secret State Police, could make all the Preissingers dance to whatever tune he whistled.

Reinhardt looked at his watch. It was not yet five o'clock. He was almost certain that, if he hurried, he would find the Protector in his office. Heydrich rarely left his office at Hradschin Castle before six. And even if he had left, Reinhardt knew which actress the Protector favored currently, and where her apartment was located.

Reinhardt took his belt from the hanger and carefully fastened it over his tunic. He patted the shining holster in which his revolver rested, always ready to be fired. He never went out without the gun. This had been his principle even in Germany, and here in Prague it was a matter of necessity. Too well had he observed the looks which people gave to his black uniform.

Before the mirror in the corner he put on his cap, carefully, so as to have the skull and crossbones insignia directly over the center of his forehead, and yet tilting it slightly so that it appeared severe and still a bit on the jaunty side.

Then he strode out of the office.

Downstairs, at the corner, he had his car waiting. Moenkeberg, the chauffeur, sprang to attention.

Reinhardt sniffed the clear air of the October afternoon. Prague, he suddenly felt, might be a good place to live in, during ordinary times, of course.

"The Hradschin," he said, "Palais of the Reich Protector."

"Yes, sir!" Moenkeberg opened the door of the big black limousine. With a sigh of relief, Reinhardt sank back in the soft, comfortable seat.

Though he was looking forward to a disagreeable interview with Heydrich, he felt good, strangely enough. Was it because of the air which was much more like spring than fall? Was it because he liked the quiet, efficient and disciplined Moenkeberg, one of the few men one could thoroughly rely on?

He had taken Moenkeberg with him wherever he went. They had first met in Hanover, in 1931, where Moenkeberg, quietly and efficiently, served the Republican Government as a traffic cop during the day, and distributed Nazi propaganda during the night. Reinhardt had been chief inspector of detectives, excelling in the collection of information on functionaries of trade unions and of the Social-Democratic and Communist Parties. At the same time he conducted a subtle campaign of intrigue against the Police Commissioner, who was a member of the Democratic Party, and who made a point of being "objective" toward everybody. Reinhardt smiled, remembering that little man who, when he had to arrest a couple of Nazis, did not feel happy till he also had hauled in an equal number of Communists. He was objective. Then Reinhardt would see to it that the Nazis were quietly released; and the Communists got a stiff term in jail.

He had encountered the Police Commissioner of Hanover once again in 1934. The little man had lost his little protruding belly, his little round head was shaved clean, and his hands trembled. That was in Oranienburg Concentration Camp. The former Commissioner was marching out with many others, into the moor, to dig peat. He did not seem to recognize Reinhardt; his eyes were staring straight ahead, little colorless eyes.

By that time Reinhardt had been put in charge of interrogating particularly difficult and important political prisoners. It was a traveling job, and Moenkeberg had been extremely useful, driving the car as well as helping in the work of exacting information and confessions. Common experiences of that kind bind men together.

Reinhardt liked the ride. Over the broad back of Moenkeberg he could see the old houses of the city shoot by. Moenkeberg always drove fast. He managed it without using the official siren too frequently, because he knew that Reinhardt hated its sharp wailing. The little flag fluttering above the hood of the limousine, was usually sufficient to bring other cars to a respectful stop, and to chase pedestrians as far away as possible.

They were now approaching Karl's Bridge. The houses of the *Altseite,* the old part of Prague, receded. The tires of the limousine began to sing on the smooth asphalt of the bridge. A golden apparition flashed by on the right—that was the famous crucifix.

The golden crucifix!

Reinhardt knew its story well. It was his practice to study the history of places to which his official duties led him. Knowledge always helped in his job.

Some Jew, in the Middle Ages, had walked across the bridge, and in passing the crucifix, had spat before the Savior. They had killed him. And they had sentenced the entire Jewish community to pay as much gold as was necessary to gild the crucifix.

A charming story. What amateurs they had been in those days! Reinhardt smiled, thinking of the much more efficient ways which, in recent years, had been developed to fleece the Jews of their possessions.

Through the big Gothic arch at the end of the Karl's Bridge, the car passed to the *Kleinseite* of the city, the part on the left bank of the Moldau River, where the narrow streets rise and wind dizzily to the top of the hill, on which stood Hradschin Castle, the Dome, and numerous other official buildings.

Moenkeberg knew his way well, and in an incredibly short time they drove past the saluting sentry up to the broad entrance of the Baroque palace in which the Reich Protector had his offices and living quarters. This had been the residence of the Presidents of the Czechoslovak Republic. Dr. Hacha, the puppet President, who now led the solitary existence of a sick and broken man, really did not need it any more. So he had been dispossessed—just one more little humiliation, infinitesimal in comparison with the big ones that mattered.

Reinhardt entered the palace and slowly mounted the stairs. He was thinking hard. It would be difficult to give a true picture of this case to Heydrich, whose irritability he had observed at various occasions. The Protector was a man of quick decisions. Even though they might be wrong, he would see to it that they were carried out to the last detail. He punished other men's mistakes ruthlessly, and he did not like to consider opinions other than his own.

Fortunately, Reinhardt had never yet incurred the Protector's displeasure. Nevertheless, he knew that everything depended on the mood in which he would find his superior.

Reinhardt did not have to wait long in the anteroom. An aide-de-camp, smartly uniformed, appeared and ushered him into the office of the Protector.

From the windows of the office, one had a marvelous view over the city, its many old towers and shining roofs. Heydrich stood at the window, his tall, gaunt figure black against the evening light.

Reinhardt clicked his heels, stood at attention. The Protector did not move. The aide-de-camp had left the room, silently closing the door.

He is playacting, Reinhardt thought. He wants to impress me. Damned if I make the opening move.

Then Heydrich began to speak, slowly, with a deep, droning voice.

"Come over here, Commissioner," he said, "I want to show you something."

Reinhardt obligingly hurried to join the Protector.

Heydrich, in the fashion of a schoolmaster, pointed his hand toward the city and made one wide sweeping gesture.

"I stand here frequently, observing," he droned. "What do you think of it?"

Reinhardt was taken aback. What did this mean? What did the Protector want him to say?

Finally, Reinhardt decided to answer as noncommittally as possible. "Quite a view, sir—quite a view!"

Heydrich turned around and, for the first time, looked directly at Reinhardt. Then he shook his head. "Oh, you— you policemen!" he said. "You have no eyes, no imagination.

42

Don't you see, all that out there is symbolic? Everything great in this city was built by Germans. We are just claiming what our forefathers created with blood and sweat. Those Gothic churches, pointing to heaven, reaching to the stars! That is German spirit. You understand?"

Reinhardt had trouble to suppress his urge to grin.

"Yes, sir," he said smartly, "I do understand. I did not know, though, that you wanted my opinion on architecture, otherwise I would have commented on it before." And to himself he thought: My God—does he talk like that to everybody? He'll make a perfect fool of himself!

Then he remembered that Heydrich was one of the intimate circle of Hitler's. Maybe this is the way they have fun, he thought. Perhaps this is a kind of fight talk they give themselves periodically. Perhaps this works like liquor— I don't know. But it would be interesting to find out what makes them tick.

Reinhardt became frightened of his own thoughts. They were decidedly detrimental to discipline.

"Well—let's get down to business!" the Protector said suddenly. His voice was different now, he sounded almost shrill. "I take it you have not come to admire my view. Have a seat and let's get through with it."

Reinhardt was deeply grateful that the tone and atmosphere had changed.

"It's concerning the affair Glasenapp that I have come to see you," Reinhardt began.

"I have heard of it," Heydrich interrupted. "Major Grauthoff of the Army called. He wants it settled quietly."

"Is that your opinion, too?" Reinhardt retorted.

"I have no opinion as yet. I want to hear what you have to say. The matter seems serious enough to merit some thought."

"It decidedly is!" Reinhardt said studiously. "After all,

the cold-blooded assassination of a German officer cannot just go unpunished, can it?"

Heydrich wagged his head. "Are you sure he was killed?"

Reinhardt hesitated for one moment. "I am proceeding on this assumption."

"Then what is your problem?" asked the Protector. "The procedure seems clear. Find the murderer, and if you can't find him, see to it that an example is made for the benefit of the population, so that an end is put to the wave of terror and sabotage."

"I am glad that we agree." Reinhardt really felt easier. He had feared that Major Grauthoff had given the Protector some ideas which would have impeded the plan as Reinhardt had conceived it. "Yet, there is a particular problem for the solution of which I need your help."

The Protector became more attentive. "This Glasenapp," he asked, "do you have any theory as to why he was killed?"

"Why! Why!" Reinhardt said angrily. "Our men get killed simply because they wear the glorious uniform of the Reich! There are elements in the population which will stoop to the most dastardly crimes to damage us. Why should we trouble ourselves to search for any other motives? Aren't the facts clear enough?"

Heydrich did not answer. He was not very much interested in the Glasenapp story. Nevertheless, he thought, the affair must be somewhat complicated. In the first place, why had Major Grauthoff telephoned him? And why did this fellow Reinhardt now trouble himself to come to his office?

Reinhardt took the Protector's silence for a hint to go on with his story. "One of my subordinates arrested everybody he found at the probable scene of the crime, the Café Mánes, down at the embankment of the Moldau River. We still have them in jail; they are fine hostages and. some of them might be the criminals.

"Among them, however, my subordinates picked up Lev

44

Preissinger, the Director-General of the Bohemian-Moravian Coal Syndicate."

Reinhardt was trying to read the Protector's thoughts. But Heydrich kept his poker face, not even his eyelids stirred.

"Now if we let this man—I understand he is quite influential in Berlin—if we let this Preissinger go, he might talk. He might spoil our prosecution. Hostages are hostages. If we once let it be known that some *can* get away, the entire system will lose whatever effectiveness it has."

The Protector nodded. "I have already received a letter from the Coal Syndicate, asking the whereabouts of Mr. Preissinger."

"I suggest that we bring the man secretly to your office," Reinhardt said. "You should talk to him. Impress him with the entire authority of your high position. Order him to shut up. Tell him that he'll be finished if he lets out a peep of what happened to him."

Heydrich sat silently for what seemed to Reinhardt a terribly long while. Then he asked:

"Why do you want to let Preissinger go?"

The question unsettled Reinhardt. He had learned that everywhere, even in the occupied countries, there were two kinds of people: the little ones who could and should be dealt with according to what seemed most expedient to the Secret State Police, and the big ones, the men of possessions and power who were to be left alone provided they did not interfere, and were satisfied to collaborate.

"Anything wrong with Preissinger?" he asked, logically spinning out his thoughts.

The Protector smiled benevolently. "What do you know of Mr. Preissinger's history?"

"Not much, really," Reinhardt muttered. He feared that he had walked into a trap. "Wasn't he a Minister at some time in the Czechoslovak Government?"

"You see," Heydrich informed him, continuing his patronizing air, "you should always inquire before you take any decisive step. If you had let him go—that would have been very disagreeable, very disagreeable indeed, to me and to others," he added carefully. "Our friend Preissinger is quite an intelligent chap. He was one of the top officials of the Czech Coal Syndicate before we took over this country. At that time the Syndicate was owned by the Petschek family, rich Jews, very rich Jews. After we marched in, the Petscheks moved out, and Mr. Preissinger succeeded in acquiring the controlling part of shares in the holding company of the Syndicate."

Reinhardt began to see daylight.

"We never, of course, asked him how he did it," Heydrich continued. "We are not interested in details of that kind. We simply dealt with Preissinger when we had to deal with the Coal Syndicate. We knew he was a safe man.

"You remembered correctly that Mr. Preissinger had been a Minister in the Czech Government. To be precise, he was a member of the Cabinet at the time of the Pact of Munich. We know that he gave the deciding vote when the question came up whether the Czechs should accept the Munich agreement. He made a little speech then. He said, 'Which would you rather have in this country—the Nazis or the Red Army?' You can see from this that Mr. Preissinger is a wise man."

"I see," Reinhardt replied, "but I do not understand why, considering his whole past, you want him kept in jail—and shot."

"Have a little patience, my man!" The Protector was oozing benevolence. "The Bohemian-Moravian Coal Syndicate is filling vast German Government orders. They are making a handsome profit. There are some very influential men at home who feel that all this money should not go into the pockets of Mr. Preissinger. People of more deserving character, Germans, should rather be considered. Don't you think so?"

46

"Certainly," Reinhardt assured.

"It therefore is in the national interest that Mr. Preissenger, in the most practicable way, be relieved of his financial burdens. I want to congratulate you, Commissioner, upon your good luck. I think I can see to it that you will be rewarded as you should be, if you succeed in settling this matter strictly and uncompromisingly."

Reinhardt felt relieved and happy. Everything worked out perfectly! He was doing a service to the Protector and to the Protector's anonymous friends in Germany. The Glasenapp case could now be settled without a single hitch. He would be promoted, he would be rich—he felt that he should shake the Protector's hand.

But Heydrich sat behind his desk, tall, gaunt and aloof. So Reinhardt kept his official attitude.

"It seems to me," he said, "that this really is an opportunity to demonstrate the socialism in the Führer's creed. We will comment on the fact that before our law, everybody is equal, the worker and the capitalist. We will dispose of them with equal justice—that is, unless we find the murderer of Lieutenant Glasenapp."

The Protector rose. The audience was obviously over. "I would like to mention," he remarked, "that you will solve this task with the same conscientiousness and reliability that your past record has shown you to possess."

Reinhardt snapped to attention. "Heil Hitler!" he shouted, almost jubilantly. The words re-echoed faintly in the big, high-ceilinged room.

CHAPTER 3

DR. WALTER WALLERSTEIN was the first of the five men in the cell to realize that they would have to die.

The idea came to him quite suddenly after he had spent the night—the second night in jail—lying on the same cot with Lobkowitz. What little sleep he had found had been restless, torturing, evil.

Now the pale light of the new day crept through the small, iron-barred window. Their cell was in the basement of the Gestapo headquarters, and this window was on the level of some courtyard where, all night, a guard had been pacing up and down in measured steps. The sound of those steps on the cobblestones of the courtyard had been digging itself into Wallerstein's brain. In the darkness he had tried to imagine the pattern of the guard's beat—left to right, then diagonally across the yard, then along the opposite wall, then back—a crazy quilt.

There—for the fraction of a second he could see the guard's boots. That was something—better, anyway, than just the tap tap sound.

And in this moment, like a flash, came the idea.

It had no rational foundation. None of them—neither

Preissinger nor he, nor his bunk mate Lobkowitz, nor the actor Prokosch nor that man Janoshik—none of them had been called for questioning. They did not know what their rôle and function were to be, and nobody told them.

Of course, Wallerstein refused to accept the idea. Every particle of his reasoning mind refused it. But the idea persisted, sat on his chest, heavy and hot.

He argued against it. Item one: What have we done? Nothing. Item two: What would they gain by killing us? Nothing.

To which the uninvited guest replied: You can't argue. Not with them, anyway. They are not open to your kind of logic. If they were, they'd be sitting at home in Germany.

True, thought Dr. Wallerstein. So we are going to die.

We meant principally I. I am going to die. To Wallerstein, other people, other beings had been alive only in so far as they mirrored themselves in his own senses. This had made him lonely, but he had known that there was greatness in his loneliness.

The coming of death filled him with regret mostly because such a sublimely sensitive and fine instrument as Walter Wallerstein, product of thousands of years of human thought, study and endeavor, should be scrapped. Scrapped just like anybody. How stupid and foolish of them! How offensive! Prisoner number so and so, he would be led to his execution, would have to die without leaving any permanent trace.

He felt uncomfortable. He turned his head, looked at young Lobkowitz who was sleeping deeply, with slightly open mouth and full, alive lips. This boy, too, would die—though what would it matter on the great ledger?

But he, who could dissect a person's soul using questions as his scalpel—? Something was wrong. Something must be done.

He was interrupted by Lobkowitz who stirred in his sleep, threw himself around and began to mumble incoherently.

49

Wallerstein could only understand: "I'll fight you—murderer you—goddamned smug face—"

A voice came from the lower bunk on the other wall: "Quiet, there!" That was Preissinger. Then Preissinger started to cough, loudly and thoroughly, like a man who is accustomed to a big sound-proof bathroom all for himself. "Morning," he grunted sourly, and sat up with effort. The wooden planks of his bunk groaned.

He stretched, yawned. "I have a splitting headache, Doctor," he said. "What do you recommend?"

Wallerstein decided not to answer. That man expected everybody to be at his service, no matter where they were, no matter what the hour. Let him think he was asleep.

But Preissinger was persistent. "Hey, Doctor Wallerstein!" he whispered loudly. "Are you awake? Have you some aspirin with you?"

Lobkowitz was wide awake now. He stared with glassy eyes at the planks over his head, which formed the bottom of the actor Prokosch's bunk.

Wallerstein figured that the others must be awake too, by now, and gave up his silence. "My office hours, Mr. Preissinger, are from three to five in the afternoon. I don't think your headache merits an emergency visit. Had you been prudent enough not to talk back to our hosts, they probably would have refrained from beating you over your thick head."

Janoshik grinned down from his bunk over Preissinger's. His heavy hair was messed up in a funny mop; he ran his fingers through it.

"I knew a man named Rudolf Holub once," he said, addressing the world in general. "He lived in Nusle, and also had a splitting headache every morning. He tried to get rid of it by beating his wife. Sometimes that helped. Then he began to trouble people by informing them that he was really the Minister of Agriculture, Blacek. When they asked him why he wasn't in his office, he said that an impostor was there. God knows why he picked on the Minister of Agriculture."

Wallerstein was interested. "And then what happened?"

"I'd rather not tell you," answered Janoshik, "it might have a depressing effect on Preissinger."

"Oh, go ahead," prodded Lobkowitz, "I never liked Blacek anyway. Stuffed shirt."

"Well, one day they picked him up in an ambulance. He fitted nicely into the strait jacket, I was told. When he died, his brain was so soft it made 'cluck cluck' in his skull. But he got a first rate funeral; his wife saw to that."

Prokosch, who had not uttered a syllable up to now, let out a dignified laugh. "A brutal story on an empty stomach," he said. "I wonder what they'll give us today."

"Same as yesterday, my dear Prokosch," announced Lobkowitz. "Scrambled eggs, coffee with cream, lovely hot rolls with plenty of butter and honey. What I don't like about this place is the monotony of diet. The Gestapo has no imagination in preparing food."

"Shut up!" shouted Preissinger, who felt the hunger the most because even under Nazi occupation, he never had suffered it.

But food and talk about food was something dear to everybody's heart—the last years, since the Nazis had arrived, had been lean. Janoshik took up where Lobkowitz had left off, and he carried on nobly. "I knew the cook in the Zlata Husa, a hefty female with one of the fattest asses in Prague—and by God, that means something! She loved me—she had a heart for the poor. Sometimes I would get last evening's special dinner for breakfast—pig's knuckles so well done the meat just fell off the bone, or goulash with paprika sauce, the real thing to wake one up."

Preissinger was genuinely enraged. Since the Kid had arrested him, he had been continuously mad, except when he was unconscious. There had been no chance to cool off—everything seemed calculated to humiliate him. The Nazis had done their best, and even his own compatriots in this cell showed no regard whatever for his position in life.

He had sworn to pay back every offense, every indignity. He was busy for hours on end memorizing them—and the more he thought about them, the more his fury rose. Just wait till he got out of this mouse trap—curse his associates at the Coal Syndicate, why hadn't they done anything by now? But today, he surely would be let out, and then there would be hell to pay!

The only one he regarded with any good will was the actor Prokosch, who was quiet and a bit pompous. If only the fellow would not talk so much of his wife, especially since she was dead. All of yesterday, Prokosch had droned on about her. Preissinger was a full-blooded man, and his interest in the dead was very limited. They were buried, and life went on, and he had told Prokosch to look around for another wife, as soon as they got out of here. Prokosch's blessed wife, Preissinger had said, certainly wouldn't wish her husband to go through the rest of his life lonely. That is, if Prokosch had to be married at all. He, Preissinger, was married, and his marriage was nothing but one long series of troubles.

Prokosch had smiled quietly. "You would not speak this way," he had said, "if you had known Mara, Mr. Preissinger."

"Oh, yes, I would!" Preissinger had insisted. If it weren't for his wife, he would not even be in this stinking wet dark Gestapo cellar. No, sir! Only to discuss his wife's mental state had he met Dr. Wallerstein in the goddamned Mánes Bar.

But Prokosch did not seem to be overly interested in the mental state of Mrs. Preissinger. He had again started to talk of Mara.

52

Well, Preissinger conceded, hers was a tragic fate. To die
in childbirth, and leave the little worm all alone.

The new day had started definitely. Even through the
strong door of their cell, they could hear the guards shuffling
outside in the corridor. A man's voice cried: "No! No!
Please—don't!" The voice died in a gurgle.

"Morning exercise—" remarked Lobkowitz.

He arose from the cot he was sharing with Wallerstein,
and tried to unlimber. From the window to the door, the
distance was four and a half long steps or six short steps.
At first, the cell had seemed terribly small to them. Along
the side walls, bunks were built one above the other. But
they were five men—so Lobkowitz and Wallerstein, who were
slightest, were sleeping together.

In the course of the first day they had become used to
these cramped quarters. After that they tried to keep out of
one another's way by staying on their cots. Only one, at most
two, would stand or walk.

Now the air was sticky from the perspiration of five bodies,
five bodies which had not been washed for two days; their
faces had assumed the prison pallor, accentuated by the
sprouting stubble of their beards.

Lobkowitz walked up and down. "Do you think," he asked,
"the fellow who cried was the same they took out yesterday?"

"How do I know?" grunted Janoshik.

Prokosch coughed to clear his throat for an important
statement. "These morbid questions, my dear Lobkowitz,"
he said finally, "don't help any of us. I am sure we all felt
the same chill running down our spines—let's try to overcome
it by not thinking of it."

Lobkowitz walked on. "What the hell do you want us to

53

think about? What do chickens think of when they're carted to market in their little coops?"

"Of digging in the dirt. And that there is no dirt around to dig in," Janoshik ventured to guess.

"That is precisely my point!" Prokosch said. "Life: Think of life! Some time we shall be part of it again. One does not appreciate life till one has met death face to face. I did. When Mara died—and you knew, Lobkowitz, how full of life she was—when she died I met death. Death was interminable emptiness, gray and without horizons. In those days, I wished to die. One more tiny dot on the great gray plain."

Wallerstein, who had been enjoying the full width of his cot, asked dreamily, "And why didn't you?"

"Because Mara believed in me. To her, I represented life. You don't dare to disappoint such belief. It was for her I had to go on. Go on living. Creating. If I played my part well, I would say: This is for you, Mara."

Lobkowitz, still walking, laughed harshly.

"Sounds banal to you, doesn't it?" Prokosch asked.

"Yes, awful." Lobkowitz turned to him. "And Mara's child? Didn't you think of the child?"

"Of course. The child was part of her. But then again the child was the cause of her death, it *was* her death. I loved her more than I ever will love the child. That's the truth."

There was a strange gleam in Lobkowitz' eyes. "You loved her because you loved yourself. She was the wall against which you spoke so that you could hear your own echo. She was the glass in which you mirrored your own goddamned big ego!"

Wallerstein sat up. His interest was aroused. He could sense a conflict a mile away. He was drawn to it naturally.

Above him, he could hear Prokosch stir uneasily. Then the actor's long legs dangled before him. Prokosch jumped.

Lobkowitz had stopped walking. The two men faced each other.

"You're lying," Prokosch said, hardly lifting his voice.

Janoshik, on his cot, made ready to prevent the fight. Not that he didn't enjoy a good fight. But he had had jail experience and knew that in crowded cells the spectators were liable to get hurt. Besides, the guards would probably come in, and it was better not to arouse their attention.

However, Lobkowitz gave in. "All right," he said, "have it your way. I'm a bit high-strung this morning. Sorry."

Prokosch retreated to his cot without replying.

Preissinger had sat motionless throughout the incident. He did not care one way or another. What did these people mean to him? All this was still a vicious dream—some strange power had transplanted him into this cell, a big fat Alice into a dark and depressing Wonderland. He did not belong, and as far as he was concerned, he would not belong. So much excitement about a woman, and a dead woman at that! These people and their petty problems deserved his contempt. He always had felt that they and their kind were far beneath him—one had to consider them in calculations on wages, dismissals, hirings. They were voters and readers of newspapers and soldiers; but they counted only when taken as numbers, groups, masses. One placed them here or there, wherever necessary. So Mr. Prokosch's wife *had* believed in him, he *had* loved her, and the other fellow said it was all nonsense; and what was the difference?

Carola Preissinger, his wife, had sometimes told him such stories over the dinner table. She had read them in books. If she hadn't read so many books, or at least had read the right kind of books, she might not have made so much trouble. Hysterical, she was. And he wouldn't have had to confer with Wallerstein, and he would be ready to drive to his office by this time of the day, instead of being forced to listen to these men.

"I want to get out of here!" He was surprised at how loud he said this.

"Don't we all?" replied Wallerstein, who was reclining again. There was silence now. Apparently nobody cared to talk.

Wallerstein took up his train of thought which had been interrupted by Preissinger's complaints and by the incident between Prokosch and Lobkowitz. He did not mind the interruptions, though, for they furthered his ideas somewhat. He discovered that he was fascinated by the reactions of his cell mates. With the exception of Preissinger, they had been strangers to him. But there was no reason why what he was observing in Preissinger would not hold true with the others.

Preissinger was undergoing a change. Of all the people Wallerstein had known, Preissinger had been the least sensitive. And here the man was becoming thin-skinned! Well, there were not many signs yet, but they would increase, no doubt.

The men in this cell were like so many stones forced by the rush of water through the narrows of a stream. They must rub one another, be thrown one against the other. It was a perfect laboratory with human samples for experiment—that's what it was.

Wallerstein was worried about himself. He, too, would be exposed to the atmosphere, to the change of soul they were undergoing. Perhaps what he was thinking now was, in fact, the result of his thanatophobia. He must get hold of himself, discipline himself. What did he want? Relief from fear? Some plan to which he could devote himself in order to escape the cruel waiting for the end?

Be honest! he demanded of himself.

Death was emptiness, gray, without horizons—Prokosch had said it. Wallerstein shuddered. It was not the act of dying he feared—that, probably, would be short. Certainly short in comparison to the eternity of utter nothing.

Once he had listened to a priest's soothing words. Wallerstein had been skeptical—he could not make himself accept the priest's belief in what he was saying. But these words made things easier, yes. They gave a definite picture of the other world, not, by any means, an attractive picture for someone whose life had been rich with earthy and spiritual values. In fact, that priest's other world had been rather bloodless—paradise, music, mildness.

There would be no priest here to tell fairy tales. And he could not accept them anyhow. Some other way must be found to enable him to stand this ordeal without going crazy.

The rattling of keys made everyone get up. They had learned that, upon entry of the guard, they were to line up before their bunks, at rigid attention. This discipline seemed ridiculous in the crowded cell which the guard could encompass in a brief glance. To the Nazis, however, this kind of discipline was a matter of principle. It had to be carried out even if its stupidity was glaring.

A black-uniformed trooper stood in the door, coolly surveying the prisoners. Apparently, this was only a routine inspection. The tension of the men let up somewhat.

A Czech warden, subservient to the German, appeared, and placed a bucket in the cell. He also carried five pieces of mealy gray matter—bread. Then he hurriedly shuffled away and returned with a pitcher full of hot liquid, and five tin cups.

The Czech repeated his instructions of yesterday: "You've got to be through with the bucket and with your breakfast in fifteen minutes. One of you will have to carry out the bucket, when we come back."

The German said nothing, he looked bored. This encouraged Preissinger to approach him and ask modestly, "Excuse me, sir. I would like to know whether somebody from the

57

Bohemian-Moravian Coal Syndicate has made inquiries on my behalf?"

Janoshik noticed the mild manner with which Preissinger addressed the Nazi. He decided to give some moral support.

"This gentleman," he explained, "is the Director-General of the Coal Syndicate and he wishes to know about his business affairs. How much coal was shipped to the Reich in the last two days, and whether the German Government is satisfied with the deliveries. He is very essential to the war effort, and would like to do his best even under the present circumstances."

The German guard was amazed and impressed. He was accustomed to stubborn silence and hostility on the part of his prisoners, or to trembling fear, but not to the amiable co-operation which he heard in Janoshik's words.

"Well—" he said, "I don't know. You'll have to find out from Commissioner Reinhardt, I guess. He's in charge here." Then he caught himself. He was talking to the prisoners as if they were people!

He shouted at Preissinger: "That is none of your business! Attention!" And turned and marched off with his little Czech assistant.

The door shut.

Preissinger turned to Janoshik, ready to jump at his throat. "Why, for God's sake, do you interfere in my affairs? Can't I take care of myself? You are trying to keep me in here, to drive me crazy!"

"Your affairs?" Lobkowitz inquired. "I thought getting out of here was our concern as much as yours."

"Go, use the bucket," Janoshik advised Preissinger. "It'll help your headache. And you have only three minutes to do it—you heard the guard."

Preissinger saw that there was nothing to do but to follow Janoshik's suggestion. He cursed softly between his efforts to move his bowels.

The others tried to eat what, by hyperbole, was termed breakfast. Even had the Nazis given the matter much thought, they could hardly have evolved a better method to make the beginning of day more miserable for their prisoners. The cells had no sanitary facilities, since the basement of the former Petschek Palais which served as Gestapo headquarters had never been planned as a prison. The Nazis' intention was merely to save themselves unnecessary work. Why serve breakfast and the bucket at different times? If their prisoners' appetite suffered thereby—so much the better. It would help the food situation.

But the men in the cell were not deterred by Preissinger's groans. They had to get something into their stomachs, and had to keep it there. The bread tasted like cotton, and the liquid, called coffee, like an extract of burned wood—and yet they hoped the stuff would sustain them.

Wallerstein, munching his piece of bread, said, "I'll volunteer to carry away the bucket today. Yesterday Janoshik did it—let everybody have his chance."

"Your offer is graciously accepted," replied Prokosch. "And let me have some more of this drink, whatever it may be, before I succeed Preissinger on his throne."

He swallowed the hot fluid and looked at Preissinger, who was buttoning up his pants. "I never lived so close to people," Prokosch continued. "It is a worth while experience. We forget what animals we are when we live too luxuriously. In most people"—he stepped to the bucket—"in most people this closeness furthers consideration for one another.... Look," he said disgustedly, "look how much of our newspaper Preissinger used up!"

Lobkowitz put his empty cup on the floor. "I want to know," he demanded, "what is going to happen to us. Even the Nazis cannot be insane enough to keep us here forever just because we happened to be in a bar from which some officer disappeared. He must have been found by now."

"Maybe they've forgotten about us," suggested Janoshik.

"I'm goddamned serious," Lobkowitz answered. "If we had conspired in any way, if any one of us were in the underground—then I could understand. But I am sure—"

"Sure of what?" interrupted Wallerstein.

"That we are innocent! As innocent as the day is long!"

"Our standards of innocence are quite different from those of the Nazis," remarked Prokosch from the bucket.

"I had nothing to do with this Glasenapp!" Preissinger said with emphasis. "And I will make this very clear. I just wait for the moment when I'll be called before this Gestapo official!"

Wallerstein sipped the rest of his coffee. "I am sure that Commissioner Reinhardt—I think that was the name our guard mentioned—I am sure that the Commissioner can't wait to lend your statements a willing ear."

"But what are we to do?" pleaded Lobkowitz. "We must do something! We must find out what we're here for, under what pretense they're holding us! The hours go by and the days. We're buried alive. . . ."

Janoshik was making himself ready to use the bucket. "As far as I am concerned," he stated, "I must say that I have made progress. I used to clean up other people's dirt. Now mine will be carried away by somebody else, a doctor, an academically educated man at that."

Lobkowitz ignored Janoshik's observations. "We have waited long enough!" he shouted. "It's time to act!"

Janoshik knew the kind of jitters from which Lobkowitz suffered. During the first few days of being cooped up, they were particularly difficult. In the jails of the Czechoslovak Republic, where Janoshik had gained his experience, pen and paper were handed to the prisoner, and he could write an appeal. An appeal helped in almost all cases, though it went into the wastebasket. It was a good expedient to let the prisoner blow off steam.

60

The Nazis were far less humane. They did not supply paper and pen. Also, Janoshik feared, arousing their attention might have sorry consequences for them all, but especially for young Lobkowitz whom he liked.

"I knew an old woman who lived in Vršovice," he said in his quiet way. "She used to sell newspapers at the corner. She was poor. When the Nazis marched in, she stopped selling papers. She said she wouldn't let people pay good money for bad lies. She meant well, as you can see."

He was standing now, having settled his business, and the very simplicity of his words made the others sit up and listen.

"So they arrested her. She's been in a concentration camp now for a little over two years. She is patient, she waits. And she has much less time left to wait than you have."

"How do you know all that?" Preissinger said, inquisitively.

"I just know. People tell me things."

Lobkowitz had become quiet.

Wallerstein's plan was ripening. He was careful not to let the others feel how tense he was. To carry the bucket away was his chance to break through the walls of his cell, to start his grand experiment which would be so singular, so audacious, that perhaps even his death would find its justification and glory in it.

But if the Nazis did not co-operate? He must not admit that possibility. He simply must succeed in impressing his mind on that man Reinhardt, whatever sort of creature he might turn out to be. This was essential.

The guards returned. The prisoners had finished breakfast and had filled the bucket.

Wallerstein, fighting down a nauseous urge, picked up

61

the bucket and followed the guards, walking, as he always did, a little awkwardly, with shuffling feet.

For the first time since he had been shoved into it, he left the crowded, narrow cell. He heard the strong door fall into its lock. The bucket was heavy, its handle cut into the flesh of his fingers. But he did not mind. With quick glances he observed his new surroundings. It was a long, dark corridor, scantily lit by tired electric bulbs. It gave the impression that one was deep down in the earth, in a world strange and gruesome, an anteroom to a hell he knew he would have to go through. Many doors like the one to his cell lined the walls; the doors were numbered and below the numerals were posted lists of names—the inmates of the cell. Some of the names were crossed out and others had been substituted in penciled writing. A short and efficient obituary, thought Wallerstein.

Occasionally, shadowy groups passed him and his two guards. The Nazi's boots resounded harshly on the stone floor of the corridor. The Czech warden hurried along on soft soles. Wallerstein quickened his pace, and finally caught up with the Nazi.

The doctor cleared his throat. "I wish to make a report in the matter of Lieutenant Glasenapp," he said.

"Get back!" the guard bellowed. "Keep that stench at a distance!"

Obediently Wallerstein fell back. Walking some ten steps behind the guard, he shouted: "Sorry I offended your sensitive nose! But what I have to say is of great importance. I respectfully ask you to take me to Commissioner Reinhardt."

The guard did not answer. The little Czech turned for a moment and looked at Wallerstein with a mixed expression of surprise and suspicion.

Wallerstein did not feel any too good. That German idiot, who wrapped himself in silence, did not seem to react to his approaches. Should he try again? He might only infuriate the man. And why had the Czech warden looked at him in that funny way? Well, maybe the Czech thought he was an informer. After all, it was an unusual request—in most cases, prisoners tried to evade encounters with Gestapo officials.

They had arrived at the end of the corridor. The Nazi opened a double door to a large room, obviously the heating plant of the building. Two boilers, which were not in operation, and an incinerator stood at the far wall. The rest of the room, however, was equipped in a particular way, and it took Wallerstein a few seconds before his mind grasped the significance of its furnishings.

In the corner was a writing desk with a typewriter carefully covered; beside the desk stood several easy chairs. In the center were two oblong tables with leather straps hanging from the sides. On the wall were two racks, similar to those in which billiard cues are placed in a pool room. Instead of the billiard cues, however, a goodly collection of steel whips, rubber truncheons, and sticks were lined up. There were whips with thick ends, and fine, straight whips and whips turned like spirals, whips to cut the flesh and whips to break the bones. On the floor stood half a dozen pails, filled with water. Also on the floor lay a heap of old rags.

Wallerstein, who had become acutely aware of where he was, had the ridiculous urge to ask the Nazi whether these rags were used to gag people's mouths, or to wipe the floor, or both—because the floor was carefully washed. The whole room evidenced the impeccable, cleanly, systematic orderliness of the men in charge.

"*Nu*," prodded the Nazi guard, "why do you stand there? Dump that bucket in the incinerator."

Wallerstein obeyed. He burned his hand on the hot handle of the incinerator door, but he scarcely noticed it.

The Czech warden sat down on one of the tables in the center of the room. He lit a cigarette. Absent-mindedly he

63

picked up a leather strap, but dropped it suddenly, having touched something wet or sticky.

"The prisoner wanted to see Commissioner Reinhardt," he remarked to his Nazi colleague. "I wonder why?"

With a deep sigh the Nazi let himself down in an easy chair and stretched.

"Why do you want to see the Commissioner?" he asked Wallerstein.

Wallerstein, holding the empty bucket in his sound hand, became conscious of the pain in his other. He blew on it.

"Burned yourself?" the Nazi asked with a show of sympathy. "Should have used one of those rags to open the door."

"It's the first time I've touched an incinerator," Wallerstein remarked. "First time I've seen the inside of any heating plant, for that matter."

The Nazi mused. "I guess we'll have to move this equipment when winter comes around. It'll be too hot to work here when those boilers are going. They should have thought of that in the first place."

"There is no other room with double doors and thick walls like this in the building," the Czech added.

"So what?" the Nazi shrugged. "There's no law that questioning must be conducted in a sound-proof room."

He turned back to Wallerstein. "Why did you say—that you wanted to see the Commissioner?"

"Just tell him it's some new information in the Glasenapp case. He'll know," Wallerstein said.

"All right with me," the Nazi yawned. "But I tell you the chief is a particular man. He'll be tough on you if you waste his time." He arose and became official again. "Forward!" he ordered. "Leave the bucket here."

Back in the corridor Wallerstein felt his knees give way. Disagreeable cold sweat broke out all over him. He shook with fear. If he had had the strength, he would have implored the Nazi guard to forget his request. But as it was, he dragged himself behind the guard to an elevator.

He did not have to wait long in the anteroom to Reinhardt's office. He wished to wait, to get a chance to compose himself. But the guard came out of the inner office hardly a minute after he had entered it, and Wallerstein was motioned in.

Face to face with the man in whose hands he was, Wallerstein gained hold of himself immediately. He did it by looking at the Commissioner as he would have looked at a patient—searchingly, coolly estimating.

The Commissioner reclined comfortably behind his desk, his dark, narrow eyes glancing past Wallerstein. Slick and ambitious he is, thought the doctor. Fellow who tries to conceal his emotions, whatever they are. Ruthless out of fear—the right man in the right place.

The piercing eyes now concentrated on the visitor.

"You're Dr. Walter Wallerstein, fifty-four years old, Aryan, single, residing at Vinohradská Street 380?"

"The same," Wallerstein bowed slightly.

"As you no doubt deduced from the lettering on the door, I am Commissioner Reinhardt."

"Honored." Wallerstein bowed again. "I regret, though, that we meet under these circumstances."

"Why? Even in my official capacity, I try to be as pleasant as possible." Reinhardt smiled, which made his weak chin seem even weaker.

Wallerstein smiled back. "Why? Because ours is bound to be such a short acquaintance."

"Not necessarily so," replied Reinhardt.

Wallerstein hesitated. He could go on fencing, but the fellow did not look as if he had inexhaustible patience. Furthermore, Wallerstein was not quite sure, as he had been in the early morning, how matters stood, and he feared to provoke developments upon which the other had not yet decided.

However, Reinhardt came to his aid. "If you have any information in the case of Lieutenant Glasenapp, who was murdered so bestially by one or several of your countrymen—I am willing to listen. If, on the other hand, you just came to ask for your release, I am afraid it will be impossible for me to comply."

"My information is not available yet, and I don't know whether it will contribute vitally to the solution of your case," Wallerstein began.

"It is up to me to judge that, isn't it?" Reinhardt lit a cigarette. "Want one?" he offered. "Why don't you sit down?"

Wallerstein nodded, took the still burning match from Reinhardt's hand—and shuddered. The Commissioner's fingernails were manicured and painted with light pink polish which stood out in terrible contrast to the rough skin of his clawlike fingers.

"Afraid?" Reinhardt prodded.

"Of course I am afraid." Wallerstein finally succeeded in tearing his eyes away from the Commissioner's fingers. "So is everybody. Including you."

"I beg to differ!" Reinhardt said sharply. "What should I be afraid of?"

"Fear, Commissioner, is an important motivating factor in our life. Why should you be an exception? Fear of death, mostly. Fear of life, by the way, is pretty much the same. If you shoot me, for instance—and I believe you will—you do it out of fear."

Reinhardt blew smoke through his nose. He was silent. Then he said, offhandedly, "I really don't know why I listen to your impertinent remarks. I don't need your information. If and when we want it, we will question you, and question you in our way. But tell me—how do you know

66

that we will shoot you? Have any of the guards been talking to you?"

"No," Wallerstein reproved mildly. "I do not inquire from secondhand sources what I can learn first hand. This morning, the idea suddenly occurred to me. And you have confirmed it."

The Commissioner was disturbed. Disturbed not so much at what Wallerstein said as at his own feelings. The doctor, meek as he seemed, spoke so unemotionally, just as he, Reinhardt, liked to speak. He knew he was met on his own plane, and he was not sure of himself. So he tried to shock his opponent.

"Want some more confirmation?" he asked, and handed Wallerstein a large, carefully folded sheet. Wallerstein unfolded it and read:

NOTICE

On the night of Thursday, October 9th, 1941, in or near the bar of the Café Mánes, in Prague
Lieutenant ERICH GLASENAPP
431st Infantry Division
was assassinated by person or persons unknown.

A reward of 50,000 Kronen will be assured those who by their aid permit the arrest of the guilty persons.
TWENTY HOSTAGES
will be shot within a week, if the murderer or murderers are not apprehended, or delivered to the authorities, dead or alive, or give themselves up.

Signed:

Helmut Reinhardt, Colonel

Commissioner, Secret State Police

The poster was printed in German and Czech; above the word "Notice" perched the German Eagle, holding a Swastika wheel in its claws.

Wallerstein refolded the sheet and handed it back. If Reinhardt had expected the doctor to show signs of distress, he was disappointed.

Wallerstein was cool and collected. "Fifty thousand Kronen is a lot of money," he said, "for a lieutenant."

"We have no scales!" Reinhardt interposed angrily.

"I did not mean it that way, beg your pardon. Do you think there might be any takers?"

"I don't have second sight, like you," Reinhardt snapped. "I don't know. But I do look forward to silencing you!"

He was annoyed with himself the moment he had said it. Why had he permitted the doctor to disturb his imperturbability? But most stupid was the fact that the usual line of bullying would not work with this man. Threatening him just proved weakness. Though what did it matter what Dr. Walter Wallerstein thought of Commissioner Reinhardt?

Yes, it mattered. It suddenly mattered terribly. I, Reinhardt thought, am master of this situation, am I not? Therefore I must listen, quietly—he wished he never had let this man in, he wished he were not so annoyed—

He felt Wallerstein's eyes searching him.

Wallerstein picked up the conversation. "Before, you wanted to know why you listen to me. Well, you listen because you are fascinated. Or interested, to say the least. It is seldom that men of our caliber meet."

Wallerstein kept a perfectly straight face. He was proud that he had been able to think up this flattery; it was good, and it would certainly entice the policeman.

"You know how bored you get with average people," he continued, "I have them right now in my cell, and it is one of my problems. And this is what I came to see you about."

"Lack of entertainment?" Reinhardt asked incredulously. "This is the first time in any Gestapo prison that anybody complained about that!"

Wallerstein let out an appreciative guffaw. "Seriously,

68

Commissioner, I am a scientist. Fate, as impersonated by you, has placed into my hands the chance for an epoch-making psychological experiment. There are four men and myself—in the face of, may I say, certain death.

"It may have happened before, but I don't know of it. A shipwreck, people in lifeboats, drifting for days on end over the wide expanse of the ocean—but till their last dying minute they refuse to give up hope. Soldiers in a dugout, artillery hammering at them constantly, their comrades dying right and left—but those who still live, hope, hope. A mine disaster, men shut off from the world, water rising slowly, reaching their breasts, their shoulders, their mouths—but they hope to live until the water has risen above their mouths. People are afraid of death, afraid to face death, therefore they refuse to believe in death. In a general death—yes, quite. But not in their own personal death. If that were not the case, the world would be different, entirely different. Your Führer, for instance—do you believe he could get any man to march in his army, if that man, in his innermost heart, did not passionately believe that death is going to pass him by?"

"We are willing to sacrifice our lives for Germany!" Reinhardt exclaimed, but it was merely a formal protest.

"Of course! Because whoever swears this oath crosses his fingers and hopes to be part of that Germany that survives the holocaust. But let's stick to the point.

"My four cell mates and I are going to be shot. That is as certain as your power over us.

"You offer 50,000 Kronen. All right. Suppose that the unfortunate Lieutenant Glasenapp *was* killed by some Czech. In that case, the attempt was organized. I know the people of this country, once they're aroused. They don't turn traitor that easily.

"I am not approving of such heroism, of course. If I knew Glasenapp's killer, I might, or might not, turn him in—but

69

I don't know him. My thinking is more abstract. I find the whole war ludicrous. We are far too busy ruling and being ruled—conquering and being conquered—collection of bugs in the fur of a minor planet that we are.

"Nevertheless, you could have saved the expense of printing the poster—the hostages are going to die. And I am among them. I have the singular opportunity of observing a group of men in the face of absolute certainty of death! As a man, I am afraid. As a scientist, I am thrilled."

Wallerstein took one last puff from his cigarette, and then stamped it out in the ashtray on Reinhardt's desk.

Reinhardt was puzzled. His animosity toward Wallerstein had been drowned in the excitement caused by the doctor's words. But Reinhardt, habitually, did not trust anybody. What the man had said, sounded intriguing enough. Was it, perhaps, some super-trick which he was unable to see through? Where did all this lead to? Was Wallerstein a fool or so damned clever that he tried to fool him, Commissioner Reinhardt?

"I want you to execute not only me," Wallerstein continued, "but also my last will. I shall write down—provided you supply me with paper and return my fountain pen— my observations on these men and myself during our last days. I shall draw certain conclusions from their behavior. You may read it, I'll be glad if you do. But I want you to forward the manuscript to the *Psychologische Monatsschrift,* to which I frequently have contributed. I know that this publication has lost much of its former quality during the last years, but what matters to me is that some record of this great experiment of yours and mine be preserved for the generations to come."

"And that is all you want?" Reinhardt asked.

Dr. Wallerstein nodded gravely.

"And if I refuse?"

Wallerstein preferred to disregard this question. "Further,

I'd like you to write an introduction to my article. You could state the facts which caused it to be written. That would make it all the more authentic."

Reinhardt pushed his chair back. He began to pace the entire width of the office. He knew that the proposal was outrageous. It was highly irregular, though he could not remember any rules or orders pertaining to it. If he told his colleagues or superiors about the project, they would laugh; if he told them that he was inclined to accept and permit it, they would think him insane.

If it was extraordinary, he reasoned, it might, nevertheless, prove helpful in the prosecution of the case. To have a trained observer among the suspects of the murder was almost as good as placing a stool pigeon in the cell. A good idea—but unfortunately the fact came to mind that Lieutenant Glasenapp had committed suicide, and that therefore no real suspects existed.

It was too damned complicated!

He stopped pacing; he stood behind his desk, his brow furrowed, his eyes trying to penetrate Wallerstein's expression. The doctor's face was friendly, almost peaceful.

"At best," Reinhardt said, "it will be entertaining to read, and at worst, I have been magnanimous. Here is a pad—I'll give orders that you get your pen. I won't give you a bottle of ink, because I've known people in concentration camps to open their veins with shards of glass. But you can have the pen refilled."

"Thank you very much," Wallerstein bowed.

"It may interest you," Reinhardt remarked, "to know that one of my colleagues in Paris, Murtenbacher is his name, also made certain observations on hostages. Of course, he is just a Gestapo functionary, but I found his article quite enlightening. It was printed about a year ago in our Elite Guard magazine, and I will be glad to write him for a copy."

"Don't bother, please." Wallerstein smiled pleasantly. "I am afraid it would reach me a little too late."

Reinhardt said, "As you wish—" and rang the bell.

The guard appeared and received his order: "Lead the prisoner back to his cell!"

Saluting. Heel clicking.

Riding down the elevator and walking along the dark, cold corridor, Wallerstein suffered a relapse into reality. Was it true or just a wild dream? It seemed too fantastic. Wallerstein wondered. He had developed his proposal from an embryonic idea, and had done it mostly while talking to Reinhardt. If the fellow served so well as a sounding board, perhaps he would have understanding enough not to throw the notes, the as yet unwritten notes, into the wastebasket. With a desperate hand Wallerstein clasped the pad of paper. The guard pushed him into the cell. For a moment Wallerstein stood dazed. Then he became conscious of the questioning eyes upon him.

"We are hostages," he announced. "In about five days we will be shot."

CHAPTER 4

THE SHOP was humming, twenty-four hours a day. They turned out armaments for the German Government, and hated it, every minute of the twenty-four hours.

Outwardly, things looked smooth enough. But once you learned to distinguish between the faces of the workers and those of the stool pigeons, you had no doubt that the shop was part of a volcano, and that the ground you walked on was thin and hot.

Though Milada Markova only recently had taken her job at the Kolben Daněk Works—for short, Kolbenka—she had learned to distinguish. Breda you could trust. Seliger was a rat. You could recognize it from the way Seliger fawned upon the gray-uniformed Nazi soldiers who were standing guard in strategic spots all over the grounds. You could recognize it from Seliger's wheedling voice, and from the fact that he had some sort of meat on his bread for lunch.

Milada worked at the Kolbenka because otherwise she would have starved. Of course, she could have gone home to her parents. But this would have meant conceding defeat— rather, she worked her fingers to the bone. Her father, Professor Jan Marek, was an editor of the newspaper *Národní*

Politika. Always a reactionary sheet, the paper had gone all-out for the Nazis since the day of their arrival in Prague. Jan Marek had joined with his bosses because all of his life he had sided with the powerful—and because there was nothing else to do anyway, don't you see, Milada, my child?

But Milada did not see. It had been an awful row. Professor Marek had called on several saints and complained bitterly: Here, he had done his best for that child; he had sent her to the University at heavy sacrifice. Had she ever had to deny herself anything? No, certainly not! What base ingratitude! But he knew the reason—too much freedom, too much running around with all sorts of people; but now, he would put a stop to it. He would set his foot down, exert his authority, and, if necessary, give her a good whipping. Yes, he admitted, it was not entirely Milada's fault. He, the father, was to blame too. He had failed by not punishing her enough, he had been too much the liberal. However, he assured her, that would happen no more. He would not tolerate an enemy in his own house, a snake in his bosom.

It was hard, back-breaking work at the Kolbenka. People did not dare help each other much—the foremen had to make sure that they talked to one another only when absolutely necessary to the pursuit of their job. Besides, there was a great turnover of workers. New faces appeared constantly. Others left. Where they went, one was not sure. There was a law which made it punishable to change one's job. Yet, men and women could not be tied to their benches. And it was difficult to stand the speed of work, sapped as one's strength was by the lack of good nourishment.

Two weeks before Milada entered the Kolbenka, a number of workers had disappeared in a very obvious way—they had been arrested for allegedly organizing a slowdown.

The management's labor policy was two-sided; the turnover meant that their production was hampered, and therefore, they opposed it; on the other hand they favored a constant change of personnel because it prevented the worker from learning to know the man next to him, from trusting him, and from organizing.

Only a small number of absolutely essential men in key jobs remained steady. Breda was one of this group.

The day shift left at six o'clock. They had been at work since seven in the morning; their faces looked haggard and tired. A long, shabby line, they filed past the guards at the steel-barred door, which was flanked by two machine guns. The guards searched every one of them, carefully, methodically. Then the workers were on their way, dragging their steps, or boarding the rattling, crowded tramway.

At the corner a silent crowd gathered around a signpost. A fresh black and white placard seemed to attract their attention. There was no muttering, no discussion. People studied the poster, and just waited. Some shook their heads, slowly.

It was the Glasenapp poster, signed by Reinhardt.

Breda and Milada stood near each other. Breda had read the poster thoroughly, had tried to weigh the significance of each line, each word. No muscle in his face moved, though his throat had become terribly dry. His mind switched back to that evening in the Mánes Bar, to the drunken officers, and his first clear thought was: Jesus—what luck! I got away just in time. . . .

He recalled the events in the bar—the rantings of the Nazis, Dr. Wallerstein's lecture on psychoanalysis, the appearance of Janoshik with bucket and broom—and seething fear shot through his nerves. Janoshik! Janoshik might have been arrested—Janoshik one of the condemned hostages!

He tried to establish some order in his thoughts. He had not heard from Janoshik since Thursday. That was strange. It was possible that, in his lowly job, they had overlooked him

If, on the other hand, Janoshik had been arrested, there was no need to worry that he would spill—of all the people Breda had worked with, Janoshik was the most unlikely to talk.

But that Janoshik should have to die among the hostages seemed inconceivable and utterly tragic. Somehow Janoshik had come to mean more to Breda than just a co-worker in their dangerous undertaking. Janoshik, with his sturdiness, his equanimity, his set and purposeful courage, his slow, clear thinking, his sly humor, had grown to be a symbol of his people. Breda felt a lump rising in his throat.

Furthermore, if Janoshik was in jail, there was nobody to pass on the Watzlik address to the longshoremen group; the planning and daring of weeks would be lost, an important project would remain unfulfilled, the munitions barges would be unloaded, their load bringing death to thousands of Russian soldiers, to men toward whom he felt a kinship nearer than to his own brothers.

The thin voice of Seliger became audible above the crowd. "Reprisals! Reprisals!" he whined, "always reprisals! We should have learned by now that one cannot buck such power! They kill twenty of ours for every one of theirs. Pretty soon, none of us will be left. Strong trees splinter in the storm, but the grass blade survives, because the grass can bend."

Seliger was quite enraged. He took every sign of resistance against the occupants as a slap in the face of his personal cowardice—a cowardice which he had to justify before himself and the world over and over again, especially because it paid him so well.

The crowd moved away from Seliger just a little. He stood in a small vacuum all his own, still gibbering, a few bubbles of spittle in the corners of his mouth.

Great excitement took hold of Milada after she read the poster. The name of Glasenapp, the fact of his death, the date of his death, the fate of so many people about to die in exchange for Glasenapp—her brain worked feverishly; the whining "Reprisals! Reprisals!" registered disturbingly.

"What do *you* know?" she protested to Seliger, forgetting where she was, and that she was about to give herself away. "Talking about Erich Glasenapp, about people you don't know...!"

She felt a strong arm around her shoulder. Somebody half pushed, half dragged her through the crowd, then took her hand with iron grip, forcing her to run. A tramway car came rattling along, and stopped. "Hop up!" that somebody commanded, and there was no resisting his order. The car started with a jerk, the thin bell tingling.

They were quite a distance away from the signpost at the corner of the Kolbenka works before Milada became fully aware of what had happened. Her abductor stood at her side on the platform of the car. He grinned broadly.

Milada recognized him. She had seen him in the shop, but he had never spoken to her. Now he said, with a pleasant, deep voice, "That was rather sudden, wasn't it? I must have frightened you—I'm sorry."

Her first impulse was to reproach him sharply, but his apologetic manner, his soothing voice, and above all his face, which was clear and open and strong, mollified her. She said, "Perhaps you will explain—"

He suggested, "Let's discuss my behavior a little later, and perhaps with more privacy. In the meantime, please, believe me—I did this to save you from considerable embarrassment."

"You're Breda, aren't you?" Milada looked at him, trying to solve the puzzle of his sudden entry into her life. "I know your face, I am sure."

"Yes, I am Breda the tool-maker," he whispered. Then, raising his voice: "Have you been on the Petschin recently? The trees are putting on their fall colors, and if you get up

77

high enough, you can see the most amazing array of reds and yellows and greens, and at the foot of the hill the Moldau, sort of silverish, and beyond the river the thousand roofs of the city—all shapes, all shades—"

Milada could not help smiling at his enthusiasm. "Are you always that violent when you ask a girl to admire nature?"

Breda disregarded her inquiry. "I go up there quite often," he continued. "The restaurant is still open. They don't serve much, these days; but perhaps we can wangle a beer from the waiter—I happen to know him."

Milada gave in. For the first time since she had lost her beloved Pavel did she again feel the sensation of being led. Pavel had been that way. The stranger, without knowing it, had touched a chord in her which had not sounded for so long, but now it began to vibrate.

The tramway car had made its clattering way toward the center of the city. It stopped at the foot of Petschin Hill before turning right to the Moldau Bridge. Breda and Milada stepped off and entered the park, slowly making their way uphill. Few people were abroad. The women who came here to let their children have some air, had long since taken them home to their meager suppers.

Some bored German soldiers strolled along, always in groups, never alone. An old woman came by, clad in a shabby coat, wearing the yellow arm band of the Jews. With a stick, she picked up odd scraps of paper from the paths. Carefully she put each scrap into a burlap bag which she was dragging behind her. The woman looked up and stared blankly at Milada and Breda. Milada tried to give her an encouraging smile; but the woman shook her head, a wisp of her gray stringy hair falling over her face; she bent over a tiny scrap on the ground, picked it up, and trudged away.

"Marked—as we all are," Milada whispered.

"You must learn to hide your feelings, curb your tongue," Breda said. "This man Seliger, for instance, don't ever talk to him. You don't know it, because you've been in the Kolbenka so short a while—but each word of his is a provocation. Every squeak he utters is planned to lead you into betraying yourself—and betray yourself you almost did. That is why I whisked you away. There was no time for explanations then and there; now, if you wish, you can scold me."

"What made you take such interest in me?" she asked simply.

He looked full into her face. Her eyes were dark and soft, a bit slanted. Her finely chiseled mouth and chin, her quiet forehead, her smooth black hair parted in the middle, made her appear strangely like one of those old ikons he had seen on the wall of peasant huts in the Karpathian mountains.

"I watched you reading the poster. Your face mirrors what goes on inside of you. You were stirred, more upset than the occasion warranted. People's feelings, you know, get dulled when they're exposed to the steady pressure of terror and cruelty. Seliger seemed to watch you, too. I may overestimate him, possibly, but he's cunning. And if his remarks were directed at you—you certainly fell for them!"

A sickening feeling rose in Milada. It made her weak, and she leaned for support on Breda's arm.

"Don't be frightened, just careful," he said gently.

"Whom can one trust?" she asked in anguish. "You give me good advice; if I apply it, you are the first one I must turn against."

"Of course," he nodded. "If you wish, we will stop at this point and part, and we will forget that we ever talked to each other."

They walked on in silence. The sun was moving toward the horizon and filled the sky with a red glow. The air was fragrant with the scent of dying leaves.

"Beautiful, isn't it?" Breda said. They had reached an opening in the trees. The city lay spread beneath them, its crowded roofs, its many towers resplendent in the sinking sun. Across from them rose Hradschin Hill, crowned by the castle and the Dome whose windows were ablaze with golden light.

"And yet," Breda continued, "one cannot live without trusting somebody. They've come here to rule over this—" with a movement of his arm he took in all the evening beauty of Prague—"they've set brother against brother, friend against friend, father against son—only this way can they maintain themselves; their tanks and guns and bayonets are powerless without this.

"If you were to ask me, I could not explain why I trust you, Milada. I had a dog once whom I called Bishop. I picked him up one night, or rather, he picked me up—just followed me. He was an incredible mixture. Now, why did he follow just me? What gave him confidence in me? Probably his nose, his dog instinct. You will pardon this lowly comparison? In this day, when recommendations must be checked, introductions carefully weighed, I have found it safest to rely on my instinct.

"There, I've given myself away. You're the one now who knows more about me than I do about you. Your advantage —and yours is the next move."

Milada felt that this man Breda was much wiser and more mature than she. She knew that it was a clever move on his part to give her the advantage—it obligated her. She resented being obligated. His superiority put her on the defensive. With Pavel, it had been different. Pavel had been her equal, their love and friendship had had its basis in their likeness and their common work at the University.

The question of why she compared Breda with Pavel at all startled her. Breda was moving in on her, subtly and with quiet strength; he was moving into the place which

Pavel had held—and this she resented too, though, she reasoned, Pavel was dead and she could not mourn him forever.

More belligerently than she had intended, she asked, "What do you really want of me?"

"I stopped you from telling Seliger what you know about the matter Glasenapp. I want you to tell me."

"Why?"

"Because I think that a friend of mine, one of the bravest men I know, is in danger, and because your knowledge might help him."

"Is he one of the hostages?"

Breda hesitated. "I'm not sure. But I'm afraid so. The Gestapo publishes the names of its victims only after they're dead—if then. However, even if all those men about to die were total strangers to me, and if what you know could be used to help them, fight for them, fight for their lives—I'd implore you to tell me."

Milada weighed his words. Their sincerity, their anxiety stirred her to the depth of her soul. Yet, a slight feeling of disappointment rankled in her—after all his words, all he wanted was information.

The heavy burden of the facts she knew had been throttling her ever since she had read the Glasenapp poster. From the moment its text had penetrated her consciousness, her mind had been full of frantic ideas.

She had even thought of telling the Gestapo that Glasenapp—but this plan seemed so childish that she had discarded it immediately.

Well, if Breda were able to do something...

"Glasenapp was not killed. He committed suicide."

Breda walked on. The equal measure of his strong steps remained uninterrupted. Milada had expected Breda to be startled.

"Aren't you surprised at all?" she asked.

Breda smiled. "No. You see, if a plan had existed to kill

81

Glasenapp, my friend, in all probability, would have warned me not to come to the Mánes that night. But I was there."

"You saw Glasenapp?"

"Yes. To me he looked bedraggled and depressed. He was quite drunk."

"Poor fellow—" said Milada.

It was getting dark. Breda tried to read her face which was full of shadows. "I am surprised, though," he said, "that you're so sure Glasenapp committed suicide. There could have been an accident. Or one of his own Nazis might have disposed of him for one reason or another."

"No, he committed suicide," Milada repeated, her voice husky. How could she transmit to this man another's emotions? How could she portray the weak-hearted desires, the touching solicitude, the reasons and motives for the great lie of Glasenapp?

"When he told me that he'd kill himself," she began, "I laughed at him. You won't do it, I scoffed, you are too weak. He was such a wretched little man as he stood in my room, guilt written all over his face."

"Guilt?" asked Breda.

They had reached the restaurant. Tables were set on a terrace overlooking the valley of the Moldau and the city. The tables were empty at this time of the evening. Nevertheless, Breda carefully surveyed the terrace and the few people at distant tables before he and Milada sat down.

"Yet I pitied him," said the girl. "It's wrong, I know. Do they ever have pity on us? He saved my life, you know . . ."

Noiselessly the waiter appeared and brought beer. Then the two were again alone.

Breda was baffled. That a German officer would save a Czech woman's life was rare enough. In what way, then, was he guilty before her? "Why did you call him weak?"

Milada sipped her beer. She sat back in her chair and closed her eyes. Glasenapp had never explained to her why

82

he had saved her life, though he had told her the story often. Once, still bedridden from her wound, she had asked him, "You must have reasons. People don't act without reasons. Was it pity? Was it your conscience? Did you want to compensate me for what your soldiers have done to my people?" Glasenapp had protested: "Certainly not. The German Army has done nothing for which I would have to make up. Ridiculous."

"There are many questions in my mind." Breda's words returned her to the present. "But it may be simpler if you tell the story, don't you think so?"

"It took me a long while to see through him." Milada spoke urgently. She had to convince Breda that her part of the relation with Glasenapp was entirely passive. "I really learned to know him only the day of his death. Then I hated him."

Breda did not prod her. He waited for her to tell him everything, because she needed to talk it out of her system. He knew he had succeeded in creating between Milada and himself the invisible current of mutual confidence.

"You remember the fight for the University?" she asked.

Breda nodded. "I know. The Nazis decided to close down the University. They knew that they couldn't order people what to think. So they sent their soldiers. And the students tried to defend the school."

Milada tugged at his sleeve, excitedly. "Do you know what Glasenapp said about it? 'As if it were of real importance—to sit around in crammed benches and scribble notes on matters and ideas of a world shelled to pieces long ago.' That's what he said. And he a teacher himself!

"In this battle for the University, he was in command of a platoon of German soldiers—and I was among the students. That's how we met."

"When I saw you at the Kolbenka," remarked Breda, "I

thought it was your first try at the machines. What did you study?"

"History and literature. German literature, at that!" Milada laughed bitterly. "Their bayonets marching upon us, glistening in the sun—and I knew their poetry!

"We had their poetry, and a few stones, but they had the bayonets."

Breda lifted his glass. "Let's drink to a time when poetry will have more weight than bayonets!"

She drank and asked sadly, "You still have that hope?— Once, my parents and I visited Nuremberg. As tourists do, we dropped in on the medieval torture chamber of the castle. There, carefully preserved, stands the Iron Virgin.

"I remember the dry, harsh voice of the guide who explained the working of this steel chamber formed like a gigantic human body. It has given me nightmares ever since. Its sides are studded with long thorns which have remained sharp through the centuries. These thorns buried themselves into the flesh of the victim inside the Virgin."

Breda folded his hands. He realized the full cruelty of the inexorable Virgin.

"We were young," continued Milada, "and we wanted to live. But before our University, we were caught inside the Virgin, her thorns closing in on us, cutting deeper and deeper. When we had no more space to move, when we saw that the Nazis' bayonets were impervious to all pleading, my Pavel rallied a few young men. They formed a spear-head to throw themselves into the bayonets to break a passage for the others, a road to escape.

"I don't think he succeeded. I don't know. Because at that moment the Nazis began shooting, and all ranks broke. I was hit and lost consciousness. I never saw Pavel again."

Breda, as always in the face of others' tragic fate, felt small and at a loss. "A brave boy," he said finally, embarrassed.

"My lover," Milada answered simply.

"And then?"

"Glasenapp was peculiar in many ways," Milada said, after a long pause. "I still can see him perched on the armchair in my room, gesticulating with his white arms. I always made him take off the jacket of his uniform. I could not stand the sight of it.

"He loved to tell me how he had saved me. The story meant a lot to him. But he spoke of me in the third person, 'the girl'—never 'you.' As if he couldn't bear to think of me as his victim."

"I can understand that," mumbled Breda. The twilight, instead of dulling Milada's features, emphasized plastically her strange beauty.

"His eyes, Glasenapp said, were attracted by a pair of heavy soldier's boots. These boots were extraordinarily large and black, and moved slowly. They were stepping on a body, the still body of a girl, lying in the dust. The boots walked off, their owner intent upon finishing whatever resistance was left among the students. Glasenapp went to inspect the body of the girl . . . my body.

"He did not know why; he seldom accounted to himself the reasons for his actions. He bent down and raised her head. The face was contorted by pain, her eyes wide open. Her lips moved forming inaudible words. From a wound in her shoulder trickled blood, discoloring her dress in ugly blotches.

"He picked her up—a burden so surprisingly light that he could run as he carried her through deserted streets, past houses whose shades were tightly drawn—till he found a taxi."

"Glasenapp reported his deed in great detail," Breda commented. "Was that his way of wooing?"

85

Milada was doubtful. "He spent so much time with me, and there was little else to talk about."

Breda was not satisfied. "Why did Glasenapp go out of his way to save you? According to their rules, pity is despicable, even forbidden. Especially pity for those subhumans who dare resist the march of Germany. His duty was to place his revolver at the girl's forehead and pull the trigger. Or, at least, to let her lie there and allow nature to take its course."

His words elicited no fear on Milada's face. She seemed placid and relaxed. She has gone though fire and has been hardened well, Breda thought.

"Why?" Milada took up Breda's question. "I don't think Glasenapp knew himself. You see, he hungered for companionship—not with soldiers, but people. Yet his uniform made him their enemy, and he became more and more lonely and frustrated. As a Nazi, he was a sorry failure, because he was open to human emotions.

"As a human being he failed, too.

"A kind of numbness had settled in his heart. He feared that this war would never end, and that his best years were flowing by without gain to him.

"I don't know what's the matter with me, he would say. Others adjust themselves. The devil may care! they think. But me? I was lost from the day they took me out of the girls' lyceum in Mainz where I taught, and stuck me into the Army. I didn't like the officers' school, and I hated being shipped all over Europe. There's no time and no place to grow roots. I don't belong anywhere but in an officers' mess —the same in every city: tables, drinks, Hitler pictures."

"And, naturally," Breda spun the thought further, "he didn't have the strength to break away from the tables, the drinks, and the Hitler pictures. The Germans are caught in this war, too."

How vividly Glasenapp stood before Milada's eyes! "If I could describe his face," she said, "perhaps you could guess

86

what kind of man he was. But he had the most nondescript face I ever saw. Like a water color on which a lot of rain has fallen."

"He fell in love with you, of course?" Breda commented.

"I came to in the taxi," Milada resumed her story. "I managed to tell him where I lived. He took me there. I was sick and weak for more than a month.

"Glasenapp often told me how his duties and routine, officers and soldiers, marching and inspecting, lost importance and became incidental—interruptions of his life with me. He said he was proud of himself for the first time in his life. He had to use dozens of different stratagems to get away from his comrades and superiors. They sneered at his secretiveness. Patzer, his Captain, warned him of the danger of strolling alone through Prague. 'A German officer—they might kill you off like that!'—and the Captain snapped his fingers.

"All these things made Glasenapp feel a martyr. He had a kernel, he said, around which to spin ideas and hopes. He nursed me. He gave the landlady money for food and medicine. To avoid calling a doctor who would have to report the case, Glasenapp asked advice from his regimental doctor, presumably for a relative who showed my symptoms."

Breda weighed the facts. This German officer gained stature. He understood that Milada wanted to justify her relation with Pavel's murderer.

"Nothing is worse than being sick and alone," she said tonelessly. "Your hands are fever hot and you keep thinking they don't belong to you. Your pain makes itself independent of you and dances about like a crazy circus. There is nobody for whom to put up a brave front—no sense in doing it for yourself. Because you know you're scared. All you want is someone who mumbles a few kind words to you. I longed for someone to come and sit by me.

"That is all I felt toward him, ever. I would let him hold my hand, yes. He kissed me, on my forehead mostly, and very shyly. It made him happy."

"Did you have no other friends?" Breda had finished his beer and was studying the bottom of his glass.

"None came. Later I learned that upon seeing a Nazi officer going in and out of my flat they decided to keep away.

"In my fever dreams, Glasenapp told me, I called for Pavel. And the moment my mind cleared, I sent the landlady to ask for him. She could not find Pavel, somebody else had taken his room. So I knew that he was in hiding, or imprisoned."

"Pavel worked among the students?" inquired Breda.

"He was one of their leaders. He was born to it. If you had ever met him, you would have become his friend right away. He was strong, full of light and life—that is why I simply could not believe him dead. It seemed unnatural for him to die.

"And Glasenapp nursed my hopes."

"Did he?" Breda was puzzled.

"Glasenapp knew that I suffered him only because I was afraid of being alone. But often I saw him ordering his soldiers to attack us. I saw the Iron Virgin carrying his face. 'Leave me! Go away!' I would scream. And then again, I'd ask his pardon, for he had saved my life.

"I was sick and torn. He saw that. He feared to lose me once I learned Pavel had gone. He knew I was waiting for Pavel, and that the will to wait sustained my life."

Milada paused, unable to go on. Breda took her hand, trying to instill strength. She looked at the last gray of the vanishing day hesitating over the towers of the Hradschin. A cool wind stroked the leaves of the trees.

"If Pavel were wounded, or in hiding, he would get word

through to me—that I knew. But his word never came. I grew more frantic the longer I was tied to my bed.

"Look for Pavel, I begged of Glasenapp. You're an officer, you can do it. Check with the police, with the Gestapo, with the General Staff. If you find Pavel, I promise to be your friend forever. You never had a friend . . ."

Breda frowned. "Glasenapp, who wanted to be your lover, was to search for your lover?"

"He swore he would do it," said Milada eagerly. " 'I am taking grave chances,' Glasenapp pointed out, 'but I'll do it.'

"As it turned out, his job was simple enough. He merely checked with the morgue."

Darkness had fallen and covered the hill. The wind, coming up from the river, grew stronger. Under its touch, many leaves tremblingly let go their hold on the branches and slowly rocked to earth.

"Glasenapp came back and lied to me. A white lie, to allow him to go on seeing me. Pavel was alive, he said, a prisoner of the Gestapo.

"I don't know you well, Breda. I hope you do not love anybody. I went through agonies, and I learned that in these times you cannot afford love. It chokes you."

Breda was silent. Then he said, "It need not always end that way—"

"But to fear that it might!" Milada thought for a moment. "I was honest, though, with Glasenapp. I told him once more about Pavel and me, and that I would not hold it against him if he withdrew and left me alone with my troubles. But Glasenapp thumped his chest. He was a gentleman, he was. He'd go out and bring Pavel back, even if he had to talk to Heydrich!

"Perhaps Glasenapp was right to speak that way. Perhaps I would have died then, weak as I was, if he had not given me hope. Who knows?"

The waiter's steps approached through the gravel of the

terrace. "We're closing now," he said, "and you better be on your way home. In an hour it's curfew time. They've clamped down on us again, since that German officer got killed."

"That's too bad, isn't it?" answered Breda, leaving the waiter to figure out whether the curfew or Glasenapp's death was the regrettable item.

Breda and the girl made their way downhill through the early night. He supported her elbow, leading her. He felt great warmth for Milada. The skin over her wound was thin and tender, and a great urge to protect her rose in him.

Breda was not without sentiment. The suffering of others affected him deeply—he was one of those men who had preserved the ability to weep unashamedly and honestly. But he also tried to do something about the suffering he saw. And since experience had taught him that alone he could do little, he had, quite naturally, come to associate with others who fought for the same end. With him, sentiment was translated into strength and sober planning and courage.

He thought about Janoshik and Milada, and how strange it was that he had encountered the one person who could provide the key to the whole affair. To him, however, she was more than an incidental instrument.

"The news of Pavel's death hit me therefore all the harder," Milada said. "I learned it on Thursday morning when I dropped in at the corner bookstore where Pavel and I often had borrowed books.

"The salesgirl was chattering away—you know. How happy she was to see me again, and where had I been keeping myself? I did not listen to her chatter; I browsed.

"Suddenly something she said struck me. 'What was that?' I asked.

"The girl repeated: 'We've been trying to get back the

books which Pavel took out. Do you know where they are? Right after his funeral we tried to inquire...'

" 'Funeral?'

" 'We were so sad!' she prattled on. 'Pavel and sixty others who died at the University—in one grave. Not even a separate hole in the ground for each of the poor kids—I cried and cried and cried about it—many were customers of ours, you understand...'

" 'Funeral? Pavel's funeral!'

"Everything about me—the books on the wall, the pictures, the lamps, the ceiling—everything swayed and crashed over my head."

The streets Milada and Breda now reached seemed bleak and without splendor. The beauty seen from the height of the Petschin had dissolved into ugly detail, flickering street lamps, tired houses and tired people.

"I awoke in my room," Milada continued. "Glasenapp was there, asking, 'What's the matter, child? You should not have gone out yet. You're too weak.'

"I felt drained of all life. How I managed to speak I don't know. I didn't say much. 'Pavel is dead. You lied. You killed him.'

" 'Milada!' he begged. His face was transparent as glass, it had lost all color.

"Woman's hate is deeper than man's, because women are weaker and cannot always translate their hatred into deeds. And so, we can express our hatred more sharply.

"I remember every word I said to him; I've said them again and again. 'You killed Pavel,' I said. 'You pretended he was alive, to play with me. You raised my hopes, only to dash them all the more cruelly.' "

Breda wished from his heart to stop her. Recounting that scene made her relive its horror. He wanted to spare her.

But the pent-up torrent of her feelings was carrying her on: " 'You beat us unconscious. Then, restoring our senses with icy water, you enjoy our pain! Can't you let us die alone?'

"Then I became quiet. I talked of myself as of some other bereaved woman. I told Glasenapp of Pavel—how wonderful he had been, how good and how wise. Pavel had wanted to become a doctor, because to help others was Pavel's main concern. I told of the baby that Pavel and I wanted to have as soon as we could afford it. Like hot lead, I poured over Glasenapp all the dreams I had dreamed, all the dreams he and his Nazis had wrecked forever.

"These weren't just my dreams, I said, not only my future —but all the little peoples' dreams and future."

Yes, thought Breda, that is how I would have said it too. She is like me and Janoshik. He adjusted his step to hers, and the sound of their steps became as one.

"Glasenapp tried to interrupt me, tried to get in a word of defense. I did not let him. To me, he had ceased being one German officer—he was a symbol. In his sorry person stood before me their entire murder machine. He had to take it.

"And couldn't. Ridiculous tears ran over his pimpled cheeks—it was disgusting. Even as the enemy's symbol he was no good."

Breda, now, could visualize the Lieutenant's baleful end, could see him staggering to the edge of the jetty, filled with whisky and sickening weakness. Then the lonely man's silhouette disappeared; only the fine black outlines of the houses on the far bank of the river against the dark-bluish sky remained.

"He tried to explain," Milada continued. "Yes, he had known that Pavel was dead. He had lied to spare my feelings. He had lied from fear of losing me. Before he met me, his life was without meaning, he said. I had become the center of his being; without me he would not go on.

" 'I am so miserable, so alone,' he driveled. 'Whatever I did, I did selflessly, with best intentions. I love you.' "

92

She was silent. Then Breda broke into the silence: "He nursed you to make you dependent upon him. He pretended to work for Pavel's liberation to bind you. A shrewd calculation."

"He threatened to kill himself, if I forced him away," said Milada.

"I asked him whether he thought his suicide would be a particular loss to mankind. I reminded him of the true meaning of his life—to make war for Hitler and a Greater Germany, to shoot defenseless youngsters, to murder and to steal, and to make up to wounded women too weak to repel his advances."

"So he left?" Breda asked.

Milada nodded. "So he left. I did not hear of him any more—till I saw the poster. And when Seliger screamed his 'Reprisals! Reprisals!' I spoke up. You understand why.

"So many people will die because of this Glasenapp. Something must be done about it. I can't just let it happen!"

"And what do you propose?" asked Breda.

"I have no plan. I haven't had time to think about it. But I feel responsible for the lives involved."

Breda, in truth, had no plan either. The story Milada had given him, the many new facts were pressing in on him from various sides.

What importance did this Glasenapp have in the whole matter? Indeed very little—about as much as the small stone which splits from the height of the mountain and sets an avalanche rolling. Would it be possible to stop the avalanche by weighing the small stone?

Yet, the Gestapo built its entire case on the lie of Glasenapp's murder. Well—practically everything it did was based on lies. On the other hand, Breda knew, there was a certain kind of warped logic which the Nazis used to justify their deeds—in this logic, theft became socialism; murder, self-defense; rape, improvement and strengthening of the race. They would burn their own house of parliament; but they had no courage to stand up to their deed, and put on elaborate trials to prove somebody else did it; they would attack country after country, each time issuing magnificent collections of documents to prove that, really, Germany had been attacked. In spite of the magnitude of their crimes, they were small-time gangsters without the grandeur of confessing to their acts—cowardly conquerors, petty crooks with the ambition to be considered gentlemen, always talking loudly about their historic significance because already they could hear the ironic laugh with which history would one day close its books on them.

If it were possible to blast their lie! If, somehow, he could get the real story of Glasenapp before everybody!

They might kill the hostages anyway; but the terror would become so senseless and stupid that it would lose its effect—because even in applying terror, a system must be used. This system may be twenty Czechs for one killed Nazi, or liquidation of the families of men working underground—but some system it must be! Otherwise terror changes its quality, it becomes a matter of mere accident, like being run over by a car, or being hit by lightning.

"If I went to this man Reinhardt and told him what I know—" suggested Milada, but her tone indicated that she herself did not quite believe in the feasibility of her suggestion.

Breda was quick to reply: "This presupposes that the Nazis are genuinely interested in the pursuit of justice. That they want to find the man who killed Glasenapp. No, their intention is to make their lives safer by frightening us."

"They are offering a reward for the murderer!"

"They can well afford it, since there is none," replied Breda. "You cannot help the hostages by telling the Gestapo of Glasenapp's suicide. You'd only risk your life. If your

94

sacrifice would free those twenty, I would say yes, go ahead, tell the Nazis.

"The Nazis, however, would simply arrest you, shut you up forever, and proceed with their fake murder case as if you and your truth never existed.

"We must let the Nazis know. There you are right. Not only the Nazis, but everybody. But how? In such a short time?"

It was fascinating to Milada to watch Breda's mind at work. How well-trained this mind was, how clear. He could transpose himself into the minds of the enemy, planning to counteract their moves before they were done, even before they were planned!

"And there is nothing I can do?" she asked.

They had arrived at the river, and through the weather-beaten Gothic arch, entered Karl's Bridge.

The city's lights were dimmed; below, the Moldau was molten black, darker even than the dark of the night. Then the searchlights began to play like stiff fingers of a trembling hand. They moved and stood still, joined and parted, and finally converged on a glittering speck in the sky—the plane. Satisfied that it was one of their own Nazi fliers, the searchlights died as suddenly as they had come to life; and darkness ruled again.

Breda and the girl had watched the play in silence. "You've done enough," Breda took up her question, "you've given me your confidence, you've given me something to work with. You see—if we could write it in the sky for all to see as they write their message of murder—"

He stopped abruptly.

"What is it?" Milada asked.

"I have an idea." He quickened his pace. "Perhaps it can be worked out. Do you mind very much if I let you go home by yourself? I will see you tomorrow."

Milada was disappointed. "No, of course not—you can go. I don't live far from here."

Breda was too preoccupied to observe the letdown in her voice. He had changed. The patient, attentive, considerate Breda had changed into a man of action, intent only on the plan he was working out. That she felt slighted, he did not notice. Purely from habit he gave her instructions: "Be careful. Don't talk about all this. Not to anybody. And if— no, that is improbable—"

"What is improbable?"

"If, by any chance, the Nazis should question you—"

"Thanks for showing so much concern! I'll know what to do."

Then he understood. He took her hands, held them tightly in his strong ones. "Oh, Milada—you are not hurt! Forgive me. . . . You want me to go ahead, don't you? I shall think of you." He scribbled a few words on a slip of paper. "Here is my address. Memorize it and destroy the paper. You'll be welcome any time—but please, come only if you think it absolutely necessary."

"Good night, my friend," she said.

He walked off briskly, the sound of his steps faded away. She watched his shadow dissolve in the night.

Now she felt very much alone, much more alone than before, when she had not known him.

The wavelets of the river broke in little ripples on the pillars of the bridge. Against one of these pillars Glasenapp's body had drifted.

CHAPTER 5

AN AFTERNOON in the cell is heavy with time.

Lobkowitz did not know whether to wish that time would go faster, or to try to hold on to every passing second like a drowning man who grasps for a tiny bit of wreckage, with hope in every nerve that it may uphold him.

The cruel news which Wallerstein had brought from Reinhardt: "We are hostages, in about five days we will be shot"—this cold and cruel news had sunk in slowly at first. It seemed incomprehensible to everyone, and everyone had protested.

You know, of course, that some day you are going to die. That is a matter of experience. You see it happen. Your grandfather died while you were still a child; much of his agony was spared your ears, you were sent around to a neighbor's house and played with the neighbor's youngsters. When you came back, he was quiet, so quiet and still that even you with your irrepressible child's jumpiness felt the cold· and just stood in awe of what had come to pass. They explained it to you: "Grandfather has died. He's gone away, and tomorrow we will bury him." There was something final in these words, you could not argue against it, it seemed

97

stupid to point at the body and say, "But look, there he is!" And when they put him underground, and when you added your own little shovel of dirt to all the other earth which already covered the casket, you knew that they were right— he would not return. Nobody could lift the heavy cover of the casket and all the earth heaped on top of it, once he was inside. Still, your consolation was easy—after all, it did not concern you, you were alive, very much so, and grandfather was an old man with whom you did not identify yourself. At night, in your bed, you fell asleep easily, because, look how much time you still have! Grandfather was sixty-nine, and you were only seven.

When your father died, you were a young man. You had read many books and studied, life and death had become an item of conversation, a subject of study, medical or philosophical, whatever the case might be. Your father died while you were away, so again you were spared the details. You learned he'd been sick, hopelessly. So, one morning, he drew his bath, took his razor out of the box, sat down in the tub, and slashed his veins. They found him dead, sitting in a purple sea, with a tired smile on his face. Your philosophy and medicine and religion did not help—you were hit, because you knew your turn was next. You did not know when it would happen, the day and the date—but between your father and you there was nobody else.

Again, you counted the years—they had diminished sadly. You went out and got drunk and tried to forget, and you managed to forget quite well; but ever so often in your days or nights you feel a cold hand reaching for your heart: That is fear.

To get away from it you build a wall called security. You see your doctor regularly. As regards women, you are moderate; too much excitement might be harmful. You go to church and exercise a little in this or that sport. And above all, you try to make as much money as possible in order to

98

care well for the needs of body and soul—in this way you create the illusion that all this is going to last forever, and you believe in it because you must believe in it; otherwise who could stand this life? Not for a day, not for an hour.

So the hostages protested.

Lobkowitz laughed. "Impossible!"

Preissinger heatedly assured everybody that over at the Bohemian-Moravian Coal Syndicate a staff of loyal employees was busy conferring with the Reich Protector, or cabling to Berlin, all to get Lev Preissinger free and back to the living.

Prokosch said that, of course, death was no new experience to him, but that nevertheless, having brushed against it once, he confidently believed that it could not touch him now—and besides why should he die? What reason did they give?

For a while, Janoshik said nothing. It was his turn to speak, and the others looked at him, expectantly. He saw their looks and scratched his head. "All this reminds me," he said, "of one Augustin Svoboda, who used to own a small potato patch near Hradec Králové. I met him sometimes, on a Saturday night, in the tavern of the village, where Svoboda came to drink beer and to pinch the waitress. Up to the fifth glass, he pinched her in the leg, afterwards, he pinched her in the ass, which was firm and had that certain resiliency needed to make pinching enjoyable."

"Did the waitress die?" inquired Lobkowitz, who felt that some reference to death should be included in Janoshik's story.

Janoshik shook his head. "As far as I know, she's still alive and getting pinched, but not by Augustin Svoboda.

"Svoboda was shot to death one morning, while digging potatoes. It so happened that his patch of land was at the edge of the forest which belongs to Baron Voblonski. Sometimes people would hunt deer in the forest, and it was a hunter's bullet which hit Augustin Svoboda.

"When Svoboda felt that he had been hit badly, and that he was going to die, he started to shout: Help! Help! I've been hit! I'm going to die!

"The hunter who had fired the shot stepped out of the forest and walked down the patch to Svoboda. Svoboda was lying on the ground, rolling his eyes and gasping for air. So the hunter bent down and lifted Svoboda's head and said, *Nu, nu,* my good man—what is all the excitement about?

"Svoboda recognized Baron Voblonski's voice and answered, I am sorry, your excellency—I was afraid I was shot by one of those dirty poachers. But yours is a legitimate bullet, and I feel much better now.

"Whereupon he died and Baron Voblonski continued on his interrupted hunt."

"Well?" said Wallerstein.

Janoshik leaned back on his cot. "I'd hate to die for the sake of this Glasenapp. I really know nothing about him except that he couldn't stand drinking. And that makes things none too satisfactory."

Thus, their reaction to Wallerstein's news. Slowly, the news sank in until it finally hit each one with its tremendous impact.

Now they knew they were going to die, their turn had come, only a few days were left, one could count the hours, the minutes. Time was heavy in the cell, and yet it raced past them in breath-taking speed.

Wallerstein was now sitting on an upper cot, his back propped against the wall, his legs screwed up almost to his chin. On his knees rested his note pad, and he scribbled.

"What are you writing?" inquired Prokosch, who occupied the upper cot on the opposite side.

"Some observations," said Wallerstein.

"About whom?"

100

"About you."

"May I read them after you get through?"

Wallerstein turned his head toward Prokosch. Prokosch was eagerly watching him.

"Certainly not," said Wallerstein, and his tone was final.

Prokosch, hurt, fell back. "Don't you think that's quite unfair?" he asked.

"Not at all," assured Wallerstein. "These are scientific observations, and the doctor is a fool who'd let his patient see his notes about him."

"I am not your patient."

"You are under my observation, aren't you?"

Lobkowitz, sitting on the floor, staring into nothingness, joined in: "What happens to your notes after next Wednesday?"

"You mean after we're dead? Why—Commissioner Reinhardt will send them to the *Psychologische Monatsschrift* for publication."

"I don't think I like the idea," said Prokosch, his hands nervously gripping the frame of his cot. "After all, I'm a private individual, have a right to my privacy. I refuse to be treated as a guinea pig."

"It won't make any difference to you. You'll be dead!"

That's right, thought Prokosch. What difference will it make? They'll burn my body, or they'll cut me apart in the anatomy class, as is often done with criminals, or they'll bury me in some corner of the cemetery, together with these men with whom I am now arguing. Lucky that they said we'd be shot—otherwise I might be hanging from some gallows for days on end, my clothes falling to pieces, my flesh rotting away, my head cocked in the funny way which hanged men have—I've seen it on pictures the Nazis have sent from the Ukraine and from Jugoslavia. And hanging, I believe, is more painful.

But this Wallerstein, he'll hang my soul, for everybody to

look at, bare of all clothes and protection, naked in the wind
—if I let him see me. Can he see me, and if so, what can he
see? He keeps his notes under his pillow at night. If I tried
to steal them.... But he sleeps so lightly, whenever I awake
at night, I know he is awake too, breathing softly, his eyes
open, the white in them shining luminously. I hate him.

Prokosch leaned over, half sitting up, using his elbow as
support. "If you want to know about me, why don't you ask
me questions? I may be quite willing to explain."

"I intended to," replied Wallerstein. "I feared, though,
that you might refuse to answer."

"On the contrary. Perhaps those who survive us will
one day be interested to know who the actor Prokosch really
was. They knew me in so many different characters—I played
Hamlet, you know, and Mephistopheles, and Hanussen, and
Santa Claus at Christmas, for the children—and to all of
them I gave a part of me, and from all of them I took a part
for myself, till I've become quite a composite, I assure you—"

"God damn your vanity," said Lobkowitz, from the depths
of his heart.

"Let me come over to you, Wallerstein," Prokosch disregarded Lobkowitz entirely. "If I sit on your cot with you,
I can speak low."

Wallerstein moved his hand in a gesture of invitation.
Prokosch clambered down from his bunk, carefully, so as
not to disturb the snoring Preissinger, and climbed onto
Wallerstein's cot.

"What do you want to know?"

Wallerstein shrugged. "Just tell me something. Anything.
Important and unimportant. What you think of little value,
may give me the key to your whole being. I don't know."

"I will tell you of my happiness," whispered Prokosch.

Wallerstein made a note: "Prokosch's happiness—frustra-
tion and self-elation." He waited, asking himself whether it

would be a worth-while task to knock the stuffings out of the fellow.

"I remember as if it were today," began Prokosch, "the scene into which Mara stepped, to enter my life. I had played Oedipus Rex that evening, in the *Staatliche Schauspielhaus* in Berlin. The curtain had finally fallen—I had had nine curtain calls, four of them by myself—and I stood backstage, between the wooden skeletons of Greek columns and the chattering of the members of the Chorus.

"And there she was—a most beautiful, almost boyish head on a lithe body, serious eyes, a stubborn forehead, and with a smile which I shall never be able to describe—a smile child-like and mysterious all at once.

"She was not quite sixteen then. I am Mara von Dubnow, she said. I will never marry you. I saw you tonight, and I decided to have you.

"This approach, you will admit, was quite unusual, and it intrigued me.

"But I am married, child, I said.

"She explained carefully that, in the first place, she was no child, and that, secondly, my marriage did not concern her at all. She had a most fascinating way of discussing highly personal matters in a cool and abstract fashion.

"She told me that she came of an old family of Bohemian nobility—the Dubnows dated back to the days of Emperor Rudolf. A Dubnow then had been administrator of the Imperial stables, a marshal, they called it. The Dubnows had furnished generals and rebels—one of them was among the thirteen Czech noblemen beheaded before the City Hall of Prague—Duchesses and Imperial whores. Though her family owned half of the Bohemian forest, she had no money, and she would have none till her twenty-first birthday. For she had run away from home, some ten months ago, to become

103

an actress. Now she was studying at the Berlin *Schauspiel-schule,* she had a scholarship because her teachers considered her their most gifted pupil.

"I was married, as I told you. I thought then that I loved my wife, and I was truly devoted to her. Our marriage, however, lacked one most essential item—and I tell you this so you will understand how I came to take up my relation with Mara. I had lived with my wife for fourteen years, and never did we consummate our marriage, due to a physical defect of hers. As far as I was concerned, I could have relieved my desires any time, but I considered that unethical, and below my dignity."

"You mean to say you never had a woman before you met Mara?" asked Wallerstein.

"Yes, doctor. And I think I had a pretty full life nonetheless."

"No doubt," assured Wallerstein, without moving a muscle in his face, "a pretty full life. And how did things work out with Mara?"

"Most enchantingly. A world opened itself to me with this child's imaginative tenderness. We both were virgins, so to speak, and had to discover our way. You know this is not always simple—especially with as complicated a person as was Mara. There were conflicts and struggles which took all my patience and understanding to overcome and endure.

"My wife divorced me when the affair with Mara became public knowledge. That was all right with me, because I wanted to marry Mara, I was proud of her, I wanted to live with her."

"What happened to your wife?" interrupted Wallerstein.

"She married again, after a few years. She seems to be quite happy—I don't know."

Wallerstein nodded. "But Mara," he asked, "Mara did not want to marry you?"

"She had her preconceived opinions, her principles. Marriage is the legalization of possession, she said. Possession kills human emotions.

"Maybe it does. She wanted her freedom—I let her have it. I thought the best way to hold her was to trust her completely.

"There isn't a man on earth who does not worry over his woman. Those who show their worry are fools.

"Look, Mara, I told her, your time is your own to do with as you wish. You are so beautiful, so pure of mind and heart and body—I know you will not disappoint my confidence in you. She loved to be with people—not always were they my kind of people. I often had engagements out of town—how could I have worked if I did not, somehow, set my mind at peace?"

"Right—how could you," said Wallerstein. "But tell me— I never saw your wife on the stage. She was such a gifted pupil at the theater school—what happened to her career?"

"I cut it short," said Prokosch harshly. "I had to, if we wanted to go on together. It was an either-or proposition, and I had to put it to her that way. Some movie producers saw her, and gave her a tentative contract. She made her stage debut as Lisa Doolittle in *Pygmalion*. A great performance. I died a thousand deaths. I am an actor and I know. You have the rôle, let's say, as ingenue. The leading man kisses you. We have the kind of theater kiss which looks hot but hardly touches. But they do it night after night, and the leading man is supposed to be charming and handsome and strong—"

He laughed.

"No, I could not stand that. I did not even want to suffer from the merest idea of the possibility of being betrayed. Mara was human, after all, wasn't she?

"I've seen the way in which men looked at her. She loved to fence. Once I entered the fencing floor. She was there, in short pants, a little white sweater more exposing than hiding

her breasts, a picture of loveliness and youth and strength—
that brought about our first quarrel. She said she'd thought
nothing of it. Have you no eyes? I asked. Can't you read
men's faces?

"She gave in. She changed her fencing habit to a more
modest one—and after a while stopped fencing altogether.

"She also gave up her stage career."

"Just like that?" the doctor inquired.

"She loved me, didn't she? She wanted to see me happy.
In each success of mine she saw her contribution. My curtain
calls were the justification of her sacrifice—I know it was
a sacrifice!"

"What a woman!" Wallerstein exclaimed admiringly.

"True—what a woman! She was amazing in many ways.
Don't get the impression that she became a submissive adjunct of my life, because I report these tributes of her love.

"She liked to torture me, sometimes. I remember once,
her telling me that she—that she—

"She loved me, she said, more than anything in the world.
But she allowed another man to make love to her, because
he had caught her fancy. I knew it wasn't true. She couldn't
do that.

"I, who never drink, went out that night and drank myself into absolute stupor. They picked me up somewhere and
carted me home. I got drunk not because I feared she had
spoken the truth but because I was desperate at realizing
that in her mind sat a devil who made her harrow me so.

"When I came out of it, she sat by my bed and cried and
asked my forgiveness and said she'd lied to me, and that she
didn't know why she had lied to me, except that it might
have been to test my love.

"I took her hand and I said, Mara—I knew you did not
speak the truth. But if you ever really did what you told
me—it would be my end. I would make it my end."

Preissinger, who had had a bad night, was still fast asleep. But neither Janoshik nor Lobkowitz could help overhearing much of Prokosch's boastful story, for the actor was simply unable to keep his voice down to the whisper with which he had started to speak to Wallerstein.

To Janoshik much remained unclear, and besides, his interest was not greatly aroused. He had a magnificent sense of the anecdotic element in life. In olden times he would have been a prankish Eulenspiegel, wandering from village to village, entertaining round-headed children and toothless little old men and women with his tales—a poet of the people, assured of his anonymity because he was one of them and remained among them.

But he never failed to marvel at the complications in the lives of such intricate persons as this Prokosch and his wife Mara obviously were. If I would try for years and years and years, I couldn't think up anything like that, he sighed to himself, quite sad over the poverty of his imagination and experience.

It was somewhat ironic that it had taken the Gestapo to throw him in with such men and so widen his horizon.

But then, what else did the Prokoschs and Maras and this fellow Wallerstein have to worry about? Only their own, exalted persons—that's probably what was the matter with them.

Lobkowitz, on listening to Prokosch, was torn by many emotions. Uppermost was hot rage at the actor's self-complacency. Lobkowitz thought he had an idea of what Mara had gone through. He had seen her suffer.

He recalled the fateful days before the sell-out of Munich, when he and millions of olive-clad Czech men made themselves ready for a decisive battle which, they knew, would bring death to many of them. He had hastily put on his

Reserve Lieutenant's uniform that still smelled faintly of moth balls, had rushed to his barracks—and an hour later they were already on their way to the Wilson Railroad Station in Prague, the train waiting to take them to the northern frontier.

There, at the Station, he had met Mara. She stood behind a wooden table, serving the men with coffee and doughnuts which were filled with prune marmalade.

Those days were charged with human electricity. Barriers, which otherwise might have kept people apart, crumbled under the current.

Lobkowitz saw Mara, and he knew, without the faintest doubt, that they belonged to each other. Such knowledge springs into being in soul-stirring days.

She left her post behind the table, motioning another woman to take up her duties. Lobkowitz and Mara merely nodded to each other, his throat was too dry even to say hello. He took her arm, and they walked along the platform, past the crammed cars of the seemingly endless train. Wives and mothers embraced their menfolk all along the train, desperately clinging to them, their beloved shoulders and hands. Lobkowitz and Mara finally reached the hissing locomotive. They studiously looked at the engineer who was checking the oil boxes.

"Do you think this engine will be able to pull so long a train?" These were the first words Mara spoke.

Lobkowitz, whose experience in railroading was limited, thought about the problem. "I guess, when we come to the mountains, we'll get an additional locomotive," he said eventually, with authority.

Suddenly, they both laughed, because they felt the futility of discussing technicalities when they had only minutes to give each other.

"You must come back!" she said. "Promise!"

"Of course I'll come back," he promised. "The bullet that would kill me has not yet been cast."

That's what he had said, Lobkowitz remembered. Now this bullet had been cast, he thought, with a little shudder.

But what had gone on between that encounter and Mara's death! What heights of ecstasy they had mounted, what abysses of torn sorrow they had endured!

And there, on his cot, Prokosch was still going strong, parading before Wallerstein in an orgy of smugness. Every nerve in Lobkowitz was stretched taut, ready to snap. He bit his lips. No, he would not talk. He could carry his and Mara's secret till that bullet shut him up for all eternity. He would let Prokosch go to his end wallowing in the blissful world of dreams the actor had woven for himself.

"When did she decide to marry you?" Wallerstein asked Prokosch.

"It had become necessary to do so. My position as a state employee required it when I signed my contract with the State Theater in Prague. The Director made it a condition that I legalize my relation with her.

"Mara refused at first. But I made it clear to her that my career depended on this formality."

This was news to Lobkowitz. So she had tried to keep one last vestige of freedom for herself—unsuccessfully of course, since, bit by bit, she had subordinated her whole life to Prokosch, and there was no limit where she could say halt.

But why, in the devil's name, did she do it? What did she see in the man?

Lobkowitz had returned from the campaign that never started. With his soldiers, he marched back through the beautiful valleys of northern Bohemia. They left their pill boxes and underground fortifications intact—behind them came the gray-clad Germans, swollen with a victory they never had gained.

Sullenly the men marched. They had sung all the way up to the frontier, they had joked when they manned their positions—now they plodded along, their rifles slung over their shoulders without regard for symmetry, their field kits heavy as if filled with lead and stones. The officers feared to enforce discipline—instinctively they realized that the men knew they had been sold out, sold out by those on top—and the officers were part of that crew on top, in the eyes of the men.

The people at home spoke in hushed tones, then, as if everybody had just come from a funeral.

Meeting Mara again had been difficult under these circumstances—to love, one must gaze openly into the beloved's eyes, but the eyes were downcast.

She took him into her arms, as one takes a wounded man, with care and warmth and tender hands. The pent-up pain in him dissolved. For this, he would be grateful to her always.

In the beginning, they hardly talked about themselves. He did not ask questions, and Mara, apparently, saw no necessity for telling him of Prokosch and her marriage. She was beautiful and gave herself with such grace, such ease, that questioning, he felt, would only have marred this rich and sweet sensation.

Her body was most harmonious. Her shoulders were broad and well-formed, her breasts, though small, were full and firm. He loved to stroke her thighs and hips which came, he told her, from the mold of a master sculptor.

At the height of love, she bit into his shoulders with little caressing bites and breathlessly called him endearing names which he acknowledged by the hard pressure of his arms.

"You son of God," she said, "you lover. Take me, lead me,

hold me." She laughed, as a little girl laughs who has just discovered a delightful new way of wearing a bandanna.

"And then she became pregnant?" asked Wallerstein.

"Oh, no," said Prokosch, "we were married almost two years when that happened. I noticed the change in her some time in January of this year. You know how women become in that state—and Mara was so sensitive anyway. Her nervousness increased to the degree of frenzy; she tried to hide it from me, but she was quite sick.

"I have eyes to see, I told her.

"You could not touch her breasts. She would not let me touch her at all.

"You are with child? I asked.

"She denied it at first. Women are remarkable—you figure them out.

"I said, Darling, I want to help you. I have such confidence in you, I am so proud of you—why don't you have confidence in me?

"She became absolutely hysterical.

"I don't want it! she screamed. I can't bear to have it! I will die, I must not have it."

Wallerstein shook his head. "She knew she would die?"

"Of course not. How could she know? It was just talk. But it choked my heart."

"You wanted her to have the child?"

"Yes."

"Why?"

Prokosch did not answer.

"You felt, perhaps, that the child would supply a tie between you and Mara—a firm link, missing up to then, to make you sure of her?"

"Of course not. I never thought that way. I was sure of

her. But I was also proud. It will be a beautiful and gifted child, I said to Mara, our child."

Prokosch suddenly turned to Lobkowitz.

"Say, Lobkowitz, are you listening?"

"You talk loud enough," Lobkowitz answered, his voice strained.

"I just happened to think of it," the actor continued. "It slipped my mind till now. So much has occurred in between —but you asked me to meet you in the Mánes to discuss a matter regarding the child, didn't you?"

Lobkowitz was taken off guard, he muttered something obscure.

"We never got around to discussing it," Prokosch insisted. "We were arrested before we had a chance. What was it you wanted to tell me?"

Wallerstein had waited for the moment when Lobkowitz would be drawn into the story. Between the two men there was a hidden enmity which, he knew, was bound to break into the open at some point.

Lobkowitz fought hard with himself. He longed to tear down the curtain, to show up the actor in all his destructive hollowness, to knock him out with the truth, to put him on the rubbish heap where the possessive despoilers of beauty belong.

But he grit his teeth. He pressed his nails into the flesh of his hands till it hurt.

When Mara was dying he had sat at her bedside, torn with self-reproach, cursing the gods who were allowing their most precious creation to be destroyed so cruelly.

"Dearest," she whispered, "I want you to promise—"

Anything, everything, he had said.

"Never must you, never—you hear me?—never must you permit Karel Prokosch to learn of us, of our love. I loved him

112

too, you see, loved him very much. Not as I love you, my darling—but if he ever knew, it would kill Karel."

Lobkowitz had sat beside her. She was bleeding to death internally. He watched her face wax more and more transparent, thin veins showing bluish on her softly curved temples.

She turned her head to him with effort.

The noises of the crowded ward in the General Clinic hemmed them in—the moaning of the sick, the hurrying feet of nurses and orderlies, the wailing of women lying in pain and labor.

Her hand moved toward him, slowly, beggingly. He had loved this hand, he had felt its love.

"Swear, dearest, swear it to me . . ."

"I will protect him, as you protected him," he promised. "It makes you feel better, yes?"

"You didn't answer my question," prodded Prokosch. The thought which had flashed into his mind took on added graveness with every second of Lobkowitz's silence.

In the midst of this silence Preissinger awoke, stretched, yawned, and inquired what time it was.

"Shut up!" Prokosch said. And to Lobkowitz: "You cannot have forgotten. You were quite excited when you asked me to come to the Mánes. I want to know—"

"It isn't important, not important at all." Lobkowitz was composed now and completely controlled. "It was about a woman I know, an excellent nurse for the child, one who would take good care of it."

"But I have already hired a nurse!"

"I didn't know—I'm sorry."

Preissinger spoke up: "You mean to say that you two fellows got into this mess because of a nurse's position which was filled anyway? Well, if I weren't in this hole myself, I

113

would laugh. I, at least, am here because of my own wife's antics!"

Janoshik said nothing. He felt that things were moving toward a climax, he did not know from where the lightning was to come, but that it would come, he was sure.

This Dr. Wallerstein, he thought, would go ahead and ask and ask, and his words were pin pricks, and he would twist the men's nerves till they tore. What power did he have? Why did they allow him to play with them, with the last days of their lives? This Wallerstein was no doctor, Janoshik thought. A doctor is supposed to heal, not to open old wounds. Me, he can't touch. Just let him try. I know a couple of stories to put him in his place.

There, he has started again!

"And what did you do about your wife's pregnancy?"

"Nothing," answered Prokosch. "The child was in her body, a child belongs to its mother much more than to its father. Doesn't it?"

What arguments! What fine distinctions! thought Janoshik. What people! A child you should bear when you have made a world for it fit to live in.

"So she tried an abortion," Prokosch continued. "We had many friends, some of them medical men we could trust.

"It was a sad story. None of them dared to help. The Nazis were prohibiting abortions strictly. The doctors were afraid not only for their practice but for their lives. Neither money nor pleading had any effect."

It was obvious that Prokosch relished telling his story. He acted it out. His cultured voice was full of doom—he was important, important as a true participant in the tragedy.

"We walked the long road to Gethsemane," he said. "And I was always questioning myself and Mara: Why? Why all the agony? Do you hate it so, this child?"

"She must have had some reason!" Wallerstein mused.

x

114

"She didn't give you even an inkling of what was behind it all? She loved you, you say—and yet—I should imagine a woman would be glad to have a child from her beloved after so many years."

"That's women for you!" Preissinger chimed in. If it came to women, he had had plenty of experience with his wife. "My Carola, for instance, one day she conceives the brilliant idea that she can paint. Carola, I say, if you want to paint, paint. It is better than playing the piano. It isn't as loud. She also had played the piano for four weeks, and progressed as far as that hideous opus *The Happy Farmer*. She got herself an expensive art teacher, one of those futuristic fellows with dandruff."

He laughed a long and protracted laugh.

"Once I came home and she shows me her latest painting. Orange triangles and purple circles, in the corner a green skeleton of a Christmas tree, and sort of fat gray bellies on top of the canvas. Carola, I say, what is this?—A railroad in the mountains, can't you see? she answers.

"Now I know something about railways, I own a couple of them, but I'll be damned if that picture looked anything like a railroad. Then she lost interest in the dandruff man and gave up painting. That's women for you. What do you make of it, Dr. Wallerstein?"

"I am after office hours, Mr. Preissinger," explained Wallerstein with patience. "And I wish you would learn that in this cell, *nolens volens,* we are equals. Among equals one respects the other's conversation and does not interrupt it with irrelevancies."

"All right! All right!" said Preissinger peacefully, because his headache was gone. "I still think it's funny, about her abstract painting. I wonder what she's doing now, she's so helpless in practical things, without me. Always trouble with servants and people . . ." His voice trailed off, muttering.

115

Wallerstein pushed the tale forward. "And so Mara had to bear the child," he stated.

"Crazy bastards, the Nazis," Janoshik said full of simple fury, "vicious and crazy. Kids dying by the thousands, from hunger and bombs and misery, but it is forbidden to save them from the trouble. I like kids. I hate to see them shrivel, limb by limb, only their little bellies getting bloated. Better to scrape them out before they're ever born."

"She had to bear the child," Prokosch confirmed with emphasis.

Lobkowitz lowered his head, fearing the others might read his face. In those agonizing months, he had seen Mara lashed by suffering, he had suffered himself because he was so utterly powerless to help her.

Once, only once, he had pleaded with Mara: "Now you must leave Prokosch. Inside you is the living testimony to the lie of your life. It will live and will grow. If you go on with Prokosch, you're undertaking a superhuman, an inhuman task. We love each other. Why don't you make a clean break?"

She said no. She said she loved Prokosch, he was kind and good and trusting and a great artist; leaving him would kill him; she would not murder him, no, never.

He had felt tempted to dispute her opinion of Prokosch, but his respect for her judgment was too great. Anyway, to belittle Prokosch in the face of her belief in the actor would have been stupid.

Now, however, living and sleeping in one cell with the actor, Lobkowitz asked himself what she had seen in that man. This vain, self-centered, walking stage prop! For the sake of *that,* all the agony, and her sad death!

Why? he brooded, and could find no answer.

116

"When her hour came, I went with her to the General Clinic," Prokosch said. "It was terrible. Crowded and dirty. The Nazis had taken over most of the hospitals for their wounded, only the ramshackle buildings and the worst equipment was left for us. The doctors, I think, tried their best.

"For more than a day she lay in labor and pain. This waiting room with its gray walls, from which the paint peeled, with its dilapidated chairs, it drove me insane.

"Lobkowitz was there, too. I met him then, for the first time. He seemed concerned, I appreciated that."

"You were a friend of Mara's?" Wallerstein asked Lobkowitz, with the insistence of a prosecutor.

But before Lobkowitz could reply, Prokosch went on: "Poor Mara, she was alone. Alone she faced woman's greatest ordeal. We and our civilization! I would have liked—in certain primitive tribes it is law that the father take his place behind the mother when she gives birth, holding her, injecting his strength into her, and accepting his share of the pain . . ."

"*You* would have done that!" Lobkowitz shouted with scorn. He felt his nerves snap. The barriers he had set himself crumbled. "What do you know of pain and suffering, what do you know of what she went through? You, whom she protected, you, for whose pedestal her life blood became the putty!"

For days, now, he had been on the verge of letting go, of shaking the self-imposed burden from his mind. He had met Prokosch in the Mánes in order to tell him the truth, as painlessly as possible, yet to tell it. It had to be told then, for the sake of Mara's child. They had met, they had sat at the table, they had talked about things inconsequential—how difficult it was to operate on another man's soul!

The arrest had been a shock—but also a relief. It saved Lobkowitz from telling the truth, at least for the present.

When he learned they'd all have to die, when he considered the various aspects of death, he began to reason: Oh, let the man die in peace and ignorance, it was good I kept the secret, I'll take it with me wherever we go.

But the temptation rose with every hour of imprisonment. Out in the world he had been able to rationalize: I don't hate him, he is as much as victim of circumstances as Mara and I. But cooped up in this cell, observing Prokosch closely, listening in on the actor's act, watching him show off his illusions—that tugged on the nerves, that bored into the mind, that galled the heart.

When you were a boy, your sister owned a doll the looks and the smell of which you hated. She knew it, she hid the doll from you. But one day when you found the doll, you were in the house all alone—smash its skull, its ugly head, murder it, burn its rags, its limp soft body—of course you did it, regardless of the punishment to come. Now you've grown older, you have been punished, you've learned to control your impulses, to erect barriers. Yet it takes only a little to break down the trappings of civilized qualms—for instance, sitting in a cell, waiting for death . . .

They all sensed the impending climax.

Janoshik, in critical moments a man of action, measured the strength of Lobkowitz as well as Prokosch. He came to the conclusion that in case of need, he'd be well able to take care of both of them. He had too much respect for the brutality of jail wardens in general, and the Nazis in particular, to tolerate an outbreak. "Ever been in solitary?" he inquired. "I hear they've got sort of upright caskets here to keep us in for the days remaining. Might as well take it easy and enjoy the comforts we have, no?"

Wallerstein was in the throes of doubt. The experiment was coming along exceedingly well, his animals were hitting their heads against the wall, and would continue to do so till they fell down from sheer exhaustion. But had he wanted it that way? This miserable, deluded Prokosch who was trying to keep himself together by stubbornly insisting that his life had had some sense, and this youngster whose nerves had been ground raw under the pressure of influences the origin of which the doctor could not yet determine—great pity suddenly swept over Wallerstein. Are we all diseased of mind? What is it that drives us to make each other suffer so cruelly? The issue was not merely Prokosch and Lobkowitz, it was all mankind jumping at one another's throats, fiendishly hurting and wounding and killing. Here, Wallerstein thought, we are going to die in a century in which we have learned, for the first time, to look into the inside of the soul; and what little wisdom we have just serves to convince us that we know nothing. I am without power, I have started something I can't finish, something I can't even face—and so little time left.

"Gentlemen!" he said, trying to give his words a strength he did not have. "This is an academic discussion, impersonal. We must take it that way!"

But Prokosch, deathly pale, sat erect, his fingers moving convulsively. With quavering voice he demanded, "I refuse to be maligned! Mara's memory is sacred! Sacred! The muck in this man's mind, I refuse to have her soiled by it!"

"Soiled! Her memory soiled! Isn't that precisely what you have done all the time?" Lobkowitz accused. "But that would be the least. The hell with memories, the dead are dead. But her life! Her life that you spoiled!"

Prokosch laughed, a forced laugh. The accusation rose and rose, and threatened to engulf him, just because he, of all men, knew the truth of it deep down inside him. "You, nincompoop," he said with acted superiority, "how I can see through you! Don't you think I know why you attempt to besmirch my love, my life? Don't you think I know that you were one of many to seek Mara's favor, Mara, who was so high above you that you couldn't even touch her foot if you stretched your dirty little soul out of joint! I saw it, I tolerated it, I smiled when Mara played with the likes of you.

"That, however, gives you no right whatever, you hear, no right whatever, even to talk of her. I'm going to die, but I'm going to die proud, and till my dying minute I'll protect her."

Lobkowitz held his head low. He tried to hang on to the picture of Mara's beggingly outstretched hand. *Never, hear me, never must he know!*

But it was too much! How could one stand it? Isn't she inside of me too? More true, more real, more mine than the fake illusion Prokosch carries with him? How can I sacrifice *my* woman? Who would demand it? For the sake of a man like that?

If he'd just keep quiet, if he'd allow me to hold on to myself—but no, he talks again!

"I am the man she loved!" proclaimed Prokosch. He took his stand before Lobkowitz, face to face. "If you have to speak your lies, why don't you? Out with them, so that I can push them back into your throat!"

Let him die in peace.... Am *I* dying in peace? Why must I bear the burden, why must I protect Prokosch? He killed Mara. He killed my beloved. Look at him, how he blusters and brags while his foundation is splitting.

Prokosch stretched his arms wide, conjuring. Slowly with pathos, he said, "I, I wanted to sit behind her in her gravest hour—"

"Stop it!" Lobkowitz begged.

"Holding her between my knees—"

"Gentlemen!" cried Wallerstein.

"Absorbing her pain, giving her my strength—"

Janoshik stepped behind Prokosch and ordered, "Shut up, now!"

Prokosch's face was red, his eyes bloodshot, his voice hissing. Into Lobkowitz's teeth he flung: "Me! Only me!"

Lobkowitz broke. He could feel it all through his body, he was two persons now, one registering the sensations of the moment: the rush of blood which seemed to overflow all dams in happy release, the threatening mask of the actor closer than ever anything had been before his eyes—and another person who laughed. It was a short, shrill laugh which remained hanging in the air.

Prokosch, with the insanity of the weak, clasped his hands around Lobkowitz' neck. Lobkowitz felt a stinging pain, felt the fingers of the man stick deep in the soft parts of his throat. He saw Prokosch jump up and down like a dervish, never loosening his grip.

"Any objection to it?" Prokosch howled. "Any objection to it?"

It happened in split seconds. Now Janoshik gripped the actor's wrists and tore his hand away from Lobkowitz' throat. Prokosch struggled, trying to free himself.

"Any objection?" he groaned.

Into the teeth of Prokosch's question Lobkowitz, hardly raising his voice, threw his answer: "Yes—because I am the father of Mara's child."

The stroke had fallen.

Prokosch was still. He had ceased to struggle. Weak and limp, he hung in Janoshik's arms. Softly Janoshik let the actor down on the cot, but his hand remained on Prokosch's shoulder. He was afraid to let go, afraid that the man would slump together like an empty bag.

None but Preissinger dared break the silence. "What do you know about that?" he asked, astonished and somewhat embarrassed.

He received no answer.

Lobkowitz had sobered up completely. Looking at Prokosch, he felt the impulse to go to him, take his hand and say something like: Great God, don't take it so hard. You'll live through it.

But they were going to die shortly. And anyway—words, words! What good were they? And he discovered, frightened by his discovery, that all his hate had gone.

Wallerstein was sad. What he had feared had come to pass. He himself, he recognized, was affected by the cell and the nearness of death. I can't go through with it, he thought. Observation, science, notes, immortality! I am losing my countenance—these men, these fighting, suffering, broken, fearful men, I am one of them! My Lord, don't let me fall, don't let me get too weak.

"Prokosch," he said, "listen to me. I know life, I've probed it from many angles. You've lived it according to your lights, and you've been happy. What difference does it make that now you find your happiness was an illusion? When is it not that? Your pride is lost—that hurts. But all those years you loved, all those moments you enjoyed, they cannot be taken away. It is your illusion that counts. It is not important what or how Mara was—important is what you saw in her. To that you must hold yourself."

Prokosch stared at the space between his feet. "Leave me alone," he said. "Let the dead be."

All his braggadocio was lost. His disintegration touched them all.

Yet it was not with pity that Lobkowitz regarded Prokosch. Rather it was aloofness. You do not pity the dead, they are on a different plane. He had no regrets either. He felt free, cleansed and purged from the depressing loyalty to Mara.

What was this loyalty? Mara had been full of fear, and she had died in fear and had left her fear with him. To this he had been loyal.

And suddenly, with a flash of intuition, Lobkowitz knew

why Mara had remained with Prokosch, to the destruction of her own life, of her love for himself, of youth and of strength. It was not Prokosch whom she had wanted to protect, but herself.

She had recognized the actor for what he was. But having built her life on a misconception, having invested her own youth, her career, her life, in this abysmal failure of a man, like a gambler who stakes chip after chip on the same number that never wins, she had refused to concede defeat. She, too, was vain and proud, and afraid to face the truth. So she had built him up, to correspond with the image she had seen, a child of sixteen, in the kingly figure of Oedipus Rex. And in protecting her image she protected herself. In trying to excuse him, she tried to justify herself.

This newly acquired clarity made Lobkowitz rebel against his fate. Knowing what he now knew, he so much wished to live. And now that he had matured, he was to be deprived of this mature and fuller life.

To Janoshik he said, "Somehow the world will go on. But how? Where to? Do you know?"

Janoshik looked at him. The astonishment in his eyes gave way to a deep, comradely understanding.

CHAPTER 6

THE AFFAIR Glasenapp was, during these days, almost the exclusive theme of conversation in the officers' mess of the 431st Infantry Division. Captain Patzer and Lieutenant Marschmann, but especially the Captain, were considered heroes who had successfully braved a vicious and unfair enemy, and who had barely escaped a most terrifying fate.

The 431st was a new division, organized under the Nazis, its officers' corps liberally sprinkled with elderly reservists who suffered from various ailments, but who made up for their lack of prowess by noisy confessions to Nazism and by the expansion of strategic wisdom of the armchair kind. The division had no battle tradition except against unarmed civilians in the occupied countries; with these, however, it had dealt sternly. The 431st was proud to represent the New Order, and worked valiantly to put it over.

"In a couple of months, at latest, we'll be in Moscow," said Lieutenant Marschmann, wiping the fat of his soup from his lips. "That means complete mastery over Europe. England? A little island, gentlemen, which we'll starve into submission, or maybe we'll send a few divisions of paratroops to occupy the City and scare hell out of the bankers."

Major Grauthoff, who was helping himself to generous slices of breast of veal, the next course, expressed his doubts: "Militarily, you're probably right, yes. But don't forget that from conquest to safe rule and profitable exploitation is a long step, several steps, in fact. We look at the map, and we get drunk from the expanse of territory, from the number of countries we've taken. What do we get out of them after we've skimmed the cream, after we've taken the goods in the shops, the food in the warehouses, the gold in the banks? A lot of headaches, gentlemen, a lot of hate. Which one of you has recently gone out at night by himself?"

None of the officers could honestly say that he had, especially after Lieutenant Glasenapp's death. So they kept silent; only the scraping of the silverware on the plates, and the sound of lip smacking and chewing were audible.

"The British," continued Major Grauthoff, "though now a decadent and decaying people, were most clever in their day. With a few strings of glass beads in gaudy colors, with the distribution of top hats and titles, they slowly wormed their way to empire. They tried to make the conquered feel that it was pleasant to be conquered, that it was an honor to be ruled by their king; only when they were firmly established did they show the mailed fist. Sly, but profitable."

"Crooks and bankers!" commented a fat second lieutenant who commanded a detachment of heavy machine guns. "That's why we're fighting them. Goddamned Jews and Bolsheviks," he added, satisfied that he had disposed of the matter.

Captain Patzer cleared his throat in preparation for an important pronouncement. The officers looked at him, the hero of the Mánes. What he said carried weight.

"Discipline! Discipline!" he began. "Before I was called to serve in the Army, I was a Postal Inspector of the First Grade. Years of service. We know what discipline means. We're born with it. That's German, it finds its highest expression in the ideals of our Führer. But these people we've conquered—and that's why we've conquered them—what do they know of discipline? We were in Norway, Poland, France, and now here; we've seen them—everywhere the same picture. Sloppy, easy going, uncultured, and full of resentment. Discipline—that's what's lacking. The British, Major, the British had time to build their empire, hundreds of years. We've got to do it in weeks and months. So we must teach them discipline. If we were to shoot every tenth man, the other nine would work for us with the greatest of pleasure. And if that's not enough, we shoot every tenth man again, and so forth, till they've learned."

"When are your hostages going to be shot?" inquired the fat second lieutenant, winking to the mess boy for another jigger of that clear Czech prune schnapps, Slivovitz.

"Couple of days," said Patzer. "This Gestapo Commissioner, Reinhardt—he's my man. No waiting, no circumstances, *durchgreifen!* He's asked me to come and see him this afternoon; I'll get the latest on the case of our unfortunate comrade straight from the source." He leaned back in his chair and folded his napkin with a show of indifference, as if a conference with a leading Gestapo official were an everyday occurrence in his life.

Marschmann, who had not been asked to see the Commissioner, was piqued. "He's probably going to ask you why you permitted Glasenapp to get drunk when you knew that the poor fellow couldn't stand alcohol."

But Captain Patzer was above slurs of this kind. He rose, bowed toward Major Grauthoff, and said to the mess boy, "I'll have my coffee on my return." Then he walked out, his shoulders straight, his chest protruding, a happy warrior.

Over at Gestapo headquarters he encountered young Gruber, the Kid, in the anteroom of Reinhardt's office. They saluted each other snappily. That being over, Patzer, in jovial mood, inquired, "Well, how's tricks? You don't look as if your responsibilities are getting you down!"

Gruber grinned, his apple face shining. "No," he said, "everything's coming along just fine."

"Any news of Glasenapp's killer?"

Gruber waxed confidential. "We're hot on his traces. But I can say nothing yet—not even to you."

"Oh, I see," nodded the Captain understandingly. "Well, I suppose Commissioner Reinhardt will tell me."

Gruber shrugged. "Maybe, maybe not. He has so many things on his mind. So have we all, for that matter."

Patzer was duly impressed. "Of course, I don't want to impose on you—"

"Not at all! Not at all! I'll announce you to the Commissioner." He strutted off and returned shortly, to usher Patzer into the inner office.

Reinhardt was behind his desk. He mumbled something that sounded like "Heil Hitler." The Captain stood near the door which had closed behind him, he was not certain what to do—whether to approach the Commissioner or to wait till he was invited to sit down. He noticed that Reinhardt was sizing him up; he felt the Commissioner's eyes moving all over him, like fingers.

A minute or so passed in this awkward manner. Finally Reinhardt motioned the Captain to the chair before his desk. The bright light of the afternoon fell full on Patzer's face, he blinked his eyes uncomfortably; Reinhardt's head remained a dark silhouette against the window.

What a *Dummkopf!* Reinhardt thought, but he knew that often it was easier to wring important facts from stupid people than from men with brains. He decided to be condescending toward the good Captain, but moderately so. If he frightened him too much, Patzer might shut up like a clam.

127

"I've had reports that you've been most helpful to us," Reinhardt began.

Patzer bowed stiffly. He felt that he was sweating, but he did not dare to wipe his face.

Reinhardt smiled a little, half sneer and half encouragement. "Unfortunately, it is not always that we get this kind of co-operation from your branch of the service."

Patzer bowed again, this time apologetically. Like most people of his class, he had great respect for the police, and besides he knew that, during the last years, the black-uniformed Gestapo had become all powerful.

"Sometimes I envy you soldiers," Reinhardt continued. "No troubles, no complications, just straight shooting. We, however, have to solidify what you gain. That seems petty, yet I assure you, without us you would have been beaten long ago."

"Oho!" Patzer said, registering a modest protest.

"What Oho!" Reinhardt snapped. "Don't you believe me?"

"I do, I do! But—"

"Then we understand each other. I am glad. You knew Lieutenant Glasenapp well?"

"As well as anybody, I think. He was a fine man—"

"No generalities, please. We don't have time for that here. Tell me, what do you do about women?"

"You mean—"

Reinhardt waited. "Oh, come on! We're no club of angels, are we? Ha, ha!"

Patzer laughed obligingly.

"Whorehouses, mostly?" Reinhardt suggested.

"Sure! We've got a pretty good one, just for officers. Every Tuesday and Friday—"

"Not interested in your schedule. Did Glasenapp ever come along?"

Patzer thoughtfully pulled his earlobe. "Come to think of

it, he joined us once, during our first few days in Prague. After that, he sort of shirked."

"Homosexual?"

"I beg your pardon!"

"It's no shame. War is a man's game. You're shut off from women—we have to consider all angles in our work."

"I'm sure he wasn't."

"I thought not," said Reinhardt. "I merely wanted your confirmation. Now I'll tell you a secret. There was a woman in the life of your friend Glasenapp, and I can't quite imagine that he'd be able to conceal that completely from you."

"Here in Prague?" asked Patzer. "What do you know! *Stille Wasser sind tief.*" There was a mixture of envy and astonishment in his voice.

"I'd be much obliged if you'd try to recollect any details which might help us to find that woman. Little occurrences, chance hints—police work, Captain, is like solving jigsaw puzzles; often we merely need one missing link to see the whole picture."

Patzer was immensely flattered that he was called upon to supply the missing link. His forehead became furrowed, his mouth twitched from the effort of thinking.

Now Reinhardt was lucky to have chosen Patzer as informant. The Captain's postal inspector mind was uncanny in its sense for detail, the training of long years in the sorting of letters, the knowledge of postal rates and distances, official regulations and orders, bore magnificent fruit.

Patzer suddenly slapped his knee. "There is a church," he said, "not an old church and not a new one either, in one of the side streets of Wenceslas Place—"

Reinhardt did not move. Only his small eyes glinted and showed that he was listening eagerly.

"We passed it once, Glasenapp and I; we watched a funeral procession. A poor funeral—a couple of monks chant-

129

ing, a shabby carriage with thin horses, wilted flowers—and then Glasenapp went off. I called after him, and he shouted back that he had to visit somebody, or words to that effect."

Out of a drawer in his desk, Reinhardt pulled a map of Prague and unfolded it. His manicured finger slid softly along a few lines, then went off to the right, and stopped at a little cross. "St. Stephan's Church?" he asked.

"Yes! That was it!" said Patzer, relieved as a student who successfully has passed his most difficult examination.

"Anything else you remember?"

Again Patzer went into a huddle with himself, but, hard as he thought, his brain produced nothing pertinent.

"Well," Reinhardt rose, "this may be of significance or may not—we'll check in any case. You've tried your best. Thank you."

Patzer was happy. He stood up and shook Reinhardt's dry, clawlike hand. "Nothing at all! Don't mention it! You don't know how pleased I am that I could help avenge the vile attempt on our dear Lieutenant Glasenapp—"

He would have gone on prattling, but Reinhardt cut him short. "All right! All right! I have work to do. Drop around some other time." And produced a croaking sound meaning "Heil Hitler" and the definite end of the conference with Patzer.

The Captain left in happy anticipation of the sensational stories he'd be able to tell his fellow officers. Now Reinhardt really was on the track of something, and he had put him on that track! He felt that this, too, added a few inches to his stature which had grown so satisfyingly ever since Glasenapp's tragic disappearance.

Reinhardt, alone in his office, was lost in thought. He distinctly disliked to dig deeper into the Glasenapp matter which, up to now, was developing so smoothly. But this Milada woman represented a possible loophole, how ever small, and it had to be plugged.

He rang a bell, and a minute or so later, a sleezy little man with a battered brown felt hat entered.

"Your Excellency?" he inquired in a voice which lay between the hissing sound of a leaky steam valve and the rasping cough of an asthmatic.

"Pan Kratochvil," said Reinhardt, "here is a job for you." Again his finger pointed to the little cross on the map, and then made a circle around it covering the territory of the adjoining blocks. "'This is what we're looking for," and he explained about Milada.

Pan Kratochvil wagged his head sadly. Somehow he managed to let even his broad saddle nose appear droopy. "Jesus, Mary and Joseph," he moaned, "why all the most difficult jobs for me? It will take time, it will take money, I must go to the stores and the taverns, I must buy, I must drink, I must talk . . ."

Reinhardt took a flat paper knife and snapped it loudly on his desk. It sounded like a shot. Pan Kratochvil winced. "I will go! I will find out. For you, your Excellency, you know, I'd do anything!"

"I give you two hours, Pan Kratochvil."

"Yes, your Excellency."

"And get yourself a new hat. Yours is becoming too much of a trade mark."

"Yes, your Excellency. But where can I buy a hat? The stores are empty."

"Get out of here!"

Pan Kratochvil bowed and left in a hurry. He walked without a sound; one could readily believe that among his kind, he had the reputation of being not only inaudible but also invisible.

And so it came that after two hours, in the late afternoon of the day, Commissioner Reinhardt was walking down the

Malá Štěpánská, Little Stephan's Street, which branched off, at the Church of St. Stephan, from big Stephan's Street, and ended in a dead end.

He was alone and wore civilian clothes, a well-tailored summer suit made from genuine English material which Murtenbacher had sent him from Paris. He had walked all the way from the Petschek Palais and had enjoyed it. It was a fine day, and he stepped almost jauntily. He wondered what this girl Milada would look like—probably not much of a woman if a man like Glasenapp could have her. Nevertheless, one could not tell—and far back in his mind a mischievous little idea was beginning to raise its head.

The Commissioner looked at the house numbers and stopped at Number 6. He examined the list of names at the side of the door and nodded. He rang a bell, waited a minute, and then entered.

The staircase was dark and cool. It was an old house, a hundred or a hundred and fifty years, he guessed, and it smelled as old houses smell, a little musty and of cabbage. It would be funny, he mused, if I should get lost here. Outside of Kratochvil nobody would know—and Kratochvil would be glad to get a less severe taskmaster. But it was better if he kept his steps in the Glasenapp case to himself; Heydrich would thank him for that. He felt for the pistol in the right pocket of his coat and tapped it tenderly.

Upstairs an old woman was waiting at the door to an apartment. "Miss Milada Markova live here?" Reinhardt asked.

"What do you want?"

"Official business, police," he said and pushed the old woman aside. "She's not in? Close the door. I'll wait here for her."

"But—"

"Come, come, you heard me. Your name is Klein and you live on a pension. I know, you see?" He entered Milada's room, followed by the landlady who was frightened out of her wits.

"Calm yourself," Reinhardt advised, looking around.

The room was small, the furniture threadbare. The afternoon sun broke through the window and fell upon a few plants. A colored dress with a flower design hung on a hook at the door, some books leaned against the wall on top of a shaky chest of drawers. The Commissioner picked them up, perfunctorily leafed through them and placed them back.

"Your husband was a soldier?"

"Yes," whispered Mrs. Klein.

"He fell in Galicia? Very regrettable, no doubt a good man. But that is war." Up to now he had spoken mechanically as if giving no thought whatever to his words. Suddenly he changed his tone.

"When was Lieutenant Glasenapp here last?"

"I knew it would end bad! I knew it would end bad!" the landlady broke down, whimpering. "He was good, not at all like—"

"Like the Nazis?" Reinhardt finished her sentence and smiled. "You must tell me more about him. Why don't you sit down?—So, when was he here last?"

"On Thursday, I believe."

"Hm. They had a fight, the Lieutenant and Miss Milada?"

"Fight?" said the landlady who was slowly recovering her composure. "Perhaps. I don't know. I've forgotten most of my German, and the door was closed." She looked at Reinhardt with shrewd eyes in which, however, fear still lingered. "I don't peep through keyholes."

Reinhardt sat down in the only comfortable chair. He crossed his legs, carefully, so as not to destroy the crease of his pants. Looking down at his well-polished shoe, he said, "I can see you're a clever woman. I'll put my cards on the table. You think that I ask about this little discussion between the Lieutenant and Miss Milada because I suspect that she may have, let's say, disposed of him?"

Mrs. Klein folded her hands in her lap. Her wrinkled face was tranquil now. She had decided to tell no more. Let this German policeman speak to Miss Milada, if he wanted to find out things. As far as she was concerned, she would not incriminate anybody.

"Isn't it so?" Reinhardt smiled.

"Maybe."

"Well, let me tell you—we don't believe that. We know that a girl like Milada could not hurt a fly. A fly!" he exclaimed and looked at the plants on the windowsill. "A girl who loves flowers and the beautiful things in life—isn't it so?"

"Maybe."

"Don't say maybe! Say yes or no!"

Mrs. Klein unfolded her hands and stroked down her patched apron. Her mouth was closed tight over toothless gums, a black line, her lips inverted.

Reinhardt, observing her, still smiled.

"So—what did they discuss on Thursday afternoon? You don't want me to take you along to headquarters?"

"No."

"You're an obstinate person," said Reinhardt, regret in his voice. "I've seen many like you. They don't last."

The landlady's hands were folded again. I don't understand this, she thought. I am frightened, I ought to run away, but I can't move.

Reinhardt said nothing; he was a master of intimidation, he could play the scales of terror like an artist. And he enjoyed it.

"What did they speak about on Thursday afternoon?" he repeated into the sunlit stillness of the room.

The questioning was interrupted by the sound of the key in the outer door. Milada entered.

She saw the stranger. Her first impulse was to cry out, but

the cry stuck in her throat. There was nothing terrible in any single feature of the visitor—his narrow, piercing eyes, the thin nose, the small, half-open mouth above the weak chin, the short parted hair cropped at the sides—yet the composite was of such discord that it shocked her.

The stranger rose slowly. She felt him measuring her. She straightened to meet his eyes firmly. His lips shifted to a smile.

"Hello," she finally managed to say. "A visitor?"

The ban which imprisoned Mrs. Klein broke. "Oh, Miss Milada," she wept, "terrible! How terrible! The police—"

"I'll introduce myself!" Reinhardt stopped the old woman to prevent her from tipping off Milada as to his line of questioning.

"Commissioner Reinhardt, Secret State Police. You are Milada Markova?"

This is it, thought Milada. This is the enemy. Here my battle begins. She felt strangely elated, a slight weakness in her knees as on the day when Pavel had taken her to the country, for the first time. She fervently wished for strength, and in wishing, she knew she would have it.

Whatever the Commissioner had imagined Glasenapp's woman to be, he had not expected a person such as Milada. She was intelligent and had the kind of beauty intriguing to him. Even the sudden shock of finding him in her room had not distorted the quiet harmony of her face. Secretly, Reinhardt always had despised the full-bosomed, pink-skinned femininity which the ideologists of his Party advertised as most desirable for the improvement of the race. This one was different, foreign, and with a touch of mystery that promised excitement. He was very pleased with the development of the Glasenapp affair.

She was exquisite—which complicated matters. For, Czech or no Czech, the relation of such a woman to the nondescript

Glasenapp must have a more intricate background than he had assumed. He moistened his lips.

"You must pardon my dropping in without having announced myself," he opened the conversation. "In our work, you know, we have so little time for the amenities that we sometimes forget them."

Mrs. Klein, trembling, hugged Milada. Whether she tried to give or receive protection was not clear. Milada, looking over the landlady's shoulder at Reinhardt, felt the irony of the cat playing with the mouse in his apologetic approach. "You frightened her badly," she said.

"Everybody seems frightened," he complained. "Why? Do I look like a wild beast?" He smiled, baring his yellowish teeth. "Nobody need be frightened of me. However, since I came to get certain information, I expect you to answer a few questions. A few only, and they won't be too difficult. . . .

"They concern the regrettable death of Lieutenant Glasenapp."

Milada freed herself from the landlady's embrace.

The Commissioner's last words which had been pronounced with significant sharpness, set loose a turbulent stream of thoughts which rushed at her and threatened to submerge her. Like a swimmer, she must try to hold her head above water, she must have time till the stream flowed quiet and orderly.

She took off her hat and placed it on the chest of drawers. Out of her handbag she took comb, powder and lipstick, and proceeded to the little chores with which women achieve delay.

The picture of Seliger, the weasel-faced provocateur at the Kolbenka, arose first. Had she given herself away then, with her protest against the outrage of shooting the innocent?

Or had Glasenapp, before his death, conceived of a plan of sad vengeance—if he could not have her, nobody else was to love her either?

It did not matter. She was in danger wherever it came from. Where could she turn?

Order your thoughts. Hold on to yourself. Not only you are in danger—there are others. There is Breda, Breda who knows, Breda and his plan. Whatever it is, it must not fail.

It is good to think of Breda; his kindly eyes, his strong face buttress one's courage. She could hear him say: *Be careful. Don't talk about all this. The Nazis are not interested in how Glasenapp died. They just want to make their lives safer by frightening us.*

Is that why Reinhardt had come? He is an important man. He signed the hostage decree. Yet he has gone to the trouble of posing as a gentleman detective. How much does he know of Glasenapp's end? How much does he suspect? What does he want to know from me?

I can't comb my hair forever. Some time I must stop and face him. All right, let him ask. Let him come on, let him show his face. The less I say, the more he must ask.

"You can go now," she heard Reinhardt say to the landlady. "I will call you in case you are needed."

The old woman left, her slippers slowly shuffling over the linoleum floor. "God and the Saints be with you, child," she whispered.

Reinhardt waited. Patience was one of his chief virtues. His eyes followed Milada's every move, as dogs follow their quarry.

He knew, of course, that she was playing for time. But he needed time too, time to work out his strategy toward her. Rarely did he go into a case with a fully developed blueprint. Experience had shown that it was more practical to decide his moves on the spur of the moment—and he was confident of making the right decisions. So much depended on the personality of his adversary. He, Reinhardt, was flexible, adjusting himself to the situation as it arose, to the other person as he or she appeared to him. He flattered himself with a gift for sizing up people in a few glances; they fell into relatively few categories, and he knew how to deal with all of them.

On his way up to the Malá Štěpánská Street, he had asked himself why, in the devil's name, he had not sent a few of his men to catch this girl and lock her up. That was the simplest thing to do. People behind bars don't squawk, neither do the dead. Murtenbacher would have done it.

Murtenbacher, yes, but not Reinhardt. Once, in Paris, they had argued about it. Murtenbacher was an exponent of brutality, a useful man. He, Reinhardt, was more genteel. He did not consider his job a routine matter to be carried out by anybody who can move a stamp from the pad to the bottom of a document.

No, the Commissioner thought, I am human, I have interests, life has its moments.

He wanted to see the woman who had driven Glasenapp to suicide; perhaps she'd be fun to deal with. And look what Murtenbacher would have missed by just burying her in the cellar!

How gracious she is! Gracious and clever. She could drive a man out of his senses, especially a weakling like Glasenapp.

Question was: Did she believe in the murder story? If she knew, or had even an inkling that the Lieutenant had killed himself—then, sorry, he'd have to use the Murtenbacher method. He also would have to chase all over town after people she might have blubbered to. If, on the other hand, she didn't know of the suicide—the Commissioner saw agreeable perspectives.

Reinhardt was a stickler for clean, smooth work. He would

let nothing interfere with the settlement of the affair Glasenapp, which was really the affair Preissinger. First came one's duty. The Protector's interests were more important than all the pleasures derived from one's work.

"Last Thursday, you were visited by Lieutenant Glasenapp, weren't you?"

Milada turned to face Reinhardt. He noticed she was calm. He felt a warm glow anticipating how he would ruffle that calmness.

Milada realized that this much he could have learned easily from Mrs. Klein.

"Yes," she said.

"You're a lovely girl. That was not his first visit?"

Reinhardt stroked his chin. A soaked sheet of paper, carefully restored by his experts, was before the Commissioner's mind. *You had grown to be something in my life which is hard to define. I am pretty desperate as you will see from the fact that I write you at all after what has happened between us.* Glasenapp's letter, never sent ... this letter would give him the wedge to open her up. "Come, come," he said. "He must have known you for quite a while."

There was no sense denying it. He had spoken to Mrs. Klein. He probably had checked with neighbors, with Glasenapp's fellow officers. She decided to sacrifice a pawn. "He did. He was very good, very friendly to me."

"No man with eyes would behave differently. And that was all? Just a beautiful friendship?"

"Yes."

"Oh, Miss Markova!" He spoke like a teacher who has caught his pupil making a stupid blunder. "My knowledge of women, especially Czech women, may be limited, but if there is one group of people I know thoroughly, it's German officers. They usually don't go in for Platonic niceties. How did he meet you?"

"On the street," she replied truthfully.

"And then?"

"We saw each other off and on."

"No ulterior motives on either part?"

"I really don't see what all this has to do with the case."

"You will," he said. "He never tried to make love to you?"

"No."

"He must have been a goddamned fool. I would have. So, I believe, would the entire officers' corps of the German Army in Prague. Check. I don't believe you, consequently."

"As you like."

"Miss Markova, your imagination isn't so limited that you can't realize your life and liberty may depend on whether I believe you or not?"

She swallowed, once. Otherwise no muscle in her face moved.

I wonder how long she'll be able to control herself so perfectly, thought Reinhardt, observing her. "In what way was he good to you?"

"In many ways," Milada said evasively. Unless he indicated that he knew of her participation in the fight before the University, and how Glasenapp saved her, she would not mention it. She had no idea where his questioning was to lead; but allowing him a glimpse into the past might mean giving away the present.

"In many ways," he repeated dreamily. "Favors? Money?"

The implication was plain. She defended herself.

"I wanted to pay him back. I was shocked to hear he was dead."

"Yes," he agreed insinuatingly. "Right after he had a fight with you, too. Such coincidence!"

Having thus baited his line, he waited for it to sink.

Milada did not notice the vicious purport of the question.

The fact that he knew of the scene she'd had with Glasenapp occupied her mind fully. How much did he know? The mere fact, only—or also what the struggle had been about? And from whom—the landlady? Some other source? If he knew the content of the dispute, how could she go on withholding the truth about Pavel, or about Glasenapp's threat to kill himself?

"Such coincidence!" Reinhardt repeated. He was now sure of his tactic. He would make her feel that he suspected her of complicity in the murder of Glasenapp; if she knew of the Lieutenant's suicide, she would be quick to offer the information in her own defense.

He saw her hesitate. He hammered home his advantage: "The Lieutenant came here, as he had come often. You had a row, a bitter row."

Curse that fellow! If only his letter had been more specific; if now one could dish out the whole story, one could knock her over in one blow. But the letter's full meaning was known only to this girl and the dead Lieutenant. He recalled the picture of Glasenapp—the nondescript face with the washed-out eyes behind thick glasses, the thin and drawn cheeks with shades of pimples. He ventured a guess: "You really didn't like him. A woman of your caliber does not go for that kind of dish rag come alive. So you had a row. About what?"

The sudden question, calculated to upset her completely, had the contrary effect. The possibility that Reinhardt himself was groping in the dark occurred to her.

"Well," said Milada, for the first time using a smile on Reinhardt, "there is no friendship without its little conflicts—"

"No generalities, please!" Reinhardt parried the attempt. "Whatever Glasenapp demanded, you knew that as a German officer he could become extremely troublesome to you.

"And a second element enters the case, my dear Miss

141

Markova. In my work, I have my fingers on the pulse of the people. You hate us, don't you?" he said, almost tenderly.

Milada wondered whether he required an answer.

Evidently he didn't. He continued: "Yes, yes—I concede we are a little difficult to be ruled by. You'll get used to it in the course of the next decades . . ."

He felt that by his provocation he had prepared the ground nicely. Now he moved in for the kill.

"Let us put two and two together—your conflict with Glasenapp. Your feelings about him. His murder. You will grant me, the pieces do fit into a neat picture."

It was a blow struck from behind. Its impact sent the blood rushing from her head; she swayed dizzily.

He's trying to pin the murder on me!

Her hands clasped the back of the chair before her until her knuckles shone white.

He's trying to pin the murder on me. She felt dry and hot. The walls of the room stood at crazy angles.

Let me think. *Put two and two together,* said the spider. This is outrageous, nonsensical.

"You're insane!" she cried. "You know I didn't kill him—".

But if he knows, why does he accuse me? If he wants his murderer, if he wants revenge for it, he has his hostages—he won't let them go. Not even in exchange for me. He has it all fixed.

"Why not?" Reinhardt asked.

Why not . . . ! Because Glasenapp killed himself! The words were on her lips, her lips moved.

Reinhardt waited. He, too, was tremendously excited. Now I have her where I want her, he thought. Now she'll break. He leaned forward.

In fever dreams, in moments of utmost danger, the human mind is capable of miracles. In the space of seconds, out of

142

the files of the brain, rush thoughts and impressions, racing, chasing each other, piling themselves upon each other. If you catch one, hold on to it, hold on, for dear life's sake!

This Milada did. In the whirlpool the immovable Breda appeared. *Be careful. Don't talk about all this. The Nazis are not interested in how Glasenapp died.*

And now, her thoughts began to take shape, a semblance of order was restored.

She realized that Reinhardt had blocked her way, right or left. If she let his accusation stand, he would nail her. If she defended herself, proving Glasenapp's suicide, he would shut her up, too—he could not permit his frame-up to be exposed; he, too, had gone out on a limb.

Her choice lay in how to perish. The decision was simple. She must protect Breda, Breda who knew and had a plan. Perhaps this plan would avenge what was to happen to her, and the death of the hostages, and Pavel's death, and everything.

The grip of her hands loosened from the back of the chair. As through a fog, she heard Reinhardt say:

"The death of the Lieutenant, no doubt, simplified matters for you. I'm not implying that you're callous. I know you felt sorry about his unfortunate end. But it came precisely at the opportune moment—didn't it?"

How flat his words fell!

Why does he trouble himself about me? she thought. He can have me without that. Just arrest me, carry me off, bury me in their cellars...

Still Reinhardt was sure of victory. Just one more little push. Then she'll blurt out that she knows of the suicide.

Or, perhaps, she really has no idea?

Basically, people are naïve. No match for a superior mind. Scare them sufficiently, and they must open up like mussels under a sharp knife.

"I didn't kill Glasenapp. I had no part in his murder." Milada sat down. She had taken hold of herself, the color came back to her cheeks. She felt that his blitz-questioning had lost its terror. Whatever the Commissioner might ask, whatever surprises he might spring on her, she was prepared, now.

Reinhardt smiled, hiding his disappointment. So the little mouse just smelled at the cheese; she wouldn't bite, yet. Don't worry, she will, be patient.

"Miss Markova," he said wearily, "I'm afraid we'll have to go through the whole thing again. . . . You see, I've done some checking on you." He skillfully inserted a pause; he wanted Milada to have time to grow anxious over the question of how much he knew of her.

His mind reviewed the results of Pan Kratochvil's expedition into the neighborhood of Malá Štěpánská Street. "You participated in a veritable street battle," he opened his new attack. "That is one reason why I don't believe you are so much above killing German soldiers—right?"

So he knew that. He probably knew of Pavel, too. Ten minutes ago, this would have upset her. Now, having overcome the frightful crisis of her nerves, she merely felt worn. Above all, she wished that he would put an end to this mental torture.

"Why don't you arrest me?" she said tonelessly. "Get it over with?"

"Ah, now," he chided. "I've been in this business for years. You're not alone, you have friends, accomplices. Any green idiot can arrest people—that's primitive. The cellars, the camp, the knife of the guillotine, I much prefer to let all that hang over your head. Fear is more efficient than pain; life under threat more terrible than death."

He worked like a boxer who softens up his opponent by short, quick jabs at the heart, in order to deliver all the more surely the deadly knock-out blow: "Who is Pavel?"

144

The same dead voice answered, "You can't touch him any more. He is so far underground you can't reach him."

"I know," said Reinhardt, using his pink fingernails to scratch the short cropped back of his head, "and here is another piece to the picture: Glasenapp was one of the officers in command when your lover Pavel was shot dead. And then he intended to take his place. An interesting height of perversion. Did you kill Glasenapp?"

"No."

"Did you have somebody else kill him?"

"No."

Reinhardt's smile began to wear thin. His easy-going air yielded more and more to harsh urging: "If you had, I'd understand you! You're a full-blooded woman, and there was that measly sample of a Nazi, responsible for all the misery you suffered—you hated him as much or more than you hate me. You would have liked to have him killed, as you would like to see me killed, if I'd give you the chance."

The Commissioner, having played all his registers, was losing his serenity. Why doesn't she speak? Why doesn't she come clean?

Reinhardt could be enraged by only one thing—the misfiring of one of his schemes. It happened rarely. But when it did, it jolted his self-confidence. He wanted her to admit: A suicide, Commissioner, Glasenapp killed himself, why are you pursuing me? He wanted her to admit it because he had worked it out that way. And he was utterly reluctant to concede that she actually might not know anything about it.

But she merely repeated, "I didn't kill Glasenapp."

He sniffed contemptuously. Of that he was sure anyway. But whether she knew of the suicide, and whether she had talked to other people about it, remained as much a riddle to him as when he had come here. It was the first flaw in the otherwise perfect Glasenapp affair. Until he had solved this

145

problem, he recognized, he was not the master of the situation. Under that he chafed.

Milada sensed the change in Reinhardt. She sat with bent head, ready to receive a blow which failed to come. What was he going to do? What else could he use on her but brute force?

Without lifting her head, she looked at him, began to watch him. His eyes had become dull, undecided. A mediocre flat-faced police official, it struck her. How, ever, could that have frightened me?

She must tell Breda about it. Breda would understand and help her to clarity. Also, she was proud. Whether Reinhardt arrested her now or not, she knew she had acquitted herself as one should: she had kept her secret, and she'd be able to face whatever was to come.

The Commissioner rose angrily. He saw the gracious line of her neck, and, for a moment, imagined the flash of the guillotine falling down upon it, severing this head from the supple shoulders. The thought consoled him somewhat. That little thrill, he said to himself, we can always arrange.

"Illuminating talk we had!" He buttoned his jacket. Then he softly put his claw on her neck. "You *are* beautiful. We shall keep up our acquaintance, I hope."

She pushed his arm away, recoiling. Disgust and nervous excitement made her feel nauseous.

He did not seem to notice. "How could a man like Glasenapp appreciate you?—Tell me. No, my dear Milada, I won't arrest you—yet. I'll keep in touch with you, in very close touch."

He left.

The landlady found Milada still sitting with her head bent, trembling as in fever.

"My poor child," she lamented, "my poor, poor child."

She led Milada to her bed, undressed her, tucked her **in**. Milada was completely passive, as though drugged.

146

CHAPTER 7

THE FIRST TIME Janoshik was imprisoned, he had shared a cell with an old tramp, who was a specialist in the preparation of chicken. The tramp gave him long and thorough lessons—how to boil, fry, broil, roast, cream, stew, fricassee and stuff the bird, under any conditions, kitchen stove or open fire, with pan or pot, potatoes or nothing.

Janoshik liked to learn, he was a willing and eager pupil. When he asked the tramp why he was in jail, the man answered, amazed by Janoshik's innocence: Why, Sonny! For stealing chicken, of course!

After that, they became fast friends. Inasmuch as the lessons, which suffered from lack of tangible accessories, aroused their appetites mightily, they searched for consolation and found it in that old device of the lonely and hungry: philosophy.

Sonny, said the tramp, if you are in the klink, you don't want to go crazy. You want to keep your wits together. Never think of nothing—put your mind on some definite thing, look at it from all sides, then turn it over and look at it again. It'll keep you alive up here—you know?

That had been the first time in jail. Now it was Janoshik's

last time in a cell. He realized it constantly, but he saw no reason to disregard the tramp's advice. The others were brooding, fighting—Janoshik devoted himself to mental gymnastics.

He did not do it merely for the sake of exercise! Times had changed since the days of the chicken-stealing tramp. Thinking had to be done with a purpose, even though, day after tomorrow, that marvelous apparatus inside your skull would stop dead.

The object Janoshik picked for his deliberations was himself. He and his relation to the outside world, which, after all, was going to go on without him. Another person in his situation might have looked back—remembering the good things and regretting that so many opportunities had been missed. Janoshik disliked to reconsider the past—not that it had been bad. He liked to look forward, in spite of the fact that he had no more future.

Whatever he had lived through in the past, whatever people he had met and befriended or fought against, whatever he had done, he had done with the future in mind. The miners of Kladno whom he had helped to organize, though they were silent now, would rise one day and perhaps recall what he had said and done, and act accordingly. The farmhands in Moravia, with whom he had lived, whose simple language he had spoken, at whose side he had sowed and harvested the wheat, the good wheat of the dark earth—they too, perhaps, one day would march on the road he had tried to point out to them. And all the others with whom he had shared the kinship of common work, common suffering, and common laughter, those with whom he had eaten and drunk, those to whom he had made love, good love, by God!—all of them now carried part of him, he was part of them.

Life had been satisfactory. One need not think about it much, except in the way in which the peasant, sitting before his house in the evening, takes account of the closing day's work, while he watches the sun go down. And even this peasant thinks more of tomorrow, and how the weather is going to be, than of what he has done.

In his heart Janoshik had hoped to see the future he had worked for. In the petty, detailed daily struggles, this had given him direction. His hopes were modest, he did not expect too much of that future. He knew that people would have to be re-formed, that this was a process of years and years, and that he was already too old to see the new age in full bloom. Just a glimpse into the beginning of it—that would have been nice. To see the day when men and women would work and eat and live as human beings should, when the kids would have a chance to develop whatever was in them, when people would own the world they had created— that would have been fun. He felt a little sorry that he was not going to have his glimpse—though, what difference did it make? Others would see it.

There were, however, two thoughts disturbing him.

He had a job to do. It was a little item only, the transmitting of an address—Watzlik, Smíchovská Street 64, he recalled automatically—from Breda to the longshoremen group. But little and big jobs were of equal importance in Janoshik's work; one depended on the other.

He was cooped up in this cellar—now, Breda knew nothing of the bald-headed longshoreman who was Janoshik's contact; and without the Watzlik address the longshoreman could not get to the package Breda had prepared—and the munitions barges would be safely unloaded, their deadly load continuing east and east—to the front, where they were fighting over the future which Janoshik so longed to see...

It was maddening.

He had fallen down on his job. Not through his own fault. He could excuse himself, he was going to die. But he never had liked to make excuses, never had liked to accept them either.

The second thought was equally maddening.

It sprang from the idea of his future, as he had seen it. If, as there always had been a possibility, he was not going to have his glimpse into the New World, then, at least, he had planned to die purposefully.

But to die on account of a certain Lieutenant Glasenapp, whom he had seen only once, and drunk at that! Of course, the best Nazi officer was a dead Nazi officer; he had no sentimental scruples in this respect. If it was necessary to eliminate them singly or collectively, Janoshik would gladly have lent a helping hand. If the organization had planned to dispatch Lieutenant Glasenapp from this earth, Janoshik would have followed orders explicitly and with pleasure. But no such order had been sent through, to his knowledge. And if Glasenapp was to be killed on the premises of the Café Mánes, he would not only have known, but probably would have arranged the action.

Therefore, Janoshik had to consider Glasenapp's death as an accident. If the Lieutenant had been killed by somebody, that person had acted for reasons purely his own.

And Janoshik did not like to die in consequence of an accident.

He wished to die in battle, as a soldier in the war for which he had volunteered. Whether he was to die with a gun in his hand, marching with thousands of others, or in lonely pursuit of a specialized task—that did not matter. This war had many phases. But—die as a soldier!

These were the thoughts which made Janoshik lie restlessly awake. Since he was a slow-thinking man, it took him some time to analyze them. But once he had arrived at his conclusions, he proceeded to work out schemes which might solve his dilemma.

For the moment, Janoshik decided to disregard his own preference as to his way of dying. That was a personal matter, and he had learned that his person was only of secondary importance.

Most important, however, was to finish his job—somehow to transmit the fateful address.

By this time, Janoshik figured, the people outside must have become aware of his arrest. The bald-headed longshoreman would rack his brain trying to find a way of getting some message from Janoshik. Poor fellow! He never was much good at brain work. He would hang around the Mánes in his Sunday best, spending his money on beer, occasionally running down to the toilet, feigning headaches, or stomach aches, opening the medicine chest, swallowing all sorts of pills—but he would find nothing.

Breda—what could Breda do? Approach strangers in or around the Mánes, asking them whether they knew Janoshik and expected a message from him? Stupid. Impossible. Breda could do nothing of the sort; he'd just fret and worry till the organization could re-establish the lost connection. That would take weeks, months perhaps—by then, the barges' deadly load would long since have reached its destination.

There was only one way: He, Janoshik, must go to the Mánes and leave the message in the medicine chest.

Janoshik snorted. His conclusions, how logical and sharp they were—and how absurd! He could just imagine the face of the Gestapo guard upon being told: Excuse, sir, but I'd like to leave this place for a while to go to the toilet of the Café Mánes.

Yet, this Dr. Wallerstein had succeeded in talking to the head man of the Gestapo, and had wangled from him paper and pen and the permission to write his notes. God knows how he had sold the Nazi on that idea, what story he had dished up—and besides, Wallerstein stayed right here, needling everybody, making life uncomfortable.

How, thought Janoshik, can I force that Nazi Commissioner to let me out of here, even if only for a short while?

Where is there a weak point that I can use?

He could find none.

The more he brooded, the more tense he become. Relax, he thought, relax. He felt his blood tingling all through him. He could not lie quiet.

"You aren't asleep?" whispered Lobkowitz.

"No," answered Janoshik, glad to let Lobkowitz take his mind off the vicious circle in which he felt himself caught. "Must be something I ate."

"Don't remind me, please," implored Lobkowitz, "I'm hungry as it is."

"Well—what do you want?"

"I am thinking—"

"About what?"

"About Glasenapp."

"Got nothing more agreeable to think about?" inquired Janoshik.

"Who killed Glasenapp?"

Lobkowitz had spoken louder than he intended. The question remained hanging in the air, heavy, unanswered.

"How do I know?" Janoshik said finally. "I'm sure I didn't do it. Speak low, anyway—the others are sleeping." But he noticed that Preissinger was awake, and listening.

"Neither did I," whispered Lobkowitz. "But somebody must have done it! He didn't kill himself!"

"And how the hell would it help us if we knew?" Janoshik inquired. "They've got to shoot us, don't you see? It's their method of government—unfortunately, we happen to be at the receiving end. Don't worry who killed that drunken bastard—try to get some sleep!"

"If Glasenapp's murderer is found, they must free us," Preissinger said suddenly.

"Sure. And Herr Heydrich will apologize to you personally for all the inconvenience you have had," consoled Janoshik, adding an energetic "Shut up!"

And who actually killed Glasenapp? repeated Janoshik's stubborn mind. Lobkowitz was right—somebody must have done it.

The importance of the question was negligible. But it was a toy to play with, a contrivance on which to practice his mental gymnastics.

He checked back, tried to re-establish the scene as he had seen it that evening, only a few days ago—and yet it seemed ages past.

Meeting the drunk on the stairs, Glasenapp sinking down beside him, reeking of alcohol. Upstairs, the mess on the floor, the bragging officers, the annoyance and embarrassment of the guests, the servility of the little barkeeper, the brush between Lobkowitz and the older officer—every detail stood engraved in his mind, though at that time he had not foreseen how momentous all this would become.

Could it be that he had overlooked somebody sneaking downstairs after Glasenapp? Improbable—after all, he had wanted to see Breda down in the washroom, and he'd been on guard against intruders.

Could it be that some person slid down the embankment of the river, swam through the breakwater, climbed up and entered the toilet through the rear door in order to kill Glasenapp? Improbable—timing that job would have been too difficult. And Janoshik, on his return to his lair, had found no traces, no dirty, watery footsteps whatever on his spotless tile floor.

Had there been intruders, there would have been a struggle. Some sign of it, some sound of it, he should have noticed!

Then what had happened to Glasenapp?

Janoshik was in a sweat, tremendously excited. He felt as a person who, a long coveted key in hand, is about to open the door to a dark, mysterious passage—where would it lead him?

Glasenapp, Janoshik concluded, had died alone.

Drunk as the Lieutenant had been, he must have opened the little side door to the jetty, stumbled out there, and walked into the river.

Janoshik, with his lively imagination, could see it clearly —the lonely figure, swaying softly against the dim sky, and suddenly swallowed up, without much of a splash, like a bag full of stones.

Did he fall accidentally? Did he jump? That was a secret Glasenapp had taken along with himself. He had wept on the stairs, disgustingly sad—this Janoshik remembered. But drunks weep frequently, booze loosens them up; or perhaps Glasenapp had had his own troubles—who knows...

There was no murder. The man had died alone.

Janoshik could not lie still any more. He simply had to get up and walk. In the dark cell, he paced up and down, an even darker, restless shadow.

"Can't you sleep?" asked Lobkowitz.

"Jesus, Mary and Joseph!" Janoshik, realizing the scope of the frame-up, cursed the Nazis. "Goddamned sons of bitches!"

"What's the matter with you?"

"Oh, nothing!" Why tell Lobkowitz? What good would come of it if the others, too, started to bang their heads against the solid wall of this cell?

He could hear Wallerstein urge: "You're rather restless, Janoshik. Don't you feel well? What's on your mind?"

Now this fellow started in! That was just what he needed!

"Did you know Judge Procháska?" Janoshik asked in reply.

"No," said Wallerstein, who was not prepared for a counter-question.

"He was a fine man," explained Janoshik, "mild-mannered, a true gentleman; you should have met him. I came up in his court once, on a vagrancy charge."

154

"What makes you think of Judge Procháska?" inquired Wallerstein.

"I think of all sorts of people, all the time. They just pop up. Is that bad?"

"No. Not exactly. It depends."

"Well," Janoshik continued gravely, "since I was picked up for vagrancy, I told the Judge that the police were quite mistaken, and that I had had a definite itinerary all the time. So, the good Judge became interested.

"Where did you want to go, Janoshik? he asked.

"To Olomouc, I said.

"So you started in Prague?

"Yes, Your Honor, I said.

"And where did you go from there? he asked.

"To Mělník, I said.

"And from there?

"To Čelakovice, I said.

"And from there?

"To Štěchovice, I said.

"And from there?

"To Beroun, I said.

"And from there?

"To Prague, I said.

"But Janoshik, said the Judge, you were going in circles!

"I can't deny it, Your Honor, I explained. You see, Doctor, in every place the police had had an eye on me.

"But you said you wanted to go to Olomouc! cried the Judge.

"Well, Your Honor, Judge Procháska, I said, that is right, I had wanted to go there, but I changed my mind!

"By this time, Judge Procháska had lost his mild manner. First he got red in the face, then purple, then gray. Then he threw me out of his court."

"Oh—" said Wallerstein.

"I like people," Janoshik went on, "I like them to ask

155

me questions. I answer them. Sometimes something happens to those people."

Janoshik felt decidedly better. He was able to lie down again, and to think. Think of Glasenapp, who had not been killed at all, but for whose supposed murder they were about to die. The whole thing was a Gestapo plot!

If one could cripple their plans!

Did anybody but Janoshik and the Gestapo know of the plot?

In any case, one must let it appear as if the carefully guarded secret were out in the open—of course, without implicating oneself. Glasenapp could have talked of it—that he planned to die, that he would kill himself. No, words were no good. Some document must exist—a letter perhaps!

A letter from Glasenapp—to whom? Well, to anybody. A letter, which is abroad, eluding the Gestapo, and which they must track down before they can go through with their plot. A letter which he, Janoshik, knows of, a letter which Glasenapp had given to him, Janoshik, to put into the mail—a letter which Janoshik had kept in the Mánes, because he had been arrested before he ever could mail it. A letter which the Gestapo must send him back to the Mánes to fetch!

Janoshik sank back on his cot, exhausted.

He knew that his was a desperate plan. It was based on a none too certain supposition. He had guessed at Glasenapp's suicide, he had guessed that the Gestapo was interested in hiding this suicide. It was just as possible that they did not care at all, or that this Reinhardt was clever enough to see through Janoshik's counter-plot, or that Janoshik might never have an opportunity to talk to Reinhardt. It was a one to a hundred shot—and yet it was Janoshik's only chance. His only chance to leave the cellar, to transmit the address on which so much depended: Watzlik, Smíchovská Street 64.

"Dr. Wallerstein!" Janoshik called softly.

The doctor raised his head, wearily.

"Let me have a slip of that paper and your pen, please," Janoshik begged.

"What for?"

"My last will."

"It's dark—how can you write?"

"Only a few lines," pleaded Janoshik. "I'll manage."

Wallerstein gave him paper and pen, pleased that finally he had found in Janoshik a reaction to the fate which hung over them.

Janoshik scribbled the Watzlik address on the sheet of paper and put it carefully in his pocket.

After that, the hostages fell into uneasy slumber, interrupted only by the groans and noises of men sleeping in cramped quarters and heavy air.

Had Reinhardt known the purpose to which the paper he had so obligingly given Wallerstein was being put, he probably would have been acutely uncomfortable. As it was, the Commissioner felt by no means happy.

His spirits, so exuberant when he had been on his way to visit the unknown Milada, had been dampened considerably after he had made her acquaintance and left her. Several factors contributed to his depression. Firstly, as part of a machine in power—and this machine, to date, never had suffered a serious defeat—Reinhardt was not accustomed to the kind of resistance which he seemed unable to break.

Secondly, he doubted seriously the truth of Milada's story, and was furious that, wherever he turned, he could find no lever to prove to himself—and to her—that she had lied or, at least, had hidden part of the truth. The specter of his secret, Glasenapp's suicide, being known to other persons, rose the stronger the more he tried to belittle the whole matter. It haunted him.

Thirdly, he felt attracted to this girl whom he had thought

to be either inconsequential or easy prey, since he was certain that even a Glasenapp had had her. Yet he had made no headway with her—neither being charming nor threatening had helped; and he was too shrewd to have any illusions on that point.

He felt tired after walking down the big Štěpánská Street to Wenceslas Place—tired of walking, tired of doing his duty. He entered the bar of the Hotel Alcron which was swarming with officers in all types of uniforms, and ordered schnapps. Some officers, astonished to see him in civilian clothes, nevertheless saluted him respectfully. He did not return their salutes, just sat and stared into his glass which reflected the light of the candelabras in the bar.

I must go through with this, damn it, he swore to himself. I was crazy to have been so cocksure of myself and my Glasenapp theory. The thing is full of loopholes, absolutely full!

"Waiter—another schnapps!"

Murtenbacher warned me. You'll end up wrong if you consider this a game of wits, he always said. Take me, for instance, Murtenbacher advised, I'm dumb; but why use your brain in this job? We're not criminologists, we're hangmen. Shoot 'em, behead 'em, hang 'em—don't differentiate, don't try to be clever—then you'll sleep well and make a career. Look at me, I rule all of Paris!

This Glasenapp business! Reinhardt frowned. I must have that Milada watched, her every move—I'll get to the bottom of it yet! I must question at least some of the hostages, they were witnesses. And how many guests of the Mánes got away, perhaps knowing what had happened, before this Captain Patzer detained the rest? Who knows....I may have to pull in a lot more people.

"Waiter—another schnapps!"

He hoped the drinks would make him drowsy, but, on the contrary, they keyed him up. He simply could not go on overworking himself as he did—what for, anyway?—one must have some relaxation, some fun.

He left his schnapps to go to the telephone booth and call his headquarters. He gave orders for Pan Kratochvil to trail Milada—with a new hat, please!—and God have mercy on him, if he lost her!

Then he told them to send Moenkeberg with his car to pick him up at the Alcron.

For a while Reinhardt stood aimlessly before the hotel on the darkening Plaza. The red street cars clanged downhill from the National Museum; a few automobiles, mostly occupied by German officers, whizzed by. He remembered Wenceslas Place when they had marched into Prague—a solid wall of people lined up alongside, and down from the Museum came the endless rows of marching German soldiers, as if on parade.

With a few of his Gestapo men he had arrived in Prague some days before the Army; unobtrusively, he had stood among the people and observed them. The people had remained stilled, with clouded faces. They just gazed at the troops in stolid grief. A small sprinkling of Sudeten Nazis, mostly students who lived in Prague, raised their hands and shouted Heil Hitler—but they were so few that the greeting seemed ridiculous.

Then, Reinhardt had felt the same prickly impatience, the same expectant unrest and anger which he felt now.

What could they do to spoil his plan, the enemies he was unable to grasp? Even if they knew of Glasenapp's suicide —so what? Hadn't he and his men things under control? Those stolid people would remain silent, they had been muffled effectively. Then why did he feel so uncomfortable and uncertain?

In its final analysis, the Glasenapp affair meant parting Lev Preissinger from the Bohemian-Moravian Coal Syndicate, thus turning the whole industry over to certain personages in the Reich without strings attached.

Anybody could do that by flagrant violence—but to wrest Preissinger's liquidation from the suicide of a stupid Glasenapp, and at the same time to administer a splendid lesson in discipline to the Czechs—this was Reinhardt's stroke of genius! It was the kind of cleverness Heydrich would remember and reward.

Maybe it was just his passion for mathematically flawless work which pinched him, because the equation did not yet solve itself....

Thank God—there came Moenkeberg. The car stopped short, Moenkeberg jumped out, saluted smartly, and opened the rear door. Reinhardt relaxed in his seat, feeling better already.

"Where to?" asked the faithful Moenkeberg.

"Let's do something tonight," suggested Reinhardt.

"Yes, sir."

"How about Willie's place?"

"All right, sir!"

Willie the Cow, as Wilhelmina Tietjen was affectionately called by her friends, had come to Prague from Holstein, following in the wake of the Army, bringing with her all her furniture which was overstuffed and mostly covered with dark velvet, her pictures which showed ample women at bath and horn-blowing Satyrs, and her two girls, Betty and Berthy. Betty was red-haired, had sickish white skin, and specialized in older men. Berthy was dark and swarthy, used strong perfumes, and was called upon to serve the perverts— those who beat as well as those who wanted to be beaten. Willie herself knew all the tricks and was able to take on any customer.

Wilhelmina Tietjen was obligated to Reinhardt. Without the protection of the Gestapo she could hardly have operated —the local competition would have killed her. The Gestapo, on the other hand, favored Willie. The Czech institutions were none too safe, officers and non-coms had disappeared occasionally, having last been seen entering one of these establishments. So the order had gone out forbidding members of the German Army of Occupation to have relations with Czech women; and while the order, of course, could not be strictly enforced, it had helped Willie's business considerably.

Therefore, she welcomed the Commissioner and his chauffeur effusively. She opened the door wide, her flowered kimono separating, and showing part of her white, mealy breasts.

"My dear Commissioner," she exclaimed, "what an unexpected pleasure! Girls!" she called Betty and Berthy out of their respective rooms, "the Commissioner has come to visit! And he brought a friend along." With an experienced eye she measured Moenkeberg's well-developed chest—"and what a man!" she added. "Girls! Bring some wine! This is a celebration!"

They went into the salon, a plushy affair with heavy curtains, shaded lights, and large mirrors at varied angles. Betty appeared with the wine, and Berthy brought the glasses. The girls giggled at Moenkeberg, and sat down near him, displaying their thighs and whatever curves their bodies possessed.

"How's business?" inquired Reinhardt.

"Not too bad and not too good," replied Willie. "We make enough money, but what can you buy for it? And then, I don't like this new crowd of officers. I'm accustomed to real gentlemen, intelligent, aristocratic. After all, education is important, isn't it? Most of them now are released husbands, glad to get away from Mamma, no refinement. You know what I mean?"

"Yes," said Reinhardt, opening his vest. He used to enjoy

Willie's chatter, her fat cackle. Tonight, he felt low. He sipped of his wine.

"Well—what do you want, Commissioner dear?" asked Willie with solicitude. She ambled over to him, perched on the arm of his chair, and took Reinhardt's hand. Then she led this hand along her thigh, exerting a gentle pressure, and brought the hand to rest in her lap. The Commissioner moved his fingers without much enthusiasm, more as a favor to Willie.

"Berthy!" she called. "Betty! Come here!" Obediently they came, swinging their hips. They stopped before Reinhardt. "Well?" said Willie. The girls opened their negligees, let them slide down, and stood nude—slowly turning around so that Reinhardt could inspect them from all sides.

At other times, something like this had been his dream of dreams—the half light, the naked women, all willing, all his for the snap of his finger. Tonight, it failed to arouse him greatly. He saw the tired skin of the girls, the oversized, ugly nipples on Betty's breast, the protruding bones of Berthy's pelvis.

He finally decided for Berthy, mostly because she was dark, dark as Milada. He nodded to her, and stood up. Berthy took his arm, snuggled up to him, and together they walked to her room.

The Commissioner sat down on the bed, and Berthy crouched before him. With caressing hands she began to undress him. "What is the matter with you?" she asked suddenly. She sensed that he was looking not at her but through her.

"You want the whip?" she said.

Reinhardt did not listen. He was annoyed, not by the sordid surroundings, not by the woman, but by himself, who had all this and was unable to enjoy it. He could see only Milada, daydreaming that he had her, naked, the slim body prostrate before him, open, with eager lips, her dark hair falling over her nude, round shoulders.

He closed his pants and buttoned his vest. "I'm afraid I'm not interested," he said and arose.

"I don't care!" shrugged Berthy. "I think you're just funny."

The Commissioner left her, breathing heavily. He was tense and could find no release.

When he entered the salon, he discovered Moenkeberg and Willie at play; Betty had disappeared somewhere. Moenkeberg, noticing his superior, stopped, but Willie did not let him out of her embrace. Her fat arms and legs, holding on to Moenkeberg, who for some reason or other was still wearing his black breeches and shining boots, were not only on the couch but also all over the room, reflected from the mirrors, mirrored again and again, an infinite chain of voluptuous limbs, holding on to a pair of black breeches. Reinhardt took a seat in an easy chair, and lit a cigarette. "Go ahead! Go ahead!" he said benevolently. "Don't mind me."

"Yes, sir!" snapped the faithful Moenkeberg, resuming his pleasures.

Reinhardt viewed the two interlocked people through half-closed eyes. Goering, he thought, invites guests for such shows, or for the mating of his bulls. Much more exciting to see them by yourself.

How strong this Moenkeberg is! How he takes her and rides her! What muscles he has! And the Cow—she actually enjoys it. Well, it *is* something when you can feel it. She wheezes too much, short of breath, she's getting too fat. And he has no finesse, just an animal....

There—now!—good man!

Willie's fingers gripped into the shoulders of Moenkeberg. Her breath came loud and fast, mingling with Moenkeberg's grunts. The couch squeaked.

163

Reinhardt felt warm and light, much as he felt when Moenkeberg got through with one of his questionings in the basement over at headquarters.

Willie patted Moenkeberg on the seat of his pants. The chauffeur got up, hesitatingly, and looked at Reinhardt. He was not certain whether he had done right to take Willie, who, after all, was the head girl of the house, and to go on nonchalantly in spite of the presence of the Commissioner.

But Reinhardt grinned and stamped out the butt of his cigarette. "We must get going," he said, half to Moenkeberg, half to Willie who was reclining on the couch still in un-ashamed nakedness. "I have some work to do. Thanks for the wine and everything. It's always a pleasure."

Willie half rose, reaching for her kimono.

"Don't bother!" said Reinhardt.

"Thanks," Willie yawned. "You know, Commissioner, sometimes I wonder..."

"Hm?"

"About the war. How long is it going to last?"

"Why?"

"After the war, I want to stop working. Buy a little house here in Prague, or in the suburbs, and just live. I like it here, you know? Of course, we must win the war. Other-wise—" she moved her flat hand across her throat. It looked obscene, the way she did it, all naked.

"You should worry!" Reinhardt consoled her and, fol-lowed by the faithful Moenkeberg, left Willie amidst her plush and mirrors.

Upon his return to the office, he changed back into his uniform, had Moenkeberg bring him some coffee, and went through the list of his hostages. He compared the list with the report Gruber had submitted, and decided to call

164

Janoshik first. Of the group, Janoshik seemed most likely to know something of Glasenapp's end.

What with his excursion to Willie's establishment, and his visit to the Alcron Bar, it was almost eleven o'clock. He preferred questioning people when they were still half asleep—their numb minds were more prone to divulge facts.

He gave the orders to bring up Janoshik. Then he had Moenkeberg set the lighting system, as they called it—Reinhardt sat in the dark behind his desk, Moenkeberg behind him in a corner, taking notes, and a powerful lamp was trained upon the spot where the prisoner must stand.

Two guards pushed Janoshik into the Commissioner's office. After they had left and closed the door, Janoshik stood there, dazed and blinking, his clothes crumpled from sleep and the long days in the cell, his hair a wild mop pointing in all directions.

Janoshik had slept only lightly, and when the guards had come to fetch him, he immediately had become wide awake. But since it was natural to him to look sleepy, and since he had planned to make as stupid an impression on the Gestapo as he possibly could, Reinhardt found the picture of the dazed man in the sharp light rather amusing.

Janoshik tried to discern the shadowy features of the Gestapo official. He could not recognize much beyond the small blinking eyes, and the reflection of the light on the silver of the uniform.

Janoshik felt the elation of a veteran going into another battle. He had met the enemy so often, and now, entrapped, in a desperate situation, he was full of fight, eager and willing to shoot it out, and with a plan up his sleeve that perhaps would take the enemy by surprise and insure his own ultimate victory. He had feared that his chance for battle would never come again—that Reinhardt would send him to death without ever questioning him. He had worried how he was to manage to get an interview with the much dreaded Gestapo man—and here, praise be! they had called him.

Reinhardt was busy studying his victim. He found in Janoshik's face and posture all the traits he identified with and despised in the Czech people—the man was obviously sloppy, none too intelligent, uncouth and evil smelling. He had a low forehead, pig's eyes which squinted even more narrowly from the effects of sleep, a broad nose, thick lips and a square chin covered with reddish stubble. Under the mop of hair, the skull was round as a billiard ball, the big ears sticking out at right angles. This head was connected by a short neck to a big hulking body slumped slightly forward. He had long arms which hung down at his sides without apparent purpose, and which appeared even longer because the sleeves of his jacket were so ridiculously short.

"Some ape!" said Reinhardt to the faithful Moenkeberg.

The ape marched forward and surprised the Commissioner by suddenly beginning to talk. He talked fast and in bad German, intermingled with Czech colloquialisms, displaying a hideous accent.

"Your Honor," he started in, "I am so relieved to see you!" He really meant it. His opening statement came with such honesty that Reinhardt was taken aback—it was the first time that any of his victims had expressed pleasure at coming in actual contact with him.

"I have to make a confession! I have been feeling absolutely terrible, really desperate, but the truth must come out, it must come out—mustn't it?" he added as if seeking assurance from his torturer.

"Moenkeberg," said Reinhardt, "will you explain to this —this—" the right descriptive word failed him, "how to behave in front of an officer of the German Secret State Police?"

Moenkeberg rose, marched up to Janoshik, grabbed and twisted his shirt, and shook him. "You—are—to—talk—only—

166

when—asked!" he said slowly and loudly, emphasizing each syllable.

Janoshik opened his eyes as wide as he could in childlike amazement.

"You—understand?" said Moenkeberg, shaking Janoshik once more; and then resumed his post in the darkness behind Reinhardt.

"But this is important," insisted Janoshik stubbornly. "If you've got to make a confession, you must make it. It is my conscience that's troubling me. My friend, Inspector Poczporek of the twentieth precinct—"

Moenkeberg was writing busily, trying to catch up with the stream of words.

"Who is Inspector Poczporek? What has he got to do with it?" Reinhardt edged in because he suspected that the unfortunate Janoshik was blubbering out some clue which might lead him somewhere.

"Poczporek? God bless him—he's dead for years. But he used to say, Janoshik, he used to say, never leave a thing unfinished. It's bad. It'll burden your conscience. Especially when he was about to win a pinochle game, he used to say that..."

"Stop!" thundered Reinhardt. "You goddamned halfwit! I am the one who talks around here! You shut up or I'll have a gag pushed into your throat—you won't like that!"

"Of course not!" said Janoshik complacently. This Commissioner was so excitable! He felt that he should give him a chance to assert himself—otherwise the interview would end with a fit of rage on the Nazi's part; and Janoshik wanted to shake the Commissioner's poise only enough to make him susceptible to his plan.

"We'll take up your stupid confessions later," Reinhardt said severely. "You were in charge of the lavatory at the Café Mánes?"

"Yes, Your Honor, the lavatory, the supply room, and Mrs. Paula Potovská, the scrubwoman."

"I take it that you love your life sufficiently to be interested in apprehending the murderer of Lieutenant Glasenapp, for whom you will die, unless we find the killer very shortly."

Janoshik wondered whether he should give the Commissioner an exposé on the value of life in general, and his own especially. But he decided to let Reinhardt go on in order to see where the questioning would lead.

"So try to remember that evening. You met the Lieutenant on the stairs, coming down to the toilet?"

"A fine man," Janoshik described the scene, "but completely boozed. At first I couldn't make head or tail of what he said...."

"He spoke to you?" asked Reinhardt whose interest was aroused, since constantly, in the back of his mind, lay his purpose to ascertain any possible leak of Glasenapp's suicide. "Can you remember what he said? And you better speak the truth!"

"I'll try! Honestly, I will!" promised Janoshik, his face showing the efforts of hard thinking.

The Commissioner watched him. The man was obviously too stupid to lie; the question was whether he'd be able to recall what Glasenapp had said. The Commissioner blamed himself for not having questioned Janoshik sooner—he had relied on the report Gruber had submitted to him, the report based on the short interrogation which had taken place at the Mánes Bar. He should have known long ago that Glasenapp had had a talk with this moronic toilet keeper! Janoshik *was* thinking hard. He knew that everything depended on the story he was about to present. It must be natural, in keeping with the situation which had prevailed then; so simple that Reinhardt would believe him; and yet it must contain the basic conditions for the fulfillment of his plan. Furthermore, nothing in his story must indicate that he had any idea or suspicion of a possible suicide by Glasenapp—on the contrary, somewhere he had to stress his unquestioning belief in the murder charges framed by the man before him.

"I want to make a confession," began Janoshik.

Reinhardt interrupted him impatiently. "That'll come later. What did Glasenapp tell you, I want to know!"

"You see, Your Honor, I owe him money," said Janoshik penitently. He tried to avoid giving his story in sequence, hoping that this way it would go over better.

He was right. Reinhardt, unable to follow the jumping of Janoshik's thoughts, despairing of the halfwit's ever answering a question straight, lost his unperturbed superiority. "What did he say to you?" he shouted. "Answer!"

"I owe him money," repeated Janoshik stubbornly. "Four Kronen and forty Heller. But I can't pay it back. You see, I don't have it any more."

"Why?"

"It was taken away. When the nice young man put me in jail, he took it away. And two Kronen of my own, and my pocket knife, and a watch which was given to me by Josef Lobsam, the pawnbroker, on his twenty-fifth anniversary in business, in recognition of my being his most faithful customer. I am an honest man, Your Honor, and I am grieved that I can't return the money, because I don't have it, and because the poor Lieutenant has been killed, so that he can't use the money anyway, and because I am going to be shot, I hear."

It was a terrific torrent of words from which Reinhardt, with effort, extricated the fact that Glasenapp, shortly before his suicide, had given money to Janoshik, and that there must be a reason for this.

"Why did Glasenapp give you money?"

169

"Because I am an honest man and he trusted me," said Janoshik, his good-natured face oozing virtue.

Reinhardt was itching to take this paragon of honesty by the scruff of his neck, bang his head against the wall, and thus shake out of him the few relevant facts which the man must be hiding somewhere among the whole rubbish of anecdotes, unimportant names, and idiotic self-praise.

"And because he wanted me to mail a letter," said Janoshik, as if this were merely an incidental item, his honesty being the main fact to be impressed on the high police.

"Aha!" Reinhardt was relieved that finally he had succeeded in extracting a tangible fact from Janoshik. At the same time he saw the implications of this letter. He remembered the other letter which had been found in dead Glasenapp's pocket, the letter never finished or sent, from which, however, he had deduced the Lieutenant's suicide. The possibility that there existed a similar letter, completed and stating Glasenapp's intentions, seemed logical and jolted him. But Reinhardt, easily exasperated by evasion and lack of precision, was never upset by complications which he could solve by police methods. If such a letter existed, he would find out where it was, and stamp out all those who knew of its content.

"What kind of letter was it?" he probed carefully.

"Special delivery," said Janoshik. "A fat letter which weighed a lot. An important letter. That's why the Lieutenant, may his soul rest in peace, gave me ten Kronen. My friend, said the Lieutenant, I trust you, you have the kind of face that bodes no ill. Then he hiccuped. He was drunk, quite drunk. Go to the goddamned post office—with your kind permission, Your Honor, these were his own words— and mail it. Then he hiccuped again and wept."

"What was the address?"

"I'll bash your skull in if you forget to mail it, he said amidst tears. You are a goddamned fool—with your kind

permission, Your Honor, his own words—but you're sober.
So you mail it. Then he hiccuped again and said, I'm so
stinking drunk I couldn't see the slit in the mail box if it
were—his own words, Your Honor—if it were as big as Hess's
asshole. I beg your pardon, Your Excellency, but the poor
Lieutenant, he didn't know what he was saying. . . ."

Janoshik was in high gear. He would have rambled on, but
he was interrupted by Reinhardt's furious: "Shut up!" To
Moenkeberg the Commissioner gave the order, "Strike that
from the notes." Then he repeated the question uppermost
in his mind, "What was the address?"

Janoshik, of course, had heard the question the first time.
He had enlarged on the description of Glasenapp's sorry
state of mind in order to think up and prepare his next act.
Now he went into it. "I wouldn't know!" he said indignantly.
"I am an honest man! You can jail me, you can kill me, Your
Honor—but insult me? A letter like this, placed into my
hands in trust by a poor innocent who now is dead—and I
should read the address? I received ten Kronen to mail the
letter, not to read the address. Reading the address is only
the first step to opening the letter and reading what is written
there—nobody can lead me into temptation, Your Honor,
nobody!"

These were new and to Reinhardt hardly believable ethics.
But he did forego, for the moment, a closer questioning as
to the reading of the address, in order to proceed. "When did
you mail the letter?"

"That is bad," Janoshik answered gloomily. He looked
crestfallen, stricken by his conscience. "Very bad. I couldn't
even do that for the poor soul. I wanted to mail it, though,
I assure you, Your Honor!"

"Stop calling me Your Honor! Did you mail it or did you
not?"

"It isn't my fault," pleaded Janoshik. "The nice young

man—he arrested me before I could go to the post office."

"Good!" said Reinhardt.

Janoshik shook his head. "No, Your Excellency, that is bad! It burdens my heart."

Reinhardt telephoned and gave orders to bring up any papers found among Janoshik's effects. They had to wait for the official's report. Janoshik utilized the pause to review his conduct and to plan his next move. Till now, everything had gone smoothly enough. Nevertheless, he thought, this Reinhardt is not stupid. But he is not used to my kind of simplicity, it confuses him; also, I know where I want to lead him; he does not. And he hasn't much time—if he were to investigate me in the Czech police files, I'd be in a terrific hole, he wouldn't believe a single word of my story—but as it is, he wants to shoot us day after tomorrow, and he wants to clear up this mess I invented for him as soon as he possibly can.

The telephone rang. "What?" Reinhardt spoke into the receiver. "No letter? No papers at all? Thank you."

He turned to Janoshik. "I'll teach you to tell me lying stories! You believe, perhaps, my imaginative idiot, that we can't make life uncomfortable for you just because you'll be dead in a couple of days? I assure you we can turn every minute you have left into such hell that you will feel relieved when you enter the real one."

Janoshik answered this threat with a look of most disarming astonishment. How can you talk that way, his face seemed to say, to me, an honest man?

"Where is the letter?" shouted Reinhardt.

"I put it away," came the dejected reply.

"Where?"

No answer.

"Where?"

"That's just it!" Janoshik confessed. "I can't remember. You see, Your Excellency, it was no ordinary letter. I was

172

very careful with it. Janoshik, I said to myself, don't lose this letter. The poor Lieutenant, he places his confidence in you, don't disappoint him—"

"Where is the letter?"

"So I hid it well, not to lose it."

"Where?"

"I hid it so well, I can't remember now."

Reinhardt, ordinarily, was not the man to show his emotions. Now, however, his fist came down on his desk with a crash.

"Moenkeberg!" he ordered hoarsely. "Tell me, how do we make people remember things?"

Moenkeberg recited monotonously: "We put them into the standing casket. Or we beat them with rubber truncheons. Or with steel whips. Or we kick out their teeth, one by one. Or we suspend them, above ground, by their fingers. Or we break their bones. Or we..."

Janoshik's expression remained as indolent and friendly as it had been all along. When Moenkeberg stopped to think whether he had forgotten any one of the more common methods, Janoshik stated simply: "You remind me of Pan Burian, my teacher in the third grade. I was in third grade for four years, and Pan Burian became sort of impatient with me. He beat me at regular intervals with a whip, cut from a young willow tree right down at the brook which runs through our village. There is, I hear, no direct connection between your rear end and your head, so I had the same bad memory before and after the beatings."

There was a short silence during which Janoshik allowed the deeper significance of his youthful imbecility to sink in.

Reinhardt, who could feel with the unfortunate teacher Burian, recognized that, with Janoshik, he would have to overstep his bounds as a policeman and enter the field of

173

pedagogy. He controlled himself and asked proddingly: "Where did you hide the letter, Janoshik?"

"In the Mánes, of course, Your Excellency, where I work!"

"In the Mánes! Where you work!" mimicked Reinhardt. "You don't suppose you could indicate a bit more precisely where you hid it?"

"There are so many places, I can't think. The storage room, for instance, you've never seen such a heap of stuff in one place. My boss, he was the one for preserving things. Janoshik, he said, even an old carton has its value. You never know when you might use it again. So I saved everything."

Patience! Patience! thought Reinhardt. "Now try hard!" he admonished. "I want you to remember where you put that letter!"

Janoshik stood before his tormentor, the pitiful picture of a dumb but willing horse, whipped to draw a heavy wagon it never will be able to move, but attempting the impossible anyhow. Finally he threw up his large hands in despair. "No. No, I can't. Not this way."

Reinhardt, at the end of his wits, was about to release a new assortment of threats, when he saw Janoshik's face light up.

"I put away my broom and my bucket, and then I fetched fresh towels, and then I bent down to tie my shoe, and then I went—where did I go? Where did I go...?

"Oh, if I were down in the Mánes, if I could see the place, I bet you I could remember. You don't bet, I suppose? Inspector Poczporek, he used to tell me: Never bet with the police, because you can't collect, Janoshik. You don't know, Your Excellency, how heartbroken I am to cause you all this trouble. But if I find that letter, you will mail it, please?"

The idea of his visit to the Mánes, so carefully planted by Janoshik, took hold in Reinhardt's mind and began to sprout.

And why not? thought the Commissioner. Don't we take a criminal back to the scene of his crime, let him retrace his steps, in order to betray himself? But the proposition was preposterous. Letting a prisoner out of a Gestapo jail, a hostage about to die! Yet, if the goddamned letter lay around somewhere in the Mánes, liable to be picked up by anybody who came upon it, the quickest way to recover it was to strengthen the halfwit's memory by placing him in his accustomed surroundings.

Janoshik was afraid his face might reflect the excitement seething in him. He had thrown the bait and the fish was swimming nearer and nearer, staring at it, considering it from all sides. Would Reinhardt bite?

Because of the strong light, Janoshik's eyes could not penetrate the deep shadow protecting the Commissioner; but he could feel Reinhardt studying him. He could sense that the Nazi was weighing the chances, searching for hidden intentions, if there were any on Janoshik's part. Had he played his role with sufficient conviction? Would the Commissioner believe that Janoshik was too stupid to plot a story so involved? Sure he was of only one thing: that Reinhardt was unable to guess why he, Janoshik, so desperately wanted to return to the Mánes.

Actually, Reinhardt suspected Janoshik. He had, however, little doubt of the existence of the letter invented by Janoshik, because he had found in Glasenapp's pocket the unfinished letter to Milada—a factor of which Janoshik had no knowledge, but which worked in his favor. Reinhardt suspected Janoshik of the usual: of attempting to escape. Therefore he warned:

"If you're planning to escape, let me put you straight. I shall give you an escort of some of my strongest men, and you'll be chained to them."

"You suspect me of such trickery?" Janoshik said with

175

pained voice. "Don't you trust anybody? You make me sad. I'm only trying to help, Your Excellency. ..."

"Don't call me Your Excellency!"

"Has ever anybody heard of escaping from the Gestapo?" He shook his head. "Oh—if you were Czech gendarmes! A certain Bedřich Kaluweit I know, when he was pulled in for picking the pocketbook of Mrs. Olga Weintraubová— though she had no cash in it—he simply invited the gendarmes to the Blue Bell Tavern which they passed on the way, and stood them three rounds of beer. Then he excused himself because he had a full bladder, and walked out through the back door of the Blue Bell. But a Gestapo man—he would have come along right to the pissoir!"

What can I lose? Reinhardt asked himself. He found no answer. Yet somewhere, deep inside of him, he felt dissatisfied. Nothing that you could lay your hand on, just an instinctive nagging within him. Was this Janoshik so complete a fool as he pretended to be? But what would he pretend it for? Ultimately, the Commissioner's reason prevailed over his instinct.

"I tell you," he said slowly, "if you don't return with this letter of Lieutenant Glasenapp, I shall personally see to it that there isn't a blood vessel in your body left whole before you die. You understand that?"

Janoshik cocked his head a little like a canary trying to catch on to a melody.

"I'll have you beaten into the bloodiest pulp that ever breathed. Because the man to fool me isn't born yet. You understand that?"

Janoshik understood. He had known right along what he would have to face. Yet he was jubilant and hard put to keep from laughing and crying and singing. Life was great and beautiful and made sense, and death was great and beautiful too.

"I give you six hours," said Reinhardt. "Now get out of here!"

Janoshik bowed formally: "Thank you so much, Your Worship!"

"Get out!"

The last Reinhardt saw of Janoshik was his big back, almost bursting out of the shabby jacket.

The Commissioner called Gruber and gave orders that the Kid and two men were to go with Janoshik to the Mánes, to help him find a letter.

"Yes, sir!" saluted the Kid.

"Also, send up another one of those hostages—yes, the actor Prokosch."

"Yes, sir. Immediately."

While they were waiting for Prokosch, Moenkeberg suddenly snorted: "He's up to something, sir!"

"Who—this idiot?"

"Yes, sir!"

"And what makes you have such a brain storm?"

"Strikes me that a man who can remember so many stories should also know where he left an important letter!"

There was, no doubt, some truth in Moenkeberg's observation. But Reinhardt would not concede this, not to a subordinate.

"And why, then, should he have wanted to go to the Mánes? I think I impressed on him that he'd have no chance to run away. No, Moenkeberg—what do you know of psychology? Better let *me* probe into the minds of my prisoners."

Before Moenkeberg could reply, Prokosch was shoved into the office. The actor straightened, pulled down the front of his coat, and walked up to Reinhardt's desk.

"I want to make a confession, Commissioner," he said, accentuating each word. "I killed Lieutenant Glasenapp."

177

CHAPTER 8

It was near midnight when Milada awoke from a restless and dream-disturbed sleep. Her head ached, her body felt as though it had been tossed about in a storm.

She sat up with a start, realizing that hours must have passed since Reinhardt left her; and that she had signally failed to do her most obvious duty: to inform Breda of the Nazi Commissioner's visit, the questioning he had conducted, and the fact that the Gestapo seemed to know a good deal of her relationship with Glasenapp.

Her dreams had been gruesome and involved, filled with fear and anguish. Some imminent, nameless dread had made her flee, but her feet became rooted in a morass. The terror then took form. Pursuing figures, sometimes bearing the face of Reinhardt, sometimes having no face at all, aimed lightning bayonets at her, coming closer, closer. With pounding heart, she wrenched herself free and escaped, only to be held immobile, only to be pursued again. Over and over this impossible flight recurred.

She dressed quickly, still feeling the hot breath of pursuit upon her. She realized that it was not only the sense of duty which made her seek Breda, but also her need for rest and strength, for shelter and the kindness this man had. For a fleeting moment she asked herself whether she should not wait till morning when she would see him at the Kolbenka, at work; but she discarded the idea knowing she was unequal to the task of waiting that long, and reasoning that Breda had to be apprised immediately; yes, should have been told hours ago.

She recalled Breda's words at parting: "Here is my address; you'll be welcome any time—but please, come only if you think it absolutely necessary."

How soon the necessity had arisen! Despite her turmoil, she warmed at the thought of seeing him again. She smiled as she pictured him with tousled hair, with eyes blinking sleepily, opening the door and saying: "Milada! Hello. Welcome—and forgive the way I look." Perhaps, because he was so sleepy, he would take her in his arms and hold her close to his warm body.

She left the house and walked down Malá Štěpánská Street. People who live there know that Malá Štěpánská is not really a dead end street, though on the maps of Prague it is drawn as such. The last house, a very old one built toward the end of the Middle Ages, has a dark passageway leading to the wide expanse of Karl's Place. This way Milada chose, since it would bring her quickest to Národní Třída which she must cross in order to reach Konviktská Street, where Breda lived.

At first she did not notice the shadow which emerged from the dark wall across the street from her house, and which attached itself to her on inaudible soles. But in the passageway where even the slightest sound was echoed, she heard the rustle of the shadow's steps.

Pan Kratochvil glided through the darkness behind her. On his head was a brand new gray velour hat. He had acquired it in the property room of the Gestapo headquarters. "Take it," the guard had said. "Its owner is in camp. He won't need it again." Kratochvil liked the hat. Throughout his long wait outside Milada's house, he amused himself with it, settling it jauntily upon his head, or pushing it back bonnet fashion, or holding it in his hand before him, elbow bent, as if in extravagant salute to the lady he was detailed to watch.

He hadn't minded the wait at all. Indeed, Kratochvil needed little sleep and was never bored. Time hung heavily on his hands only when there was nobody to be pursued.

He had always been that way, from the very beginning of his career. In those days, he'd been a check-up man for the streetcar company. His job was to ferret out people who stole rides by hiding their faces behind newspapers in order to evade the conductor's scrutiny. When Kratochvil caught such a chiseler, he made him pay twelve Kronen, tenfold the price of the ride.

But after several years of faithful service to the company, Kratochvil got tired of the paltry sums involved, and entered the field of labor relations. He learned that trade from the ground up, starting as a mere agent provocateur, and ending as vice president of a union. After he had successfully sold out his members in the course of a long and bitterly fought strike, his usefulness in this field was over, and the Czech police, eager to acquire the services of so substantial a citizen, gave him employ. When the Nazis marched in, Pan Kratochvil adjusted himself quickly to the new conditions. Now, more than ever, people of his abilities and character were needed. The rewards were greater, and the speed with which his information was acted upon was entirely satisfactory. No comparison with the old times when the police, in certain cases at least, had to fear parliamentary intercession or the protests of meddlesome organizations.

Milada stopped in the dim light of a street lamp on Karl's Place, opened her handbag, took out a little mirror and proceeded to pick a nonexisting speck out of her eye.

What an old trick, thought Kratochvil, stepping back into the shade of a door. His job, as it had been explained to him, was twofold—to prevent Milada from disappearing, and to check on the people she called on. If in the course of this the girl discovered that she was followed by him, it did not make too great a difference. But he liked the cat and mouse play, and he figured that this little mouse was not too difficult an opponent.

Milada saw nobody in her mirror. But she was almost sure of being followed—it was the thing for Reinhardt to do to her. She upbraided herself for having fallen asleep; if she had gone to Breda directly after Reinhardt's departure, she might have escaped before the Commissioner could have arranged his shadowing service. Should she go back home? But she knew that now, no matter when she left the house, her shadow would trail along, watching her. And tomorrow, Breda might approach her in the shop, without knowing that she was being watched. . . . No, she must see him now, and she must shake off the noxious, dangerous pursuer.

Karl's Place was a square, enclosing a small park. Milada decided to sit down on one of the benches, as if she had come out of her house to catch a bit of fresh air.

Kratochvil came ambling down the pathway, a little tramp, with a newspaper under his arm. He did not seem to notice the girl on the bench. He formed his newspaper into a modest pillow, took off his gray velour, yawned, and lay down to sleep on the bench opposite Milada's, turning a most unconcerned back to her.

He looked so harmless, so peaceful, with his worn-out shoes and his crumpled pants; only the gray velour, resting at his feet, furnished a discordant note in this portrait of a poor tired wanderer.

Milada sat motionless for a while. If this resting tramp really was her shadow, she could try to elude him by avoiding the gravel-strewn path. Her steps would not be heard on the grass which she was able to reach by climbing over her bench.

Kratochvil did not stir. He had an unfailing sixth sense for what went on behind his back. He would give her an advantage. He would let her go ahead for about four hundred feet, provided she wanted to go anywhere; he would let her think that she successfully had shaken him off—why not?

There—now he could hear her move. Ah, she was careful, she avoided the gravel road, walking over the grass. But here and there, a dry leaf which October had made to fall from the trees, crackled at the touch of her foot.

Milada glanced back. The tramp was still lying on his bench, had not changed his position—she could hurry now, hurry out of his reach. It had been much simpler than she had expected. No, nobody was following her. The street was absolutely empty. She quickened her pace.

The dark night of Prague embraced her, swallowed her. Milada loved her city, now all the more, with the warm pitying love tendered to the sick. The city was sick, even though, up to now, it had been saved the horrors of bombardment, and no craters yawned in its streets, no burnt-out houses stared through blind windows at each other, all the landmarks still were standing—the proud dome on Hradschin Hill; the Rokoko gardens behind the palaces of the nobility; the Karl's Bridge spanning the silvery Moldau, its low arches built for the centuries; the huddled, narrow-breasted, medieval houses.

The city was sick; although looking at the pale, wasted face of the beloved, you still could see the old beauty which once enthralled you. It was a conquered city. It was not the first time that foreign conquerors had come and occupied it. The Swedes had come and the Papists, the French and the Austrians and the Prussians, and many others—but their marks had been evanescent, and what they took from the city, they gave back in many different ways. This time, however, the conquerors' boots sounded strange and hollow on the cobblestones of the old streets, the sharp commands and orders re-echoed mockingly. This time, its spirit was being defiled.

The people were finding pitiful ways of showing their bereavement. On some days, the statues of their heroes blossomed forth in flowers, and sullen policemen, directed by black-uniformed Nazi guards, removed the wreaths and bouquets placed there over night. Or for no reason intelligible to the conquerors, the sirens of factories began wailing simultaneously, symbol of mourning and of warning. Or strange inscriptions appeared on the walls of houses and shops, words of defiance, words of threat.

Before Milada approached the house in Konviktská Street, she again looked around carefully, but could find no trace of her shadowy pursuer. So she rang the bell to Breda's apartment. She had to wait. Then she heard his steps on the stairs and saw a light. He opened the door with a big noisy key.

"Why—Milada!" he said. "Don't stand there like a frightened child—come in!"

He was fully dressed. He took her by the hand and led her, supporting her when she faltered with weariness.

"I'm not prepared for guests," he joked. "I have only a little bread, but I can brew some of the stuff that's now called coffee—it'll be warm, at least. You're shivering!"

Breda's apartment was really only a room leading from a long, musty corridor. A basin and small stove were screened off in one corner; in another corner stood a table, above which a rough-hewn book rack was fastened to the wall. A bed, a couple of chairs before the curtained window, a mirror, a cupboard and a picture of a man with an Emperor Francis Joseph beard, completed the furnishings.

He invited Milada to sit on the bed. "It's the only soft place around here," he apologized. "I used to live better, had lots of books, but—you know—"

183

"I like it here. The room could stand a woman's touch, though," she added with an attempt to smile.

"Really?" He seemed embarrassed and busied himself with a pot, which he filled with water and put on the stove.

Milada sat silently, at a loss to begin. The room was so filled by his presence, the measured steps with which he moved, the way he did things. Pavel had been different, much more like her, her own age. This man Breda was as she would have liked her father to be, he was wise and considerate, and because of that, it was difficult to find a bridge to him. She felt small in his presence; her worries, her problems seemed petty. Yet everything in her was opening up to him; she felt as though the outer covering of her heart had been removed, and with every beat her heart sent a wave of seeking warmth to him.

The water in the pot began to simmer. He sat down on a chair facing Milada, one hand on his knee, the other stroking his chin. He looked at her, his large, greenish-gray eyes reflecting the light of the electric bulb.

Then he spoke: "I'm glad you came. I was lonesome."

"I feared you'd reproach me for having come," she replied, immensely relieved. "You said I shouldn't visit you without grave reason."

And if you'd come without any reason at all, he thought, I'd be grateful. Aloud he said: "You may not find me good company. You see me dressed, because, in a couple of hours, I plan to leave to start work on a job.

"I've been priming myself for it. I have to. Often I think I'm not a brave man. I'm jittery before action. So I was marking time, trying to hold onto my nerve, trying to read. I can't sleep."

Without knowing it, he had built the bridge for her. He had told her of his weakness and fears, he had shown her that they belonged on the same plane, he had aroused in her the welling desire to protect and comfort him. She clasped her

184

hands—Mother, you send your son off to battle, you give him the old medal with the picture of his saint in crude enamel—there he goes, strong and tanned by wind and sun, your little boy.

Breda put the brown, finely ground *Ersatz*-coffee into the boiling water. "Soon it will be ready," he said, fetching two blue cups with gold rims almost worn off by frequent handling. "And what happened to you? I can see you've had a harrowing time."

"I ran all the way. I was being followed. But I shook him off."

Breda turned off the light. Then he went to the window and drew aside the curtain, just enough to look out without being seen.

The fire in the stove shed a warm, lively glow over floor, walls, and the few pieces of furniture. Breda poured the coffee and handed Milada her cup. "Little man with gray hat?" he asked. "Steady! Hold onto your cup. You'd burn yourself if you spilled this brew."

She drank a little, and her trembling subsided.

"Now I've pulled you with me into this mess!" she said. "I am so stupid! I should have known better than to come and see you after Reinhardt was in my house—"

"Oh—the Commissioner himself!"

He sat down beside her on the bed, took her free hand and stroked it. "You don't mind if we keep it dark for a while?" he said. "There aren't many lights burning in the house at this hour, and I'd rather not make your whereabouts too plain to that fellow downstairs."

"What will they do to you?"

"Listen, Milada—there are some fifty people living in this building, some in flats facing the street, some in flats facing the back yard. Gray Hat does not know whose bell you rang, because he was not close enough when I opened the door—we would have seen him if he had been. Gray Hat probably made sure that the house has no back exit—which it doesn't have—and now he simply waits out there till you emerge. If he or his master wanted to catch you and your host, whoever he might be, we'd have the police ringing door bells by now."

"But they'll follow you, too!"

"Possibly! I've learned to elude stool pigeons. Prague is a wonderful city; just think of all the crooked streets and interlocking passages, the dark stairways and the pillared niches of its solid old walls. And I know this city, grew up in it."

"And if they keep watching this house?"

"According to my plan, I was not to return here anyhow. You stay in the apartment till morning. And when I go, in about two hours, I'll have a good look at Gray Hat. Somehow, I may be able to get rid of him for you."

He swallowed his coffee. "This is terrible!" he exclaimed, making a wry face. "I can taste the acorns, and there is barley in it, and charcoal. But what else does it contain?—What did Reinhardt want?"

His way of asking important questions as if they referred to wholly irrelevant matters made it less difficult to answer them. He had succeeded in putting Milada at ease. Reinhardt, with all his slyness and threats, with all the power he represented aligned against her, seemed somehow less terrifying.

She tried to find the reason for this, because she knew that her future held in store more of the tribulation she had overcome that very day. She wanted a lodestar, a guiding light on which to fix her eyes when the enemy tried her again.

The silent man beside her, this Breda, what was it that gave him strength, that made him live this way, shifting from one dismal room to another probably more dismal, without love, without anchor, joking about Gray Hats and pursuits through the crooked streets of Prague? And not even a brave

186

man! She had disturbed him while he was fighting his nerves. What if he slipped only once? From the way he behaved toward her, she knew how sensitive he was; the calloused ones could walk without fear, that was no miracle. But Breda was no hardened professional.

The darkness brought them closer. He seemed to have divined the road of her thoughts. "If you have to face the enemy, you have fear, of course. Of the people I know, there is only one without it—a man named Janoshik, and he's in prison now, one of the hostages. But we ordinary humans? In the war, when we went over the top, we were terribly afraid. But then you saw that you were not alone, there were many like you—and we shouted. We shouted from the depths of our throats as primitive man must have shouted ten thousand years ago. You were drunk with the feeling of being many, and suddenly you lost your fear.

"Now when this Reinhardt comes again, or any other one of them, or several—think of that. I do. Think of the many others marching with you. You don't know them, I don't know them, I just know they are there. I get drunk with that feeling, I get a lump in my throat. Oh, well—I'm talking big. Though, sometimes, one must see the whole picture so as to not lose sight of the tiny sector in which one happens to be working oneself.... Now tell me, what did Reinhardt want?"

Things were clear now. It was easy to speak. She felt sheltered and protected. The wood crackled in the little stove; occasionally, a cake of ashes fell through the grate and landed noisily in the ashbox.

She told Breda of the shock of finding Reinhardt at her house; how he knew of her quarrel with Glasenapp, of Pavel and the street battle before the University; how the Nazi subtly at first, and later quite openly had tried to accuse her of Glasenapp's murder; how to defend herself she had almost flung the fact of the Lieutenant's suicide into Reinhardt's face, but had stopped short of it; how he had threatened her when she neither admitted the murder nor let on to her knowledge of the suicide; how he had attempted to approach her—"with his terrible hands, dry like claws, but with pink manicured nails!"—and how, finally, the Commissioner had left her, dissatisfied, and announcing that he would keep in close touch with her!

Breda listened intently. Throughout her story, he had to fight his urge to take Milada into his arms, to shield her with his strong body. Yet, he must shut out his pity for her, his pride in her, in order to think through this story in all its consequences, all its angles.

"Why?" asked Milada. "Why did he keep hammering at me with the charge of murder? He has his case all cut and dried, his hostages all locked up and prepared for slaughter. . . ."

Breda put his cup on the floor. "Reinhardt neither believes you killed Glasenapp nor that you were an accomplice to the murder," he stated slowly. "He wanted you to confess what you know of Glasenapp's suicide."

Breda thought on. He could realize his desire to protect the girl at his side only by arming her mind, by showing her fully the depth and the intricacy of the problem as he understood it.

"You see," he explained, "the Nazis are peculiar in their conception of justice. They consider any act against them justification for retributions, and so they kill people, hostages, though these have nothing whatever to do with the particular act. But in this case, the whole thing is a fake— Glasenapp was not killed. Therefore, Reinhardt is forced to keep up the pretense of murder, once having proceeded on the basis of his fake. He must eliminate all those who possibly may know of the suicide.

"And he's afraid that you know.

"What puzzles us is why they care at all? The Nazis have

the power to shoot and hang whom they want; they're not obliged to present reasons, or to justify themselves. Yet they do. It must be a mental quirk, a perpetually bad conscience. Or, perhaps, German thoroughness which says: You can steal and plunder, but give the owner a receipt with an official stamp on it; you can torture and despoil and kill, but pretend there is just cause, no matter how threadbare."

"I understand," nodded Milada, "but does that explain why he did not arrest me?"

"No, it doesn't. But his reasons are simple enough. He lets you walk around on a leash instead of keeping you behind bars, because he's not sure that you know of Glasenapp's suicide. He merely suspects it. If you remain free you may lead him to others who also know—me, for instance. And the second reason—"

He stopped, embarrassed.

"Tell me," she pleaded. "You are so clear. You seem able to think with their logic. If I must face them, and face them alone, I want to know."

"He'd like to go to bed with you."

Milada couldn't sit quiet any longer. In the dim light of the fire in the stove, he watched her pace the floor, her flickering shadow, large and distorted, rushing along the walls.

"Forgive me," he added hastily, "forgive me for saying that, Milada. But it supplies a good explanation for his ostensible laxness."

He hated himself for expressing Reinhardt's depravity. He was hurting Milada. But he owed her clarity. He tried to soften the blow.

"I judge Reinhardt from your story. You are beautiful. Reinhardt assumes Glasenapp was your lover. He might prefer to think you not dangerous to his plans, and step into what he supposes to be Glasenapp's shoes."

189

"So trapped! So absolutely and helplessly in their power!" she said forlornly.

His heart ached. Breda buried his face in his hands. Oh, to tear down the clouds from the night's sky, to uproot the foundation stone of all this wickedness!

"Don't, Milada!" he begged. "I'll try to help you."

I love her, he realized, and can't protect her. Man wants to protect his woman, to build around her a wall of warmth and comfort, a house. But they bomb our houses and burn them, they push in our doors with the butts of their rifles, and defile our women.

"You mean much to me, Milada. That's why I had to be frank."

Oh, to tear open with our nails the invaders' throats, to beat their brains against the stones of our streets! But we are silent and shackled and without arms, waiting in agony.

"I must tell you of the work I will do tonight," Breda said, "because it affects you, it endangers you even more.... Please, come and sit with me."

She obeyed. It was as if his voice had hands which drew her to him.

"You remember the night we met?" he asked.

"Yes. It gave me strength."

"When we walked over Karl's Bridge, the searchlights cutting the sky—do you remember them?"

"That was when your mind turned away from me," she answered. "It made me feel alone."

"I thought of Janoshik, who stands for so many who have died and will die, and I thought that somebody somewhere must arise and accuse—not when it is all over, but now, now!"

Milada, with all of her own fears, was carried away by the emotions of the man. She knew that in his work, emotions are of small importance, often even a deterrent. She knew

190

that he acted on reason in whatever he did. But with womanly instinct she also felt that she and her crisis were the cause of the upheaval in Breda.

"You said: If we could write it in the sky!" She smiled at him. She knew his words by heart.

"Yes," Breda replied, "if we could write it in the sky, as they write their message of murder.

"I have a friend who works with me—Frantishek, a technician at the Prague Radio Station. Through him, I have the chance to make a broadcast if really great things are at stake. And I think they are.

"We will expose this hideous plot of the Gestapo over the radio. We need not talk about terror as such—the terror is known to everybody. But we must expose the perversity, the complete lack of principle in the Nazis' application of the terror. Once people have learned that no matter how they behave, the terror will hit them indiscriminately—once they've learned this, the terror loses its effect, its sting. You can shrug it off.

"And thus, we may avenge Janoshik. And you. And all the others."

His purpose and determination fascinated and frightened her. Because he was a fighter, she was drawn to him. Yet, she trembled with apprehension. She had lost Pavel. She did not want to lose Breda too. "What about you?" she asked. "You don't think of yourself; but I do."

He felt humbled. She could forget her danger which he was about to increase, and think of him!—What could he give her? He had nothing, not even his life. His life was not his own. What could he tell her? Of a future which was uncertainty? Of his feelings which could lead them, the girl and him, nowhere?

"I love you," he said.

Milada was silent. She had waited for these words as the

191

ivy waits and searches for the tree around which it can grow to the sun. She had wanted these words to give her the strength to face a world of Reinhardts; but now that he had spoken them, she felt nothing but fear, fear for the man, fear of his leaving her.

Her hot hand gripped his.

Breda, too, was afraid of his confession. "I love you," he repeated, "I shouldn't have said it. It doesn't help us, does it?" He rose and walked to the window. Gray Hat was still on guard.

He turned and almost shouted at her, "Don't worry about me, will you, please? *I* won't speak over the radio, of course not!"

"I'm not afraid," she whispered. "I believe in you."

"Tonight," he continued, more quietly, "we're making a recording. Then tomorrow, we will get hold of a certain Nazi announcer who happens to bear some resemblance to me. I will simply take his place, walk into the studio, put on the recording, start the machine going, and walk out. That's all."

He laughed. "Just imagine their faces when they find out how we fooled them!"

She joined in his laughter, relieved and with childlike delight. Then, her anxiety returning: "And if you don't succeed in kidnaping the announcer? Or if the guards at the station, the men in the studio, anybody, if they recognize the masquerade? I imagine the radio station is thoroughly policed. My God, your plan has so many chances of failure! And any slip may mean your death."

"There is always danger," he tried to reassure her. "But I've been lucky so far. And should we stop our work because we might fail and be killed? What do we have to lose? Is this life?

"I love you more than I can say. And I must sit by helplessly, must see you delivered into the hands of this Reinhardt. Is this life?

"We can't move, we can't speak, we can't breathe—is this life?

"Over there in the east, thousands die every day. In our country, men are condemned to slow death in the camps or executed by the hundreds. Life is not precious any more, it has become cheap.

"And I'm not a hero. I'm desperate, that's why I fight."

"Forgive me," she said. "I am a woman. Somehow I know how hard it is to give birth to life, just one life. How much pain! How much love!

"Let me worry a little for your one life, because you have only this one, and it is precious to me."

"Oh, damn it all," he laughed, "in a minute you'll have me weeping on your shoulder, weeping for myself and for you, and for all the things we miss and will never have. Don't soften me, please, I can't stand it, certainly not now. Think of yourself! Think how much I jeopardize you!

"The moment the broadcast comes over the air, Reinhardt's carefully guarded secret is out. Millions will know of Glasenapp's suicide which Reinhardt suspects you alone know.

"I am in much less peril than you, poor Milada."

This was true, she realized. Her mind was obsessed by so many things that when he outlined his plan, she had not thought of how it would involve her.

But I am not afraid, she observed with amazement. In the course of this day I must have run the gamut of anguish, so that now I'm unable to feel greater fear.

"Is this life?" she paraphrased Breda's own words, jokingly. "Gray Hat waits for me, a Gestapo Commissioner pursues me either for my information or my body—and I refuse to be intimidated."

She became serious. "Now is the hour that counts. You see, Breda, I want to live. I, the tiniest cell in the great bleeding, starving, tormented body of mankind, want to live. I'm

193

not cynical, please, my friend, you must understand me. You know the song to the Red Morning Sky?

> *Red Morning Sky, Red Morning Sky,*
> *You say that soon I'll have to die.*
> *Soon, when the bugles raise their call*
> *Must I and many comrades fall—*
> *Red Morning Sky, Red Morning Sky.*

> *Red Morning Sky, Red Morning Sky,*
> *I haven't lived, why should I die?*
> *The girls so young, the wheat yet green,*
> *So few the Springs that I have seen—*
> *Red Morning Sky, Red Morning Sky!*

"It's an old song..." Her voice broke.

Such a wave of hot compassion filled Breda that it burst the floodgates of his reticence. He closed Milada into his arms.

Tomorrow lay somewhere beyond them. This room was their island, the dancing fire in the stove their sun, this desperately brief span before they must part, their lifetime.

Tomorrow meant separation, he doing his work, Milada facing Reinhardt. Harvest the hour before it falls into time, to be lost forever.

Milada's trembling body pressed against him as if he were the only thing in the world. Yes, that he was. All around them was darkness, the only light was in his eyes. The only strength was in his arms, the only tenderness was in his hands, the only consolation in his lips.

Their union was as natural as the elements; as the stars, drawn together through limitless space, unite to form a new sun; or the molecules that clash and erupt into flame.

Oh my God, she thought, this is my need. Close around him, his strength, his warmth, never to let go, never. She caressed the softness of his skin, his hair. Like freshets the blood of her heart inundated him, who was in her heart. To give yourself, to lose yourself, to merge yourself indelibly, eternally—this was hers, this nobody could take away, this triumph over death and fear, this love!

My flesh is burning, sweet, consuming fire. A thousand sense-threads bind me to him, each one seeking him, tasting him, drinking him. Let there be no single nerve orphaned! Each one must receive him, his immense glowing wonderful life, each one must be blessed.

Feel him, his shoulders and his thighs, his belly and his chest. Drink his warm breath, the honey from his tongue, the blood from his lips, the life from his limbs. This is the sea, the wild, joyous sea. We swim exulting, borne by its waves from unfathomable depths up into the sky, the clouds. We soar like birds, strong birds with wide-spread wings, supported by the storm, flying to the sun—up and up and up.

I am a fireball. I am light, oh so light. This man in me, this beloved child. I carry him with me to unscaleable heights, to infinite azure. I can do it, I am the master, the mother, immortal, receiving and giving. Now I have reached it. Nobody ever, ever, ventured so high. How lonely I am, this man in me is just a cell, a kernel of life, a fetus. I shall bear him. Look at the space, the nothingness!

The rocket bursts. Oh, the joy of unfolding and of diffusing yourself and of shedding yourself the world over, spending, spending.

She sank back. The man in her arms, how helpless he lay. He smiled and kissed her, shyly, as one kisses the hem of the blue gown of the Virgin.

With gentle lips she brushed his cheek and eyes and brow, murmuring words of comfort and endearment, until her love, like some exquisite lullaby, cradled him to rest.

Then nothing was said. In the stove, the fire died. Breda got up to fetch a blanket to cover their bodies.

They lay close, breathing evenly, her head in the hollow of his shoulder.

"Darling," she whispered, "when you go away, the world will stop."

He took her elbow into his big hand, pressing it hard. "You're the closest thing I've ever had. But it's impossible, we cannot afford it today. This is the age of aloneness. Good luck to both of us."

She thought that woman's love must be greater than man's. Had he never forgotten reality, not even in her arms? Then she realized he was trying to break away; he had to. He was gentle and did not want to hurt her.

"I love you," she said.

"You are brave and natural."

"Why shouldn't I be? I'm only conscious of one thing; you must live on for me."

He sighed. "I couldn't love you this much if that weren't the end of the story."

"You must go?"

"I want you to know: We belong. Like day and sun, night and moon, dawn and colors."

"Yes."

"That I'll take with me, wherever I go."

"I, too."

He kissed her. Then he arose. He covered her carefully. With drowsy eyes, she watched him dress.

All in all, the day had been too much for her. Her body lapsed into the state of exhaustion where it skims along between sleeping and waking. That was good, it made their good-by less painful.

Breda, with the understanding created and nurtured by love, knelt down at her side. "Sleep well," he said, "and don't forget, at the shop we don't know each other."

"Don't leave me, dear!" she embraced him with warm arms.

"We'll see each other again," he consoled. "Take care of yourself. You are so beautiful, Milada; your hair is like

196

winding, black rivulets. Let me look at you, engrave you in my mind as you are now—"

Then, determinedly, he freed himself from her arms, rose, walked out, closing the door softly.

It took a while before Milada realized that she was alone. The sound of his steps had died long ago. "Darling!" she called. "Oh my darling!" For the first time during the staggering day she wept; and weeping she fell asleep.

Pan Kratochvil had waited before the house with the patience of a hunter who knows that, some time, the deer must emerge from the thicket, to go to the brook and drink. He kept his powder dry, thinking pleasant thoughts of how he would spend the additional pay due him for his long hours of work. One must credit it to this Reinhardt that he was not stingy with money. On the other hand, Kratochvil considered sorrowfully, there was not much that one could buy with this money—either there were no wares, or the money had lost in value. In his small way, Kratochvil had run up against the iron laws of economics. Hard as he tried, he found no solution for the problem posed by the regrettable lack of consumers' goods due to Nazi appropriation, and by the oversupply of shiny banknotes still smelling of the printing presses. The middle classes, of which Kratochvil regarded himself as a member, always get it in the neck. No chance of real, solid prosperity. He therefore decided to spend the money, much as he hated to do it, on bribes for the guardians of the property room in the Gestapo headquarters. In return, they'd let him have his choice among the belongings collected from the victims of his own and his colleagues' activity.

To pick the crumbs from the tables of the new rulers, Kratochvil reasoned, was better than to pick no crumbs at all.

In the midst of his excursion into philosophy, he was interrupted by a man who courteously but firmly requested a match for his cigarette. The man, Kratochvil's watchdog mind registered, had come from the house into which his quarry, the Milada girl, had disappeared.

Kratochvil lit a match, and for a second or so, the two men looked at each other with probing eyes. Then the match went out.

"Thank you," said Breda.

"My compliments!" replied Kratochvil, lifting his gray velour.

"Pleased to have met you," said Breda, turning away.

"You seem to be in a hurry!" continued Kratochvil.

"I'm a busy man."

"That's fine! That's fine!" beamed Kratochvil. "Where does your business take you so late at night? What line are you in?"

"You're such a pleasant little man," said Breda. "How can you ask so many questions of a stranger? One might almost think you're connected with the police. But, of course, if you were, you wouldn't be alone on the street, at this hour!"

"Why not?"

"Because it's dangerous."

"Really?"

"You see, if you were connected with the police, and you were alone, and if I disapproved of your connection—all these, my friend, are only suppositions—I might put my fingers around your throat—like this! and close my fingers—like that!"

"Stop! You're hurting me!" Kratochvil's voice was choking.

"I beg your pardon!"

"Don't mention it," growled Kratochvil.

"Well—thanks for the light!" And before Kratochvil had

recuperated from his shock, Breda vanished in the night. He chuckled. For the rest of his watch, Gray Hat would feel decidedly uncomfortable. How easy it would have been to kill him! Just a little more pressure of the hands—but Breda's purpose was not to kill the spy at this moment, which would have meant alarm, a police raid through the neighborhood, and very likely Milada's arrest. By approaching and frightening Gray Hat, Breda ascertained that the little man was alone and could not immediately detail another member of his brotherhood to follow him.

Now he knew the spy's weasel face; he promised himself to see to it that it was smashed soon.

How I have changed! Breda mused. Here I am contemplating coolly and even with satisfaction the disposal of a man I never met before. And I used to be a peaceful, law-abiding man. Now I am prosecutor, judge, jury and executioner—feeling no compunction whatever.

What have they done to us that we have become jungle beasts? They've taken something from us that our generation never will recover. If they had stolen only our property, our land, our books, our machines—their plan might have succeeded. One must admit, theirs is a gigantic conception: A whole continent starving, producing, sweating for a few anonymous men somewhere in Germany. Still, it might have worked, because people are so goddamned complacent; just give them something, even an illusion, and the people will feel that a bad life is better than no life.

We had little enough under our betrayed democracy: but we were modest. We worked and lived, and laughed and hoped.

But in their eagerness to suck the honey from the rose, they've sucked us dry, and no more flowers will come. They've taken our hope, our dignity, our humanity. If you treat humans like beasts, they will turn into beasts. If you rule us by murder, we will murder our rulers. Granted, a slave's life

199

has no value, but in the slave's mind, nobody else's life has value either.

They have defeated their own aims, they will be caught in their own brutality. History has its sly way.

If one could step outside this globe and watch the whole process from some heavenly balcony, one could get an Olympic laugh. But I am in the midst of it, one of millions of participants in this drama. I will have to do the killing and the dying, I, Breda, once a lover of sunsets, rivers, and quiet meditation. But I won't lose sight of the great plot of the drama; if I considered my small scene alone, I'd have to fear I were trapped. But I see the end and the future, I see my efforts merging with those of the many, forming an irrepressible stream, ultimately breaking all dams.

Before entering the basement to Frantishek's house, Breda once more made sure that he was not followed by one of Gray Hat's deputies. He had reached the house by round-about ways, designed to shake off any possible pursuer, though Breda was reasonably certain that he was unmolested ever since he had left the frightened man in the gray velour. But in the hard school of illegality, Breda had learned to be thrice careful.

He was let in after he had knocked in the prearranged manner.

The radio mechanic Frantishek, a short, powerfully built man with small and lively eyes, and the weatherbeaten skin of a Carpathian peasant, was a member of Breda's cell. The other member was the druggist Podiebradsky. Between the three of them, there was hardly a mechanical or chemical gadget which they could not produce—they were a good team and trusted one another implicitly.

They shook hands.

Breda inspected the recording machine which was connected with a microphone on the table. Beside the microphone the thorough Frantishek had set a glass of cold water —"as in a real studio," he explained. "Speakers always get a dry throat."

Podiebradsky, who had furnished the blank disk on which Breda's speech was to be recorded, laughed his full-throated laugh. "One would think you are a prima donna, old boy. Now you should gargle with peppermint and start making Mi-mi-mi-mi!"

"Mi-mi-mi yourself," protested Breda good-naturedly. "I have no intentions of singing, though I once was a soprano in the chorus of St. Mary's in Brno."

Turning to Frantishek he praised the mechanic: "It must have taken you months to steal all those parts. It's a shame we can use this apparatus so rarely."

"It'll be worth it," said Frantishek.

"One day," Breda felt that even in this work a good job should receive its due credit, "one day, Frantishek, we shall have a museum, a liberty museum, a museum of the Czech Revolution. It won't be as stuffy as our old National Museum, it'll be far more interesting, and we shall take our kids to see it. And in a place of honor shall be this recording machine, crude as it is, put together from stolen parts. I can see the little slip on the glass case: A simple worker, named Frantishek, built this machine in months of diligent labor to enable his friends to broadcast an important message over the Nazi Radio Station of Prague."

"Oh, forget it!" said Frantishek, but he smiled with pleasure.

"Maybe I should keep a sample of the false hair you're to wear tomorrow?" inquired Podiebradsky. "I had planned to sell it to Mrs. Konetzková, a widow, who is losing hers rapidly. But the museum is more important, I can see that."

"You're a cynic," commented Breda.

"But a practical one. You know what I have here?" he

pointed at two circular labels, printed in gold lettering on red. *"Hohenfriedberger Marsch,"* he read, "played by the Band of *Leibstandarte* SS, conducted by Giselher Kaltbauer. Just in case some wise Nazi might want to have a look at the record which you'll carry into the station tomorrow."

"By God, I hadn't thought of that!" Breda admitted. "That was very good of you. After we make the recording, we must check back over everything, to see whether we overlooked any other detail...."

"I spent fifteen Kronen for that lousy thing," Podiebradsky reported serenely. "The salesman told me he hadn't sold a Prussian march for at least half a year. Even the German Army seems to have little interest in its musical products."

"Are you ready?" Frantishek asked Breda.

"Just a moment. Let me go over my notes once more."

Breda sat down before the microphone, reading the sheets covered with his clean, laborious handwriting. The words seemed cold, dead on paper. He must recover the burning spirit of hatred and fight in which he had conceived those sentences. He thought of Janoshik, he thought of Milada, he thought of the dead buried in nameless graves. In this basement, with two men of equal devotion, he was about to raise the call which would penetrate these walls and all walls. His feeling was almost that of reverence.

"Ready, Breda?"

"Ready, Frantishek."

The disk began to spin.

"Citizens of Prague! Tomorrow, twenty hostages are to be shot for the murder of one Nazi, one Lieutenant Glasenapp. This man was never murdered. He committed suicide.

"Not even the motive of petty revenge for their dead remains to the Gestapo; your fellow citizens have been framed and are to die at the cruel whim of the invaders.

"There is no more law, not even Nazi law. There is no more security, be you as peaceful as you may. Your lives, the lives of your loved ones, are at the mercy of unprincipled, power-mad murderers. They kill for the sake of killing, they torture for the sake of torturing, their wrath strikes you, any of you, as a hailstorm does.

"There can be no more reason for trying to live with the invaders. We must fight against them. We must sabotage the work they want us to do, derail the trains they want us to run, burn and explode the stores they keep, the cars they drive, the houses wherein they live. Crush them, as they crush us! Beat them, as they beat us! Choke them, as they choke us! Kill them, as they kill us!

"It's we or they! Citizens! Each one of us has his chance, each one has his day! Use it—fight! Alone or in groups, fight! Till the last of the murderers is driven off our land, forever!"

CHAPTER 9

PROKOSCH's dramatic confession of the killing of Lieutenant Glasenapp struck Reinhardt with bewildering suddenness.

His careful planning, his work, his investigation, his plotting, his fateful conference with Heydrich—all toppled like a house of cards.

No! his mind protested. It can't be true. It must not be true.

This confession jeopardized his whole position. He, who pretended to search for Glasenapp's murderer, had based everything on the theory of the Lieutenant's suicide. That's why he had promised the Protector to liquidate the hostages, to liquidate Preissinger, to teach the population the great lesson of Nazi justice before which everybody, rich or poor, had the same chance of being shot.

And now he was cursed with this self-confessed murderer. The man whom the police were ostensibly hunting, the man whose apprehension radio and newspapers demanded, the man for whom his posters promised a reward of 50,000 Kronen, stood before him, disrupting the whole works with impudent unconcern.

With a shock, the Commissioner perceived the tenuous

path he had tramped so unwarily. He had relied on Gruber's report, on the observation of a simpleton like Captain Patzer, on a half-finished letter written by Glasenapp in a mood of depression. On such circumstantial evidence he had built his clever edifice! How in the world could he have blundered so thoroughly! How could he have exposed himself to such fatal danger—to the fury of the ill-tempered Heydrich, to the ridicule of his colleagues, to demotion, shame, and—he shuddered—to a possible transfer to the Eastern Front!

"So you killed Glasenapp!" he exclaimed with disgust. His voice expressed little doubt—for who ever heard of a man voluntarily taking upon himself the punishment which would be meted out to the murderer of a German officer?

"Yes!" Prokosch said firmly, even proudly.

The Commissioner lapsed into silence.

He had to make a decision, and he had to do it quickly. Moenkeberg was beating his pencil on the pad on which he had been taking notes of the questionings. Well, these notes Reinhardt could dispose of. Moenkeberg, the faithful Moenkeberg, knew well enough that his life was inseparably tied to Reinhardt's; so he'd keep his mouth shut.

Reinhardt decided to construct a new floor of deceit upon his foundation of falsehood. First, he had changed the suicide into murder; now, he had his murderer. Since, to his plot, a murderer was fatal, there must be no murderer. Simple. He would let him disappear.

Too bad that Murtenbacher was not here. There was nobody to whom he could boast of the dispatch and skill with which he had fenced off this unexpected attack upon his plans. But isn't it always so in life? Our greatest thoughts are developed and our wisest deeds are done without the knowledge of the public, without credit and applause. Perhaps one day, when he wrote his memoirs....

Reinhardt smiled again. He was proud of himself, a conscientious, intelligent official striving in the service of Greater Germany.

"And what makes you confess?" he asked Prokosch.

Yes—what made Prokosch confess?

He was no man of courage. He had always evaded conflicts which challenged him to take a stand.

In the center of the universe stood the actor Prokosch, the world his audience, his life a stage. It was doubtful whether an individual unit named Karel Prokosch really existed—he was a hero today, a sinner yesterday, a saint tomorrow. He could wear all the colors of the rainbow successively, the expression of his face, his mind, his character changing with the shade of the hour and the day.

"Isn't that what you love in me?" he once had said to Mara. "That I am not a drab one-sided affair, but that I'm able to transform myself into my rôles—sometimes, Faust—sometimes, Oedipus—sometimes, Lear; but always a living being. This is my greatness. My art and I have become one."

Mara, upon listening to such fatuity, had been torn between admiration and bitter laughter. Admiration, because Prokosch had the ability to place himself on a pedestal and derive inspiration therefrom; bitter laughter, because in his self-centered blindness he did not see that the theater, even if he carried it around as Andersen's fairy-tale king carried his imaginary clothes, was not the world, was not life, but a house of artificial lights and hollow props.

When she tried to bring him back to reality, he complained: "This world you talk about, it's not my world. And if I had to live in it, I would die. I see things with my eyes. What I consider green may be red to others. Quite possible. But where is the man wise and impartial enough to judge who is right? I prefer my image of the world, in which I am great. That's the image you yourself made of me. That's why you love me, that's why you gave up your individual life to merge with mine—I don't thank you for it, it was only natural."

At that point, Mara would become silent. Doubting him meant doubting herself. That she could not do.

The man thus grown in dimensions which never existed had died in the basement of the Gestapo jail in Prague. The truth had killed him. He had always been a walking illusion. He had nourished himself with illusions, and when the truth was flung in his face, the giant of clay had crumbled.

This world he had despised had struck back with vengeance. His own wife, his beloved, had betrayed him, had allied herself with a scribbler of no consequence; even the child, born of her womb, was not his own.

He had failed in his biggest rôle, his life. He was a buffoon, a pathetic product of moth-eaten costumes, grease paint, and studied phrases.

In the long hours following his defeat, lying on his cot staring up at the narrow wet stone ceiling of the cell, he recognized himself for what he was: A fool, not a hero—and not even a lusty, positive, compelling fool such as Shakespeare had created, but a sad cuckold in an average farce.

What difference did it make that the others despaired of their approaching death? He was dead now; deader than dead because he never had lived.

In the midst of these thoughts the guard had summoned Janoshik for Reinhardt's questioning. Prokosch had not joined in the good wishes which accompanied Janoshik on his difficult way, the good-bys—for who knew whether Janoshik would ever again be seen alive? The cell door had long been closed before its clang registered in Prokosch's mind.

So this uncouth man had gone, taking with him his stories which were designed to be funny, but which had struck the actor as utterly vulgar. What difference did it make? One more, one less. He, Prokosch, was deader than dead.

But the human mind is a peculiar machine. It picks up an impression, a sound—you don't even know, at first, that you've seen or heard it. And then, against your best intentions, the mind begins to play with this impression, with this sound; it weaves its own pattern, it creates its own picture. At length, you become conscious that your mind has played you a trick, and despite yourself you become involved in its creation.

So, thought Prokosch, Janoshik has gone to be questioned by the Gestapo. It was about time they started. Soon my turn will come. Well—let it. I don't care. They can question me, they can kill me—I shall welcome it. Anything is better than to be dead alive, alive dead. Kill me, I'll urge them—kill me! Make an end!

For how can I go on, even these few days which are left? Living means believing. I believed in my greatness, and I believed in Mara. Fool that I was—I believed in the image I made of her. Now that this image is broken into a thousand fragments, I've had to lose faith in myself. The hangman's face will be a friendly face, the sound of the death squad's rifles will be harmony.

Kill me! I'll tell them—make an end!

It should be a great scene—my last and my greatest.

He could see the back of the stage—a bleak, gray wall. The sun rising in reddish glow. The others, little extras, standing in numb desperation. But he, the actor Prokosch, throwing up his arms in a spine-thrilling gesture, calling with all his power: Kill me! Make an end!

Or better—he must play his scene alone. Get rid of the extras. Why should they die? They'd spoil his great rôle! Whatever guilt they had, he had taken upon himself, the hero, sacrificing himself for the others, the little ones. What a curtain!

Now he must give his sacrifice some motivation. For the very reason that he was smashed to the ground, he must rise and show his overwhelming humanity. Jesus died this way, taking upon himself the sins, past and future, of all mankind. What glory! Love thine enemies, and die for them.

Who was the enemy? Whom did he hate most? Whom could he shame for all days to come?

Lobkowitz. Too bad the man was not of greater stature; but there was no one else, he'd have to do.

He, Karel Prokosch, by his sacrifice, would free the man who had robbed him of his wife, who had fathered her child. What a plot! For the rest of his days, the scoundrel would have to walk with head bowed. What a revenge!

And when the volley was fired, when the curtain came down, there'd be nobody to step on the proscenium to accept the applause. He would lie in his blood, with a knowing smile on his lips, finally and perpetually justified.

Reinhardt could have no idea of the motives prompting Prokosch to confess. But Reinhardt, in his years of service, had come upon thousands of people, people of most diverse backgrounds and character; and, for a policeman, he had a surprising insight into the minds of others.

That's why he asked, "What makes you confess?"

He did not doubt the confession of the murderer, disagreeable though it was to his plans. But if Prokosch killed Glasenapp, he must have had some reason; also, how did he do it? Furthermore, Prokosch could have retained the anonymity of being one of many hostages. Or did he assume that his confession would free the others? Reinhardt had, in his long practice, encountered heroics of similar kind. He considered such heroics ridiculous, they belonged to an age long passed. But, thinking of this possibility, the Commissioner's logic went one step further: what if the whole confession was an act? An act designed by this Prokosch to free the hostages by sacrificing himself?

"Step nearer!" he ordered Prokosch. Now the sharp light of the lamp was focused on the actor's face; but Prokosch did not blink, he was accustomed to the brilliancy of spot-lights.

Reinhardt studied the actor. The man looked pale and wasted under the glare, his cheeks were baggy, his eyes red-rimmed, his forehead pasty-white. The actor's lips were color-less, the stubble of his growing beard deepened the shadows in his face. The man is sick, thought Reinhardt. It may be merely the atmosphere of the cell—it may be actual sickness. Also, he is unbalanced, a weak intellectual cracking under pressure. It should not be too difficult to get the facts from him.

"Now, my dear Prokosch," Reinhardt resumed his ques-tioning, "why don't you tell us in a little more detail why and how you killed Lieutenant Glasenapp. You can't just tell us: I killed him! and assume that, with these few words, the matter is settled. We are here to find the truth, the whole truth. If you give us the truth, you have nothing to fear."

Prokosch, who had had lots of time on his cot to think up details, went into his sordid story.

"I hated him. He was such a beast. He was ugly and swag-gering, nauseating and drunk. I'm a sensitive man. So I killed him."

Reinhardt interrupted: "Is that a habit with you? I mean —kill people who strike your fancy the wrong way?"

"No," said Prokosch, "but he was a Nazi, and as such un-worthy of the usual consideration with which one regards even the most obnoxious."

"Well—you don't mince words!"

"Why should I? I know my life is forfeited whatever I say. In fact, it thrills me to let you hear the truth."

Reinhardt nodded. "The truth . . . Go on!"

Prokosch gesticulated: "You belong to the masters. You don't know what it is to be ruled by you."

"You bet I know," Reinhardt smiled. "I have imagination!"

"One reaches a point when one begins to think: The next one of that gang I meet, I will kill. Just to release all the stifled longings inside, all the words one must not speak, all the thoughts one must not have, all the feelings one must not harbor, all the deeds one must not do. It's such a marvelous relief to kill, to feel life ooze out of the scoundrel in your hands—"

And suddenly, a step nearer to Reinhardt: "Terrible, isn't it?"

Reinhardt was not quite carried away by the actor's passion. "You are very convincing," he said. "Too bad I never had the opportunity of seeing you on the stage. And it is a most extraordinary confession. In my profession, I have heard many men and women confess, but you are the first to do it with such gusto. Isn't that so, Moenkeberg?"

Moenkeberg grunted. "Can't you make him speak a little slower? I have a hell of a time writing all that down."

"You heard what Moenkeberg wants?" said Reinhardt. "Ordinarily his job is much easier—I ask questions and draw the answers out of my prisoners; so Moenkeberg has time to catch up. But you talk so enthusiastically—pardon our shortcomings, please."

Prokosch was somewhat nettled by the Commissioner's answer. He felt the ambiguity in Reinhardt's well-mannered criticism, but could not decide whether the man believed him or not, whether the story had gone over, or whether Reinhardt was subtly ridiculing him.

The truth of the matter was that Reinhardt, the longer he listened to Prokosch, doubted him the more. The Commissioner's intercourse with actors had been limited and he thought: perhaps they are that way. But there was a good

211

chance that Prokosch was lying, lying magnificently and with great flourish, but lying.

Reinhardt, however, was not the man to stand up and shout: You bloody bastard, you lie! Oh, no—he sat back and enjoyed the show, and waited till the liar trapped himself in his own story, gently steered into the trap by Reinhardt the Wise.

"And that is all the motivation you had?" he inquired. "If it hadn't been Glasenapp, any other German would have done?"

"Yes," said Prokosch, "hate does not discriminate."

"You seem to be a dangerous fellow!"

"I might be considered that, yes."

"I have already asked what made you confess—you haven't told me. I'd like your answer now."

Prokosch was prepared for this question. He raised his right hand in eloquent gesture. "Your basement prison, Commissioner, is not conducive to increasing the lust for life. On the contrary. And when I learned from Dr. Wallerstein that all of us were to be shot as hostages for Lieutenant Glasenapp unless the murderer is found, the simple thought occurred to me: Since I am the murderer, and since I have to pay in any case, let me confess! While my death may be made more painful, still, I can suffer it only once. And I will have the satisfaction of knowing that others, innocents, will go free."

Reinhardt smiled. He looked at his fingernails, and brushed them against the lapel of his black tunic. "So you rely on our decency?" he asked. "The decency and fairness of the same people you so deeply hate, the same you said you'd kill whenever you had the chance. Why should we act on your wish? Why should we not take the same viewpoint you just espoused: kill you, whenever we have a chance? You— and the hostages?"

From under his lids he watched Prokosch's reaction. He

212

was satisfied—the actor lost countenance, and there was no prompter to give him the next line.

"You can't do that!" Prokosch stuttered. "I have confessed! Punish me! Shoot me!"

"We will, we will! But first tell us how you killed Glasenapp. And I'd like to hear the truth without theatrical accouterments—you know, Moenkeberg must write it all down."

It became frightfully clear to Prokosch that instead of his playing with the policeman, Reinhardt was playing a devilish game with him. Poor Prokosch's mind was not trained for adventures in logic and criminology. And how could he, lying on his uncomfortable cot, torn by the thoughts of his wasted life, construe a web of facts which would stand up under Reinhardt's sharp scrutiny? How could he know what facts the Commissioner had at his disposal? How could he think up answers in advance to questions he could not foresee? He had hoped that his confession alone would be sufficient, with perhaps the addition of an insolent account of his motives.

But now he was called upon to give details, circumstances, facts—he, for whom small things had been of utter unimportance.

"How did I kill him!" he protested. "I killed him—isn't that enough? Do I have to give you the gory details?"

"You're getting tender-hearted, eh? You amaze me, Prokosch! Yes," Reinhardt spoke pleasantly, "I want the gory details."

"I don't remember. Everything happened in such a whirl of emotion." He pleaded with the hard man before him: "Don't you understand—blood rushes to your head, everything you see is distorted, everything you hear is shrill..."

"Believe me," assured Reinhardt, "I know considerably more about killing than you do. It just isn't as you describe it. Most of it is done very coldly, very determinedly. You want me to accept what you say, don't you? Well, as a man to whom the security of life and property in this city is entrusted, I have to know precisely what happened. If you can't tell me, I must assume you are lying."

Prokosch was on the spot. He knew it. Whatever story he told, could be right only by lucky accident.

"He went down to the toilet. He had vomited on the floor of the bar, and he was weakened, I could see that. So I followed him." Prokosch spoke haltingly, pausing after each sentence.

"When?"

"When?—A little while after the handy man had come up to wipe the floor. I figured that perhaps, outside of Glasenapp, nobody would be in the men's room."

"You see how right I am?" remarked Reinhardt. "Killing is done in cold blood. You considered most of the possibilities quite reasonably. Go on!"

"I went down the stairs."

"Nobody saw you leave?"

"Nobody that I know of."

"Had you come alone to the Mánes?"

"No, I was with Peter Lobkowitz."

"I see," said Reinhardt. "Go on."

Prokosch realized with fear that he would have to inform Lobkowitz of the confession, and that he would have to beg his enemy to substantiate the story before Reinhardt. Prokosch winced.

"Go on! Go on!" prodded Reinhardt.

"Down in the toilet I found Glasenapp bending over the basin, very sick. I was disgusted and all the more determined to get rid of him. I don't think he heard me when I stepped behind him—he was too busy with himself.

"I put my hands around his neck, I pressed the soft part of his throat—" Prokosch's imagination had taken hold of him. He thought not of Glasenapp whom he hardly had noticed in the Mánes, but of Lobkowitz and Lobkowitz' throat—"I pressed and I pressed, hard. And suddenly he went limp. He was dead."

"Without struggle?"

"He was drunk and surprised; he did not struggle."

"You grasped him like this?" Reinhardt put his hands around Moenkeberg's thick neck, illustrating the scene.

"Yes, like this," confirmed Prokosch.

"And how did you dispose of the body?"

"I threw him into the river."

"You mean, you carried the dead Lieutenant out onto the jetty and pushed the corpse into the Moldau?"

"Yes."

"Weren't you afraid somebody might see you?"

"It was dark. I don't believe I was observed."

"So there are no witnesses..." Reinhardt leaned back. Then he went through the sheaf of papers on his desk, the file marked "Erich Glasenapp, First Lieutenant." He looked at the medical officer's report—there were no marks on the body. Choking fingers would have left their imprint.

Reinhardt smiled. It was a vicious smile. He had closed the trap.

"I may have to give an order, my dear Prokosch," Reinhardt explained smoothly, "which I hate to give. But you will understand! We must keep you isolated from your cellmates so that you cannot report to them the interesting and enlightening conversation we have had. Now, our arrangements for solitary confinement are not exactly comfortable—in fact, you will be confined to a rather small space, in which you will neither be able to lie down nor even to sit. It will be dark, and the ventilation leaves much to be desired. As I said, I hate to do this to you—I give the order only in the interest of truth. In case you decide to add further details to your confession, or perhaps to change your story, I shall

215

have one of the guards inquire after your well-being every three hours or so. Is that agreeable with you?"

Prokosch's knees buckled. He closed his eyes—for the first time in the actor's life, the light on his face hurt him. He thought of the standing coffins of which Janoshik had spoken. To that he was now condemned. His last scene, his great exit, would not be easy to achieve.

"Don't despair," consoled Reinhardt. "I know quite a few people who have gone through it and who are none the worse for the experience." He rang a bell, and the guards came to lead Prokosch away.

The actor heard Reinhardt chuckle: "Moenkeberg—this affair Glasenapp gets more absorbing by the hour. Don't you think so?" Then the door closed, and the mild twilight of the corridor embraced Prokosch.

Now there were only three of the hostages left in the cell, Preissinger, Lobkowitz, and Dr. Wallerstein. And none of them could sleep, although the cell seemed much more roomy, and each had a cot for himself.

It was pitch dark, which dismayed Wallerstein especially. He could not write. He could not lose himself in his precious notes.

Preissinger tossed and writhed. The noisy movements of his heavy body mingled with the tap tap of the guard's steps outside in the courtyard, a disquieting duet full of foreboding.

Lobkowitz' mind was with the two who had been called for questioning, and who had not returned. All he had heard of cruel tortures and endless grillings came alive before his eyes; in fearing for Janoshik and Prokosch, he also feared for himself whose turn would come soon. He did not hate Prokosch any more, he pitied him. How would the actor, shaken as he was, stand up under the whip of the Nazis?

216

Lucky enough that there was no secret Prokosch was supposed to keep. All that the Nazis' most intense efforts might wring from Prokosch would be the confession that he knew nothing.

With Janoshik it was different. They never had talked about it, but Lobkowitz sensed that there was more to Janoshik than he admitted. Lobkowitz prayed for strength, strength for himself and for Janoshik; he prayed to a God in whom he had never believed and who, reason told him, could not exist. Yet he prayed in the crazy hope that He, serious and fatherly, was enthroned somewhere in lofty heights, and that desperate words could reach His ear.

And another crazy hope entered Peter Lobkowitz' mind: Could it be that the questionings meant a chance for life? What if the Gestapo's case was not all cut and dried? What if they had found a clew to Glasenapp's murderer, what if they'd found the murderer himself?

"If they got hold of the man who killed Glasenapp, do you think they'd let us go?"

No answer.

"Did you hear me, Dr. Wallerstein?"

"Yes, I heard you, Lobkowitz."

"Then why don't you answer me?"

"Because there is so damned little hope. We are just victims of an unfortunate fight between fanatics. Whoever killed Glasenapp will not come to the Gestapo and confess. Those who harass the Nazis know it will cost lives. And if it's the lives of men like Preissinger and you and me, what of it? Such lives are not worth much. And the Nazis, in the perpetration of their terror, must take our lives; only thus can they demonstrate the ruthlessness by which they maintain themselves. It's a vicious circle, and we're caught in it."

"Suppose," continued Lobkowitz stubbornly, "one of us hostages *were* the murderer! In fact, it is a most logical thought since we all were in the Mánes when Glasenapp was killed."

"Would you denounce him?" Wallerstein was interested in determining how far these days had undermined this young man of obvious quality. "Provided you knew who he was? Provided the Nazis would let you free, eh?"

Lobkowitz considered that his life was at stake. Would he sacrifice another man to save it? Or would he sacrifice his life to save another man's? But the alternative was unrealistic—if the murderer was among the hostages, he would die anyhow.

Therefore, Lobkowitz gave an evasive answer. "Since I don't know who killed Glasenapp, the question is academic. Nevertheless, I would expect the man to confess. His life is forfeited, and he could save us all."

"Maybe you expect such grandeur; people, unfortunately, do not always come up to your expectations, my young friend." Wallerstein placed his hands between his knees, as he often did during the tense pursuit of an elusive symptom. "A man like Preissinger, for instance—he'd hardly confess. He's a coward at heart. Would you denounce him?"

"I don't like your questions, Dr. Wallerstein. He's in the same boat as we are—"

"All sorts of people can be in one boat," replied Wallerstein pleasantly.

Preissinger, whose annoyance and dejection had grown deeper with every minute of the conversation, shouted, "Sadist! I know how you hate me! You want to drive Lobkowitz into denouncing me to save your own skin! Well, let me tell you that I'll come out on top yet. I shall be freed, I know it! I know it! I am powerful, I have connections....*You* may have to die, and I'll be damned if I feel the least bit sorry."

"If you're so powerful," said Wallerstein, "why are you still here?"

Preissinger laughed, a demented laugh which startled Lob-

218

kowitz. "I am here just because I am so powerful. You don't see that, you two—you think I'm crazy, don't you? But I'm not—I know what I'm talking about. You two, you are infinitesimal pawns, you only exist to be pushed around. But I am not merely a man, I am mountains and mines. I represent Coal. If you take a piece of coal and shove it into your stove you don't realize that you bought it from me. I own it, and through it, I own you. I am Coal—that means I am railroads, electricity, steam; I am the wheels that move, the presses that stamp, the pistons that push."

"Very impressive—look at yourself now!"

"That's nothing!" triumphed Preissinger. "I got myself into this, I will get myself out of here! . . . They had to make me a minister of the Cabinet—don't you remember?"

"Yes, I remember," admitted Lobkowitz, the newspaperman. "It was quite a scandal."

"Scandal—nothing! You can't imagine how exasperating it is to see those politicians dilute your well-planned orders. So I decided to take a hand in it myself.

"Now I'll tell you the most important thing I did. When the Big Four met in Munich and told us to hand over the Sudeten to Hitler, I was in the Cabinet. I knew, and we all knew, it meant handing over Czechoslovakia. But the issues were far bigger than this little country of ours.

"You are not accustomed to political thinking. I'll have to explain. The Soviets offered us help if we'd resist. They figured in Moscow they'd have to fight anyhow, and they preferred doing it with an airplane base a few hours from Berlin. We held the fate of Europe in our hands, then.

"Opinion in the Cabinet was tied.

"I am Coal, I am power.

"So I stood up and said, Gentlemen, I said, do you wish to have the Nazis in the country, or the Red Army? In both cases we lose. With the Nazis we lose those intangibles: democracy, national independence, free press, free speech, what have you. With the Red Army we lose very tangible things— I for instance lose my coal mines; you, Mr. Premier, your estates, you, Mr. Blacek, your newspapers and bank accounts. Help from the Soviets means that all those little people whom we are here to rule will raise their heads and become very difficult. With the Nazis, we can deal.

"We have to choose between two evils. As far as I'm concerned, I prefer the Nazis and shall so vote."

Lobkowitz was appalled. To him, those intangibles had meant something. And he had believed that his government, weak and vacillating, as it often had been, somehow represented the will of the people.

He was enraged, and his voice was hoarse with fury: "You deserve to be shot—shot by the Nazis."

"Don't fool yourself!" laughed Preissinger. "They remember me. I've had the most agreeable relations with them. Before they came, the Jews, the Petscheks, owned the controlling stock of the Coal Syndicate. When the Nazis took over, the Petscheks were kicked out. I got the stock. So you see, in that Cabinet meeting, there were far bigger issues at stake than just our little country."

"I can see that," conceded Wallerstein. "You interest me as a phenomenon, Preissinger. The stock, the Coal Syndicate—you can't eat it, you can't go to bed with it. You sold out your people—what did you get out of it? What sensation? What satisfaction?"

"Power," said Preissinger. "The knowledge that you are the mover, not the moved; the pusher, and not the pushed."

"You are mad!" cried Lobkowitz.

But Wallerstein, who knew the world better than did the young newspaper man, remained cool. "This is," he said, "a wonderful joke. Mover and pusher, Preissinger the Almighty. And with all your power, you have one more day and one more night to go. Then you'll be extinguished like any ordinary dirty melted down candle."

And turning to Lobkowitz: "Now would you denounce Preissinger?"

"Who would believe me? The Nazis know him too well."

"Preissinger, I assure you, would denounce anybody to regain his precious life, his wonderful power, my dear Lobkowitz. Wouldn't you?" he asked the man who was Coal.

Preissinger was exhilarated and exhausted at the same time; he did not reply.

Wallerstein went on: "It would be such a small matter compared to the great deeds you have performed; I even think you are entitled to it. Who are we? Infinitesimal pawns you shoved around by the millions; but you, Preissinger—can you imagine a world without you and your kind?"

"I can!" said Lobkowitz. "And, by God, a better world!"

Preissinger scratched his head. "We are all egotists, aren't we? We all like to be on top. But it takes ability, initiative, energy, character, to get there and to stay there."

"And ruthlessness, depravity, corruption, cruelty," continued Lobkowitz.

"But look at what we built!" Preissinger argued. "The industries, science, civilization, progress—of course, that costs blood and sweat and lives, but mankind multiplies so prolifically...."

"And then you call the Nazis, and the War, and you destroy it," said Wallerstein.

And Lobkowitz, screaming with indignation, retorted: "You built it? Hell! You never did a day's decent labor!"

"I don't have to," said Preissinger, and yawned. "I run the show."

Janoshik sat in the back of the big open staff car between two sturdy, steel-helmeted SS soldiers who had little regard for his comfort and showed **this** by using him as a buffer whenever one of them desired more space on the seat. In front sat the chauffeur and Gruber, the Kid, who led Janoshik's expedition to the Mánes. None of the guards liked his task particularly; they had been rooted out of the pleasantly smoky atmosphere of the Skat game in the guard room to accompany this slit-eyed, round-faced Czech ape on a wild goose chase to some bar or other—and the worst of it was that the bar would be closed at this hour, and that they were not supposed to drink on duty anyway.

Gruber, upon meeting Janoshik again, had sneered; he recognized him as the man who had given him so much mental trouble on the evening of the hostages' arrest. He'd have some fun with the fellow now he had him in his power again!

The car raced through the darkened streets, its siren screeching. The few pedestrians it encountered huddled close to the house walls, thinking: Poor man, God knows what he has done, God knows what they will do to him.

But Janoshik was quite happy. The fresh air of the night, beating against his face, blowing through his thin jacket with the velocity of the car's speed, was delicious. After the murky atmosphere in the cell, it cleared one's head, it braced one's heart. Released from a dungeon, one almost felt free!

He hummed a little melody he once had heard sung by the young voices of Moravian peasant girls with firm buttocks and breasts. It was morning and they walked to the fields to begin harvesting. Janoshik was not musical, he hummed it wrong, but with all the more expression. And, in his mind, he gave the lusty melody new words:

Yes, you scoundrels—today is the day—when we will win our battle!

Yes, you scoundrels—doing my duty—I give the fateful word, the address!

Yes, you scoundrels—against your brute force—we set cunning and firmness.

Oh, you scoundrels—how you shall fly—when all this blows up under your asses!

As poetry, it was unfinished and poor; as a battle cry for Janoshik, a battle cry which never was born in sound, it was triumphant. An officer leading his men over the top with a call inspiring them to victory is sometimes honored and remembered by posterity. Fortunate man! The Janoshiks, fighting their battles no less bravely, planning them well, carrying through their tasks conscientiously, they die nameless, knowing only that they have contributed their bit to a future embracing millions.

"Stop that yowling!" orderer Enzinger who sat to Janoshik's right. "What do you feel so goddamned happy about, anyway?"

"It's this city, this Prague!" explained Janoshik. "You see, I am saying good-by to it, because tomorrow I will be shot. If you were born here, and if you had to die tomorrow, wouldn't you be happy to see your city once more?"

Enzinger turned to Walters, the guard on Janoshik's other side. "Can you make out these people? We shoot 'em, and they sing."

Walters grunted: "They don't know what it's all about. It's an inferior race, that's what it is. They got no culture, no nothing. And we have to cart them around in the middle of the night."

The car swerved around a curve. They had reached the river and now drove along the embankment of the Moldau. The moon was behind them and cast its frosted light over Petschin and Hradschin hills on the opposite shore; a few clouds with silver fringes stood still in the starless sky.

Janoshik saw the river, the quiet wide river which reflected the light of the night in its myriads of ripples—it took his breath away. All mischievous thoughts, all irony, all the hardness he had acquired in years of struggle dissolved. Nothing was left but great peace and this: *How small I am, how insignificant!* This city and this river will go on, living and flowing, ageless, majestic. And I am merged with them, like the pillars of Karl's Bridge, like the stone figures on the Dome.

Three long, solid, heavily laden barges were gliding along the river in silence, recalling Janoshik to reality. Perhaps these were the barges which he would help to explode, perhaps not. He had ceased to worry. He was so strong, so sure of himself and the purpose of his life that no doubts and no fear could ever again enter his heart.

They reached the Mánes and stopped. The place was dark and deserted; on its terrace, the chairs were piled upside down upon the tables.

Gruber, his foot on the running board, his elbow propped on his knee, and his chin propped on his fist, struck the pose of a field marshal lost in thought. His thoughts led nowhere. So he turned to Janoshik and inquired, "Who has the keys?"

"The Boss."

"And where is the Boss?"

Janoshik, still hemmed in by his two guardians, ventured the information: "I hope at home, in bed with his good wife."

"Is there no superintendent or such?"

"There is. It's me."

"Why didn't you say that in the first place? Who has your key?"

"You have it, sir."

But Gruber had never thought of taking along the key he had confiscated upon Janoshik's arrest. And he had no desire to drive all the way back to headquarters, search through the property room, fetch that miserable key, and return.

"We'll have to break in the door," he announced, changing his marshal's pose to that of an active commander in the field. "Forward, men! Take along your rifles!"

"Good!" said Janoshik, trotting behind Enzinger and Walters. "Let's show them that we have an important job. What's the fun in searching if afterward nobody can see that we were in the place, no?"

Enzinger and Walters got busy with the butts of their rifles, and since Janoshik was shackled to them, he had to wave his chained arms in the same jerky moves as theirs—a strange marionette, a helpless parody.

The door splintered and gave. Janoshik, preceded by Gruber and his two guides, entered the darkened, ghostly halls in which he had once worked so modestly and unobtrusively. There was poetic justice in the fact that he, the lowliest of all, now was to have the run of the house.

"Lights! Where are the lights?" Gruber shouted.

Janoshik saw no reason for hurry; the more time he could spend in the Mánes, the less time he would have to suffer in Reinhardt's torture chamber. Let Gruber bump his shins if he was in such a rush!

"The main switch is in the basement," he suggested helpfully. They moved gingerly along the blacked-out corridors, a thin segment of which was cut out by Gruber's flashlight. Janoshik, who knew every nook and cranny, felt his way as awkwardly as the others.

"Enzinger! Walters!" commanded Gruber. "Watch out for the prisoner!" But these two experienced men, foreseeing how dangerous a blow from his manacled hands would be, had already tightened their grip on Janoshik.

For a short second the idea flashed through Janoshik's mind: Beat them down, kick Gruber in the guts, take their arms, and run! To be free! He could hide, the Gestapo would never find him in this city whose thousand secret haunts he knew. But bigger than his freedom loomed his task; the chances that he'd win a pitched battle with the three armed huskies were few. What was his life compared with the many he might save by having the barges blown up?

And then light flooded them, the sharp light of the unprotected bulbs in dusty sockets. They were in the basement storeroom, part of Janoshik's kingdom. Here were all the old boxes and cases which the Boss had made him save, broken down furniture, empty bottles, piles of out-of-date menus, rags, pails, brooms, baskets—the motley collection of a restaurant's backwash. To find anything, but especially a letter, in or behind this jumble, was a policeman's nightmare.

But Gruber had not been a policeman for long, and was therefore of good cheer. "Well—start!" he said, and looked at his watch. He did not suspect that, before the night was over, his experience would be considerably enriched.

Janoshik was still tied to Enzinger and Walters, and he went at his work with a vengeance. With the two guards in tow, he dived into the boxes. The heavy dust flew up in clouds. He shifted the cases, he stumbled over and behind bottles, he pushed the old furniture around with the complete unconcern of a man who has little respect for the property of his Boss.

Gruber fled to the door and kept his nose outside. But Enzinger and Walters had no such relief. Their lungs filled with dirt, their eyes watered, their faces grew grimy. Janoshik, enacting a furious search, showed no mercy.

"I must find it," he kept mumbling, "I must find it. What will the poor Commissioner say if we come back without this important document? Now this corner—perhaps it is here!" And down came the piles of menus, so that they had to wade through paper. Janoshik went down on his knees. "I must find it!" And the sheets flew right and left while he dug deeper and deeper.

Enzinger and Walters were choking. The discipline drilled into their bones began to wane. They were rapidly approaching the point of mutiny. Gruber was holding a handkerchief

226

before his face, taking it off only long enough to take a puff from his cigarette. But no such luxury for Enzinger and Walters—they had to hold on to Janoshik!

Finally Enzinger stated for Gruber's benefit: "This is nonsense! This is a way to hide things, not to find them!"

And Walters moaned: "Goddamn the crazy ideas of that sonofabitch!" without explaining whether he referred to Janoshik, Gruber, or Commissioner Reinhardt.

Gruber had not merely been taking it easy, he had been thinking. Now he sped up his brain work and arrived at a result. "Stop!" he said. "At this rate we'll still be here tomorrow afternoon. We must use a system. System!" he repeated, remembering chance crumbs he had picked up from Reinhardt's occasional lecturings.

The four men came together near the entrance of the storeroom where the mess had not yet reached such dimensions that one could not remain standing. The war council began with another repetition of Gruber's demand for "system!" But Janoshik interrupted him by declaring modestly that the best system was one in which everybody worked. This struck a sympathetic chord in Gruber who recalled the speeches of his leaders in which, for the consumption of the common man, the socialist end of National Socialism was stressed. And since Gruber as the commander of the expedition would have the rôle of supervisor, he had no objection. However, he did not give credit to Janoshik for the latter's contribution; rather, following the example of the most famous of his leaders, he appropriated the idea and said: "We will divide the room into three sections. Enzinger—to the left; the prisoner in the center; and Walters to the right. Then we'll go through the room lengthwise, searching it foot by foot." And taking his revolver out of the holster, he continued: "You can let go of the prisoner, I'll keep him covered all right."

Janoshik felt the time had come for some laudatory remarks. "That is excellent," he exclaimed, "never could I have devised such a clever system; now, we'll have this letter in no time..." and added a little more thoughtfully: "If it is in this room."

Gruber, flushed by the effort of designing such complicated orders, overheard the last "if"; but not so Enzinger and Walters who were in dark despair and fury over the prospect of having to co-operate with Janoshik in the search through this filth; and they let him feel it by making the removal of his handcuffs as painful as possible.

Janoshik remained friendly; he smiled at them with his most winning, benevolent smile, hiding his sinister pleasure at his success in putting to work the two representatives of the superior race.

For a long while they labored intensely, without results; and mighty thirst befell them. A vicious nervousness came over Enzinger and Walters, especially after they noticed that Janoshik was falling back in the competition. So they began pushing him and cuffing him and beating him whenever they had a chance; and Gruber looked on, cigarette in the corner of his mouth.

Finally Janoshik, who did not like these extracurricular activities, declared that, try as he may, he could not go on without a glass of beer. The bar upstairs, he said, was open and accessible, and he had watched the barkeeper so often that he thought he could serve as one easily enough. Enzinger and Walters took up the clamor.

Gruber smelled a rat. "So you want to get us drunk, eh?" he sneered. Did Janoshik imagine this was a pleasure trip? The nerve, the impudence!

Janoshik was not discouraged. Soon he would have to steer his guardians into the men's room, so that he could leave the note with the Watzlik address in the medicine chest. It would not hurt if their mood was somewhat lightened.

"No," he told Gruber, "nothing is further from my mind.

Don't I know that the members of the Secret Police are seasoned fighters and that a few glasses of beer won't have the slightest effect on them?"

It was not so much Janoshik's argument as the sour looks of Enzinger and Walters which convinced Gruber. He wanted to keep his men in line.

"All right," he said, "beer it is!" And they trooped up the staircase on which Janoshik, it seemed to him ages ago, had seen Lieutenant Glasenapp for the first and last time in his life.

Up in the bar Janoshik took his place behind the siphons and began to serve—first Gruber, then Enzinger, and then Walters. He served graciously, looking forward to the moment when he would pour himself a glass of the cool drink to wet his parched throat. Gruber let him fill his glass, but just as Janoshik lifted it to his lips, he said, "Oh, no, you don't!" And beat Janoshik over the hand with his whip so that Janoshik dropped the glass, and the beer flowed over the polished bar.

Enzinger and Walters roared. Janoshik bit his lips. His look crossed Gruber's, and the Kid saw the hatred in Janoshik's eyes before he could lower his lids.

"I don't know what is behind the Commissioner's order for your moonlight expedition to the Mánes," said Gruber, "but I will see to it that you won't enjoy it. Another round, come on!"

"Another round!" echoed Enzinger and Walters.

Janoshik obeyed. This Kid, he thought, can't be much over twenty. Look at his baby face, his pink cheeks, his round eyes. How do they make 'em that mean, so young? It must be a major science to instill that much cruelty into a boy's heart in so short a time. Suppressing his own thirst, he placed full glasses before his tormentors. It may not be possible, he speculated, to re-educate them; the ones who are as spoiled as this one will have to be exterminated entirely. He wiped the spilled beer off the bar. How much blood yet, he asked, till this world will be fit to live in?

"Wouldn't you like to drink?" inquired Gruber. "This is good beer!"

"Yes, wouldn't you like to?" cackled Enzinger and Walters. Janoshik raised his brows: "I am thinking."

"Thinking!" parodied Gruber. "Fancy that!"

"I am grateful to you for keeping me from indulging in alcohol. I was almost forgetting that I am here to find the letter of Lieutenant Glasenapp."

"Another beer!" demanded Gruber.

"And now I know it isn't in the storage room."

"What!" exclaimed the three Nazis in unison.

"A friend of mine, a certain Vladislav Peterka, also suffered from lapse of memory. One day his wife told him to bring home some cleaning fluid for her teeth; she had a full set of most beautiful false teeth, you see . . ."

"Do you mean to say," asked Walters who simply could not comprehend that he and Enzinger had gone through all the dust and trouble for nothing, "do you mean to say you made us dig around in that dirt for no good reason?"

"So Vladislav Peterka went about his business, and on his way home he remembered that he was to get something for his wife—but he had forgotten what."

"So you think you fooled us!" cried Enzinger.

"He thought and thought—could it be hairpins? Or potato flour? Insect powder? He was desperate."

"Answer, damn it, answer!"

"So he came home, empty-handed. But the moment he saw his wife open her great big mouth, with her false teeth staring into his face, he knew what he had forgotten—the cleaning fluid!" Janoshik laughed.

"Don't excite yourself," Gruber said darkly to his two men, "we'll fix him yet." And to Janoshik, he said with artificial restraint, "What, if anything, is the connection between the goddamned false teeth and the Glasenapp letter?"

"That's easy enough," explained Janoshik. "When I saw you denying me the drink and beating me over the hand, I was like Peterka looking at his wife's false teeth. I suddenly remembered the other night when you arrested me. You had the same expression. And I remembered that I never entered the storage room after the Lieutenant had given me his letter, and that the letter, therefore, must be in the toilet."

Gruber and his two henchmen were of one desire—to beat the daylights out of this Czech who not only had deprived them of a night's comfort in their quarters but also had added insult to this injury by making them work, and work hard. Gruber, who hadn't done a thing, was especially outraged. Further, he suspected the irony in the Peterka story though he was unable to say exactly wherein the affront lay.

But he restrained himself and his men. The orders he had received from Reinhardt were definite: To see to it that Janoshik found the Glasenapp letter. "There are ways," the Kid hinted darkly, "to get even with you!" Ending the recess he commanded, "We'll search the toilet—forward!"

They went downstairs again. Janoshik felt in his pocket for the small slip of paper, which rustled gently and consolingly. The crucial moment had come.

The sourish smell of the toilet, a mixture of acid and disinfectant, surrounded them.

Janoshik entered each of the four small cubicles and went through the motions of searching; the top of the water container; behind the wooden boxes holding the toilet paper; behind the seats. He wanted to give the impression that he was honestly investigating every possibility.

While he was in the last booth, he put his hand into his pocket and grasped the slip with the Watzlik address, holding it flat in the slightly curved hollow of his hand.

Then he walked to the medicine chest and went through it from top to bottom; into the corner of the lowest level he dropped the slip for the bald-headed longshoreman to find. His excitement had mounted so that he could hear his heart pound against his chest. The three Nazis were watching him; he felt their eyes on his back and asked himself over and over: Do they notice it? They did not stir, they were frightfully still. He was so tense that he almost wished something would happen, if only to break the tautness of his nerves.

He knew he was lost if he showed the slightest sign of the storm raging within him; with superhuman energy he suppressed the trembling of his hands and closed the medicine chest as casually as if the relaying of an underground message right under the eyes of the Gestapo were an everyday routine.

In turning he saw that none of the three guards had caught on to his trick; the expression on their faces showed contempt and arrogant impatience, but not suspicion. Relieved, he went through his shoe-shine box; through the closet which held the towels, soap and brushes—and now there was no place left where he could search. He had to face the wrath of the Gestapo. His work was done.

He stood before the three scornful uniforms, and shrugged his shoulders in a piteous gesture of helplessness.

Gruber, without a word, pushed him aside into the arms of Enzinger and Walters, who took painful hold of him. The Kid, ambitious, his amateur detective instincts aroused, did not trust Janoshik's eyes and efforts, and wanted to check for himself.

There was nothing of interest in either the closet or the shoe-shine box, which he furiously kicked over so that its contents were spewed out all over the floor.

Janoshik was on the verge of collapse. His mind worked furiously. The fate of thousands of men depended on how sharp Gruber's eyes were.

The Kid was approaching the medicine chest.

If only he had drunk more!—Janoshik leaned against Enzinger for support.

Luck! Luck be with me!

Then Gruber, glancing over the bottles, the packages of gauze and cotton, spotted the small piece of paper.

He took it out, held it between his fingers for what seemed to Janoshik an indeterminable length of time, and finally read it.

He furrowed his brow. "What the hell is this?" he asked, his voice showing more curiosity than suspicion. His words fell like thunderstrokes on Janoshik.

"You!" Gruber called Janoshik. "Come here!"

Janoshik felt as though he had no legs. Later, during his hours of punishment, he kept puzzling how he ever managed to approach Gruber, but manage it he did.

Gruber did not know, and never would know the importance of the little slip he was fingering. But he liked to play the inquisitor.

"And what does this mean, please?" he queried importantly.

"This?" asked Janoshik hoarsely. "Oh, this? . . . Nothing, nothing important!"

Gruber slapped Janoshik, hard. The blow made Janoshik's ear ring. "If I ask you something," announced the Kid, "it's important—understand?"

"Yes, sir."

"Well?"

"It's an address."

"I know that much myself. Whose address?"

Janoshik hesitated. "It's the address of a doctor—a doctor for social diseases. We keep it here just in case. Do you need it?"

Janoshik saw the Kid's fist come down again. The blow landed on the same ear, intensifying its ring and pain.

"Czech swine!" shouted Gruber, crumpled the slip and

threw it on the floor. "Enough of this comedy!" Gruber raved. "Take him back to headquarters! We'll show him what it means to play with us!"

Janoshik closed his eyes and breathed deeply.

The crumpled bit of paper was forgotten. It remained on the floor of the Mánes toilet, casual and innocent, and nobody could see how much heartache and suffering, how much planning and hope, how much blood and fate were contained in it.

Enzinger and Walters, urged on by Gruber, rushed their prisoner back to the staff car.

For a fleeting second, Janoshik saw a shadow detach itself from a house door on the other side of the street. It looked faintly familiar. It was tall and awkward, like the bald-headed longshoreman.

CHAPTER 10

JANOSHIK's absence from the cell intensified Dr. Wallerstein's consciousness of him.

Wallerstein had always approached people as actual or potential patients. But in Janoshik he had run up against someone outside of the established categories of his psychiatry. He had been unable to discover in Janoshik even the slightest element of fear.

This was a new experience and could not be explained away easily. His first superficial observation had classified Janoshik as undeveloped in social attitudes—a primitive. Either the man's psyche was calloused, or else it had not been exposed to twentieth-century madness in a like degree to that of the other hostages, himself included.

On reconsideration, Wallerstein dispensed with this theory. Knowing that the more primitive the man the greater and more varied his fears, he could arrive at only one conclusion: Janoshik, instead of being more primitive than himself and the others, was more civilized, having reached a state of inner security, of peace within himself—a peace entirely outside Wallerstein's reach.

The doctor was not at all pleased with his discovery. It

upset everything he had learned. Fear, fear of death, the defense mechanism against fear, the flight from fear, had given him the key to his analyses and diagnoses. Everything was based on fear.

Society made its laws out of fear. Fear of being deprived of possession, property, power. The Nazis killed out of fear of being killed. The very brutality of the political terror now victimizing himself and his cell mates derived from the fact that the Nazis' fear burst all normal bounds.

The war, Wallerstein knew, had been started because certain powerful interests wanted more power. But why did they want more power? Why were they not satisfied with the tremendous possessions they had? Because of fear, excruciating fear that the people might rise and take away some of that power. So the Powerful placed themselves in receivership, making the worst hoodlums in the country their receivers, exerting from them only one promise: To let them keep what they had and prepare the war to gain more—more lands, more industries, more people to exploit. All that was called fascism, and was by no means restricted to Germany. Preissinger was a prize example. He, a Czech, had called in the German hoodlums to protect him from his fear; that his calculation turned out wrong, in no way affected the validity of his motives.

This world, in which people now murdered each other by the millions, was the product of fear. The little man feared for his job, his savings, his food; and in the struggle for these he learned the greater fear: that his life was a vicious circle of trying to feed himself and his family, and that he never, never really achieved living. The end was hysteria.

Men and women feared for their breeding. Since they lived in dread of death, they wanted to make the best and the most of their love. So they scrambled into each other's arms, sowing rotten oats into a rotten ground, ill-fitted to each other, chasing and whoring and drinking. Those who had any balance lost it quickly, but most of them had little to speak of in the first place. The end, again, was hysteria.

Many fled to religion. Life being what it was, the idea that a better and more peaceful world lay beyond this valley of misery seemed consoling. God and heaven were nothing but an escape from the devil Fear; and ultimately the devil got them anyway, because God was persistent in His refusal to meddle with their little affairs, and He left them to their own devices whenever the situation became critical. Hysteria, again.

So they invented new panaceas. Some believed in astrology; others, in their being a selected people—selected to torture or to being tortured which were merely two sides of the same coin. Some believed in leaders and others believed in nothing. The end was hysteria and the waving of symbols, killing and dying.

When the epoch of the dinosaurs was nearing its doom, when unbearable heat and sandstorms were drying up the luscious marshes and meadows on which these beasts had thrived, they, too, embarked on the confused quest for a solution. Senselessly they began their trek over the continents of drought, dying by the wayside, leaving their skeletons for a wondering, shuddering posterity.

Had the same time come for mankind? Had there arisen a special kind of heat, creating a psychosis affecting the multitude? Were we haphazardly rushing around, using our planes, our radios, our machines, our brains only to annihilate each other? How far had we gone on the trek, destroying ourselves by the wayside? What right do we have to complain of a Hitler who is only the most terrible product of our panic?

And I myself, how ridiculous I am. I see the disease, and am unable to heal it. What kind of doctors are we who can heal, partially perhaps, the one or other person, but not the billions of men and women who may not even be conscious of their ailment? I am full of fear myself. Fear of death. All my living thoughts circle around this fear. I write down my observations in the hope that somebody, sometime, may read them and transmit them, absorbing thereby a particle of the being I was, rendering me immortal. How little this is! How modest I have become—and even this modest glory, this tiny immortality is probably an illusion created by my own fear of death, of nothingness.

That is why I can't comprehend a Janoshik. I *know* what he believes in: himself. He has faith in himself as part of a race that makes sense, as a cell in a world the existence of which, even for the future, *I* must doubt. My experience makes me disbelieve in people, and therefore in their ability to build something new, something better out of the ruins which they now produce in such extravagant fashion.

But Janoshik exists, nevertheless, he exists as that unbelievable mammal existed in the dying world of the dinosaurs. With their dust-caked little brains and their sand-filled, inflamed eyes, those giants must have thought that the lively, healthy thing hopping about where they were perishing, was nothing but a vision. They could not understand it—as I cannot comprehend a Janoshik. I can only bow my head in humility and admiration, before the advance guard of a new, fearless world.

His existence, of course, cancels out mine; the two of us preclude each other. I shall die together with my executioners; but he may have a chance to survive and really become immortal.

Having thought that far, Dr. Wallerstein, with an angry motion of his hand, tried to eliminate the whole complex from his mind. From sitting in judgment over the world he had ended up by indicting himself—an impossible procedure.

He was almost grateful when his train of thought was interrupted by the noisy opening of the cell door. The same

238

loud-mouthed, heavy-voiced guards, who previously had come for Janoshik and Prokosch, now returned.

The three remaining hostages lined up before their cots and stood at attention. Preissinger's as well as Lobkowitz's face showed their agitation—who next would walk the path the end of which none could foresee?

"Which of you is Lev Preissinger?" snarled the guard with the silver stars on his collar.

Now that the time had come which Preissinger had anticipated, the time when he'd be arraigned face to face with the Gestapo official in authority, his defiant nerve, his self-reliance suddenly left him. He was frightened. The high and mighty words he had used so prodigiously before his cell mates, now failed to carry him. He paled and his eyes moved furtively, as if seeking help.

But the guard was not in a mood to dally. "Preissinger!" he shouted. For the Director-General of the Bohemian-Moravian Coal Syndicate, there was nothing to do but to step forward and to accept whatever was to come.

The other guard grabbed Preissinger's arm hard and shoved him out of the cell. No "Good-bys" and "Good lucks" followed him. Wallerstein had little interest in Preissinger's good or bad luck once he left the cell and so ceased to be an object of medical observation. And Lobkowitz' mind was preoccupied with the question of whether the man who was Coal would actually succeed in what he had so confidently predicted: extricate himself from the fangs of the Nazis because he was rich and powerful and a traitor to his people.

Reinhardt's reception of Preissinger immediately dispelled the latter's despondency and fear. The Commissioner felt decidedly jovial after proving to his own satisfaction that Prokosch's confession to the murder of Glasenapp was nothing but a desperate and childish lie. Preissinger profited by this; and when he saw the Commissioner rise, and heard the courteous greeting, "How do you do, Mr. Preissinger?" he concluded at once that his days of suffering were over, and that this friendly official was about to make profuse apologies in the name of the German Government, prior to releasing him.

Reinhardt beckoned Moenkeberg to bring a chair for Preissinger. Moenkeberg moved it from the wall to a place before the desk which the Commissioner indicated. Preissinger, all dignity, sat down, his knees spread apart, his stomach resting on his thighs.

Suddenly Reinhardt trained the sharp spotlight on the Director-General. The shock of the blinding glare made Preissinger feel like a criminal on line-up; but he quickly dispensed with this impression. He was inclined to forgive the Commissioner. The police are like that, he made himself think, blinking and trying to protect his smarting eyes.

"My name is Reinhardt," began the Commissioner, leaning over his desk to get a close look at Preissinger. He never before had seen the man who was the centerpiece in his cabal; the king-pin for the sake of whose possessions the suicide Glasenapp had to be murdered, hostages had to be manufactured and killed, charming girl students pursued, nights spent in exhausting interrogations...

Gazing at Preissinger's apoplectic face with the little vein network of arteriosclerosis showing sharply under the light, at his stubby gray hair, his big fleshy ears and his hard chin, the Commissioner really saw a chess board on which he was playing—and winning—a game with most complicated moves; a game which he relished because it was fascinatingly played with human pieces, and with himself, Reinhardt, determining the rules.

Preissinger coughed modestly to compel Reinhardt's attention. "The arrest and the abuse I received from your men, and my involuntary stay in the basement cell of your headquarters, Herr Reinhardt, were not exactly pleasant. I hope—"

"I know," interrupted Reinhardt, "there is always room for improvement. And you must understand the Gestapo has so many duties, especially since our work is all too often gravely impeded by your countrymen, that it becomes difficult to give everybody the individual attention he deserves."

"I understand," confirmed Preissinger with a conciliatory smile. "I quite understand." Then he paused expectantly. He hoped that Reinhardt would now give the momentous word setting him free. But when the Commissioner made no move to talk, Preissinger continued: "Nevertheless, for a man of my background, influence and position, it was a humiliating experience."

"No doubt," smiled Reinhardt. "I hope you made the best of it. Even our Führer, as you know, was once detained in prison. There, he wrote a great book which you certainly have read."

Preissinger had not. But he found it politic to reply that the book had given him many moments of serious reflection and of uplifting thought.

The Commissioner, Preissinger observed, devoted regrettably little attention to the tribute paid to his Führer's literary product; he seemed absorbed in the study of a little dagger engraved with the SS initials of the Elite Guard. He held the dagger so that the light was reflected from its steel blade. Suddenly he shot a most unexpected question at Preissinger: "When did you last see Lieutenant Glasenapp?"

Preissinger, surprised, stuttered: "Why—what do you mean —last?"

"Please answer concisely and truthfully!"

"You don't think I have anything to do with this crime?" protested Preissinger.

"When did you see him last?"

"I didn't see him at all!—that is, perhaps—I may have seen

him—but how do I know? I don't even know what this Lieutenant looked like; there were a number of German officers at the bar, I don't remember how many; I never looked at their faces. I didn't observe what they did or where they went. I have my own troubles, I assure you. I was most surprised and most annoyed when your men took it into their heads to arrest me in connection with this matter. And I must ask you—"

"My dear Mr. Preissinger!" Reinhardt raised his hands appeasingly. "You seem to labor under a misapprehension, really! In this office, in this building—and if I may say, in this country—it is I who does the asking, not you!"

Preissinger rose, enraged. But in rising he noticed his bedraggled, wrinkled pants, the gray rims on the cuffs of his once impeccable shirt, his mud-spattered shoes; he felt his dirt and his sweat and the stubble of his beard. "Oh my God!" he said aloud, and to himself: What am I doing? I am in the hands of this man, I am an old prisoner like any other old prisoner. As long as I am here, I must not let myself go!

He sat down again, grateful that he was allowed to sit.

"I beg your pardon," he pleaded meekly. "I am not used to this—this—"

"Treatment?" continued Reinhardt.

"No—oh, no! That's nothing." He laughed, as a dog would laugh, if it could, after having received a vicious kick from its master. "Permit me, though, to ask—there must have been inquiries on my behalf from my associates in the Bohemian-Moravian Coal Syndicate? I am the Director-General of the Syndicate, and after all, I can't just disappear without a word, without a trace, without people instituting a search!"

Reinhardt picked up his dagger again. "As regards that, you can rest assured that your colleagues and your employees have shown the most touching loyalty. We have received a host of inquiries, visits, intercessions. Even President Hacha, who, I am glad to hear, is a personal friend of yours, has begged an audience with Protector Heydrich and has asked for your release."

"Ah, I am glad!" sighed Preissinger. He was not lost, not forgotten! They had set the machinery in motion, and this petty Gestapo officer was merely one of those long-winded fellows who waste so much precious time before coming to the point. "Of course," Preissinger hastened to assure, "I shall be only too glad if I can be of assistance in the solution of this heinous crime, the murder of Lieutenant Glasenapp."

"I expected no different attitude from you," Reinhardt said with a slight bow.

"And now—will you give me the necessary papers—?"

Reinhardt put his dagger back on the desk. In the silence, the slight thump sounded terribly heavy.

He raised his eyebrows in apparent amazement. "What papers?"

"For my release!"

The Commissioner frowned as if he did not understand at all.

"Don't you have to issue some papers so that I can pass the guards—you know—?" Preissinger's voice sank to a desperate whisper; finally he had no voice at all.

Reinhardt laughed, loud and prolonged. He was enjoying himself greatly. He slapped his hand first on his own, then on Moenkeberg's solid thigh. Moenkeberg, upon being slapped, began to cackle too.

Reinhardt rarely laughed that way—he was not the laughing type. He laughed because he knew it would break Preissinger. He had recognized from the first that Preissinger expected to be set free; outside of learning from the industrialist that there was nothing he knew of Glasenapp's end, Reinhardt had only played with him. He did not ask himself why he wanted to break Preissinger; it was not necessary for his plan. But it tickled him to see the man squirm, see him lower his bull's head in total misery, see his knotty fingers move convulsively.

Reinhardt thought he had laughed sufficiently. With a dainty handkerchief retrieved from his inner breast pocket, he wiped the perspiration off his forehead.

"Did you actually think," he said with a show of astonishment, "did you think we'd let you free? Merely because you're Lev Preissinger, Director-General of the Bohemian-Moravian Coal Syndicate?

"My dear sir—how you misunderstand us National Socialists!

"We are a movement of the people, our Führer is a man of the people! What kind of socialism is it in which only the poor get shot, eh? What kind of people's justice in which a man escapes his sentence because he is a millionaire? What would your own countrymen, whom we are trying to educate to collaborate with us, say if we took every Karel, Johan or Peter hostage, but made an exception of Lev Preissinger?"

Preissinger let the storm of reproaching questions break over his bent head. He sat on his chair, stricken. He felt empty, absolutely empty. Before, he had been high in hope and low in desperation, he had been swinging from one extreme to the other. Now the rope which held the swing had broken, and he was falling and falling.

"Exceptions!" hammered Reinhardt. "Our brave soldiers are dying at the front, fighting against bloody bolshevism. We Germans, we march into this country, to save it and to save men like you—and you want us to make an exception with your life! Wherein is it different from the life of the lowliest Pomeranian infantry man? I ask you!"

Preissinger had no answer.

"If we let you go our whole system would break down! We arrest hostages to have some means of retribution against those of your compatriots who refuse to accept our protection."

"But I collaborated with you!" pleaded Preissinger. "I increased my coal production so as to fulfill the war orders of your Government. I did my best to support you, to help you!"

"I know! I know!" Reinhardt smiled regretfully. "You don't appreciate the terrible situation *we* are in. If we release you, those *Untermenschen* will say: Hostages, ha ha—the Nazis don't mean it anyway. Look at Preissinger—they let him go scot free!

"This is a matter of principle, and we are as much the prisoners of our principles as you, my dear Mr. Preissinger."

Reinhardt's mention of principles stopped Preissinger's sensation of falling into endless space, and brought him back to the world of sober reasoning. "Principles" he knew. Whenever somebody wanted him to pay a higher price, the question of principles was thrown into the negotiation. There were principles of patriotism which were worth approximately ten per cent. Principles of business practice cost anywhere from fifteen to twenty per cent, and principles of morale were, at most, twenty-five per cent. He did not know the Commissioner's scale of principles; but he recognized the outstretched hand, palm upward, ready to be smeared.

"Prisoners of our principles—" he said. "How true, how very true! I'd feel much freer if you dismissed your secretary, Herr Reinhardt, for the time being..."

"Moenkeberg? Moenkeberg is a very trustworthy man, as silent as a tombstone."

Preissinger squirmed. It might offend Reinhardt if he attempted to bribe him before his subaltern. Or was Reinhardt so naïve that he laid himself open to possible later blackmail by this Moenkeberg fellow?

"It's personal, concerning only you and me—don't you see?"

"Ah," smiled Reinhardt, "I get you. Moenkeberg, you can go. I shall call you when you are needed." Moenkeberg marched off, and Preissinger, having made sure that the door was closed, moved his chair forward and leaned over the Commissioner's desk.

"You're on the spot, Commissioner," he began in a confidential whisper, "I appreciate that. It's bad publicity for you if you let me go. Your career, your principles, mean a lot to you, I understand that. But I think the matter could be arranged. I'm a businessman, and I have dabbled in politics, so I know how these things are. If you released me, I'd have to disappear for a while—nothing easier than that. I've worked pretty hard, and these last days have not improved my health. I need a rest cure. I could go to Baden-Baden, or to Switzerland, wherever you suggest, and under a different name—just take it easy and wait my turn. What do you say, Commissioner, what do you want me to do for you, in return for this little favor?"

Reinhardt did not answer. He was curious to learn how much Preissinger thought his life was worth. He knew that this play of give and take had become quite common in Germany and the occupied regions. He knew the tables compiled by industrious agents, in which the various Governors, *Gauleiters*, military commanders and their amounts were listed. Copies of such lists were in his files. It was a convenient means of holding the whip hand over the bribe-takers, and a certain percentage of that income went, in due course, to the leading Gestapo officials, for their bank accounts in Switzerland and Sweden, real estate, precious stones, stamp collections...permanent values.

Preissinger was encouraged by Reinhardt's expectant silence. "A million Kronen?" he offered tentatively.

Reinhardt smiled.

"Five million?

"Ten million?

246

"I don't have much ready cash—I'll have to float some of my assets if you want more; but that will take a little time..."

Reinhardt again picked up the dagger and twirled it pensively.

"I can see," probed Preissinger, "that with the present uncertain monetary situation, you may, perhaps, not be so much interested in cash. You're a clever man, Commissioner. But don't expect too much. My properties, as such, are less than you'd think. I control the Coal Syndicate because I control the strategic shares in the strategic holding companies. Nevertheless, there is a little coal mine, a pearl, I tell you, a pearl among coal mines, near Moravská Ostrava—I could sign that over to you."

He paused.

"Why don't you answer, Commissioner?" he asked nervously.

The twirling of the dagger stopped. "How do you expect me to manage a coal mine from my desk at Gestapo headquarters?"

"That's right," conceded Preissinger. "I did not think of that. Though, some time, after the war you may want to go into this business.... All right then, it'll have to be stock, I suppose. Common stock will bring you more returns, but preferred stock gives you a better chance to manipulate and make money. I'll be glad to advise you ..."

Reinhardt grew impatient. "You value your life very little, don't you? From what you say, I infer that you have it in mind to get free by sacrificing *part* of what you own. How ridiculous! When you're dead, you own nothing at all!"

"You want to rob me!" shouted Preissinger. "Me, who is responsible for your easy conquest of this country; me, who has done more for your Führer's New Order than any ten dozen Gestapo *Herren* taken together! Is there no gratitude? No recognition of merit?"

"No. And I suggest you lower your voice. It is against the law to buy a German official."

"How much do you want?" whined Preissinger, outraged over so much shamelessness.

"Everything."

"Everything...?" Preissinger's mouth fell open. The veins of his throat thumped with the pressure of his ferment. He rose with effort and stood before Reinhardt, more stoop-shouldered than ever. His fear of poverty already made him look like a beggar, and his pitifully broken voice was like that of the blind man at the corner of Wenceslas Place, quavering and miserable. "Why? Why? And what am I to live on? Have you no pity, no heart? Are you human or stone? I have obligations, a wife, family, household..."

Reinhardt rose too. He felt great and important, he was Justice and Fate, mightier than the money changers and property owners, the dancers around the golden calf. Money was nothing. Power was all. He felt religious, as he had felt when he watched the giant march of endless Party members at Nuremberg, rows upon rows of splendid fellows, in the great arena before the Führer, with their standards and glistening helmets, before the streaming red banners with the symbol of the Swastika. For this fleeting moment, scotching the louse Preissinger, he passionately believed in the greatness of the idea, in National Socialism!

"And your life?" he asked sternly.

Preissinger closed his eyes. His body swayed. "Take everything," he croaked, "take it! Take it! I want to live!"

"So!" said Reinhardt. "It seems that finally you're able to talk in a realistic manner. I'm glad you have come that far! Imagine the time you and I could have saved. I wonder, though, whether you can rouse yourself to think your situation through to its logical end. I'm a great friend of logic. That's why I joined the police."

248

"Not yet enough?" Preissinger laughed insanely. "Do you want the gold inlay of my teeth, a pound of my flesh?"

"I want you to think, my dear Mr. Preissinger. Think! You offer us all your possessions in return for your life. What kind of offer is that? Are you in a position to offer anything?

"Don't you see that we will get whatever we want the moment you are dead?"

Lev Preissinger felt a hand reach for his brain and dig its fingers into the soft matter. It was a pain, throbbing and agonizing, which he hoped would kill him then and there. But, on the contrary, he seemed to live more intensely, see every detail, hear the slightest noise, distinguish sharply the devilish face which stared back at him from the dark background of the shadowed wall, the silver buttons on his tormentor's uniform, the belt with its engraved buckle—an etching of gruesome translucence.

Live! I must live! he thought. Reinhardt was death, black death with silver buttons. Lev Preissinger, in his pain, grasped for life. Hang on to life, with every nerve, with your teeth, your fingernails!

And with the clarity that comes in the moment of dying, Lev Preissinger saw his salvation. He remembered Wallerstein, and Wallerstein's sneering words: *Preissinger, I assure you, would denounce anybody to regain his precious life.* ... Yes, I would! By God, I would! If I am no hostage they can't kill me! That's as clear as the devil's face staring at me.

His pain eased. He snickered to himself. How foolish to despair! Lev Preissinger, the man of a thousand ideas, of a thousand schemes, who had built an empire of Coal, a fortress of power—giving up hope and himself before an inferior policeman! If he had learned anything in his years of business, and business had been an obsession with him, it was this wisdom: There is always an escape, always a last resort, always a hidden ace. Find it, play it cleverly, at the strategic point—and you must come out on top.

Reinhardt noticed Preissinger's recovery with surprise. He saw him sit down again, cross his legs, and adopt the position of a man at ease with himself and the world. The Commissioner, against his will, began to respect Preissinger, and to understand why the industrialist had reached the height of wealth and power of which he now was to be deprived.

Preissinger rapidly considered his candidates. He must make a choice probable from the viewpoint of character as well as of circumstance. There was only one man who fit all the specifications, and who, in addition, enjoyed Preissinger's enmity.

"Janoshik!" said Preissinger. "Janoshik killed Lieutenant Glasenapp. He admitted that much in the cell. To be quite frank I would have preferred to be released without having to inform you of this, Herr Reinhardt. However, since you blocked any other way out, I must tell you the truth. Here is your murderer. From this moment on I cease to be your hostage, and I expect you to do your duty."

The esteem which Reinhardt bore for Preissinger now approached the degree of admiration. The Commissioner, no mediocre soul himself, appreciated a thorough scoundrel who stuck to his guns.

"Never say die, eh, Mr. Preissinger?"

Reinhardt did not believe a word of Preissinger's denunciation. But he thought further. What reasons had Preissinger to pick on Janoshik? Janoshik had impressed the Commissioner as a naïve nitwit, not a potential killer. Yet Preissinger, who had had several days in which to observe Janoshik, and who in denouncing anybody had to consider the credibility of his story, had chosen the harmless keeper of the toilet. Reinhardt began to worry about Janoshik who had not yet returned from the Mánes.

He picked up his telephone and gave a few short orders which were unintelligible to Preissinger. Then he turned to the Director-General: "How will you prove your accusation? If I should question Janoshik, he is sure to deny it."

"Of course!" admitted Preissinger. "And the men in my cell will probably support him. It'll be my word against his. But let me warn you—this Janoshik is not as stupid as he acts. He is sly. He uses his moronic appearance to hide his real thoughts and activities. Among us Czechs, this type of person appears frequently. Don't be taken in by him!"

"I won't," said the Commissioner firmly, though he was not at all as sure of himself as he appeared to be. Was it possible that Reinhardt, with all his experience and ruthless cleverness, had been hoodwinked by Janoshik? But for what purpose?

No, he decided. Preissinger was not telling the truth. The Director-General was building up Janoshik as a dangerous individual only to bolster his denunciation.

"Men like Janoshik," continued Preissinger, "hate authority, yours and mine. They're against the established order and try to undermine it. If I remember rightly, Janoshik appeared in the bar to clean up *after* Glasenapp had gone to the toilet. There must have been sufficient time and opportunity to kill the Lieutenant, don't you think so?"

Preissinger felt that he had, at least, succeeded in sowing the seed of doubt which would make the Commissioner reconsider his decisions. "And furthermore..."

Preissinger stopped, interrupted by the sound of dragging steps behind his back. In the intensity of his argument, he had missed the opening of the door. He turned around.

Moenkeberg was ushering in a man whose every move seemed concentrated pain. Something about him was vaguely familiar. Then, in a horrified flash of recognition, Preissinger realized that the stranger was Prokosch.

The actor never had been a picture of health, and Preissinger knew that the days in the cell and the destructive clash with young Lobkowitz had affected Prokosch more than any of the other prisoners.

Yet this was Prokosch's ghost staring at him, not possibly the actor in flesh and blood!

"What—what happened to you?" stammered Preissinger.

Prokosch was barely able to stand; the faithful Moenkeberg supported him. Preissinger wanted to get up and offer his chair to the actor, but he could not move.

Reinhardt regarded this ruin of a man with utmost placidity. He gave his two hostages time to view each other. Then he asked Prokosch: "Have you reconsidered your story?"

Prokosch spoke with difficulty. First his lips moved inaudibly. Only after several efforts was he able to make a terribly strange and tired voice speak:

"I killed Glasenapp."

He freed himself from Moenkeberg's arms, and with faltering steps he staggered to Reinhardt's desk and repeated:

"I killed Glasenapp!"

"All right! All right!" said Reinhardt. "I heard you!" He turned to Preissinger, and his face was completely disinterested: "And now, sir, will you please repeat your statement?"

Preissinger was bewildered. He was relieved at Prokosch's confession which meant that he would be released. He was upset because he imagined the means by which Reinhardt had wrung the confession from the actor. He was disturbed because this confession contradicted his denunciation of Janoshik, and he saw all his chances endangered. He was angry because Reinhardt must have known of Prokosch's confession all along, and had put him, Preissinger, in the position of making a fool of himself.

"Well, Commissioner," he laughed awkwardly, "you see that I am innocent."

"I see nothing of the sort," retorted Reinhardt with bitter scorn. "Repeat the statement you made before, please!"

"But you don't want me—!"

"Better do it voluntarily," warned Reinhardt.

Preissinger dared not look at Prokosch. He whispered something.

"Louder!" urged Reinhardt.

"Janoshik killed Glasenapp!" Preissinger slumped forward in his chair. He looked at his mud-spattered shoes. He felt miserable and pitied himself as a victim of the cruel game of the Gestapo.

"You lie!" said Prokosch with deadly voice. "You lie!"

Preissinger's misery changed to cold fury. He raged not so much at Reinhardt, who had engineered the confrontation, as at Prokosch who had spoiled everything. "You lie yourself!" he shouted. "This dirty Janoshik is the murderer, and you know it! This is a conspiracy! A lying, malicious conspiracy against me! Believe me, Commissioner, this Janoshik—"

Reinhardt rose. Erect with triumph, he seemed taller than he was. He smiled.

"Quiet, please, gentlemen. Quiet. It seems to me that both of you are lying. You have your reasons for doing this, no doubt. Your reasons are of little interest to me. The facts are sufficient. I want you to know that we of the Secret State Police, to whom the security and the welfare of this country are entrusted, cannot tolerate this frivolous play with the truth. I will have to punish you both, you understand that, don't you?"

The door was torn open. He stopped.

Janoshik, disheveled, was thrust into the room by Enzinger and Walters.

Gruber made his way to the desk, stood at attention, saluted.

"Beg to report, sir," he said, "we have returned from our search."

"Hand me the letter!"

"Beg to report, sir, no such letter was found. With your permission, I believe the whole thing was a hoax. No letter of Glasenapp existed."

"So!" cracked Reinhardt. He placed his hands on his hips, and the cloth of his uniform stretched itself dangerously tight over his chest. Balancing himself on the balls of his feet, he moved up and down. "Another liar!" he bellowed. "What do you think this is? Fools' paradise? Kindergarten? Ah, you've seen nothing yet, nothing!

"Moenkeberg! Gruber! Take those three—to the caskets! And make it tough on them! Tough! I said—Tough!"

He watched them being marched off—Prokosch dangling on Moenkeberg's arm, Janoshik pushed hard by Enzinger and Walters, and Preissinger whose hesitant steps were sped by Gruber's short but expressive German oaths.

Then the Commissioner sat down. Suddenly he realized how tired he was. He had been driving himself for almost twenty-four hours.

He looked out of the window. A tender gray stole down the street. Morning had arrived, beclouded and listlessly.

The hostages had only one more day to live. He was glad of it.

CHAPTER 11

Milada left Breda's house refreshed and strengthened. Within her she carried, a tender secret, the memory of the palpitating sensation the man, her man, had given her. A warmth, flooding her with delight, made her close her eyes and tremble. Breda's love, like a liberating thunderstorm, had cleared her world from its dark and threatening mirages; everything was lustrous and light and serene. Whatever might happen to her, she could face with equanimity; she had ceased to be alone.

Pan Kratochvil, seeing her come out of the house and walk toward the streetcar line with youthful, swinging steps, was also of good cheer. A real huntsman—and that he was—does not hate his quarry. Rather, he has toward it a feeling of perverted affection, as if he had created the nimble animal he is about to kill. The kill itself becomes unimportant. The hunt—the planning, the waiting, the closing in, the jockeying for position—affords the thrill.

The streets were full of hurrying people. But their steps were heavy. They went to jobs they detested, because the jobs meant work for the oppressor, nerve-sapping hours without relief. They went to shops to stand in line and wait, wait for the little food of poor quality which was to be doled out in insufficient rations. They went to offices to sit around in anterooms, hoping to be received by arrogant officials who only half listened to their pleadings, pleadings for fathers and husbands and brothers—some kidnaped to Germany to slave in the conqueror's plants, some arrested and dragged to concentration camps and prisons, others forcibly inducted into the German Army to dig trenches and build concrete fortifications on the Eastern Front and in the Balkans. The New Order was the disorganization of human relations, a criss-cross migration of individuals who were shuttled east, west, north, south. The old ties were being torn, the old roots uprooted to meet the grotesque needs of further attacks which the conqueror planned, or to assuage the disquieting fears which deprived him of the enjoyment of his victories.

Kratochvil hid easily among the crowd. He boarded the trailer of the streetcar on which Milada rode. Pressed in by the people on the crowded platform, he cleverly evaded the conductor collecting fares, using the methods he knew so well from the time when he had been on the other side of the fence. On his expense account, of course, the fare would appear as "paid."

Thus he was taken to the Kolben Daněk Works. Following Milada through the big entrance door, he was stopped by the guard.

"Identification, mister?"

Kratochvil fumbled through his pockets and brought out a much stamped document, carefully enclosed in a cellophane folder, which he pushed under the guard's nose.

"Take me to your commanding officer!" demanded Kratochvil.

The guard, recognizing the seal of the Secret State Police, became flustered and servile. "Right away, sir! I beg your pardon, sir!" He led Kratochvil to a small one-story house, before which a bored soldier with fixed bayonet marched up and down.

Inside the house, Kratochvil was received by an elderly German lieutenant who had been lounging on a couch, his stockinged feet on a pillow. Lieutenant Schinklein was reading the morning edition of the *Prager Deutsche Zeitung*. He looked up, recognized that the visitor was a mere civilian, and continued his study of the paper.

"Good morning," said Kratochvil. "Are you in charge here?"

Schinklein wiggled his toes. Then he put two fingers of his free hand under his collar and began to scratch his neck with evident pleasure.

"What do you want?" he grunted.

"There is a certain Milada Markova working here," explained Kratochvil carefully.

"What business is that of yours?" said the Lieutenant, again concentrating on his newspaper. He turned over a new page. "Thousands of people work here, all with names that nobody can understand and pronounce. It's a bother. And who let you in here anyway?"

"I don't like your attitude," announced Kratochvil.

Schinklein was jolted. "What?" he said and sat up. "You don't like—that's splendid! That's a new one on me!" He approached Kratochvil with the waddle of a flatfooted man in socks. He looked like a tobacconist on masquerade. "I'll have you know, you Czech louse, that I'm an officer of the German Army..."

Kratochvil flashed his document.

Lieutenant Schinklein gave it one glance and uttered a surprised "Oh!" He dropped his paper and buttoned his uniform hurriedly. He searched for his shoes, but was unable to find them. He bent down to fish for them under the couch, emitting from this uncomfortable position, inarticulate noises of embarrassment.

Finally, he was in shape to pay his respects to the agent.

The two gentlemen sat down to business. Kratochvil who, thanks to his job, had achieved social and racial equality with the scion of the *Herrenvolk,* explained carefully that he was delegated by Commissioner Reinhardt to keep a watchful eye on the girl he had mentioned, Milada Markova. Had the Lieutenant any suggestions as to the least obtrusive way to perform this duty?

The Lieutenant, flattered by so much confidence, thought long and hard and came up with a plan of which Kratochvil approved heartily. Overalls and a wrench would transform Kratochvil into a workman—but, pinned to the overall would be a supervisor's badge. The badge would enable him to stand around wherever he deemed necessary, he could observe Milada closely or from afar, whatever was more convenient, and he could check on the people with whom she talked, and in general have the run of the house. Satisfactory?

Quite so, quite so. A firm handshake gave testimony to their mutual pleasure at having met each other. A check-up in the files showed that Milada was working in the shell cap department. Kratochvil was advised as to the nearest way to this department, and then proceeded to don his proletarian attire. Lifting his gray hat courteously, he bade good-by to Lieutenant Schinklein who, satisfied with this morning's work, was all smiles and amiability.

To Kratochvil the Kolbenka was a new and amazing world. Since his existence was purely a parasitic one, he was accustomed to consider people outside of their relation as social beings. Here he saw them at work, busy as beavers, either running around with hurried steps, fulfilling various errands; or standing glued to their machines, their limbs performing the same motion in monotonous repetition. He felt subdued and proud at once. The giant organization and its power which ordered all those little beavers to spend themselves filled him with awe; on the other hand he was proud because he, Kratochvil, was a necessary part and adjunct of the organization, contributing his bit to keep the beavers where they were. Kratochvil was the element of order. In his eyes he gained tremendously in social significance.

He sauntered through the wide halls of the Kolbenka, his gray velour hat from which he did not want to part in sinister contrast to the patched overalls covering his scrawny body.

In the shell cap department he saw the endless stream of the conveyor belt carrying rows upon rows of unfinished shells through the length of the room. The skylights were painted black so that work could go on during air raid alarms; the gloomy artificial light spread by tired bulbs gave the pale faces of the workers deep shadows which emphasized the more their pallor. Women stood at short intervals behind the belt, young women, middle-aged, and old, but all with the same look of concentrated fatigue. Behind the women the foremen busied themselves, occasionally checking on one or the other shell, but mostly driving the women with short, sharp orders.

There was Milada, her hair hidden under a tight blue cloth. Her face, though she could not have worked long, was already perspired and grimy. Kratochvil leaned against a pillar in easy comfort, pushed back his hat and stared at the girl. After a short while Milada became conscious that she was being observed and looked up. She instantly recognized her tramp of yesterday, and dropped the shell cap she was holding. Inexorably the conveyor belt moved forward, as she remained stupefied.

"Hey, you!" shouted one of the foremen. "What do you think you're doing? Wastage! Always wastage! Goddamned women—whore around all night and sleep in the day! Here! Catch up! Catch up!"

With mechanical obedience, Milada turned back to her work. Her hands flew, trying to make up for her loss. But her shells had gone too far. The attempts of several of the others to help her threw the whole row of women into disorder. The foremen had to stop the belt.

"Sabotage!" one of them yelled. "Every hour that happens!"

A woman with a dark voice grumbled, "Why don't you reduce the speed? Nobody can work that way."

"Who said that?"

No answer.

"I'll call the guards and have all of you arrested!"

"Yeah—why don't you?" said the dark voice. "You can run your machines yourself, maybe?"

But at that moment the conveyor belt started again, order was restored; only the purring of the belt and the clanging of the metal parts striking against each other were heard.

Through the room passed Breda the tool-maker. He walked along the conveyor belt. Nearing Milada, he stopped for a moment, bent down and adjusted a screw; when he righted himself he looked at her and greeted her with a slight nod.

He noticed that she was disturbed and raised his brows questioningly. Imperceptibly she moved her head in the direction of Kratochvil. Breda did not indicate in any way that he had taken cognizance of her gesture. He walked on, picked up a conversation with one of the foremen, and only then, as if by chance, did he glance over at the pillar where Kratochvil waited, observing everything.

Breda raised his hand in friendly greeting. Kratochvil, surprised, lifted his gray hat. "I didn't know you worked here!" shouted Breda over the din of work.

Kratochvil pointed at his badge. "Supervisor!" he shouted back.

"Good luck!" came from Breda.

"What?"

"Good luck!" he repeated.

Breda left. Kratochvil's spirits slumped; the exchange of greetings suddenly dispelled his cheerful mood. He felt nervous and uncomfortable, and decided a change of scenery would do him good. Milada could not leave her post at the conveyor belt until lunch time. He could take it easy and phone in a report to headquarters.

But he got lost in the maze of complex buildings. Partly, it was his own fault; the remarkable encounter with the man who had almost choked him during the night, so occupied his mind that he took the nearest exit from the shell cap department instead of finding the door through which he had entered it, and walked on without regard for the direction of his steps. With a start he realized he had lost his bearings.

He asked a worker the quickest way to the guard house. The answer he received was courteous but complicated. He took the indicated route, crossed a courtyard and found he was lost again. The man he now questioned showed him a different way—right, left, around this building, then straight ahead. Kratochvil started to sweat profusely.

The walls of the shops looked bleak and forbidding, their dust blind windows seemed to say: We don't see you, we don't want you, you don't belong. He hurried. He crossed narrow-gauge rails and was frightened by a locomotive which drove past from behind him with extraordinary speed. Then another locomotive—or was it the same—came at him on the other track, tooting angrily, and he had to jump.

He ran with stumbling steps, as if pursued. His breath came hard and fast. He thought he heard somebody behind him and turned, but there was no one. The deep disquieting noises of machines at work, grinding, stamping, rolling, hammering, hemmed him in. I am caught! he quavered. Caught! Caught!

There was an open door! He fled through it and found himself in the foundry. It was a giant hall, its walls and roof supported by steel girders. Under the roof was a network of rails along which cranes glided carrying steel bars, wheels, barrels of heavy caliber guns and mortars, silently and with ghostlike efficiency.

Few men were around. They looked like dwarfs who had strayed into the land of giants; they seemed senseless and helpless, unnecessary in this empire of iron superhands with hooks for fingers, roller bearings for joints, and steel cables for muscles.

Kratochvil felt himself utterly small and lost. Hesitatingly he walked toward the other end of the hall, where the big compressed air hammers were rising and falling, crushing and crunching whatever was beneath them.

Again he had the feeling of being pursued. Again he turned and saw nobody. But then, something in him made him jerk up his head, and he saw—saw one of the cranes gliding along directly above him. There was nothing extraordinary in that, it was above him, so what? He stopped. The crane stopped. He started on his way, the crane moved too. He went to the right as soon as he could discern an opening between towering machines—the carriages of the crane above him turned right, too. What was it, a game? Who directed those cranes? He could see nobody; those machines seemed to go by themselves, remorselessly, cold and heavy. Kratochvil ran. The crane increased its speed—faster, faster. It was a race for his life, Kratochvil knew it. The machines were after him, the machines! He stumbled, his knees gave, he pulled himself up in desperate fear, spittle on his lips, his eyes burning.

Suddenly he heard somebody shout, "Watch out!"

He looked up—

The terrible cry which was forming in him never was uttered. Pan Kratochvil was smashed under tons of steel. Above him stood the crane, its fangs open, quiet and innocent.

The gray velour hat, Kratochvil's pride, lay beside his tomb of steel, as the helmet of a Nazi lies on his grave.

Work in the foundry stopped. Men hurried to the scene of the accident, stretcher bearers, a Works doctor, the foreman of the foundry.

One of the workers examined the hat.

"Who was he anyway?" he asked. "None of our men wear such hats at work!"

"We'll have to raise all this stuff before you can get at him," said another to the stretcher bearers. "Won't be much left of him, I guess."

"How did it happen?" inquired the doctor.

"I don't know. Short circuit, perhaps."

"But the lamps are burning!" said the doctor.

"There can be a short circuit in just one of the carriages. We don't have enough forces to check and repair. It's a miracle that this doesn't occur every day."

"All right! All right! Back to your places!"

The men returned to their jobs, the cranes resumed their movement, the hammers picked up where they had left off, and everything was humming and purring.

From the roof, the fangs of the crane were lowered. The load of steel was lifted as if it were so many matches.

The doctor, who watched the procedure, noted that the crane seemed to be in perfect order again. He wondered—but decided to say nothing. Better not to get involved in these affairs, times were dangerous. And what concern was it of his? A short circuit. What did he know of things electrical?

Averting his eyes, he directed the stretcher bearers to collect the flat, blood-smeared remains of Pan Kratochvil. Then he took the orphaned gray hat, the mute witness of the tragedy.

The hat gave Lieutenant Schinklein the clue to the victim's identity. When it was placed on his desk in the guard house, he remembered Kratochvil, and a hasty search was instituted. The results of the search left no doubt that sinister forces were at work disturbing the peace in Schinklein's domain.

The Lieutenant did not like this at all. His assignment to the Kolbenka had pleased him because it promised to be a quiet job. He was no warrior, he was a family man, and he tried to adjust the war to his way of life. Kratochvil's anomalous accident upset Schinklein's routine, filled him with foreboding, and, above all, burdened him with a responsibility which he was ill-equipped and unwilling to bear. In this crisis of his military existence, Lieutenant Schinklein was mainly concerned with shoving the responsibility on someone else's shoulders; that's why he called the Gestapo.

He had to wait while his call was switched from one department to the other; he had to repeat his report three times before he finally found a man who became sufficiently excited to tell him that this was a matter for Commissioner Reinhardt himself, and that he should please hold the wire; he would try to reach the Commissioner immediately.

Reinhardt had caught a few hours of unrefreshing sleep. The hostages had followed him into his dreams which had been a veritable danse macabre of grinning Prokosches, squirming Preissingers and gabbing Janoshiks. Wallerstein had come up shedding notepapers everywhere, burying the Commissioner under white sheets covered with writing he desperately tried to read but could not. And suspended above the whole medley hung Milada in mid-air, without visible support, as he had once seen it done in a Variété show. In fact, she was wearing the tight gaudy costume of the performer, displaying the charms of her body; but he could not reach her, hard as he tried; and suddenly she did not have her own face at all, but Glasenapp's, and she was under water, swaying and turning, while Reinhardt attempted to jump in after her. However, Gruber would not let him jump. Gruber held on to his shoulder, and he could not shake him off.

He awoke to find Gruber actually shaking his shoulder. Reinhardt was lying on the couch in the room next to his office, in which he held conferences or rested when time did not permit him to go to his apartment.

"There is a telephone call, sir," said Gruber. "Urgent. Something has happened, and I thought you better deal with it yourself." Gruber remembered the trouncing he had received when he had arrested the hostages on his own hook. "You certainly were asleep, sir!"

Reinhardt's shirt was crumpled, he looked exhausted, his breath was evil smelling. He threw the jacket of his uniform over his shoulder and tumbled rather than walked to the telephone.

"Hello?" he said, his voice hoarse with sleepiness.

"This is Lieutenant Schinklein at the Kolben Daněk Works. I am in charge here, you know—"

"Yes, yes!" said the Commissioner impatiently. "Come to the point, please, will you?"

The Lieutenant, tired of giving his story again and again, felt slighted and complained irritably:

"Well, if you people don't care that one of your snoops got killed here, I don't give a hang either. But what'll we do with the body?"

"Listen, Lieutenant, this is Commissioner Reinhardt. In case you don't know, my military rank is that of Colonel, and I expect you to submit your report in proper form and with due respect, understand?"

"Yes, sir! Sorry, sir!" Schinklein clicked his heels mentally and thought: Oh Jesus, I knew this damned business would bring nothing but trouble. "This morning," he reported, "a Czech man appeared, identifying himself as an agent of the Secret State Police. His name was Kratochvil."

"Kratochvil?" asked Reinhardt, shocked. "What happened to him?"

"He's dead. An accident."

"I don't believe it!" said Reinhardt.

"I assure you, Commissioner, he is very dead. There isn't a single little part of him left in its original shape. He was smashed flat. Please, believe me, sir," the Lieutenant pleaded.

"I meant that I don't believe it's an accident," explained Reinhardt with angry voice. "And what was Kratochvil doing at the Kolben Daněk Works? And why did you leave him alone?"

Lieutenant Schinklein defended himself: "He seemed quite able to take care of himself, sir. Besides, it is quite outside my authority to interfere with the affairs of the Secret State Police."

"All right! All right! What was he doing?"

"He was watching a certain Milada Markova in the shell cap department."

Schinklein could hear a long low whistle. Then the Commissioner continued: "And what steps have you taken?"

"We had the body identified. Inquiries were started as to the cause of the accident. A short circuit, it seems. Kratochvil was buried under a load of steel."

"I am no longer interested in Kratochvil!" shouted Reinhardt. These army officers—what boobs! "Even you, Schinklein, should be able to guess that the usefulness of a dead stool pigeon is strictly limited. What have you done with the Markova girl?"

"Why—nothing!"

"I thought so. Will you be kind enough to have her arrested and brought to Headquarters immediately? Can I trust you with this or do I have to send over a special detail?"

"Yes, sir! No, sir! I mean we'll arrest her, right away, you can rely on us!" Schinklein wanted to go on assuring the Commissioner of his efficiency and making profuse apologies, but he heard the click of the telephone receiver being hung up on the other end. Schinklein was disgusted with himself, with the Kolbenka, with Kratochvil, and with fate which condemned him, who used to be second cashier at the *Handelskreditanstalt* in Osnabrück, to being blamed for all sorts of things with which he had no connection. He half planned to be disgusted with Reinhardt, too, but somehow he did not have sufficient courage for that.

In his office, Reinhardt finished dressing, helped by the Kid who brushed his clothes and polished his boots. While the Commissioner shaved, he frowned in thought. Kratochvil's death, he saw distinctly, could not be taken as an isolated incident. It fitted into a pattern, it was part of a conspiracy of which he could discern neither beginning nor end, neither shape nor scope. This opening of the Glasenapp case had been a jab into a hornets' nest, and now they were swarming and stinging.

He must take stock of the various events and try to link them. Prokosch's self-denunciation—Janoshik's supposedly purposeless trip to the Mánes—Milada's stubborn reticence—Preissinger's accusation against Janoshik—and now the death of the one man who was actually pursuing one of the hornets.

But what did it amount to? Who was hiding what? Who was protecting whom? What did they plot, what did they plan? Who else was in the game?

Murtenbacher was right. Kill them all. But killing them did not solve the problem—always, a part of the network remained, new threads were woven, and shortly, one was faced with the same situation again. One must get to the bottom of it, to the root, to the men who pulled the strings on their side as he was pulling them on his side. But those men were elusive.

It was as if one tried to fight the fog. You could walk into it, punch holes into it, but the fog closed in again, you could not grasp it, it surrounded you, taking away your breath, your vision, your safety.

The fog, he thought. Nobody tells the fog how to act. Is it possible that there is no bottom, that there is no root, that there is no master mind in back of it all? Just the people?

But then, the task grew to desperate dimensions. It ceased being a police problem and became bigger than all the Reinhardts in the world. This he could not, he would not concede.

He had to search for the pattern of the scheme. But its component parts contradicted each other. If Prokosch wanted to appear as Glasenapp's murderer, why had Janoshik brought up the story of the second Glasenapp letter? If Milada knew of the suicide why had she refused to admit it even though she had been threatened with involvement in the murder case? Why did Preissinger denounce Janoshik and not Prokosch? Were they all in the plot, or only some of them, and what was the connection between Milada and the hostages? Was it possible, by any chance, that Glasenapp actually had been murdered?

Nothing was certain any more, everything was in flux, and he felt as if he were sucked under by the waves.

I must return to a solid foundation. I must be able to stand somewhere, otherwise I will not only bungle the case but go crazy on top of it. The more he thought, the less he knew.

Fear rose in him. Fear that he was faced with something far above his power to conquer. And fear he must not have. He must not lose his head. He must get down to earth, to the solid, well-tried, safe methods of police work—questioning, searching, arresting, torturing. He must get results!

Some time today, he would put Milada through the mill—and this time, he promised himself, he would break her. And Janoshik—Janoshik he would pull to bits. And if he had to tear out the man's heart to get his secret, he would do it! His plan must remain the same as originally conceived: *Glasenapp was murdered by persons unknown. And Preissinger together with the other hostages must be shot!*

All preparations for Janoshik's inquisition had been made before Reinhardt went to the boiler room in the basement of the Gestapo headquarters to add the finishing touches.

Janoshik had been taken out of the casket. Gruber, by means of vicious kicks in the kidneys, had made him drag himself the entire way down. In the boiler room, he was received by Moenkeberg who, with sleeves rolled up, examined the prisoner. Janoshik was ordered to strip. The Nazi guards present, among whom he recognized Enzinger and Walters, grinned and cracked jokes about the hair on his body, about his genitals which—though his mind was not afraid—were contracted by the physical fear of his nerves.

Moenkeberg touched him. He felt the muscles in his back, the resiliency of his skin, the strength of his shoulders. Moenkeberg's hands were experienced. They seemed to say: This man is strong. He is not young any more, but his flesh is still firm, and he can stand a lot of pain. He appraised Janoshik as the cattle buyer appraises the steer he will purchase for the slaughter house.

On the basis of his findings he selected the whip which would do the most good, a long elastic steel affair that would cut deep if swung with the right amount of power and at the right angle. He let the whip glide through his hand, almost caressingly. Then he lit a cigarette and waited. Whenever the ashes grew too long, he carefully flicked them off on the whip.

Janoshik observed all this with detached mind. It seemed unbelievable, unreal. He had to remind himself that it was he, Janoshik, standing bare and alone before these men who were so businesslike and who, apparently, viewed him with as little concern as the laundry worker feels for sheets he is about to put through the mangle. The clearest sensation he had was the roughness of the cement floor under his soles; this tickled him somewhat and he moved his feet to relieve them of his weight.

"What the hell are we waiting for?" asked Gruber who was intent upon action. He saw in Janoshik his special enemy, since the Czech had never shown much respect for the Kid.

Moenkeberg turned dreamily. "For Reinhardt," he announced. "The Commissioner himself is going to attend."

"How about making him ready?" suggested Gruber.

Moenkeberg had no objection: "All right with me. Strap him good and tight. I don't like it when they move."

He talks about *me*, thought Janoshik. Making *me* ready. Strapping *me* down, good and tight. He doesn't like *me* to move. Why should I move? I've got to lie quiet and relaxed. The more relaxed I am, the less I'll feel it.

Enzinger and Walters approached him. "Come along," said Enzinger, not at all unfriendly. To them, this was no new experience. To them, Janoshik had ceased to be an individual with mind and heart, soul and nerves. He had become something to be worked over, to be utterly destroyed. Had Janoshik resisted, they would have made short play with him. But he seemed pliable enough.

They led him to the table. Before he knew it, they had grabbed him and hoisted him up on it, belly down. His body defended itself. It rose and flexed its muscles to prevent the closing of the straps, but again the brutality of the guards proved stronger than the obstinate flesh; a blow at the back

270

of his neck made his muscles slacken, and the straps closed in on him, anchoring him to the oblong table which had become smooth by the trembling and quivering of the innumerable predecessors of Janoshik.

His head lay pressed sideways on the table. He could see clearly a small section of the wood, and beyond that a part of the floor, a corner of one of the boilers, and a few feet of the dark gray wall. There was nothing consoling in this view, it was bleak and was to dig itself indelibly into Janoshik's mind.

Now he heard hurried steps and salutes. He guessed that Reinhardt had entered. Soon thereafter, a typewriter began to clatter, the Commissioner's dry voice dictated: "Glasenapp case—interrogation of Janoshik, male, Czech, continued." There was a pause. The voice asked: "What time is it, precisely?" Somebody answered: "Ten minutes past eleven, sir." The voice droned on: "Eleven ten, Tuesday, October 14, 1941."

The typewriter stopped. There was a silence which seemed ages long to Janoshik. Slightly squeaking shoes announced someone's approach. Then, the breeches and boots of a man entered his field of vision. A chair was placed behind the breeches. The man sat down. Janoshik was staring into the pale face of Reinhardt.

"I've come to keep my promise," said Reinhardt. "Remember?"

Janoshik felt no need to answer.

"We've been extremely liberal with you, Janoshik. That was a mistake. We are willing to concede mistakes where we make them. You have abused our humanity, our magnanimity, and have told us a number of lies concerning the end of Lieutenant Glasenapp."

The typewriter in the corner clanked noisily. The hard rasp of its carriage at each start of a new line gave a jerky accompaniment to Reinhardt's sermon.

271

"Now don't think that you will get away without punishment. I am known as a man who stands squarely to his word. But you can save yourself quite a bit of suffering by telling me now why you instigated that seemingly unnecessary search through the Mánes."

The two men glared at each other, face to face, but they saw each other at a ninety degree angle. To Janoshik, the Commissioner's thin nose seemed horizontal, and his bloodless lips the obscene frame of a black vertical line, his mouth.

The Commissioner, who had a larger view of the whole situation, saw his enemy's two eyes above each other, but both filled with the same hate, the same contempt. In his previous interviews with Janoshik, those eyes for the most part had been veiled by heavy lids, or they had looked out at the world with indolent sleepiness. It seemed to Reinhardt that, in this distorted perspective, he recognized Janoshik for the first time, a different, a dangerous Janoshik, a Janoshik unmasked.

Again he felt the same queer emptiness in his stomach, the same foreboding which he had experienced upon receiving the news of Kratochvil's sudden accident.

Janoshik moved his lips. Reinhardt could not understand what he was saying. He bent forward, close to the other's face.

Janoshik whispered, "Why don't you begin, Reinhardt?"

The Commissioner shrank back, appalled. The man was tied securely to the torture table, no question about it. And yet Reinhardt, for a moment, had believed that somebody was attacking him. Then he controlled himself.

Janoshik saw Reinhardt's lips close even tighter.

That was the last impression he ever had of Reinhardt—lips, pressing upon each other, like the shells of a clam.

Reinhardt left Janoshik's side and took his place in one of the comfortable chairs near the typewriter. The dry voice dictated: "Since the prisoner proved unwilling to answer, the questioning was taken over by Sergeant Moenkeberg."

The faithful Moenkeberg, who, up to now. had remained

quite motionless, smoking one cigarette after another, took off his tie and opened the collar of his shirt. He looked at his chief.

"Proceed," said Reinhardt.

Gruber wet his lips. His eager young eyes watched the tall Moenkeberg's catlike approach to his victim. He saw the live skin of Janoshik divided into sections by the straps holding the body. He saw Moenkeberg lift his arm, and with a flash swing it down.

The whip whined through the air and thudded against the flesh. The guards breathed more easily, as if relieved. Reinhardt stretched his legs comfortably and looked at the tips of his splendidly polished boots. Moenkeberg's arm rose for the second stroke.

Janoshik, too, had a feeling of relief. He had expected the pain of this first stroke to be so overpowering as to be unbearable. To his surprise, he found that the pain was composed of several sensations all of which registered perfectly in the fraction of a second. There was the shivering of his skin and the immediate tautness in the strip across his back, where it was hit. There were the waves of pain, emanating from the impact of the whip, and flowing from there over the tips of his nerves to the back of his head. There was the violent reaction of his muscles, over which he had no control; they contracted and tried to throw up his body, in vain since the straps held him down. There was the urge to scream; from deep down within him something seemed to push up against his vocal chords, forcing itself through his throat. And against this urge he set himself. Now his mind began to work. Now the struggle between mind and nerves began. He had to have some point of concentration. And it was this around which he rallied all his conscious forces: I won't scream!

He felt his skin break where the whip had raised a welt. The blood, rushing to the swelling; burst through the taut skin and trickled out, moist and warm. Cold sweat covered

273

him, its salty taste registering on his tongue as he licked his upper lip.

Janoshik was astonished that his brain functioned under the impact of the pain. It functioned as a seismograph recording the convulsions of his nerves. I might be able to stand it, thought Janoshik.

Then came the second stroke. Again the earthquake of pain, again the shock and the shattering of his nervous system. And the third stroke. And the fourth, the fifth, the sixth stroke.

Moenkeberg was systematic, quiet and resolute. That's why Reinhardt entrusted him with important work. And Moenkeberg had received extensive training. He had perfect aim. He planted his strokes parallel to each other, about one inch apart. He was careful not to hit the open wounds again, because this would make the prisoner pass out too quickly. And over an unconscious man, he knew, one has no power.

No, Janoshik did not become unconscious. He did not scream, but he had no control over his groans which forced their way from the depths of his chest and penetrated his tightly gritted teeth. Their sound compelled Enzinger to remark, "He's goddamned strong, like a bull."

Walters answered, "Primitive, you know. These uncultured races, they got no nerves."

Gruber was pale. His hand shook when he lit a cigarette. He dropped the cigarette from his quivering lips and had to pick it up. He found it had become dirty; he cursed, and stamped it out.

The seventh stroke. The eighth stroke.

Still Janoshik's mind fought his nerves. The pain had taken on sound. Deep chords came from somewhere, increased, reached a high pitched fury, and floated away.

He heard the dry voice of Reinhardt ask: "Is he still all right?"

And he heard Moenkeberg grunt, "Yes, sir—yes!"

All this came from afar. Theirs was a different world, while he had entered some plane where they could not follow him.

The ninth stroke. The tenth stroke.

He could feel the pain, but it did not matter any more. His eyes were so full of water that he couldn't see, as much as he tried to keep them open. Still his mind fought.

Everything now centered on the little slip of crumpled paper on the floor of the Mánes toilet. The Watzlik address. He thought of the shadow of the bald-headed longshoreman, and the shadow assumed gigantic proportions, swallowing the scrap of white paper. Then Breda's hands appeared, those strong reliable hands. Then the hands receded and he saw flashes of yellow and red and white, shooting up wildly to unbelievable heights.

The eleventh stroke.

He laughed. He actually laughed. It was a thin and tortured laugh. It sounded so terrible that Gruber looked around inquiringly—where did the laugh come from? It took the Kid a while to realize that Janoshik was laughing.

At this moment the door opened. The new visitor wore a white smock over his black uniform. His head was closely shaved, and he had a glass eye, which remained stationary while the other eye looked at Reinhardt.

"Hello, Doctor!" greeted the Commissioner. "You came to have a look?"

The doctor nodded. He walked over to the table on which Janoshik, his back bleeding profusely, his legs twitching convulsively, lay.

The doctor's one sound eye counted the pattern of wounds.

He followed Moenkeberg's whip which came down for the twelfth stroke. He saw Janoshik's body reel under the blow. He saw Janoshik's bowels discharge a mess of blood and feces. He put a handkerchief to his nose and in a tone of fatherly reproof chided, "Stop it, Moenkeberg, my boy. You'll kill him."

"He's conscious yet," answered Moenkeberg, picking up a rag to wipe his whip.

The doctor turned to Reinhardt: "What are your intentions with the man?"

"He's a hostage. We'll shoot him tomorrow."

The doctor's eye looked straight at the line of Reinhardt's mouth. "You won't need a bullet, if you go on like that."

"I don't want to kill him now!" The Commissioner seemed to be on the defensive. "I want to find out certain facts from him."

"Pour some water over him. Unstrap him. Give him half an hour's rest," ordered the doctor. Then he bent down to the Commissioner and whispered, "I appreciate your motives, sir—but there are certain limitations to the endurance of the physique." And aloud he added, "An interesting medical problem, very interesting.

The typist was sent to fetch some schnapps. The doctor settled in the easy chair next to Reinhardt's, crossed his legs, and continued: "An obstinate people, physically and otherwise. Having any trouble?"

"No."

The doctor lowered his live eye while his glass one stared at the Commissioner. "You look worn. Maybe you need a vacation. Any time you want to, I'll be glad to give you a thorough check-up."

Reinhardt did not believe the doctor's solicitude stemmed from altruism. "Come on!" he said. "What do you want?"

They were interrupted by the arrival of the schnapps. Reinhardt poured it into small glasses. "Well—to the Führer!" It was the custom to down the drink at one gulp.

The glasses were refilled, and the two gentlemen drank to each other's health.

"An obstinate people," repeated the doctor philosophically. "I've been doing some research in the field. I've compiled endurance tables; but imagine my hard luck—I never come to a final result. I have to revise the tables continually, and upward, mind you! The longer we practice our methods, the tougher, it seems, our patients get. Disgusting! Absolutely disgusting!

"*Prosit!*" Another drink. Gulp.

"Well—what do you want, I said?"

"It's about a colleague of mine whom you're holding, my dear Commissioner."

"Wallerstein?"

The doctor nodded.

"I'm afraid I can't do anything for you. He and the other hostages will die tomorrow." Reinhardt spoke with finality.

The doctor managed to give his one eye an expression of amusement. "No, no, no! What do you think I am? I have no charitable intentions whatever. But I wanted to ask you— the man did a lot of interesting research work. What happens to his property? I'd like to have a look at it."

"I'll say he did!" smiled Reinhardt. "In fact he made me a most amazing proposition to which I agreed. He is writing his psychological observations on himself and his fellow hostages in the death cell—what do you think of that?" Reinhardt's face showed his pride. He could prove to the doctor that he, too, had intellectual interests and in addition was a patron of the sciences.

The doctor's eye glinted greedily. "And what are you going to do with Wallerstein's notes?"

Reinhardt thought it better to be noncommittal. "I don't know. I'll read them some time, I suppose."

"Listen, Commissioner—we always have been good friends, haven't we?"

"I have no enemies," smiled Reinhardt.

"Let me have those papers," pleaded the doctor.

"For publication? Under your name?"

The doctor's glass eye was unashamed, while his real one

seemed to show a slight embarrassment. "I don't mind if I do. I'll write an introduction, you see. It's quite common."

"I don't think I need a vacation," said Reinhardt.

The doctor grinned. "Maybe you don't, at that!" Then he bent forward. "You'll do me the favor?"

"Provided I approve of the contents, it's all right with me." Reinhardt refilled the glasses. *"Prosit!"* Gulp.

"And as regards that man," the doctor pointed his thumb over his shoulder at Janoshik, "take it easy. Change your medicine, and don't administer overdoses. That's from one scientist to another!"

And closing both his glass and his live eye, the doctor laughed, and laughingly departed.

This laughter brought Janoshik back to full consciousness.

Now, because he was not being beaten, only his pain was with him. This pain seemed to have a personality of its own. It stood over him like a terrible taskmaster, pressing him with every heart beat; it enveloped him with remorseless heat from which there was no escape.

He was lying in something wet and sticky. He tried with effort to ascertain what it was—till the idea hit him that this must be his own blood.

The straps had been loosened and he attempted to move. But this attempt made his pain so shrill that he gave up and lay perfectly still. He felt utterly weak and exhausted and began to ask himself: Is this my end? That would stop this pain against which he was defenseless. It would stop everything.

But he knew that they would not let him off so easily. Reinhardt had made clear what he wanted to know. What Janoshik had gone through, he was sure, was only the initial softening-up process.

He wondered that he was able to think about himself so rationally. There must be a part of his brain which could reason even now, while the other part was taken up with the pain. I must try to blot out the painful part with the thinking part, he demanded of himself. I must think of matters so important, so great that they can overwhelm the pain.

Important was whether the Watzlik address had been picked up by the longshoreman.

He heard the talk of his tormentors. He heard their approaching steps.

Important was whether the munitions barges would blow up in time.

He heard Reinhardt's dry voice saying something about strapping him down again.

Important was whether he was able to bargain his stubborn silence for the lives of thousands of Russian soldiers on the Eastern Front, against whom the load of the barges was to be used.

He heard Reinhardt say: "Well—how do you feel now?" He guessed that the question was directed at him.

Important was that those Russian soldiers fought on, and, with their fight, helped to free his little country, his Prague, and the miners of Kladno, and the farmhands of Moravia.

"Your silence seems to indicate that you don't feel too well. Obvious, isn't it? Now tell me—did Glasenapp ever give you a letter? Yes or no—"

Important was that he held his post. Others before him had done it, and he would do it, too. Yes, he would.

"What was your agreement with Prokosch?"

Important was—Prokosch? Why did he ask about Prokosch? How did Prokosch get into this?

"What do you know about Glasenapp's death?"

Important—what silly questions the man asked! I am long past all this, it is far below me, I have a wall of pain around me, impenetrable, insurmountable.

"Moenkeberg!" said Reinhardt, shrugging his shoulder and leaving Janoshik's side. "Moenkeberg, take over."

Moenkeberg, who had rested well, viewed the prostrate body critically. "I guess I'll start here," he grunted.

He placed his first stroke across Janoshik's thighs, and gradually worked down to knees and calves.

His whip had reached the soft flesh in the hollow behind the knee, when an orderly appeared and reported to Reinhardt that Milada Markova had been brought in.

The Commissioner rose hurriedly. "Gruber!" he shouted over the groans of Janoshik. "Here is a list of questions. Continue asking them and let me know when our man breaks.

"Moenkeberg!"

Moenkeberg, now shirtless, his chest glistening with sweat, interrupted his activity long enough to snap to attention.

"Yes, sir!"

"Stop when he faints. Bring him to and change your methods frequently. And—he's got to stay alive till tomorrow morning!"

"Yes, sir!"

The Commissioner stalked off, confident that he had left Janoshik in good hands.

CHAPTER 12

THE STREETCAR approached its last station, slowed down, and stopped with a final screech. The few passengers got off and dispersed.

Breda gripped his tool box firmer and set out on his way, first along the road which the car had come, then cutting left between suburban houses, following a pretty tree-lined street. It was obvious that he had familiarized himself with the neighborhood so as to avoid asking directions from strangers.

Yet his steps were not firm and resolute as usual; he walked wearily. Sometimes he stopped and looked forlornly at a hedgerow or at a pile of stones which children had built to dam the rain water running along the gullies; now the water had dried up and the stones were left, relics of laughter and childish excitement.

He was lost in thought, and his thoughts were not concerned with the business on hand—the visit to Otokar Simek, the Nazi announcer of Radio Prague. Other times, when Breda was about to launch an important action, his mind was concentrated on the project. He tried hard to think of Simek, Simek whose features and stature were supposed to resemble closely his own. Simek who had been a dissatisfied bathhouse attendant in Karlsbad, Simek who had considered it a personal affront to have to serve constipated Jewish businessmen who suffered from overweight or diabetes or both. So Simek, though demanding and accepting ample tips, had joined the local Henlein-Nazis, and soon had risen to prominent rank since he possessed a glib tongue and a wide experience with Germany's enemies.

After Munich, when Karlsbad and the whole Sudeten region were incorporated into the Reich, Simek served faithfully under the *Gauleiter* who had been imported from Koenigsberg by the new rulers. Simek took terrible vengeance on the Czech director of the bathhouse who, because he owned a little house, did not retreat into the Czechoslovak rump state, with the other Czech civil officials. The director of the bathhouse hanged himself in the attic of his home, his wife and children were taken in by charitable relatives, and Simek moved into his house, always careful to avoid the attic.

Then came the day when Hitler decided to take over all of Czechoslovakia, and Simek, since he spoke both Czech and German and had the highest recommendations from his *Gauleiter,* got the job at Radio Prague to which he was eminently fitted. The heat in the bathhouse, the steam from the healthful waters of Karlsbad, and above all the noise which he constantly had to overshout, had made his vocal chords practically untiring. He could repeat Hitler's speeches in Czech, giving them the same intonation as the original, and could scream the strategic passages even louder than his Führer.

All this Breda knew; Frantishek had told him the case history of the Nazi announcer whose place he was to take. He attempted to think of it, to envisage the surprise of

Otokar Simek when, suddenly, he would be confronted by the very underground against which he harangued every day.

But always his thoughts returned to Milada, to her arrest.

After the settlement with Kratochvil he had passed the shell cap department. She was still behind the conveyor belt, her arms moving mechanically, her face tired, so tired. Then and there he had decided that he would try to get her an easier job. Just as he was about to leave the department, in marched a detachment of German soldiers, led by Lieutenant Schinklein.

The conveyor belt was stopped. Into the dead silence of apprehension, the Lieutenant's fat voice asked, "Which of you is Milada Markova?"

The next thing Breda saw was the frail girl—his girl—standing between the soldiers. She did not speak, she did not even look at him. She seemed the only bit of humanity among the gray uniforms. If the dogs corner a deer, the deer doesn't speak much either, thought Breda. But what goes on inside of it, you can see in the deer's eyes. That's where you can see it.

He looked at the children's abandoned play dam. Then he gave the stones a vicious kick that sent them splattering in all directions. Simek could look forward to an unpleasant time.

He came to a small park and found Podiebradsky and Frantishek sitting on a bench. Frantishek was munching a piece of bread. He had pushed back his cap and let the afternoon sun fall full upon his face. Both, like Breda, were dressed as workmen, and the casual passerby might think—if he gave the matter any thought—that here were hardworking people taking a well-deserved rest during lunch hour.

The two moved and made space for Breda. Wordlessly Breda sat down, putting his tool box on the ground.

They sat in silence. Two women, pushing baby carriages, ambled by. Everything seemed peaceful enough.

Then Podiebradsky, after ascertaining that nobody was within hearing distance, said, "I want to report good news."

Frantishek chewed. Breda continued in glum quiet.

"I said good news!" repeated Podiebradsky.

"Well?"

"Watzlik's little boy dropped into my store this morning. He said that a tall bald-headed man had come to pick up the packages. The boy was home alone, and the man gave him some money to buy candy."

Frantishek stopped chewing, carefully wrapped up the rest of his bread and replaced it in the bag which he had brought along.

"What is the matter with you, Breda?" he asked. "Don't you realize what this means? Your Janoshik, that magician, has actually succeeded in contacting the longshoremen! And from the Gestapo prison! Why don't you say something?"

Breda folded his hands. "Good news," he said. "Good news."

"Why, it's marvelous!" replied Frantishek angrily. "I feel like laughing and crying, like jumping and dancing! And you say: Good news, good news—as though you just were told that the wife of your aunt's third cousin had her tonsils cut out—successfully."

Breda realized perfectly that Janoshik had performed a superhuman task. He remembered their last good-by down in the Mánes, the handshake without words, though he had been full of the wish to express something strong and warm and comradely. But this memory arising now, in addition to the vivid picture of Milada's still face among the soldiers, choked him and he was unable to speak.

Podiebradsky, more sensitive than Frantishek, saw that Breda was deeply troubled. "Everything all right, isn't it?" he asked. "You look all upset."

The two women with the baby carriages, having made their rounds through the park, came by again. Breda looked after them till they disappeared. It gave him time to steady himself.

Then he said, "Don't let it worry you. It's nothing concerning our immediate job. It's the girl."

"Which girl?"

"Milada. She gave me all the information on the Glasenapp suicide. They arrested her today, in the Kolbenka, right before my eyes."

"Milada was her name?" mused Fantishek. "Was she as lovely as her name?"

Breda winced as if hit by a hard blow.

Podiebradsky noticed it and, trying to break away from the emotional, inquired, "Are they after you, too?"

Breda did not seem to listen. "The worst is that you have to stand there and see it happen, and can't help. Can't raise a finger, can't lift a hand, can't call to her—nothing. And then you torture yourself. You keep on asking: Was I careless? Was it my fault? Am I, perhaps, to blame?"

"And why should it be your fault?" inquired Frantishek who was a man of practical bent.

"The Gestapo chief, Reinhardt, somehow discovered that she had known Glasenapp. He questioned her, and didn't get very far. He did not arrest her, but had one of his men trail her. This man had a fatal accident, this morning, in the Kolbenka . . ."

"Oh!" said Frantishek.

Podiebradsky tried to reason: "No sense in reproaching yourself. Suppose the fellow were still in perfect health—she might have been arrested anyway. On the other hand, if you wanted to protect her, you had to liquidate that stool pigeon. Furthermore—how will they prove her connection with the accident?"

His arguments, valid as they seemed to be, made little

285

impression on Breda. "I know!" he said, "I know! All that I've told myself time and again. It doesn't make me feel any better."

Frantishek was hurt and disappointed. He was one of those men who have unqualified belief in the leader of their own choosing; and he demanded that this leader live up to his expectations. Therefore he was severe: "You always preach that personal feelings must not enter where the work is concerned. But now that it hits you..." He stopped, sensing that Breda was suffering more than he let on.

"I preach?" said Breda sadly. "Do I? A bad habit. Stop me next time I start sermonizing, will you?"

Podiebradsky laid his hand on Breda's and spoke with the tenderness which grows from the understanding developed by men working with each other in common danger. "Don't be cross. Frantishek means that people like you have an obligation. What would become of fellows like him and me, if we were to see you falter and get weak? We look up to you; you must not fail us."

They're good men, thought Breda. They're right too. They're the stuff to build a world with. Salt of the earth. As long as they and their friendship last, I'll manage to go on. I will.

He looked at his watch and said, "Time to start. We'll take the short cut. Won't little Otokar be surprised, eh?"

"I listened to him, last night," remarked Podiebradsky. "He was in great form. He told the story of the German sergeant who singlehandedly, armed only with his service revolver, captured sixty Russians, equipment and all. And then, he said, after the sergeant had brought in his prisoners and booty, he looked at his revolver and was surprised to find that he had forgotten to load it.... Amazing, isn't it?"

Frantishek, with grim humor, objected to Simek's careless selection of material. "Broadcasting about a Nazi who forgets to load his revolver—inefficiency! Rank inefficiency!"

286

Breda grinned. "That sergeant, I would say, has a fat chance to become Chancellor of the Reich. Hitler got his Iron Cross for the same kind of tale, twenty-five years ago. Thus history repeats itself."

They continued their historic discussion with great studiousness and came to the conclusion that, really, there was very little new under the sun, with the exception, of course, of matters technical. Tanks and dive bombers, poisonous gases and flame throwers doubtlessly were the achievements of the twentieth century.

They were a tiny bit regretful that they had to stop their deliberations, because suddenly, out of the gardens before them, loomed Otokar Simek's summer villa. He lived there by himself, occasionally throwing parties which, so it was whispered at the radio station, excelled in debauchery. There was a cleaning woman, but she came only mornings and disappeared around noon time; this was Frantishek's information.

Expecting Simek to be alone, they were disagreeably surprised when they heard a loud voice through the open window. Apparently a heated political conversation was afoot. Simek was declaiming: "If we do not want the name of 'Czech' to be effaced from the world and from history, we must change our attitude toward Germany. It serves nothing that we should proclaim our fidelity and submission to the Reich if we do not feel it and live it. It is not enough to submit; we must co-operate!"

"Bastard!" said Frantishek, louder than he intended.

Podiebradsky put his finger to his lips, warningly.

Apparently nobody in the house dared deny the truth of Simek's statement, for the announcer repeated, this time with different intonation: "It is not enough to submit; we must co-operate!" The last word he pronounced with a particular drool; it seemed that his tongue had become too wet from licking spittle.

A light of understanding gleamed in Frantishek's eyes. "Boys," he whispered jubilantly, "the bird is alone! He's rehearsing! That's one speech he won't deliver!"

They walked around the garden to the front entrance of the house and rang the bell. The declamation stopped. Somebody shuffled through the hall. The door was opened, just a slit. Through it, they saw a small section of Simek, his one visible eye scrutinizing them carefully.

"What do you want?" he asked.

"We're the plumbers!" said Breda, and before he had finished his answer, Frantishek threw himself with full weight against the door and forced it wide open.

"Your tub is leaking!" he announced, walking in.

"Your drain is broken!" said Podiebradsky.

Breda caught on to the spirit of the moment and informed Simek that not only his tub and drain but the entire pipe system was decidedly in need of repair.

Simek protested: "It's an error! How dare you come in like that! My house is in perfect condition, I bought it only recently. You have the wrong address. Get out, now, I have no time to waste!"

"Neither have we!" said Breda.

These were the last words Otokar Simek's consciousness registered. He tried to reach for the pistol which he, like most other Nazis in Prague, carried with him. It was too late. Breda and Frantishek tackled him. A blow from a wrench which Podiebradsky had taken from Breda's tool box made Simek slump.

They stood beside the body, panting. Podiebradsky was the first to regain his composure after the struggle. He knelt down, lifted Simek's eyelids, and looked at the yellowish matter of the announcer's eyes. "He'll be out for a little while," said Podiebradsky. "There, the big chair—let's tie him up there. He'll have to be a very quiet model, understand?"

288

Simek was securely tied and fastened to the chair. His head was propped up and his hair, disheveled from the blow, re-arranged.

"Now, my friend," Podiebradsky pulled up another chair beside Simek's and motioned Breda to sit down, "now we'll create Simek's alter ego!"

"Simek's who?" asked Frantishek.

Podiebradsky took off his coat, pulled up his shirt sleeves and produced a make-up kit from the package he had brought along. "Latin, my friend, Latin!" he said. "Don't worry—he'll look like Simek himself!" He studied Breda, then Simek.

"You know," he mused, "this is an interesting job, really. They say the devil looks like God, but in·reverse. Where God is benign, the devil is vicious, where God smiles, the devil grins. You see, Frantishek—now consider the mouth. The shape is alike, in Breda as well as Simek; but the little mustache, and the way Simek presses his lips—they make all the difference in the world."

Podiebradsky attached a mustache to Breda's upper lip. Clipping the mustache to the size of Simek's, he admonished Breda, "Watch that mouth! Try to imitate its expression!"

And to Frantishek he said, "See how Breda changes? His mouth becomes mean, bitter, ruthless."

Podiebradsky worked like an artist. Scrutinizing his model and his object, he stepped back to study his work.

"Listen, Breda!" he pointed out. "When you enter the studio, you must keep in mind to hold your mouth thin as Simek's. . . . Now the hair!" He produced a reddish-blond wig. "A simple matter of shortening the forehead. You have a well-formed forehead, Breda. Looking at you, one somehow feels that good thoughts are behind it."

"Stop the flattery!" Breda felt embarrassed; but he was fascinated by Podiebradsky's activity.

Podiebradsky placed the wig over Breda's thin, straight hair, and with his comb, parted its reddish wool in the center.

"Some transformation!" he exclaimed. "A shifty, vicious, underhanded plotter! If I were a philosopher—I'm not, to be sure—I'd say: How little divides the great from the ridiculous, the fine from the vile!"

In the midst of Breda's metamorphosis Simek began to stir. Frantishek picked up the wrench, ready to deal the announcer a second blow. Breda looked at the man he was to replace and frowned. He knew that Simek would scream if they allowed him to come to; on the other hand, something in him rebelled at the beating of a defenseless man.

He was delivered from his scruples by Podiebradsky, who put aside his scissors and comb to take a syringe from his bag. "Help me!" he ordered Frantishek. They untied Simek's left arm and pulled up his shirt sleeve. Then Podiebradsky jabbed the needle into the announcer's flesh, and slowly pressed down the handle of the syringe till all of the thin, clear fluid had entered the patient's vein.

"That'll put him to sleep," he mumbled. "He'll be very quiet, very quiet." Podiebradsky's cheeks were flushed, little drops of sweat stood on his forehead.

"Don't work so hard!" admonished Breda. "We have plenty of time."

"I want to get out of here!" said Podiebradsky gruffly. He labored on, conscientiously. Finally he seemed to be satisfied. He led Breda to a mirror in the corner of the room.

Breda viewed himself. He felt strange. The face which greeted him from the mirror was his—and yet it wasn't.

"Maybe there is something of that scoundrel in me," he thought aloud. "How otherwise could you succeed in transforming me so thoroughly?"

Podiebradsky, proud of his work, evaded the question: "Make-believe—that is all. I'm glad I used to dabble in dramatics; once I staged a whole play with my family, and a good performance it was...." He stopped, thinking of his son who had died in a concentration camp. It had been this death which led him, a peaceful druggist, to seek and find a new content for his life: Revenge.

"Now for one of Simek's suits!" he exclaimed, with forced cheerfulness. They left the mute body of the announcer and hurried upstairs to search the closets. They chose a trim blue serge for Breda, complete to the Swastika button in the lapel. While Breda changed, Podiebradsky warned, "Don't perspire. Don't touch your mustache. In case your coiffure gets ruffled, repair it before you enter the broadcasting station. And above all—rely on me. You can be confident—you look exactly like Simek!"

"And how he does!" confirmed Frantishek. "Disgusting. A face you'd like to slap for hours on end. No wonder Simek hates to have the engineer stare at him from the control room and insists on broadcasting from his private office.... You remember, Breda, how to get there—don't you?"

"Main entrance, elevator to the right—don't speak to man at desk, just nod and raise hand mechanically—third floor, down the hall, office 318."

He had gone through this examination a good dozen times. Knowing how important absolute knowledge of locale and procedure was, he submitted good-naturedly to this repetition. Besides, it made Frantishek feel good.

"Go on!" urged Frantishek.

"The phonograph is to the right of the door. On it, ready to be played, I will find the record of Simek's theme music, the *Hohenfriedberger Marsch*. I wait for the green light over the door to flash On The Air, and I start the phonograph. After ten bars of Simek's march, I substitute my recording."

"And then?"

"Run like hell!" said Breda, chuckling. He buttoned his coat.

"There's nothing funny!" admonished Frantishek. "Walk slowly, look unconcerned. Don't use the elevator. And good luck!"

The pseudo-Simek, impeccable to the point of the announcer's choicest silk tie, picked up a briefcase from a chair. "That, I think, is everything I need," he said. "You both had better leave now. I want to thank you, you've done your job well. So well that I expect the rest to go all right too. If, however, I should not return, you have your instructions."

"Not return? Don't be silly!" joked Podiebradsky.

Frantishek grabbed Breda's hand and pressed it. "What I said before—you know, about your disappointing me—forget about it. I think you're a great fellow."

"Now! Now! No preaching—you remember? Just keep your fingers crossed for my radio debut, yes?" He laughed.

He accompanied his comrades down the stairs, to the door.

"Good luck!" said Podiebradsky.

"See you soon!" said Frantishek.

"Thanks—oh, Podiebradsky, before you go—when do you think Simek will wake up? I want to be out of the house before that time."

"Simek?" asked Podiebradsky. He hesitated. "Oh. Well—he won't wake up. No. Never."

"What? But—" Breda could find no words. They had discussed the possibility of having to kill the announcer. But they had made no decision, one way or the other. Podiebradsky had acted without orders! No, thought Breda, it wasn't a matter of breach of discipline. It was—what was it?—his own softness? But Kratochvil.... No, with Kratochvil it was different. A machine, a load of iron, had killed Kratochvil. Had Podiebradsky sensed Breda's inherent weakness? Was that why he had gone ahead on his own?

Frantishek said, "Simek saw me. He might have recognized me at the studio."

That was true. Frantishek had to be protected. Breda nodded.

Podiebradsky, stern of face, looked at Breda. There was

no avoiding that look. "Listen," he said. *"Crush them, as they crush us! Kill them, as they kill us!"*

Breda embraced the old druggist, kissing him on both cheeks. There was much in this gesture—apology, thanks, and above all the warmth of a friendship which knows that, whatever the one friend does, is done out of concern for the other.

Then they were gone. Breda was alone in the house. He sat down at Simek's desk, picked up a newspaper, tried to read. Impossible. So he decided to face himself—to face the dead Simek. He pulled up a chair, relaxed, and set his eyes on the announcer's wasted features.

It was not difficult, not difficult at all! You see, he said to Simek, we have caught up with you. You're just a little cog in the Nazi machine, and it is pure accident that you were called upon to pay your debt before the other, bigger cogs. And you don't pay only to me—I'm just the cashier. You pay to Janoshik, and to Milada, to her Pavel, and to the son of Podiebradsky. You pay to all the others whose names I don't know, and who'll rise from their unmarked graves to demand: An eye for an eye, a tooth for a tooth. I was brought up with the Ten Commandments. Thou shalt not kill. Ha, ha! You, Otokar Simek, have shelved this and the other nine. Now I am judge, and I am judging according to a new set of laws which will remain in force till the world is purged of all the Simeks and Kratochvils and Reinhardts and of their taskmasters. I will be a good judge, a hard judge. Our Justice will not be blindfolded, she will have sharp eyes, and look into the most secret corners of your minds.

Are you listening, Otokar Simek?

The dead man, who looked so much like a Breda in reverse, did not answer.

Breda rose and took one of Simek's cigarettes from the box on the announcer's desk. He lit it casually. He was not bothered any more by the presence of the body. He finished the cigarette in due time, took the briefcase into which the careful Podiebradsky had slipped the recording of the speech, and left the house. A man on the street, apparently a neighbor of Simek's, greeted him deferentially. Breda replied to the man's greeting with a jovial wave of his hand. "Fine afternoon, isn't it?"

"Yes, sir," said the man, and lifted his hat again.

"Milada!" said Reinhardt dreamily, smacking his lips as in the aftertaste of some agonizing sweetness.

He was alone in his office; had been alone for more than ten minutes without a word, without motion, just thinking. The guards had taken her to solitary after the questioning— "so that you will have time and quiet to consider my questions again and, perhaps, volunteer some positive answers," he had said.

It seemed to him that a bit of the fragrance of her being was left hanging in the room; a faint sound to which he was listening, the rustling of her steps.

He had displayed great patience and mildness toward her, and had admired himself in the process of her interrogation, because he, who so short a while ago had been supervising the treatment of Janoshik, with her possessed the versatility and self-restraint required of a true gentleman.

Nevertheless, he had made perfectly clear to her that this time, no denials or subterfuges could help her; she was firmly in his hands, and through her own fault. He regarded, he said, as rank ingratitude on her part the liquidation of poor Pan Kratochvil whom he had detailed as much for her protection as for his own. He could conclude therefrom only that she refused to be co-operative and that, furthermore, she was a desperate and dangerous woman which, of course, he had suspected.

When she protested that she had not even known of the

existence of Pan Kratochvil, Reinhardt conceded that this statement was quite in line with her previous stubborn behavior, and that she must forgive him, but he preferred to disbelieve her.

Reinhardt, reviewing his manner toward the girl, was satisfied. Tonight he would call her again; he was sure he would harvest what he had sown; to wring a confession from her would be so fascinating and thrilling as to be a reward in itself.

In the meantime, he would go through the routine of questioning Lobkowitz and the other fifteen hostages. This would assure him that no point had been overlooked, that no loophole remained through which his secret of the Glasenapp suicide could slip. And Wallerstein—Wallerstein and his notes!

Wallerstein's notes had steadily gained significance in Reinhardt's mind. The Commissioner considered himself quite an expert in soul-searching. He used different methods than did the medical profession, and used them to different ends; but a certain relation existed nevertheless. And the more entangled the Glasenapp case had become, the more Reinhardt hoped to find some clue in the observations of the psychiatrist. This expectation was especially strengthened by the one-eyed doctor who wanted to appropriate the notes; the man was no fool and knew the value of Wallerstein's work.

So it came about that Reinhardt, in spite of the apparently adverse events, was quite cheery when Wallerstein was brought in. Confident that the case would shape up as desired, he beamed at his prisoner. "Well, Doctor, I hope that in the welter of life in a Gestapo cellar you've had sufficient leisure to concentrate on your work!"

Wallerstein, Reinhardt found, had deteriorated considerably since their first interview. His eyes were shifty and red-rimmed, his cheeks sagging, his lips distorted. He had aged. For a fleeting moment, the Commissioner tried to imagine how he himself would feel in the expectancy of death—for a moment only, then he waved away the idea. Everything he did was done toward the end that he would never fall into this situation; he was strong and a fighter, he could mete out punishment—the hostages were weak and had to take it; and he would see to it that he remained with the strong.

"Thank you," said Wallerstein, "I have tried my best." He swallowed. "When—when may we expect our end?"

"Tomorrow at daybreak," informed Reinhardt. "Around six o'clock."

"You haven't found the murderer of Glasenapp?"

Reinhardt smiled. "Surprisingly enough, we've had several candidates. Fortunately we could prove their confessions a hoax."

"Fortunately?" Wallerstein's eyes rested on the Commissioner. Reinhardt averted his face. He had the disagreeable notion that the doctor was seeing right through him, he was afraid of Wallerstein's shrewdness.

"Fortunately," he said gruffly. "Of course fortunately! We are not interested in blood *per se;* we don't want just any murderer—we want the right one!"

"Your motives do you honor," declared Wallerstein.

Reinhardt sensed the irony very well. "It is by no means too late," he countered Wallerstein. "You yourself were present in the Mánes Bar when the murder occurred. If you have anything to contribute to the solution of the case, why haven't you spoken up? Why don't you speak up now? What do you know about it? At this point your life is still in your hands!"

Wallerstein felt tired, tired and weak. Standing before the Commissioner's desk hurt his legs, and he wished the whole futile procedure were over.

"What do you want me to do?" he asked, tormented. "Confess that I killed Glasenapp? Denounce somebody else? Tell you that Glasenapp never was murdered but committed suicide?"

"What!" interrupted Reinhardt, aghast.

But Wallerstein, too much immersed in his own misery, did not notice the Commissioner's reaction, did not know how near he had come to the truth. He went on: "Tell you tales only to have you prove conclusively that I was lying? In what way, I ask you, would such a desperate attempt change my affairs?"

Reinhardt recuperated quickly from his shock. But something in him tempted him to ask, "Why did you mention suicide? Do you actually believe in that possibility? Do you know anything of it?"

"Of course I do!" said the doctor. "Suicide is one phase of psychic sickness, the final phase as it happens."

"You mean—theoretically spoken."

"Of course! What else should I mean? What should I know of Glasenapp? I never was and, I suppose, never will be much interested in the inner life of German Army officers." He paused. Then, with slight amazement, he asked, "How come we talk about suicide, Glasenapp's suicide? Do you suspect...?" He had grown unnaturally pale, and a glimmer of hope shone in his eyes. "Are you not sure?"

The Commissioner rose. He was now certain Wallerstein knew nothing. "No!" he assured the doctor, "I am sorry to disappoint you. Glasenapp was most definitely murdered. Suicide, my dear doctor, is typical of a decadent race. We are Germans, about to conquer the world—we don't commit suicide.... And now, I'd like to see your notes."

Wallerstein handed them over with hesitant hand. "You will be careful with them," he begged. "It's the only copy. It's the only thing I leave. I have also written a letter to the editor of the *Psychologische Monatsschrift;* it's attached to the manuscript."

He would have continued his pleas, if Reinhardt had not motioned him to stop. Scanning the first page of careful, even writing, the Commissioner said, "Sit down. And let me read, will you?"

With intent, anxious looks Wallerstein followed the Commissioner's eyes which were gliding along the lines, his hands which were turning page after page.

NOTES ON DEATH AND THE DISINTEGRATION OF PSYCHIC STANDARDS

By Walter Wallerstein, M.D.

Greater and more incisive, more cataclysmic than any other experience in human life is the one which ends it: dying.

Not only the body, but also the psyche stops functioning. For reasons of convenience Medical Science and Society in general have established a qualitative deadline for the process called death. We issue a certificate when the heart muscle has permanently ceased to pump blood. We know, however, that dying and living are processes complementing each other, that parts of our living tissue die off constantly. We say, speaking of certain clinical cases: He takes a long time dying. Plato, in describing Socrates' death, tells graphically how his teacher stopped living limb by limb, part by part. (This, by the way, is one of the few reports we have of the reactions of a man who knew he was going to die, and who could measure "when the stiffness would reach his heart," i.e. when he would reach the qualitative deadline. We do know that Plato was a good reporter, but we do not know how thorough an observer, especially from the psychological viewpoint, he was.)

Death is the most cardinal taboo mankind has established.

The individual, from observation on himself and on others, learns he must die. Conscious and semi-conscious are geared to this fact. The traffic light on the corner is a very conscious means of precaution against death; the instinctive ducking of the soldier, when he perceives a shell whistling overhead, is clearly a semi-conscious reaction.

These are simple and everyday defense mechanisms against death. One can safely say that most of the medical profession derive their livelihood from this same source. We are, however, concerned with the psychic defense mechanisms against death—or the dread of death—and with the struggle between the conscious and the subconscious in the face of the certainty of a predictable death, predictable to the minute and the hour.

In the ordinary course of affairs, a doctor would be cruel to let his patient know that his death is expected, let us say, at midnight. We rather strive to maintain the patient's hope to the end, also, perhaps, taking into consideration our own fallibility as medical men. We want to save the patient the psychic agony of awaiting his death.

In some cases, as for instance the execution of criminals, the "patient" spends some time in the death cell and knows when he is going to die. We know that some such criminals suffer fits of rage, or of depression; some eat their last meals with gusto, others throw perfectly good food at their guards; some take consolation from the priest, others curse him. These reactions, obviously, depend on past history, development, and other circumstances of the "patient."

Unfortunately, we do not know of any case where a psychoanalytically trained observer was permitted to spend with such a patient his last days and hours. We know almost nothing, therefore, of the changes taking place in the psyche of an individual facing the certainty of dated death.

Thanks to the friendly co-operation of the Secret State Police in Prague, and especially its esteemed Commissioner, Helmut Reinhardt, it has been my good fortune to observe and analyze a group of men in just such position. This group includes myself, and I must beg the reader's indulgence if I have not succeeded in completely eliminating my own feel-

ings. I am sure that, considering the circumstances, he will give me a posthumous pardon.

The facts, in short, are these: We were arrested on Thursday, the 9th of October, 1941. The next day, we learned that, after five days, we would be shot as hostages. In my cell and under my observation were four men—Mr. L., a young newspaperman, Mr. P., an actor, Mr. Pr., a businessman, and Mr. J., without profession. All were informed by me of the impending execution. I had ample opportunity to talk with them, to ask questions which seemed of importance to me, and to observe their reactions.

I stated above that death is the most cardinal taboo established by mankind. Society, its laws, its moral relations would undergo quite basic changes if this were not so. A man about to die knows no inhibition, for there is no more possibility of punishment, either by society or by himself. He is above retribution.

In other words, the conglomeration of inhibitions and educational drill, of established behavior patterns and consideration of others, this thing called "conscience" ceases to function, because there is no more necessity for it. In the face of certain death, man is utterly alone and, therefore, becomes a super-egotist.

This development could be observed in perfect clarity in Messrs. P. and L. It so happened that both gentlemen had been in love with the same woman. Mr. P., the husband, did not know of the relationship between his wife and Mr. L., though he might have suspected it.

Under ordinary circumstances Mr. L., no doubt, would have kept his secret to himself. Knowing, however, that he was to die, and provoked by Mr. P.'s constant, possessive talk of his wife, he announced that he was Mrs. P.'s lover and the father of her child. This led to an outbreak of physical violence on Mr. P.'s part, which was difficult to stop.

But why had Mr. P. provoked Mr. L. and thereby con-

300

tributed to the complete breakdown of the latter's inhibitions, weakened as they were by impending death?

Here I had the opportunity to observe a secondary trend, also, of course, based on the taboo. Close familiarity with death means the touching of the taboo, the breaking of the inner law. Mr. P., therefore, tried to find a justification—a justification for his life. His life was bound up in his relation with his wife, which had been unsatisfactory. Consequently he was interested in picturing this relation as a highly successful one before himself and everybody.

The reader who has not had our chance to approach so closely the finality of death, will ask how it is that five sane men willingly gave up the fight for life as long as there was breath left in them. There are two answers.

The one is highly complimentary to the Secret State Police. We knew, once we realized the judgment, that this organization keeps its word, at least in so far as a promise of execution is concerned.

The second answer is more complicated. The fight was not abandoned. In trying to realize the inevitability of the end, in overstepping the boundaries of the taboo, such horror was experienced that the individual shrank from the acceptance of the fact that it would be extinguished completely.

This provides the basis for the frequent change in mood and temperament observed in all the hostages except one. I shall, later on, deal with this one exception more extensively. We wavered between fatal depression, expressed in long lapses of brooding and silence, and on the other hand, frantic activity. This activity concerned itself not only with attempting to save oneself and one's "soul," but also with hurting one another. The reader might assume that a group of men, thrown together in the same small room, facing the same fate, would develop solidarity and a closeness to one another akin to comradeship. However, just the contrary

301

took place. Hostility, excitability, antagonism were the main traits developing.

The most calloused and self-assured of the men, before his entry into the cell, Mr. Pr., the businessman, became the most irritable. He who, due to his position in life, was accustomed to having other people do the work and the suffering and the dying for him, seemed, up to the closing of these notes, unable to perceive that he would have to suffer and die himself. An extrovert, he sublimated his fears by hectically denying that he would be dealt with as would the rest of the hostages. Unwilling to concede that he was stripped of his former power, he tried to convince himself and his cell mates that strong outside forces were at work to save him. Interestingly enough, he did not rely only on those outside forces. He, who in the course of his self-consolation, opened up and gave his cell mates a fairly thorough picture of his unscrupulous past and the means by which he had achieved his power, indicated clearly that he would stoop to the lowest level and stop short of nothing to keep himself alive.

Mr. Pr. demonstrated, most clearly of all, the absolute breakdown of moral, psychic, and social standards under the impact of certain death. The conclusion seems in order that this reaction is typical not only of Mr. Pr. but of all men riding the wave of power and defending, to them, quite valid interests. This, however, verges on the political and, therefore, is outside of the present considerations.

The others continued to fight for life, but on a different plane. It seemed impossible to adopt the resigned attitude of a Socrates, much as we tried. The impulse to preserve dignity, while certainly felt by some of the men, did not prove strong enough—mainly because there was nobody before whom it was necessary to preserve dignity. We knew that no witness to our agony would tell future generations: they died like heroes (or something to this effect). We had no

302

Plato watching us, we were reasonably certain that no immortality such as Socrates' was our lot.

Yet we made feeble attempts at establishing our immortality. I assure the reader that this statement has no religious content whatever. We try to allay our fears of death which, if we realize it honestly, is a complete and to the human mind almost inconceivable and unbelievable nothingness, by creating the illusion that something of us will continue to live on, as the hair and nails continue to grow even after the heart muscle has given up its steady pumping.

Mr. Pr., most primitively and unimaginatively, pined only to live on in the flesh.

But Mr. L., following man's instinct to live on in his progeny, in dying defended and claimed his child, which nominally was Mr. P.'s.

The actor P., whose name and art were of significance in the world of the theater and who therefore could expect a few regrets and a little glory from his public, tried to magnify his greatness as an artist and his success as a man before his cell mates—a pitifully weak crutch on the last walk to meet extinction.

And I must confess that these notes are written because I myself, in fear of oblivion and unable to accept death, want to leave behind something of lasting value, though I know my limitations to which the reader will agree.

We are very miserable and try to hold on to ourselves by, perhaps, ridiculous means. Isn't the scientist, too, a human being? I could afford to be casual with my patients from behind the smugness of my desk in the office, or the galley proofs of my articles. But now I am haunted myself, there is no hole into which to creep, no father confessor, only these papers, and frankly, they are of little help. This is no science any more, I realize it, this is an outcry. I am choking and I just put down what I feel—somebody else, some day, may

303

have the time and inclination to analyze my last desperation, and have mercy on us.

I have not mentioned Mr. J.

There is good reason for it. Medical science knows of rare cases where men may move in the midst of raging epidemics, touching the sick, eating their food, drinking their water, breathing their air—yet they are not infected. Their bodies seem to possess a priori sufficient antitoxins to counteract the influences of the disease.

Supposing that our fears are a disease, Mr. J. walked through them without visible signs of being affected. He was no idiot impervious to human emotions; he seemed to me to possess shrewdness, understanding, kindness and warmth. He was able to hate and despise; his relation to Mr. Pr. gave testimony to this. He would, however, have reacted to Mr. Pr. in the same way if they had met on the street or in an office, instead of the narrow cell where the meeting took place.

But Mr. J. seemed to be impervious to the fear of death. He accepted death as one accepts temporary setbacks in life— it's too bad, but we'll get over it.

He refused to live up to the rules of my game. I, an experienced observer of matters psychic, trained by years of practice to ask the questions which reveal, to the doctor, the state of the patient's mind, was unable to find any more than what I said above.

There were times when I had to curb a stupid and unfounded feeling of hate toward Mr. J., merely because he appeared superior to me, the doctor who himself was torn by the disease. On the other hand, as a worker in so young a field as psychiatry, I cannot afford to be narrow-minded and assume that what is not on the books does not exist.

It exists!

What motivates such a man?

*Has he faced death so often that he has established a close
enough relation with it to be free of fear?*

*Or has he knowledge of a future of which the rest of us
know nothing?*

*Is he, perhaps, that rare specimen called hero, and has it
been my good fortune to meet him before my seeing days are
ended?*

Or do all three reasons apply to him?

*I am trying to dispense with my feeling of inferiority, to
be objective. It may well be that from him I can derive the
strength which my life lacked and which is failing me now.
For Mr. J., in his modest way, not only cheats death of its
triumph over man—but also the powers wielding death of
theirs!*

At this point the Commissioner stopped reading.

This can't be, he thought. Impossible! his mind repeated.
Doesn't this Wallerstein say himself that his brain is diseased
with fear? These papers—a mad concoction of a scared intellectual, that's what they are!

But the analysis of Prokosch gave Reinhardt the perfect
solution for the actor's confession of Glasenapp's murder!
The actor was out to glorify his death! If the doctor was right
in that, he was right, too, in his observations on Janoshik;
and here lay the deeper reason for Preissinger's false denunciation of Janoshik!

All of them had seen through the bumpkin's act—only he,
Reinhardt, had been a sorry fool.

Much as he wished to disbelieve the papers, in his heart
he knew their truth. He knew that the hub of everything
moving against him was Janoshik, Janoshik the harmless
halfwit, the roundhead, with his tattle-tale stories and the
innocent look in his watery eyes.

Most maddening of all was that while he knew a plot was

unfolding against him, and that Janoshik was the spearhead of it—yet, where did it come from? What was it? Who were the other conspirators? This remained unanswerable. Again he was pushed into the whirling fog; certain outlines he was able to discern—but nothing was firm and concrete, so that he could arrest it, hold it and stop it.

His fury turned against the notes which confronted him with his own failure. He still held them, a number of pages unread.

Wallerstein, attempting to penetrate the Commissioner's masklike face, moved restlessly in his chair.

"You suppose you've done a great job, don't you?" asked Reinhardt. "Well, let me tell you—this is a lot of poppycock, and it makes me sick. I'm wasting my time. From the day you and the whole bunch were arrested, I knew you were shivering in your boots, during your waking hours and at night, in your sleep. Cowards! Cowards all!"

"If you open a man's stomach and look into his entrails," replied Wallerstein, fighting for the validity of his notes, "it's not a beautiful view either."

"And your Mr. J.—a hero! Laughable! I tell you who's a hero: The man who's on top! Because he is the one in control, he is the one who makes history and who writes it. He's the one who'll be talked about when all of you are dust and forgotten. Right?"

Wallerstein rose. "I don't think we understand each other."

"I understand you!" shouted Reinhardt, standing up likewise and pushing back his chair. "You're not stupid, Doctor!" He came around the desk and placed himself closely before Wallerstein, hissing his hatred into the doctor's face. "A sly kind of vengeance you wanted to take, didn't you? Couched in your scientific language, so that I, the policeman you despise, would not catch on, you tried to make me out a perfect fool!"

"No! No, sir!" asserted Wallerstein, torn by fear for his notes. "I swear you misunderstand me . . ."

"Janoshik—a hero! You want to see your hero? Maybe tonight I'll give him back to you to look at; there'll be a bloody pulp left of your hero, if that! And I'm in the best mood to give you a dose of the same medicine for daring to present me with a collection of impudent lies!"

Galileo, it flashed through Wallerstein's mind, also stood before the Grand Inquisitor to deny that the earth moves around the sun. Yet the earth moves . . .

"And I," Reinhardt continued with embittered voice, "I, a supposedly serious and intelligent official of the Secret State Police, should send off this drivel for publication. No, Doctor, your little plan miscarried!"

Reinhardt tore the notes into shreds, threw them on the floor, trampled on them. "That's what I do to them, you see?—that!"

The full realization that his work, his heritage, was utterly destroyed, did not immediately come to the doctor. Instead, the phenomenon of the frantic Nazi tearing up words and thoughts aroused his medical interest.

"Your behavior indicates," he said meticulously, "that you are trying to stamp out something you do not have the courage to face. The truth, Commissioner. Don Quixote, remember, also charged the windmills. That didn't stop the wind."

Reinhardt went blind in fury. Only after Wallerstein's emaciated body had toppled down before him, did he become conscious of the fact that he must have hit him on the temple with unexpected force.

He rang for the guards.

"Take him back to the cell," he ordered, pointing at the body. Then, without looking back, he strode off to the basement, firmly determined to crack Mr. J. and his secret.

CHAPTER 13

EVENING comes sooner to the basement cells of the Gestapo headquarters than to the world outside. Its messengers, dusk and darkness, arrive there first as if in pity for the days of the prisoners.

Wallerstein and Lobkowitz, alone in the cell, silently watched the twilight settling. Wallerstein softly massaged the left side of his face and his temple which were still swollen from Reinhardt's blow. The doctor tried not to think of tomorrow, and clung to any fleeting thought in the hope of being carried away to forgetfulness. Isn't this body of mine amusing? he asked himself. It goes on burning oxygen and feeling the dullness of the blow, concerned only about its own business, truly a busybody! It doesn't bother about apprehensions, it keeps on functioning with animal stubbornness—as if this state would last forever!

My body is more reasonable than my reason—conscious and subconscious, the whole goddamned complicated mechanism which makes me unhappy. If only I could make myself see myself in the perspective of history, as the unimportant speck of matter which I really am. But my subconscious refuses to accept the wise lesson my mind is attempting to administer. The two worked out a compromise, very cleverly. A sly dash toward a little immortality; but we all were stopped by the brute, Reinhardt.

And now we are naked, as naked as when we were pushed into this world. We are shorn of the protection which we so carefully built up in a lifetime of labor. Our philosophy, our knowledge—what good are they in these last hours? Wherein do I differ from a creature like Preissinger who cannot grasp that he, too, must stand naked before his fate, minus his coal and minus his power? Death, Mr. Preissinger, is a most democratic institution. Even the Nazis, who deal in death, feel it, feel the contradiction. That's why they try to bribe death by throwing before the All-Embracing hecatombs of victims. Memorials of bones and ashes they are building; in vain, in vain—all in vain.

Remember the pharaohs with their pyramids and mummies—what magnificent illusions! Remember the imperators with their triumphal arches, and the pious kings with their Gothic domes—all forgotten. Stone piled upon stone, and yet they departed naked.

Naked and alone. Just as I.

Lobkowitz, he thought, this poor boy, sitting on his cot, staring at his feet. "What are you brooding about? We all have to die some time!"

"I wish I were as cynical as you, Doctor. I suppose one must have lived longer than I to be able to give up hope, painlessly. The years you've had—what I could have done with them!"

"You're wrong, my boy. No matter how long you live, always you expect that tomorrow is the day when the great things will start happening to you. Mark my words, if only for the few hours we still have to go; Goethe was lying. The moment of complete satisfaction with life which he lets his Faust reach at the end—this moment never, never comes. I'd like to confess, whether you believe me or not, that I, Walter Wallerstein, am as unable as you to accept resignedly this death of ours. So if, in the course of the night, I cry and scratch the walls with my nails, tear my clothes or hammer my skull, you will know that I am going insane for the same reasons as you."

"No," said Lobkowitz, "I wouldn't give the Nazis that satisfaction. I was lucky, I suppose. I've had only five minutes of questioning by Reinhardt—enough for me. I won't let this sneering petty despot have the pleasure of triumphing over me! No!"

"You see," said Wallerstein, "how much stronger you still are than I? I don't give a damn whether they have to carry me out before the squad with all my reflexes out of control, kicking and screaming and foaming at the mouth. You have a child, Lobkowitz, you are lucky. Perhaps some day, somebody will tell this child of yours: Your father stood upright before the executioners' rifles. But why should I keep myself to the established forms? Who cares?"

"I should leave a letter for that child!" Lobkowitz, suddenly animated, jumped up. "May I have some of your paper and your pen?"

"Don't bother! I tried to leave a letter for the whole world —they tore it up. They took the drowning man's straw and used it to tickle him!"

"Your notes?"

Wallerstein nodded.

"Serves you right. Don't you think I know that all the time you considered us your rabbits, inciting us, playing one against the other, all for your precious letter to the world? You tried to sell our souls, our suffering, to the Nazis for the proverbial lentil soup of glory. You forgot that the Nazis are in the market for glory only for themselves. Poor Prokosch. Poor Mara."

"Why pity him? That's the good thing about this execution—tomorrow you and he and all of us will be beyond pity and sundry emotions. Or are you afraid that you might be called to account for your sins?—Don't be childish. The sins we commit, pleasant and unpleasant, find their punishment only inside of us, only as long as this outmoded rating system, implanted in us by dissatisfied spinsters of all sexes and ages, functions."

"But I am still alive!" shouted Lobkowitz. "What you call my rating system, it still functions and will function till those bullets—"

"Tear your heart," finished Wallerstein. "I know. Because you are the youngest of us hostages, you have not broken down completely. And far be it from me, this last evening, to subvert what remains to you. I merely endeavor to convince myself that all my living cleverness, wisdom, brains—whatever you want to call it—won't amount to a jot after 6 A.M. tomorrow. Something in me refuses to believe it, and I have been trying to reason with this something because I'd like to sleep, or because I don't want to be like you, one minute riding high in hope, one minute dying in desperation. One death is sufficient."

"Prattle! Prattle!"

"That's what it is! Despise me, go ahead!" Wallerstein rubbed his smarting face, and felt the stubble of his beard—the stubble which would keep on growing, growing till the flesh rotted away.

Abruptly, he stopped massaging himself. The clang of the jailer's keys presaged momentous developments. Despite their mental agony the two men fell into the ridiculous jail routine, snapping to attention.

Preissinger and Prokosch tumbled into the cell. Preissinger, his knees buckling from the excruciating hours and hours in the standing casket, barely reached his cot to fall prostrate upon it. A smell of excretion rose from him, nauseating even Wallerstein and Lobkowitz, although their nostrils had become adjusted to the ordinarily stifling odor of the cell.

Prokosch was as enervated as Preissinger. But he remained on his feet by clinging to the metal framework of the upper cot. Standing like the Crucified, and with the same emaciated face, his first, hardly intelligible words were: "Where is Janoshik?"

The brutal evidence of the torture the two had suffered aroused in Wallerstein and Lobkowitz the immediate impulse to help them. But Prokosch's repeated question: "Where is Janoshik?" kept them from administering what little aid one prisoner can give another.

"Why—we don't know!" Wallerstein explained slowly. "He was called to Reinhardt, last night, right after you had been fetched—and he hasn't returned since."

"He hasn't returned," repeated Lobkowitz gravely. And then, with haste, he asked, "Do you know what happened to him?"

Prokosch's wristbones, straining at the pull of his weight, shone white in the last twilight of the cell. "I fear the worst," he mumbled, "the worst." Suddenly he let go the cot's frame and slid down opposite Preissinger. "You," he said threateningly to the twitching hulk of flesh trying to find rest, "you! There's no name for a beast as low as you! For hours, standing in that dark box, without air to breathe, bathed in my sweat and piss, all my body one burning pain, one tiredness—I racked my brain to find the word for you!"

"What happened?" asked Lobkowitz. "What did he do?"

"I couldn't find it!" laughed Prokosch. "There is no such word!"

He turned to Lobkowitz. "Behind my back, you took my wife and gave her a child, destroying me in cold blood—you're well versed in the ways of evil. Perhaps you know the word for one who goes to the torture-master of us all and denounces one of his fellow victims?"

"Judas!" said Lobkowitz.

Wallerstein, hardly believing that Preissinger actually had committed what he, the psychiatrist, had foreseen but dared not predict, wanted confirmation. "How do you know? Whom did he denounce?"

Preissinger, apathetic to their talk, whimpered: "Water! Water!"

"Water! Water!" aped Prokosch. "Did you care who'd cry for water when you bargained with Reinhardt? That's what he did! Bargained away Janoshik, in return for his own cheap life. Said Janoshik killed Glasenapp . . ."

"He must have been at the end of his rope," offered Wallerstein, "to attempt such a desperate trick. Reinhardt didn't believe him?"

"Of course not!" coughed Prokosch. "He called me out of my box into the office, and had us throw our lies into each other's faces."

"I don't follow you. What lies?" asked Lobkowitz whose anger at Preissinger and concern for Janoshik were rising rapidly.

Prokosch was very weak. He had to fight the pain of his muscles, the rasping of his breath which had been throttled for so long. But he rose to his story, deriving satisfaction not only from reporting the perfidy of Lev Preissinger but also his own sacrifice. How he took upon himself the blame for Glasenapp's murder, because to him, life had ceased to be livable. How he wanted to free all of them, including Lobkowitz, the father of Mara's child. How he had stuck to his story in spite of Reinhardt's doubts—"In the end, I am sure he would have had to believe me!" And how Preissinger, by his despicable lie, had given the Commissioner the lever to disprove the confession and to seal the doom of them all.

When he had finished, he slumped down on the cot, completely spent. "So we will die," he said, "and it will be without meaning." He wept unashamedly, from pity for himself, from rage, and from weakness.

Lobkowitz did not believe that Prokosch's dramatic confession would have wielded the slightest influence on Reinhardt's decision. His short interview with the Commissioner had given him the unalterable impression that the Nazi knew what he wanted and would not be swerved from his purpose by any wriggling on the part of his hostages. Consequently, Preissinger's denunciation of Janoshik likewise had its significance not in its effect on the fate of the hostages but in the way it exposed Janoshik to Reinhardt's wrath. The more Lobkowitz thought about what Preissinger had done, the higher his fury rose.

Lobkowitz was a young man with strong moral principles. He perceived poetic justice in the fact that Preissinger, the man who had helped to engineer the betrayal of their country, was caught in his own net; that no amount of tossing and shaking was going to get him out of it. That the Nazis themselves were the incidental executors of this justice gave it all the more point.

He understood that the sell-out of Janoshik was infinitesimal compared to the historic crime of Preissinger. But it loomed bigger because it was so purposeless. The reward for Preissinger's collaboration with the Nazis had been his few years of unrivaled power and unlimited profits. But in delivering Janoshik to the knife of Reinhardt, Preissinger must have realized that this would not free him. Or was Preissinger, the man who was Coal, actually possessed of a blindness not known to ordinary humans—a blindness created by power and by the belief that everybody could be bought and paid off?

Tomorrow all of them would be dead. To Lobkowitz' mind, there was no hell in which a Preissinger could be made to pay for his crimes. Only this night was left to even up scores. It will do me good to punish him, thought Lobkowitz. It will pay for Janoshik and for our sad retreat from the border fortifications. For everything.

When does Fate hand one a whipping boy who is the actual cause of the pitiful distortion and destruction of one's own life? It would be sinful to pass up this chance.

Preissinger, in spite of his stupor, felt the animosity of the others. When Lobkowitz approached him, he turned upon him like a snarling dog: "Leave me alone!"

"I hate to soil my hands in bilgewater which, I conclude from all you have said and done, runs through your veins." Lobkowitz stood before the industrialist, the beautiful fire of righteousness in his eyes. "God, or whoever arranges these affairs, has laid it to me to settle a few long-standing accounts. You're a businessman, you understand that there comes a day when old debts must be paid. Meet the collector!"

Preissinger understood only half of what Lobkowitz said. Lobkowitz had spoken with ironic restraint; Preissinger mistook the irony for jest.

"What accounts?" he said with difficulty. "I have nothing left. It was taken away. I am poor."

"You've watched the allegory told by the clock of our city hall, haven't you?" continued the inexorable judge, Lobkowitz. "Every hour, out of the wall, come the manikins symbolizing life—the knight in his armor, the miser with his money bag. And on the last stroke, Death swings his scythe and cuts them down."

"I've seen it," admitted Preissinger unable to grasp Lobkowitz' point.

"That's good. Remember it. But there's a short pause before Death moves—that is the moment of judgment.

"Most people find judgment in themselves. They've eyes to see and ears to hear, hearts to feel and minds to weigh what is good and bad, decent and perfidious. A few, however, are without sensibilities."

"You tire me," complained Preissinger. "I've taken all

315

the punishment the Nazis could hand out. I'm a sick man. Let me rest."

"Without sensibilities," repeated Lobkowitz. "They have no conception of social responsibility. It is a crime that they are allowed to run loose. Unfortunately, they are not only at large, but often assume great powers because they know no restrictions; lawless, they determine the laws, asocial, they impress themselves upon society.

"For these, Death allows the pause of judgment before he strikes."

"All right, all right!" Preissinger squirmed uncomfortably. "I am listening. I have to. I can't run out. I know I'll die. So why the speeches?"

Lobkowitz' fury was not of the rash kind which flares up and dies down in a matter of seconds or minutes. His wrath was sustained; it grew slowly, nurtured by its own reasoning.

"So you denounced the poor and defenseless Janoshik, because, as a matter of course, you assumed that your life was incomparably richer and better and more important than his."

"I'm sorry for it," mumbled Preissinger.

"An excellent bargain, you figured—throw Janoshik to the wolves, and save yourself."

"I tried to give him money!" Preissinger defended himself weakly.

"Whom?"

"Reinhardt."

"Blindness!" exclaimed Lobkowitz. "A man who can't conceive that he has lost all—offering money." He waved his hand. "Not good enough. Have you no better excuse to offer?"

Preissinger suddenly realized that he was being judged. He rebelled: "And who gives you the right?"

"Nobody. I assume it. I, too, will be dead tomorrow. I, too, know no restraint.... Well?"

Preissinger did not answer. He had reached a mental impasse. The world he had lived in had turned upside down. The Nazis who were supposed to protect him had forsaken him. The people he was accustomed to rule usurped the right to pass sentence on him. This was chaos. He wanted no part in it, neither active nor passive. He wanted to close his eyes and rest after the terrific strain of the day, he wanted somebody to tell him—somebody like his mother—that all this was not true, that there was no firing squad and no jail—drink some tea, Lev, and forget the nightmares.

Lobkowitz, the implacable, continued his demand: "What defense have you?"

"My life—" moaned Preissinger.

As the toreador's cloak infuriates the bull, so this argument affected Lobkowitz. He was about to throw himself upon Preissinger to vent his stored up emotions upon the vicious old man, when again the clank of keys reached into the cell. Like marionettes attenuated by the sudden paralysis of the puppeteer's hands, the hostages stood stiffly at attention.

Janoshik was thrown into the cell like a bundle of old rags.

The center of attention shifted immediately from Preissinger to the formless, stilled, blood-smeared mass. Preissinger rose in horror. He comprehended that this was Janoshik and that he, somehow, was responsible for the man's terrible state. He broke into hysterics. He wailed like an old woman, his wails rising and falling.

"A disagreeable manifestation of guilt." Wallerstein threw the observation into the uproar. Then, with all his might, he slapped Preissinger's face. As abruptly as it had started, the wailing ceased.

From the control switch out in the corridor, a dim little bulb was turned on. It shed a sickish light over the pale faces of the men and the distorted body of Janoshik. Dead silence reigned in the cell.

317

The four men seemed to wait for something.

What an exquisite torturer this Reinhardt is! thought Prokosch. Making us spend our last night with this thing, which once was a man, and which now has lost all human semblance.

Doctor Wallerstein was the first to notice the faint whimpering of this thing. He bent down and put his ear to the hideous maw that used to be Janoshik's mouth.

Then, in feverish haste, he tore off his own shirt and began to wipe off the caked blood from Janoshik's face and body. "Water!" he said, "I need water!"

Lobkowitz hammered at the door. He hammered with the force of desperation. Shortly, the Czech warden entered the cell, carrying a bucket of water. "Stop that noise!" he warned. "I'm not supposed to do this." Averting his eyes from Janoshik, he hurried out.

"A shirt, somebody!" ordered Wallerstein, tossing his own soiled and soggy one into the corner.

Prokosch quickly complied. "It's not so clean," he mumbled apologetically. "One sweats in those coffins—"

Under Wallerstein's deft hands Janoshik's face slowly took form. Swollen and discolored, one eye gouged, his nose shapeless, stumps where teeth had once been—it was, nevertheless, a face.

"Let's lift him up!" ordered Wallerstein. Prokosch, Lobkowitz and the doctor carefully raised the body and placed it on a cot. Out of two jackets they formed a pillow to prop up his head. "Careful! Careful!" said Wallerstein. "His back is one single wound. He should be in a water bed ..."

"Water bed!" Lobkowitz pursed his lips. "You talk as if we'd have time to heal him."

Wallerstein wiped his hands on his pants. "He'll live—for a while at least. His body was so strong and healthy, the strongest of us. I don't think any of his basic organs have

318

been critically hurt. The Nazis were careful not to spare him one moment of agony. He'll live—to die with us."

"Will he come to?" asked Prokosch.

Wallerstein shrugged. "I'd just as soon he wouldn't. If I had anything available, I'd keep him drugged for the rest of his time."

The doctor sat down beside his patient and felt his pulse. "High fever. The poor body is fighting.... Just look at this hand!" he exclaimed, horrified. "They broke his fingers!"

What remained of Janoshik's face began to twitch. The eye they had left him opened with effort. It was solidly red with blood. He closed it again.

"He's awake," said Lobkowitz.

Wallerstein nodded. "Take it easy, Janoshik," he said. "You'll feel better shortly."

With his unmaimed hand, Janoshik motioned the doctor closer. Wallerstein leaned over him. Janoshik's mouth was trying to form words.

"What?" the doctor asked. He could not believe his ears.

Janoshik repeated, struggling for each word: "Never—felt —better—in my—life...."

A scraping sound rose in his throat, like a caveman's first pitiful attempt at laughter.

Lobkowitz began to laugh, too. Wildly, shaking all over, tears in his eyes. "Bastards!" he laughed, "Goddamned bloody sons of bitches!" He turned to Preissinger, grabbed him by the collar, and with the strength born of outrage, hurled him wildly into the corner. He didn't see Preissinger the man who, like all of them, had to die; he saw Preissinger the personification of the enemy's ruthlessness.

Preissinger dared not utter a sound; he picked himself up and remained hunched in the corner, trembling.

"Lobkowitz!" whispered Janoshik.

With two steps, Lobkowitz was at Janoshik's side and knelt down.

Janoshik's heavy tongue was adjusting itself to the missing teeth and the unwieldy lips; his words came a little easier.

"I didn't talk!" he spoke thickly, "I didn't ... Nothing!" He paused to catch breath. "Don't beat the walls ... don't. They'll fall and crumble ... You will see ... !"

Was he talking in a delirium, had his racked brain snapped out of the bounds of normal perception? "Yes," said Lobkowitz, "of course. You're right."

Actually, Janoshik's mind was working with painful clarity. But it concentrated on one objective, to the oblivion of everything else. As in moments of highest tension the hand will grip and hold onto a single mainstay, so Janoshik's mind in the hours of torture had revolved around the two imperatives: I must not talk! The munitions barges must be destroyed! The explosion must occur!

Yes, it appeared to him that his steadfastness was the condition for the explosion; that the explosion depended on him and only on him, and that it would be his personal reward. Thus he established a personal relation with fate, a whole new set of values wherein his superhuman suffering was exchangeable for the success of a venture over which, if he still were able to think objectively, he had no more control than over the flow of the Moldau.

Back in the cell, his thoughts were still on that other plane where they had fled to maintain his life. To Lobkowitz and the others, this gave his words a prophetic significance. Pain and suffering create veneration; you have suffered for your cause, so your cause must be worth suffering for—were it not so, why would you have taken the burden upon yourself? Now you speak with the authority of sacrifice, the crown of thorns is really a crown and not the mockery intended by the torturers.

Thus the mantle of leadership fell on Janoshik's torn shoulders. At first, he did not notice it; he was concerned with himself, with the ceaseless pain scurrying through his nerves, with anxiety for the success of the explosion. Soon, however, he became conscious of the fact that the others were watching him expectantly, especially Lobkowitz. He sensed that they felt more for him than sympathy, and that he was called upon to say something important.

Collecting his thoughts slowly, he regretted the need to keep his secret. For the first time he realized how cruel death must be to a Lobkowitz, a Prokosch, or a Wallerstein who, despite their surface superiority, could neither see the future as he saw it—bright and worth dying for—nor even up the score with the Nazis.

Not he, Janoshik, was in desperate straits, but the others who were going to die what to them was a senseless death. Could he not give them a little of his strength, a particle of his hope? Was it not his obligation to lift a corner of the great curtain which veiled from their view the thousands upon thousands of fellow humans who, regardless of how many fell, ultimately must win over darkness and death?

Lobkowitz in his aimless revolt, Prokosch in his sad ambition, Wallerstein in his one-sided search—were they not striving, too? Why let them die alone? Were they not, each in his way, a part of the teeming picture he wanted to show?

The trouble with me, thought Janoshik, is that I can think out all these great things, but I can't speak them. Even if my tongue were not a great sore, and my throat a dry flame—how can I express the hopes of the soul, the aspirations of the heart without sounding like a penny orator?

"Ever heard of Vladislav Vančura?" he asked, wringing every word from his smashed lips.

"No," said Lobkowitz.

"You don't have to talk," Wallerstein had torn a sleeve off Prokosch's shirt and used it as a compress on Janoshik's forehead, "if it's a strain on you."

"Vančura from Vyšehrad," insisted Janoshik, "a shoemaker."

"It's all right," said Prokosch, "let him talk, he loves to tell stories."

"He was a joiner, Vančura was, president of the singing society, color bearer of the local *Sokol*, trumpeter with the auxiliary fire service—his wife didn't like it—"

Janoshik paused to catch his breath. The others waited with compassion. They knew there wouldn't be many more stories he'd be able to tell.

"He was away from home so much, you know—"

"Yes," said Lobkowitz, "women don't like that, they're funny."

"If there was a uniform and a band, Vančura joined—a joiner—" Janoshik felt drowsy. But he forced himself to go on. Vladislav Vančura, of whom he had not thought for so many years, and who probably was dead long since, again had a function to fulfill.

"One day, in 1918, he goes to pick up a pair of shoes, goes along the street, the way he walks, slowly, looking at people, saying hello and my compliments and nice day today, you know..."

"A fine fellow, this Vančura," said Prokosch.

Janoshik waited. He was weak and the ache tried to overpower him. Finally he mumbled: "A fine fellow? Yes and no. Just average, like me. A shoemaker."

There was silence again. Preissinger edged out of his corner toward the group. "Go away!" said Lobkowitz. Preissinger flinched and retreated before the finality of the other's tone.

Janoshik resumed his tale with difficulty: "Along comes a group of men. They have a banner and are trying to sort of get in step. But it isn't the real thing."

His voice sank to a whisper. "So Vančura starts hollering: Hey, slackers, have you no marrow in your bones? What kind of marching is this?

"One of them who knows Vančura shouts back: Why don't

you join in? Show us, Vančura, how to march, you can carry the flag!"

Janoshik stopped. He tried to chuckle, but it hurt him. He could see old Vančura, tall and lanky, gingerly entering the ranks, taking the flag pole into his bony hands, sticking out his chest. . . .

"Well, of course he did. He was sorry that he didn't have his *Sokol* uniform on him, or at least his fireman's helmet, but this thing had to be improvised."

Wallerstein moistened Janoshik's lacerated lips. "He started to sing *My Czech Country* and *Christmas Comes Once a Year* and *The Black Girls and the Blond,* all the songs he knew, and he had them going pretty soon. The demonstration grew by leaps and bounds. Once he turned around, and as far as he could see, there were people marching."

Janoshik opened his eye and looked at Lobkowitz. "He was mighty proud of all those people, though he had no idea what they were marching for. And he had no time to ask. He was leading them, you see?"

Lobkowitz nodded. "He was carrying the flag, I understand."

"When they came to the center of Prague, there were gendarmes and soldiers with machine guns. That astonished Vančura; what were they standing around for? They blocked his fine march! The gendarmes and the soldiers expected him to stop, because they had the guns and thought he knew what that meant. But he didn't, you see?"

Janoshik paused, trying to break the barriers of his pain. Like Vančura, he succeeded. "He knew only that he had all those people behind him, and that there would be an awful mess if he stopped and the people were stuck on the street, unable to move either forward or back.

"So he shouted: Don't block the way! Don't you see this is a parade? I am Vančura the shoemaker! And he began singing *From the Tatra* which has a snappy melody.

Wallerstein took Janoshik's wrist and felt his pulse. It was hammering fast.

"Finish your story another time," he pleaded.

"The officers started shooting, but the soldiers looked at Vančura and saw that he would march on, because he carried the flag and had all the people behind him. So they didn't fire and some even marched with Vančura. . . . That day the Government fell."

"What happened to Vančura?" asked Wallerstein.

Janoshik thought for a while. This doctor—always he wanted to know the details.

Then he said, "Vančura? He saw that the people had learned to march without him. So he handed over the flag. He met somebody he knew, I think the man who sold him nails, and they went to the Blue Goat for sausages and beer. Because marching makes one hungry."

The light in the cell went out.

In the darkness, Lobkowitz asked, "What does it mean?"

Janoshik did not answer.

Lobkowitz continued: "You mean to tell us that whatever we may be—shoemakers, doctors, actors, toilet keepers—whatever we do, wherever we are—we don't know what we may start with our actions, as long as we march, as long as we move forward. Is that what you want to tell us?"

Prokosch grumbled, "Can't you find your own answers?"

But after a little while, Janoshik whispered again: "When they shoot us tomorrow, somebody, perhaps some Vančura, will hear the shots. Bullets through good people's hearts make a long echo."

The nervous tension under which Commissioner Reinhardt labored had reached such proportions that he saw complications and threats even where there weren't any. He longed for the hour when the platoon commander's me-

chanical "Fire!" and the ensuing crack of bullets would end
most definitely the case of the hostages. At the same time he
was full of apprehension.

Working over the balance sheet of the case he had to admit that now, the night before the execution, he knew no
more than he had known when he decided that Glasenapp's
exit must be not that of quiet suicide but of murder. Neither
Janoshik nor Milada had opened up under his most skillful
pressure. Wherever he turned, he found a dark blank wall
and, like the king of Babylon, Nebuchadnezzar, he saw in-
scribed on that wall the fiery *Mene Tekel*.

Now he could comprehend what other colleagues had told
him: The numb desperation, the blind rage that befell them
when they found themselves fighting shadows. Yes, he had
laughed at them, he had bluntly informed them in so many
words that they were stupid and that he, Reinhardt, in a like
situation would have proceeded to solve and clear up the
case and then, knowing where he stood, exterminated the
enemy to the core.

Where did he stand?

He had ordered Milada brought back to his office not so
much because he wanted to question her anew. Neither the
Wallerstein papers, nor the interrogation of Lobkowitz and
the other fifteen hostages, nor the final torturing of Janoshik
had given him material for any further questions he could
ask the girl.

Rather, he desired to assert himself and his power. Shaken
as he was he needed the tonic that flows from crushing the
weak; their cries must be music to his ears, must heal his
wounded self-confidence.

Therefore, when Milada entered, he was haughty, almost
gruff. He stared at her as if he wanted to annihilate her with
his cold, merciless eyes—and he wanted to! But he was di-
verted by her strange beauty which had been heightened by
her ordeals. Kratochvil's pursuit, Breda's hasty love and

farewell, her arrest and the loneliness of the damp cell had added a new, translucent quality which, to Reinhardt, was enchanting and painfully maddening alike; for hers was now a beauty which seemed to remove her from his reach.

"Have a look at this!" he began and pushed a photograph across the desk. She followed his order but failed to identify the picture. "This," continued Reinhardt with a show of emotion, "is the remains of my man Kratochvil."

She recognized now what the picture meant. It was ugly and cruel. She replaced it on the desk, as far away from her as she could.

"You shudder!" he said. "You! He was smashed flat under a load of steel. And you're responsible. You and the others whom we'll ferret out of their holes and smash.

"You say we're ruthless and cruel. We are not. The war, yes, the war is cruel and senseless. But why is there war? We Germans are the only ones who have a sufficiently large conception of the world as it must be. One economic, political and spiritual unity, determined and governed from Berlin, administered by a generation of physically and psychically superb German warriors whom we now are raising, led by the super-mind of the Führer.

"Then there will be peace, the only peace possible—a peace enforced by the iron fist of ourselves, the rulers, the organizers. This war began only because people like you refused to recognize and accept the reasonable basis for the new order we are establishing.

"Your fight is so desperate because it is lost. The means you use are so vicious, the darts you shoot so poisoned, because you are weak. We accept your defiance. But don't cry if we retaliate!"

He paused. He had been carried away by the magnificent flow of his words. He had tried to instill in them all the sincerity and conviction of which he was capable. Yet he was afraid that what he said sounded hollow. Milada's face remained unchanged, indifferent. Searching for new arguments for his thesis, he continued, "Our superiority as Nordics—"

Milada interrupted him: "You're wrong. I did not shudder. I've forgotten how to be horrified. I knew I was lost the minute you entered my house. From then on, I have lived on borrowed time.

"And on borrowed time, I'll answer you. You can stop me easily enough. You carry a gun, and nobody will call you to account if you draw it and shoot me."

"Go on! Go on!" he urged, a thin smile on his lips. "As long as you know your position, I don't mind the squeak of the mouse in its trap."

"You have everything on your side. The arms, and the machines to produce arms. You have the Kratochvils to watch us; you yourself are only a super-Kratochvil.

"But you forget on whom you're trying to stamp your New Order. We are people, humans! Certainly we're weak, and it's easy for you to get the jump on us because we prefer the tranquillity of home and love, of working and singing and fishing, to years of planning and scheming war. But just this tranquillity, this minding our own business—this it is which people will rise to defend."

"With what?" he heckled.

"It takes people a long time to become aware of your schemes, they're so fantastic, so full of delusions of grandeur. At first they were unbelievable to us. Now we've learned, now we're fighting, all over the world. You know it yourself. You say we started the war—and in a certain sense we did. We started the shooting as does the aroused farmer who looks out of his window and finds thieves carrying away his livestock, and setting fire to his barn.

"You offer peace—the kind of peace in which the farmer returns to his bed and wakes up in the morning, forced also to sell his land to the thieves, at their price, and in the bargain, to give himself up as a slave in order to have a loaf

327

of bread for his kids. That kind of peace is not acceptable."

Milada stopped, taken aback. Who had made her speak so audaciously? Who had told her to be the spokesman before this uniform? What was it that carried her away with her own words? Where did those words come from?

She had given thought to such ideas before. But never had she formulated them as a system, a system opposed to the power and the slogans of the conqueror.

She could speak because she was lost, and any sentence might be her last. At the same time she felt the ridiculousness of going all out before one person, and this, a person by nature and training unable to understand her. Reinhardt could grasp only one point—that she had confessed to being the enemy of everything he stood for, and that he must act upon that point.

Reinhardt had suffered a letdown after having expounded upon the plan for a world with the Reich Chancellery in the Wilhelmstrasse as its hub. He, however, knew why he had gone out of his way to hold forth upon the beauties and the magnitude of the New Order. As a representative of this immense new world conception he expected to impress Milada, either as a sincere fighter or as an inexorable terror. And his disappointment arose from the fact that she, too, paid in the inspiring currency of philosophy.

If he had failed to impress her, she did impress him. He was tired of cowering and silent victims whom he could dispense with by the usual means. The physical attraction which the girl exerted changed and became a definite challenge.

A challenge to him as a man.

It was vastly more interesting that the woman he wanted to conquer also was his enemy, and that both knew it. Taking her meant breaking her. And since she was delivered into his hands, inescapably, he would enjoy the process to the hilt.

Milada, observing the whip-hand expression in his eyes when he rose and approached her, withdrew instinctively. She remembered his claw which once he had placed on the nape of her neck. This claw was extended now.

"It is good," he smiled, "that we understand each other. Of course it is my duty to dispose of you because you belong to the most dangerous species—the idealists. But how and when is entirely up to me."

He measured her with cold eyes around which he tried to lay some friendly wrinkles.

"The time limit is up to you."

He wet his thin lips. The lips remained open.

Milada inched away from him, which did not disturb him at all. He was careful to keep the same distance throughout the dialogue in which her part consisted of tense silence.

"We could work out a schedule, starting with the smallest unit—a friendly smile from you, let's say, is worth an hour of your life. An effort at sincere love-making—a day; and an act completed to my satisfaction—half a week."

He pulled a pad out of his pocket, produced a pencil, and proffered them: "I'll let you do the bookkeeping. I have confidence in your honesty."

She shook her head violently.

"No? You don't want to be burdened? I understand. These small items might disturb the flow of your great ideas."

Still the distance was maintained. His eyes glided over her, undressing her. He was aroused to the point of offering more substantial advantages.

"I will see to it that you get good food. I'll have a comfortable bed placed in your cell—I don't want your beautiful body bruised by the hard flatness of the prison cots. I think you should appreciate my solicitude."

Reinhardt did not feel like making ironic quips. He wanted her desperately but had enough sense not to make himself ridiculous by pleading. Besides, he figured that irony backed by brutal frankness would break her soonest.

He saw the terror in her wide eyes. But he also saw that just because he was terrible and repulsive to her, she responded in those dark corners of the mind which react to the lure of repulsiveness.

"You'll be surprised," he offered, "to learn a few thrills at the end of your days—thrills which, in all likelihood, you would have missed if we had not met...

"Stop running away!" he shouted, suddenly impatient.

This shout broke the almost hypnotic spell enveloping Milada.

She saw him with appalling clarity, as the little fly sees the spider in whose net it is caught. Every detail it sees—the sharp angularity of the legs, the white cross on the spider's fat body, the suction mouth ready to bear down and drain the juice of its life.

He had maneuvered her against the wall. He smelled acidly of sweat. His breath came fast. He emitted short grunts of desire, as he edged nearer and nearer.

Milada tried to push him away, but he did not budge. Suddenly his arms, overlong, shot out and constricted around her, holding her in an unyielding grip. Her arms were crushed to her body, and held immobile. She tried to turn and squirm, struggling to free herself, attempting to kick his groin with her knee.

She wanted to bite him; but he was taller than she, and her teeth caught only the smooth cloth of his tunic. The more she struggled against him, the stronger became his hunger for her; each movement of her body tantalized him the more.

His closeness revolted her; she not only had to fight him but also her stomach's urge to unburden itself. Her head began to swim. The perspiring, panting, evil animal towering over her grew and grew. His members were like chains, unbreakable, heavier with each second, bearing down on her and throttling her flesh.

She made one more effort to free herself, straining her muscles and nerves until the blood shot to her head and she thought her veins would burst. Then, with a vicious twist he pinned her arms to her shoulder blades. She cried out loud from the pain flooding her. Her knees gave in. She would have fallen if he had not held her.

He tore her poor dress. She felt his dry claw fingering her skin, rasping down her bosom; she felt his hot breath on her naked scratched shoulder. She shivered as if in cold fever, her throat grew parched and clogged, her tongue swelled to a heavy gag.

She fainted.

Finally the Commissioner arose from the couch, warm and disheveled, and deliciously tired. Softly he whistled through his teeth the melody of a song hit he had recently heard in a night club. He began to dress.

He looked at Milada who lay sprawled on the couch as he had left her. A few strands of her dark hair had fallen over her white shoulders and gave her skin a wild and tortured design. Her nipples were still stiff from his sucking kisses, and between her spread legs, on the dark green cloth of the couch, a few drops of heavy blood were drying.

Pleased and satisfied he looked at her. While attaching his suspenders he lit a cigarette and inhaled the smoke deeply.

He regretted that the girl had been unconscious throughout. On the other hand, it was precisely her stillness, and the fact that he had had to set each of her limbs according to his purpose which had given him the longed-for sensation of power and ownership. Yes, she was a most beautiful thing,

331

and he had broken her. Tightening his breeches, he moved his hands caressingly along his thighs. It was as it should be! He was the master and everything had to bend to his will.

Milada was slowly coming to. He went to his desk in the office to fetch a bottle and glasses. When he returned, her eyes were open, and she had thrown her slip over her nakedness.

"Well, well, well!" he said, welcoming her back. "Was it so bad, my dear? Next time we'll stay awake, won't we? So that all the fun is not on my side, eh?"

He poured the drinks and handed her the glass.

She shook her head.

He raised his brows in friendly scolding. "You deserve a drink, don't be childish. It'll help you to get over the shock. You were difficult, my dear. Almost like a virgin. Almost—" he laughed. "If I hadn't known that you and Glasenapp, and Pavel, and probably quite a few others—"

She began to sob. Dry, hard sobs. She did not want to cry. Her hate and her shame made her cry, and she succeeded soon in suppressing the convulsive throb of her throat.

"Have your drink," he urged.

This time she drank, with greedy haste. The alcohol warmed her, brought back her spirit. "I want to dress," she said. "Please go into the other room."

He laughed. "That's a cute joke. In case you don't remember—I've just seen you naked."

"Go!" she said.

He shrugged his shoulders, bowed derisively and went to his office. She heard him switch on the radio; a few seconds later a Viennese waltz full of nostalgia came over the air. He hummed the melody.

Every move was painful to Milada. In his unconcerned lust, he had injured her; she winced, contorting her face. She did not think, did not want to think. What were the present and the future but loathing and humiliation? Sunk into ob-

livion were Pavel and Breda and the light she had known,
the hope that had filled her.

She was utterly, utterly alone. She could not bear touching
her own bruised flesh, she was repellent to herself. I must
kill myself, flashed through her mind.

"Coming soon?" Reinhardt's voice called.

She did not answer. She slipped into her torn dress.

"Cigarette?" he asked.

Then he came and stood in the doorway, measuring her
coolly. She shrank together, wishing only to be as small and
as far away from him as possible.

"We'll have to get you a new dress," he announced. "What
color do you like?"

The Vienna waltz broke off. An announcement came over.
Then the strains of the *Hohenfriedberger Marsch*. The news
broadcast was due.

"Want to hear the news?" Reinhardt asked pleasantly.

"You don't have to ask me," she answered bitterly. "You
seem to do what you want."

"Damned right you are!" he laughed. "It never hurts to
be courteous, though . . ."

Then the miracle happened to Milada. Suddenly the room
was filled with Breda's voice and presence. His strong, warm,
passionate voice. Clearly, unmistakably.

*"Citizens of Prague! Tomorrow, twenty hostages are to be
shot for the murder of one Nazi, one Lieutenant Glasenapp.
This man was never murdered. He committed suicide."*

Reinhardt paled. Within a second, he lost countenance.
Frantically he ran to his desk, lifted the receivers of his telephones, got the wires entangled, cursed, shouted.

*"Not even the motive of petty revenge for their dead re-
mains to the Gestapo; your fellow citizens have been framed
and are to die at the cruel whim of the invaders."*

Milada followed into Reinhardt's office. She stood in the
door, laughing, jubilant. The Commissioner was still trying

333

to establish a connection, excitedly shouting into the phones.

"There is no more law, not even Nazi law. There is no more security, be you as peaceful as you may. Your lives, the lives of your loved ones, are at the mercy of unprincipled, power-mad murderers."

Milada was joyous. Her clothes and her body in tatters, her heart sang. It sang over the fear of the man Reinhardt who now had to listen to his own crimes, fretting in anguish, desperate because he could not stop the voice.

"They kill for the sake of killing, they torture for the sake of torturing, their wrath strikes you, any of you, as a hail-storm does."

The words were addressed to all, but the voice of Breda spoke to her. In her hour of deepest abasement, she was avenged. Beloved, her heart sang, I am here. I am with you.

"There can be no more reason for trying to live with the invaders. We must fight against them. We must sabotage the work they want us to do, derail the trains they want us to run, burn and explode the stores they keep, the cars they drive, the houses wherein they live."

"Stop it!" Reinhardt howled into the telephone. "Stop it!"

"You can't!" exulted Milada. "We are here, there, every-where!"

"Crush them, as they crush us! Beat them, as they beat us! Choke them, as they choke us! Kill them, as they kill us!"

Reinhardt pounded his desk. His eyes seemed to pop out of their sockets, the words he shouted fell over each other in a twisting, swirling confusion.

Then a sharp click sounded through the loudspeaker. A breathless, tremulous voice made embarrassed apologies. A mishap. The Russians. A mistake in transmission.

Furiously, Reinhardt turned off the radio.

He had sufficient presence of mind to realize what had happened. The enemy had struck. His secret, so carefully guarded, was out. Millions of people knew it. Everybody.

334

His plan, his clever scheme, his work—lost! He was the laughing stock of Prague, of Europe.

He folded his hands on his desk and buried his head. Heydrich! he thought, and cold fear gripped him. Murtenbacher had told him stories of the Protector, the man was relentless.

He heard somebody laugh.

Laugh! he thought. Go ahead! All will laugh.

Then he looked up and saw that it was Milada who was laughing.

"You?" he said. He had forgotten that he was not alone. He straightened immediately. Seeing her triumph, he rose and set his face in his customary smile.

"An unfortunate accident," he said. "I'd hate to be in the shoes of those radio people."

"Now, if you are still so kind," said Milada, "you may give me a cigarette."

He opened his cigarette case, came close to her, and extended the hand holding it. "Light?" he asked.

"Thank you."

Pensively, she exhaled. His eyes followed the smoke. He had one overwhelming desire: to clamp down on her, to show her that he was still himself, Helmut Reinhardt, the all-powerful.

"To correct a perhaps mistaken impression on your part." he announced, "I should like to mention that things are as they were—this radio joke notwithstanding. We shall shoot the hostages, as planned. It is action that counts, not words.

"I hope it will not spoil your fun or hurt your feelings if I invite you to attend the execution?"

She dropped her cigarette.

Reinhardt stooped to pick it up. "I hate to see these beautiful rugs burned. The people from whom we took them showed excellent taste. . . . I insist on my invitation."

She bowed her head. He had beaten her again.

CHAPTER 14

CAPTAIN PATZER possessed a strong feeling of loyalty and esprit de corps.

Although Glasenapp by no means had been his friend, the Captain nevertheless considered him as a comrade who had been vilely assassinated almost at his side. He believed it to be a matter of honor to have a hand in settling the account, and had applied for special permission to command the firing squad on duty this morning.

It promised to be a glorious morning. The sun had not yet risen, but in the east, a pale gray was vanquishing the flickering starlight over the roofs of Prague. The Captain felt chilly and drew his greatcoat closer. The spurs on his well-shined boots, hitting the cobblestones, jarred the quiet of the streets.

He had no eyes for the beauty of the departing night. His mind was set on his function. It was the first time that he was to order the fateful command despatching a number of mute, blindfolded people from this world. Major Grauthoff, upon informing Patzer that his application had been granted, had rehearsed the rigmarole with him carefully.

Patzer coughed, cleared his throat thoroughly, and spit. He must not be hoarse. His voice must ring like a clarion call avenging the dead Glasenapp—a call echoed by shots.

"Fire!" he shouted. And again: "Fire!" His voice resounded from the dark walls of the houses. Somewhere, a window lit up. The silhouette of a head became visible and disappeared immediately. The witness of Patzer's short soliloquy had recognized his uniform and preferred not to have seen or heard anything.

Patzer marched on. The world became lighter; the street lamps lost their aura; a few old women silently entered a church for morning mass.

Before the barracks, Patzer found his platoon waiting. The sergeant stepped forward. "Sergeant Hollerahn and twelve men, sir!"

"Thank you!" Patzer saluted. "Forward, march!" It was an illusory command. The sergeant pointed toward a truck which came lumbering up the street. The truck stopped, the men piled in, with Patzer and the sergeant taking their seat beside the driver. Throughout the rumbling trip, Patzer moved his lips, forming the word "Fire!" in all possible shades and intonations. He dared not pronounce it aloud fearing that the sleepy sergeant might get the impression that the Captain, after all, was a newcomer to this business.

About this same time, the Czech warden entered the cell of the hostages, carrying the bucket, coffee and bread. The Gestapo administration saw no reason why people should be fed better than usual before their last walk. Since they were to die shortly, the good food would be wasted.

On his own initiative, and from his own meager food allowance, the warden had brought from home a pot of beef broth for Janoshik. It was the same broth which he and the family had had the previous night. Little strength was left in the bone from which it was cooked, and few were the fat eyes on the surface of the soup. But the warden had remembered Janoshik's helpless mouth. Nobody should be executed on an empty stomach, he thought, because he had had his training in more humane times.

Lobkowitz, who had not closed his eyes during the night and who looked as wretched as he felt, took the pot from the warden's hands.

"It's for him!" said the warden, nodding in Janoshik's direction. The first light of the morning was not yet strong enough to tear away the merciful veil of shadows from Janoshik's distorted, smashed-up face.

"I want to feed him." Lobkowitz shifted the hot container to his other hand. "I'm his friend."

"Take care you don't burn him!" The warden gave a spoon to Lobkowitz. "I carried the soup under my coat to keep it warm."

He looked once more at Janoshik, shook his head, and went out, closing the door softly.

Preissinger noisily swallowed his coffee. He bit a piece of his bread, tried to chew, and stopped dead. The bread stuck in his throat, gagging him. He spewed out the half-munched mass.

Prokosch, holding his cup, was staring at the wall. His long legs dangled from the cot as if they were dead already. He raised his brows and said to Wallerstein, "You are sure death comes instantaneously?"

The doctor looked grayer than usual. "If they hit you right. But they will. They do this every day."

"Suppose they tremble?"

"After it's all over, the officer in charge checks up. He has a pistol. If he finds that you still show signs of life, he puts a bullet in your head."

"I'm not afraid," said Prokosch apologetically. "Even an experienced actor has stage fright, but he loses it after his first few opening lines. This is the last act. I'm interested in a perfect exit, and wanted to know the cue."

Lobkowitz, supporting Janoshik's head, was feeding him. He concentrated on his self-imposed Samaritan task, trying to forget himself and his distress in the helplessness of the other. Speaking to him with little endearing words, as the nurse talks to the baby she feeds, he tried at the same time to do penance for the feeling of repulsion which gripped him whenever he looked at the disfigured Janoshik.

Janoshik had slept. The pain and exertion of the previous day had made him sink into a comatose sleep from which he awoke to feel the stronger the burn of his wounds, the throbbing of his nerves. Lobkowitz' solicitude touched him.

"Today's the day?" he asked, half-jokingly. His stomach responded gratefully to the warmth of the soup. He managed to give his remaining eye an expression of wistfulness. "So many things will happen today. Children will be born. Young men and women will kiss each other. A number of people will contrive to get drunk in spite of the thin beer we're having now. Some hostages will be shot. And, perhaps, this or that surprise will come through."

He swallowed another spoonful. "You never can tell. Any day brings surprises which nobody can predict."

Wallerstein and Prokosch, having finished their meager breakfast, joined Lobkowitz at Janoshik's cot. It seemed as though a quiet strength emanated from the sick man; they rallied around him to derive part of that strength.

Wallerstein said "Good morning!" Taking Janoshik's unmaimed hand, he felt his pulse. "You're on the best way to recovery. You have a marvelous physique!"

"Yes?" replied Janoshik, not very attentively. He was listening. He had one desire: To learn the success of his expedi-

339

tion to the Mánes, before he was shot. He was afraid that the sound of the explosion might not be able to penetrate the thick walls of the basement prison.

"I'm proud to have such a patient," continued Waller- stein.

"I'd hate to be taken there in a wheel chair." Janoshik, supporting himself on his elbows, sat up. His eye closed to hide the pain which swept through him. "I want to walk with you and stand with you." Again he tried to listen. Only the thick silence of the earth embedding the cell surrounded him. Like a grave, it struck him.

Preissinger sat on his cot in miserable isolation. Nobody spoke to him; he was an outcast. A spark of hope glimmered, that a special messenger from Berlin or from the Protector's office might yet arrive to save him and make amends for his mortification. But this flickering hope could hardly survive the grim trickling away of the seconds and minutes. To face death alone is cruel punishment. The walls of the cell seemed to close in on him, choking him. He wanted to cry out loud, he needed consolation, a hand to guide him, pity, warmth.

He rose to make the few steps across the abyss which parted him from the others. He wanted to kneel down be- fore this Janoshik and beg everybody's forgiveness. Not that he wanted forgiveness—he wanted to be accepted into the fold of mankind as represented by the tortured Janoshik and the three administering to him. He wanted to hear a few words addressed to him, Preissinger, kind words, feeling words.

Edging his way to Wallerstein, he accosted the doctor: "Let me help, too. Can't I do something?"

The suppliant, sniveling, pious tone of Preissinger dis- turbed the little community. Lobkowitz, having finished the feeding of Janoshik, placed the pot on the floor and threw the spoon into the pot. The metallic clang, harsh and shrill, made Preissinger flinch.

"It is unfortunate," said Prokosch, "that you will be executed with us. To the world this will give the impression that you belong to us. You don't. Your blood will soil the cleanliness of our death. The fact that your greasy name will appear beside ours on future death lists, fills me with disgust."

"Doctor Wallerstein!" appealed Preissinger.

The doctor turned to glance at him. Preissinger's self-abasement and dissolution was a welcome diversion in their bitter, last hour. It is a great help to know that there is somebody more desperate, more torn than oneself.

"I would not advise you to interfere with our farewells. Men dislike being disturbed in moments of deepest emotion. You know that much psychology, don't you?"

Preissinger lowered his bull-head. He would have to tackle the core of the antagonism, Janoshik. Pushing the doctor aside he stepped to Janoshik's cot. "A word!" he pleaded. "A word! Say something! Don't leave me alone!"

Janoshik was listening for the thundering message he hoped for. He saw the figure of Preissinger as through fog.

"When I worked in your mines at Kladno," he began, "I knew a certain Petka. A kid. He was driving the blind horses which pull the cars with coal.

"He died. A mountain of stone fell on his legs and belly. Crushed.

"We'd wanted new wood from you to back up the shaft. But you thought that new wood cost money, and lives are cheap."

He coughed. The figure in the fog shrank in dimensions.

"I was with Petka when he died. I held his hand. A kid."

Preissinger had never heard of Petka. He could not see what Petka had to do with his loneliness.

"There are many Petkas," said Lobkowitz. "They're rising now to ride your heart, Goddamn you."

"You're all against me!" shouted Preissinger.

"Yes," nodded Wallerstein, "we are."

The Commissioner's restless night had been made more restless by a special memorandum from Heydrich which arrived toward two o'clock.

Upon his return to his residence on the Hradschin from his current inamorata—the second girl from the right in the ballet—the Protector had found the report of the broadcast about Glasenapp, and had dictated his note. The memorandum breathed the wrath of the man. Tart, sarcastic words requested Reinhardt to appear at nine sharp before the Protector.

Reinhardt had crumpled the sheet and thrown it into the wastebasket, furiously. Now he picked it out and smoothed it, to read again what Heydrich threatened:

"I entrusted you with an important task for the fulfillment of which discretion was of prime necessity. You not only let out the secret of the case, but also allowed it to be broadcast all over the protectorate. Congratulations...."

And on and on and on.

The Commissioner considered. It would help him little to point out to the irate Heydrich that the policing of the radio station against uninvited speakers was outside his domain. The connection between the clever stroke of the enemy and the case he was working on was too obvious.

The worst was that he had to concede to himself that he had made the cardinal mistake of all police work: He had underestimated the opponent. He had been unable to uncover the links between the hostages and the outside world. Certainly, there were mitigating circumstances. Murtenbacher, even Heydrich himself, could not have cracked the iron perseverance of a Janoshik. To run up against such an unfeeling creature was simply hard luck. But could he reply to the scorching derision of Heydrich with the schoolboy's excuse of hard luck?

Thank heaven, the Protector did not know of the most inexcusable of Reinhardt's blunders: To have sent this Janoshik on the fool's errand to the Mánes—to search for the elusive letter of Glasenapp! Now the Commissioner saw clearly what Janoshik had wanted: to seek contact with somebody, to arrange for the bold counter-stroke of the broadcast. But how, the Commissioner asked himself, how did Janoshik know of the suicide? Had he been present? Or was he a genius able to divine the truth from some remark which he, Reinhardt, had made in the course of the questioning? Or—after the broadcast the Commissioner was willing to believe almost anything—was Janoshik the murderer of Glasenapp? Was Reinhardt's suicide theory a stupid, rashly conceived notion?

These questions went through his mind with rapid sting. He knew no answers. The Glasenapp case remained a riddle, and the only man who could give him the answers would not speak and, shortly, would not any more be able to speak.

For a moment the idea occurred to Reinhardt to stay the execution in order to continue to work on Janoshik. His policeman's conscience was ill at ease at shelving a case without having solved it. But the man Reinhardt felt simply unable to live through any more of the uncertainty and tension which he had experienced since reading Glasenapp's letter to Milada, retrieved from the waters of the Moldau.

Perhaps at the bottom of his troubles was the spirit of this melancholy river which brooked no interference with the affairs of its dead once it had embraced them. But this was rank romanticism, and no proper thought for a safe and sane police commissioner.

How much sanity, he asked himself, had he left? His interest in the Wallerstein papers and, in the first place, his permission to have them written—how morbid! His feverish quest for motivations and background of the pimpled Glasenapp—how abnormal! His overwhelming urge to win the Milada girl—how insane! Had he held on to the routine and the tried methods of his years of fruitful labor and steady climbing, the Glasenapp case, instead of becoming more entangled with every step, would have solved itself almost automatically.

What was the matter with him? Was he falling down? Had this old city with its history of cranks and madness, its dark corners and secrets, affected his brain? Or was he bucking up against a power stronger than he—a power subtly proceeding to break his spirit and strength, a conspiracy without limits, frightening him out of his wits?

No, for the sake of his sanity he must have the hostages executed—now! He must bury them and kill their ghosts; that was the main job ahead. And then: return to normalcy! What if Heydrich raved! He would sit still and listen and say yes to everything; somewhere the Protector's irascibility would reach its end.

Milada was brought in. She wore the new dress he had requisitioned for her. Reinhardt had not known how to describe what he wanted for her, and had sent Moenkeberg to shop without specific instructions. Moenkeberg, no specialist in ladies' fashions either, had broken into the first shop his eyes had met, and carried away over a dozen dresses of various sizes and styles, leaving with the scared shopkeeper a scribbled note to collect from Commissioner Reinhardt of the Gestapo, if he dared.

Thus Milada had acquired a richer wardrobe than she had owned since she left her father's house.

She picked a simple blue dress, its only adornment a little white collar—my execution dress, she thought.

The Commissioner was agreeably surprised. Nothing buoys a female as much as a new dress, he reflected, no matter what she has gone through.

To Milada, the new dress and the air of well-being it lent her was a means of defiance. She knew only too well the Commissioner's intention in forcing her to view the execution. She had set her mind against his. Again, as during the first questioning in her dingy room, it was a matter of pitting strength against brutality, will against torture. He had debased her by raping her unconscious body; her conscious must rise the higher to overcome her defeat.

"Stunning!" said Reinhardt.

He was again enraptured by her; and his mood was mellow after the self-reproofs he had made.

"I am trying to honor the men you are killing," she announced.

Her enmity restored the full viciousness of his hate.

"Mourning seems to become Milada," he jeered, rubbing his hands. "I wouldn't mind having you attend these functions regularly, just to admire you dressed in this fashion and to enjoy the expression of dignified hostility on your face."

He lifted the receiver of his telephone and ordered breakfast for two. A guard appeared shortly, carrying a tray with eggs, hot rolls, coffee, sugar and cream. "To be on the right side of the fence," Reinhardt remarked pointing at the tray, "has its advantages."

Expertly, he spread napkins over his desk, and set the table. He opened her soft-boiled eggs, buttered the rolls, and poured the coffee.

At other times, Milada would have given much for such a meal. But the company and the foreknowledge of the second part of the program made even the coffee, which she tried, taste bitter.

"Would you like to have your breakfast after the execution?" he asked. "You are too sensitive. Think of Kratochvil

345

whom you had crushed flat. I daresay our shooting squads do cleaner work."

He wolfed his food, smacking his lips. A bit of the yellow of the egg remained in the corner of his mouth, his fingers shone with the fat of the butter. Milada, determined not to show any signs of weakness, fought down the urge to vomit. Finally he pushed his empty dishes aside and folded his napkin neatly. Seeing that Milada's food was untouched, he took one of her rolls and nibbled it thoughtfully.

Gesturing with the half-bitten roll, he said, "This is an important day to me. Today the murder of poor Lieutenant Glasenapp will be paid for at the current rate of exchange: twenty Czech lives to that of a German officer. The lies which were spread in yesterday's unfortunate broadcast do not alter the facts."

He paused, expecting a reply from Milada. None came. He repeated: "Facts!"

Milada looked at her knees. They trembled slightly. She knew that he could not believe that Glasenapp had been murdered. Or did he? Was he caught in the plot which he himself had spun? Did he want to provoke her?

Breda's broadcast had changed her position. She could speak of the suicide without revealing that she had furnished the material for it.

"Glasenapp was not murdered," she said slowly, "and you know it. Your last pretense for killing these men has been spoiled. The execution is an act of unbridled perversity."

"Not quite," he smiled. "Not quite. You are wrong, because you forget that it is we who determine the facts. If I say that Glasenapp has been murdered, then my saying so automatically makes it a fact. This, like our breakfast, is one of the advantages of power....And why—" his piercing look forced her to raise her head—"why should he have committed suicide? Do you know?"

His surprise question caught her off guard. If she told him

346

the truth, he would learn that she knew of the suicide before it had been broadcast.

"Perhaps you do know?" he asked, still friendly.

She turned her face to the window. From the street came a dull noise, as of many voices in subdued excitement.

"I don't know," she whispered. "Except that he was a candidate for suicide as much as you. It must become tedious to ravage and conquer and violate, from country to country, again and again. It makes you lonely, and pride is no substitute for love. Ultimately you will choke in your own successes."

"Really?" he said with a show of sarcasm. But inside, he was astonished that this girl, who could not know him well enough, had put her finger squarely at his wound of doubts and hesitations, at the basic reason for his failure to solve the Glasenapp case. His amazement changed into anger, his anger grew to cold fury—nobody, and least of all this girl who was his conquest, his property, had the privilege to divine the squirming abyss of his quandaries! This was his own dark province, into which he himself rarely dared to glimpse!

"What romantic bosh!" he cried.

The noise outside grew.

"I will show you reality!" He motioned her toward the window.

The street, on which the window opened, was filled with a milling crowd of people. They seemed to wait for something. They did not shout, they bore no banners. Many women were among them, carrying market baskets. The people talked to each other, gesticulating. Some pointed at the Gestapo building, in the courtyard of which the executions were to take place.

The black-uniformed, steel-helmeted guards paced up and down, in seeming unconcern. Czech gendarmes appeared, trying to disperse the crowd. But the crowd had reached a

347

density and resiliency by which the gendarmes were simply swallowed.

"This is the whole effect of your broadcast!" sneered Reinhardt. "A numb mass, disorganized, not knowing what they want, leaderless, littering the street."

He went to the telephone and gave a few orders.

Milada saw a truck with soldiers drive up and stop before the building. Captain Patzer jumped off, followed by his platoon. Sergeant Hollerahn directed the men to the door. The people who had pressed close willingly opened a passage.

Then, suddenly, Elite Guards came rushing up the street. Brandishing submachine guns and swinging rubber truncheons, they advanced. She saw people falling. The mass of men and women retreated, stepping on each other, pushing and shouting.

Milada felt Reinhardt's horny claw on her neck and cried out. He stood close behind her, pointing at the street scene. "Power!" he said. "Reality! Machine guns!"

Milada turned, tears in her eyes. He grinned. The silver embroidery on his black lapel grew hazy, the shining splendor of his buttons was like knives tearing her heart.

They were alone. She could kill him. It would be easy. Fingers around his throat, don't let go till he slumps dead. Or rush to the desk, grab the dagger, bury it deep in his chest.

She thought of Breda, wishing desperately to receive his strength.

But Reinhardt took her by the hands before she could realize any of her plans. "It's time to go," he said, "they are waiting."

He had to support her faltering steps.

The courtyard of the Petschek Palais which housed the headquarters of the Gestapo in Prague was not laid out for

348

the purposes of the Secret State Police. In summer, the former owners of the palace had given magnificent garden parties, and in other seasons, the space was used to walk the dogs and to store carriages and automobiles.

Under the new, more severe regime the trees had been cut down to make room for the movements of the platoons and companies of the Elite Guard or the Army who drew up, presented arms and, ordered at ease, were distributed over the building to their various purposes.

A heavy door led from the main part of the building to the courtyard. Opposite this door the windows on the ground floor had been hastily bricked up with ugly red bricks splotched like blood on the gray coat of the walls.

This door now creaked open. Two black-uniformed SS Guards appeared, and behind them, in single file, each one flanked by SS men, the five hostages were led out.

Dr. Wallerstein marched in front, his big head hunched between his shoulders. He walked awkwardly, more shuffling than usual, because during the long days in the cell he had had no exercise whatever and had almost forgotten how it feels to move one's legs without hitting a wall after a few steps. Then he looked to the square of sky glorious in cobalt blueness, without a single cloud, over the courtyard. The morning was cool, and he shuddered slightly.

Behind him came Prokosch. The actor used his best walk. Thus he had come on stage as Othello, a victor, strong and upright, a stranger to the vicious plot which was to unfold against him. The guards appeared small in comparison. He tried to shake off the pale hand of fear which gripped him, by carrying himself regally. He thought of Mara—not the Mara who had betrayed him to Lobkowitz, but the Mara who had approached the portly Oedipus and thrown her life as a mantle under his feet. He felt great tenderness toward her, a tenderness which, in spite of everything he had learned,

349

made him want above all to live up to the magnificent picture she had created of him. He raised his hands as if he were blessing the sky and the land, and the life which would continue on it; and shrank in shock when one of the guards snarled: "Hey, what do you think you're doing?"

Lobkowitz, who followed him, also thought of Mara. But he saw her differently, lighter, as he had seen her at the railroad station, going to the front. It seemed to him that this Mara was entirely his own, and had no tie to Prokosch. Having possessed her and suffered for her had been the essence of his life. The finality of the backs of the soldiers in the firing squad which they approached slowly set an end to any continuation of this life; he had to be satisfied with what he had done and tasted. And, remarkably enough, at this moment he was satisfied. The gray backs of the soldiers, one exactly like the other, made him resigned and, as after a rich meal, want to say: Thank you. It was all I desired. It was good.

Janoshik dragged his wounded body, limping, suppressing his groans. He was tense and expectant. Alternately, he quarreled with his fate and implored it to fulfill his last wish for which he had endured all the torture any human being could take upon himself, and to—please—let the great moment occur before the bullet set the final, unalterable period behind his modest life. What had he ever asked? What favors, what rewards? The broken fingers of his hand dangled helplessly. He used his unmaimed hand to hold the wounded one in a mute gesture of pleading, his shapeless lips mumbled unintelligible words. He cocked his head in order not to miss the slightest sound penetrating from the outside world into the closed square of the courtyard. So little time was left for the thunder of the explosion to reach his living, hearing ears. The hostages had almost arrived at the stiff line of the firing squad.

Suddenly Janoshik wanted to laugh. He remembered poor

Franta Horak from Kladno, a miner like himself, who had told him the saddest story of his life. Too bad that now it was too late to retell this story: How Franta Horak, on a Sunday night, had slid dead drunk into an irrigation ditch at the road to his home and had slept for a solid forty-eight hours. During that time a disaster occurred at the mine where he was supposed to be at work. And how, when he woke up, he sleepily had ambled into his house to find a message that everybody had gone to church, to hear memorial mass for him, Franta Horak. How he had hurried to church to be on time to listen to his own mass, eager to hear what the priest would have to say about him, and to see how many candles were burning for him. And how, upon reaching the church, the people were just streaming out after the services. Oh, this Franta Horak! Coming too late even to his own memorial mass!

He laughed and, for a moment, forgot the harrying question of whether the bald-headed longshoreman actually had retrieved the message with the Watzlik address, and had succeeded in time to get his group to plant the explosives on the munitions barges. . . .

The rigid line of the firing squad opened to let through the five hostages and their guards.

Wallerstein was the first to perceive the brick-windowed, shadowy wall, scarred by the bullets of past executions which had missed their aim.

At the foot of the wall stood fresh puddles of blood. The ground was muddy, and the foot tracks of the previous batch of hostages, as well as the indentations where their bodies had fallen down and the trail as they had been dragged away, were terrifyingly clear.

Wallerstein stopped short. His eyes closed. He tried to extinguish this picture, so real and unreal alike, from his appalled mind. But the image remained. There was only

351

one means to wipe it out—to kill the mind which had perceived it.

Preissinger, walking last, took a few seconds to understand the meaning of the wall and the plastic mud at its foot. At first it seemed as if his buckling knees must swing him to the ground.

But then, with the strength born of deadliest fear, he pushed aside his guards, broke loose, and careened across the courtyard in fantastic jumps. With a voice scarcely human he cried, "No! No! I can't die! It's an error! I am Lev Preissinger!"

In the ensuing chase, the squad standing at attention and the four hostages were the only firm figures. They formed a T—the soldiers the horizontal, the hostages the vertical beam of the letter.

The SS Guards ran after Preissinger, shouting orders to each other, trying to cut off their quarry's path. Preissinger moved from corner to corner, wildly breaking through the guards whenever they formed a semi-circle to catch him. His face was scarlet, his hair bristling, his fast wheezing breath sounded all over the yard.

It was a ridiculous as well as a tragic scene—these uniformed men, hunting lust in their eyes, chasing the fat animal. Finally, one of the guards lifted his revolver, aimed, and shot Preissinger in the knee. He folded and sprawled on the ground, kicking with his sound leg and his arms, biting and scratching. It took four guards to lift him and hold him and pull him to his post. Since he could not stand, they made him kneel, his face toward the wall, his hands upraised, the dirty jacket over his broad back showing the pattern of his last hopeless fight.

Then the other four were marched up and ordered to stand against the wall. Still Janoshik cocked his head, listening, listening. Before his one eye was a small field of rough stone. He could see the dust which had collected in its grooves. A tiny bug was crawling along, black and shiny. Suddenly it unfolded its wings and whirred away.

Reinhardt led Milada into a sparsely furnished office whose windows afforded a good view of the courtyard and the execution wall on the opposite side. Rows of filing cases extended the whole length of the office; a badly reproduced print of Hitler in the position of a knight errant in shimmering armor, his clumsy hand holding an overlong sword, a poison-yellow sun rising behind his pomaded hair, was the only ornament in the room where some minor officials seemed to work. The morning being so young, they had not yet arrived. Reinhardt and his prisoner were alone.

Like the gourmet among the urchins, who saves the tastiest candy in the bag for last, Reinhardt had arranged for Janoshik's group to be executed after the other fifteen hostages.

The firing squad did its deadly work with automatic precision. Thrice Captain Patzer, in perfect form, raised his shiny saber and, with clear, disciplined voice, commanded: *"Achtung!"* The soldiers snapped to attention. *"Legt an!"* They raised their rifles. *"Feuer!"*

Thrice the volley of shots rolled over the yard, resounding from the walls, rattling the glass of the windows.

Thrice five hostages tumbled down in weird contortions, and their bodies were dragged away, their faces trailing through mud and dust.

Reinhardt observed the spectacle in stony silence. A cigarette hung in the corner of his mouth; its ashes, falling to the floor whenever they had grown too long and heavy, lent the only movement to his statuesque figure.

Milada, beside him, had been unable to take her eyes off the petrifying scene. The reverberation of each volley had shaken her body to its very depths; her lips were as white as her face, the nails of her fingers dug into the flesh of her hands.

When the last group of hostages, led by Wallerstein, made its appearance, she suddenly turned to the Commissioner and said tonelessly, "I can't go on."

Reinhardt, absorbed in his thoughts of grim retribution for all the wrong done to him, continued his silence.

She left his side to sit down, to fix her eyes on something else, anything ... anything but the bleak wall of the shooting gallery with its popping figures.

"Come back!" he ordered, not even raising his voice.

She shook her head.

"I want to show you Janoshik," he said, "an extremely stubborn fellow, and how we break his stubbornness once and for all."

The name Janoshik registered with Milada. She heard Breda say: *Of the people I know, there is only one without fear—a man named Janoshik....*

A great sadness and weariness overcame her. She was tired of struggling. But she roused herself. It seemed to her that she had been given a mission—to witness the last moments of the life, and the death, of the fearless Janoshik. And thinking on, she felt certain that she, the witness and recorder, was going to live to tell the tale—as Breda had said: *Janoshik stands for so many who have died and will die, and I thought that somebody somewhere must arise and accuse....*

She, Milada, surviving even the fatal embrace of Reinhardt, would be the accuser. To accuse, she must go through the hell of seeing and witnessing, with wide open, dry and burning eyes!

"I'm coming," she said, and with leaden feet walked back to the window.

She arrived there just as Preissinger made his dash for life. Viewed from their window upstairs, this break seemed all the

354

more tragic and hopeless, surrounded as the yard was by un-scalable walls.

To Reinhardt, Preissinger's clumsy running and jumping was a source of utter glee.

"Look! Just look!" he cried, following with his manicured finger the torturous route of the hunted one. "This is Preissinger, my dear, Bohemia's most powerful man! You did not want to believe me, my dear—here is a graphic illustration. This is how we chase them merrily, and catch them, and eliminate them. There is no power but ours, today in Europe, tomorrow—"

"Which is Janoshik?" she interrupted him.

"There!" he pointed. "The one who appears slightly mauled."

Janoshik was turning his face toward the pursuit. Thus, Milada caught a glimpse of his manhandled, misshapen, scarcely human round head. She saw that his poor jacket was darkly spotted by the blood trickling from the wounds of his beating, she saw how he held up his maimed, twisted hand, she saw that he had only one eye left, and that, where the other eye and his mouth had been, there were only gaping cavities.

Then Preissinger was caught and pushed against the wall. Janoshik turned and limped to the place assigned him to die at.

I must not cry, she thought, I will not cry. This I must see to the bitter end; it is my fate and my task, and the meaning of my life.

Reinhardt threw away his cigarette. Impatiently he fingered his buttons; the sweat of excitement stood out on his nose and forehead.

"Now they're made ready," he commented. A guard was walking along the wall, adjusting the hostages at proper distances from each other. The guard then hurriedly moved out of the area of fire and posted himself beside the platoon of soldiers.

Captain Patzer, his cheeks flushed with the satisfaction of his importance, his eyes shining with righteous hate for his victims, stepped to the left of his squad. He set one foot forward so as to distribute evenly the weight of his body for the erection of his arm and saber.

The saber flashed. *"Achtung!"*—*"Legt an!"* The soldiers moved, twelve men as one.

A terribly cracked voice shouted: *"Pravda Vítězí!"*—Truth will conquer!

Thus Jan Hus had died, the prophet of Czech liberty, centuries ago.

"Feuer!" answered Patzer.

"Pravda Vítězí!"

The rifles spoke.

Thus died Janoshik, a plain man, a son of his people, October, 1941.

The cackle of the shots evoked a tremendous echo. Crashing thunder rose from the river. Yellow, shooting flames crisscrossed the cobalt sky over the yard. Billowing black smoke soon obscured the square of sky. Explosion followed upon explosion, rocking the building to its foundations.

Panic gripped the officers, soldiers and guards. Jolting, pushing, lunging, clamoring, they stumbled toward the building, seeking protection against the elements which seemed to have broken loose. Somewhere, anti-aircraft artillery began to yelp against an enemy they could not see. Sirens screamed and fire engines rushed clanging through the streets.

Only the hostages were still. They lay as they had fallen, each one his way. Lobkowitz, in death, was gripping a piece of earth. Wallerstein reposed neatly on his side, a thin smile around his open lips. Prokosch's arms were entwined in an uncanny, not at all theatrical gesture. Preissinger was flat on his back, his fat stomach overtowering his head.

Janoshik's head was cocked as though, dead, he still was listening for the thunder which had come too late for his life.

Up in the empty office, Reinhardt had thrown himself to the floor. He held his hands over the back of his head, in an effort to protect his most precious parts against bombs, falling stone or whatever was to come hurtling from the heavens with the vicious intent of hurting the Commissioner.

Milada stood enthralled by the gruesome beauty of the catastrophe. She tore open the window to taste the faintly acrid smell of the air. She wept and laughed and laughed and wept. Bubbling words formed on her lips. Somebody greater than the black-uniformed man cowering on the floor of this room, somebody greater than he and all he represented had thundered an irrefutable reply. And she had been blessed to behold the mighty conversation between the cackling rifles of the firing squad and the roaring antagonist from the river.

"Listen, Commissioner!" she cried over the noise of the continuing explosions. "Where is your power? Where is your greatness? Listen to me! Out there—your hostages are dead. But the men who killed them huddle behind doors in fear of the millions of Janoshiks you can't reach. And you lie in the dust, your whip beaten out of your hand, your shining dagger blunted, your guns barking ridiculously. And this is only the first slight tremor of the earth. There will be a time when it opens up under your feet, and you perish in darkness and oblivion."

The Commissioner was too concerned with thoughts for his own safety to heed Milada.

Finally, the noise outside ceased, and he heard people running along the corridors, telephones ringing, voices shouting. He rose clumsily, a foolish, apologetic smile on his face. He

357

brushed the dust from his pants and tunic, and picked up his cap.

"What were you saying, my dear?" he asked.

There was no answer. He looked around, dumbfounded. Milada had gone.

Moenkeberg was driving with extraordinary speed. On the approach to Karl's Bridge he turned on the sirens full blast.

"Stop that infernal screeching!" shouted Reinhardt, his nerves on edge.

"I can't," answered Moenkeberg, gruffly. "The entire length of the river embankment is blocked off, and we have to get through to the Hradschin."

Reinhardt sank back in his seat, holding his hands to his ears. How could he think under such circumstances? Everybody and everything were against him. Milada, in the confusion following the explosion, simply had walked out of the Gestapo headquarters. Chagrined, he had issued a warrant with her detailed description, but he had little hope of catching her again. The friends she no doubt had would hide her safely.

Then the preliminary reports of the explosion had come in, claiming all his time and attention.

All three munitions barges anchored in the river had been blown up. The soldiers detailed to guard them had disappeared without trace—no wonder, they must have been torn to bits. Munitions in the value of millions of Marks destroyed. The whole city quivering with malicious delight.

He could well imagine the mood in which he would find the great Heydrich. And there was nothing he could tell him but the fact that his men were searching, and that up to now no trace of the perpetrators of the crime nor of the way in which it had been carried out had been discovered.

The big car hobbled over the cobble stones of the Hradschin and came to a halt. Reinhardt, briefcase in hand, slowly emerged, unresponsive to the salutes of the guards.

Each step of the wide staircase leading to the Protector's suite of offices seemed to him more difficult than the previous one. Finally he halted to rest and think. But no lifesaving thought occurred, his head was heavy and ached.

His name had been called several times before he took notice. An aide-de-camp came rushing down the stairs to meet him.

"Commissioner Reinhardt!" he reprimanded. "How long do you think you can let the Protector wait?"

"Sorry!" said Reinhardt. "You know—the explosion..." He had to hurry to follow the aide-de-camp's quick steps. Then the door to Heydrich's office was torn open, and he was ushered in.

Heydrich was again standing at the window, striking the same pose he had used upon receiving Reinhardt the first time. But today he turned to face the Commissioner as soon as the door had closed.

He began immediately. "I have here two documents, one of which requires your signature. Your signature is needed to your letter of resignation. The other document is your transfer to the SS Regiment Deutschland, at present in battle on the Eastern Front.

"Please sign here."

Heydrich threw the resignation across his desk. Reinhardt picked it up gingerly and read.

"Having failed miserably at my task of protecting the interests of the Reich and the Führer in Prague..." it began.

Reinhardt's hand was ice cold. The letter slipped from his fingers and fluttered to the floor.

Heydrich had walked back to his window and was staring at the landscape. He, too, was thinking of the consequences of the Glasenapp affair with which, he suspected, the explosion was somehow connected. He thought of Himmler in

Berlin, and of the Führer who was liable to do anything if he saw fit to fall into a rage. Somebody had to be the scapegoat, and he had decided that this conceited careerist, Reinhardt, would make an excellent one.

Transfer to the front—this was all Reinhardt could think of. This short order revolved in his head, spinning around wildly. Everything else—the hostages, Glasenapp, Milada, the broadcast, the explosion—was blotted out. Important was only that he, Reinhardt, a man in his middle years, and certainly not a good soldier, would have to leave his desk to go out alone and face those monsters, the tanks. The tanks were terrible. They rolled toward you with inexorable sense of direction, pointing their machine guns, their cannons, their crushing weight against you. Wherever you turned, there was a tank. The tanks had faces. One looked like Janoshik, as he lay on the torture table in the basement, his mouth grim, his eyes filled with hate. One looked like Wallerstein, superior with the knowledge of something which Reinhardt feared. Another bore Prokosch's face as he confessed to the murder of Glasenapp, resolute, willing to sacrifice. There was no end to these faces, there were so many. The Police Commissioner of Hanover, Milada, and the prisoners in the concentration camps whom he had questioned and beaten. The dead whom he had shoved underground, the living who cursed him—tanks, tanks, tanks.

"Why?" he cried out in his need. "I have served you faithfully. I have done my best. It is not my fault that here and there I failed. The others are strong, too—you know it—your Excellency."

Heydrich spoke out of the window. He did not deem it necessary to face the fallen Commissioner. "Why? Do you question my decisions?"

"No! No!" Reinhardt assured him. "How could I! But not to the front! This punishment I do not deserve."

Heydrich came back to his desk. "Apparently I must explain the graveness of your failure to you," he said sitting down. "It was important, wasn't it, to eliminate Mr. Preissinger in the most correct manner? Instead of that, you managed it so that certain forces were able to publicize, over the official radio station of Prague, that the Glasenapp case involving Mr. Preissinger was a despicable frame-up. I, of course, had no idea of such a stupid, criminal plot. But you will agree with me that the official responsible for it must be punished severely."

Reinhardt did not answer.

"So you agree," the Protector continued. "If I did not punish *you*, Mr. Preissinger's friends in Berlin would hold *me* responsible. You don't expect me to jeopardize my position to protect a blundering idiot?"

There was nothing Reinhardt could say.

"In addition to which," Heydrich's hawk nose was drooping over his chin, "this morning a mysterious explosion occurred, destroying considerable government property. I prefer to suspect a connection between the explosion and the Glasenapp case. But even if this were not so—again, *you* are the official entrusted with the protection of the munitions barges. Again, you failed miserably to do your duty.... You see, Commissioner, I have no alternative."

"But not to the front!" squirmed Reinhardt.

"You're a coward," said Heydrich, "but I expected that. I have good reasons for sending you there. I cannot afford to have enemies alive. And, my dear Commissioner, I have no illusions about the fact that from this second on, you are one of them."

Reinhardt rose. With Heydrich's last words, the image of the onrushing tanks disappeared. His head was clear. The hawk nose and he were enemies.

"Your Excellency!" He bowed and picked up his letter of resignation. He took a pen off the Protector's desk and signed his name in firm, upright letters. "In taking leave of you I would like to say a few words of farewell."

"Proceed!" replied Heydrich, accepting the letter.

"In my work it has been my misfortune to encounter people who were not cowards. On my side, I've had everything—a vast police machinery, communications, arms, and soldiers. The others had nothing but perseverance, the will to sacrifice, more—to die—and cunning. I have had occasion to learn that there are many of these people, many more than we suspect and can conquer.

"I have failed and concede my failure. I am going to a horrible death. But I tell you, Your Excellency, that my successors, and even you yourself, must fail in the same way, and that you will meet a more violent end than I."

"I think I've heard enough!" Heydrich pointed toward the door.

Commissioner Reinhardt snapped to attention. His silver embroidery and buttons looked faded. He raised his hand. But before he could utter the customary "Heil Hitler!" the Protector shouted:

"Get out, you!"

Reinhardt turned and ran. He was bathed in sweat.